NIGHT
PLAYERS

THE SEQUEL TO
THE VAMPIRE NOVEL
NIGHT PRAYERS

BY

P.D.

THE DESIGNIMAGE GROUP, INC.

All alone and struggling to master her newly acquired powers (and limitations) in a rollicking tour of the underbelly of L.A., Allison ends up in the most unlikeliest of places, "The Fur Pit", a sleazy Hollywood joint where the exotic dancers are only part of the draw. There she reluctantly strikes up an unlikely friendship with the unlikeliest of guys: Mica, a Bible-thumping street corner preacher who just happens to be one of The Pit's own bouncers. But not even Mica realizes that The Pit's dancers are actually bloodthirsty, shape-shifting vampires, or that their nightly routines are just a front for an orgy of bloodletting and violence.

"A steady, IV-like drip, drip, drip of verbal and situational humor...an entertaining read."
C. Krusberg, The Vampyre's Crypt

It isn't long before a newborn vampire and naïve preacher-wannabe are wrestling with their own mutual attraction. But there's no time for romance once Allison and Mica end up on the undead dancers' bad side. Now it'll take more than a nightful of prayers to fend off the catty coven of strip club vampire vixens. Even after a sinisterly slapstick climactic battle , Allison and Mica are both on the run from the L.A. law and the long reach of the evil undead when they hide out in Las Vegas...and NIGHT PLAYERS picks up...

"A wild ride into the seamy world of the undead...a perfect mix of helter-skelter humor and horror."
Michael McCarty, Horror Magazine

The Design Image Group, Inc.
PO Box 2325
Darien, Illinois 60561
www.designimagegroup.com

ISBN: 1-891946-11-0

First Edition

THE DESIGNIMAGE GROUP, INC.

Printed In The U.S.A.

10 9 8 7 6 5 4 3 2 1

To Tom,
A true believer in dreams

CHAPTER 1

"And I say unto you, O My Brothers and Sisters, that you may THINK you know the Lord, but I can tell you right here and right now . . . this very minute . . . that you DON'T know nothing about the Lord or His plans!"

The words filled the luminescent hall, ricocheting off the many-faceted arched windows and hovering in the air above the upturned faces of the congregation. *His* congregation. So many of them crowded into the great tabernacle of glass and gold — hundreds of men and women and children staring up at him with eyes full of hope and joy . . . and, yes, just a little fear because they knew what he was saying was true. They didn't know diddly about The Lord and never would without his help.

Mica smiled down at his people. But solemnly. It wouldn't do any good to make salvation too easy. He knew that from experience.

"No, my dear friends in Christ, you DON'T know. You think that just because you look up every now and then you think The Lord is listening and that help's always going to be there. For you. JUST for you and nobody else. That's what you think, isn't it?"

Mica paused and let the corners of his mouth fall into an angry scowl.

"Well, ISN'T IT?"

Voices gasped and the fear he'd seen in their eyes spread across their raised faces like the waters of the Red Sea that had parted for Moses and the Israelites then fell back upon the heads of the Pharaoh's minions. Mica let go of the scowl and lifted his arms in benediction. They were sinners, oh yes, no doubt about that, but they were his people and they would learn.

With his help. And The Lord's, of course.

"Of course it is. You think The Lord's only there for you because you think that's the only power He has . . . to help you when you drop that quarter into a slot or try to draw into an inside straight. I know, and The Lord knows, because we've heard you: 'Come on, God, all I need is the Jack of Clubs.' 'Oh Lord, just let me win back enough to make the house payment.' That's the truth, isn't it?"

Mica's smile returned in full as the humbled sinners gathered below began muttering. Suddenly inspired by their contrition and shame, he tipped back his head and shouted to the glittering glass dome 80-feet above the altar.

"Hallelujah!"

Someone in the congregation, maybe a couple of someones, it was hard to tell in such a huge edifice, began thumping the floor at the back of the pews. It was a soft sound that steadily became the beating of his own heart when Mica lowered his gaze and saw her. An angel in a diaphanous gown, come down from Heaven to walk among mortals. Her golden hair shone with a radiance that dulled the voltage of the thousand electric candles illuminating the life-size statue of Jesus that stood directly behind Mica. Her eyes, bluer than the cornflower robes of the Holy Mother herself, met his with a rapture he knew he'd only find again when The Lord met him at the Pearly Gates.

"Hallelujah," he repeated.

Mica held out his hand and watched her ascend the white marble stairs to his pulpit. The clinging gown whispered as their fingers entwined.

"Now, do you really think The Lord's going to help if the only time He hears from you is when you're only asking for material things? Well, DO you?"

He hadn't wanted to shout, but he did want to make his point. She understood and, gripping his hand tighter, lifted her flawless face to the power of his words and closed her eyes; falling back against the golden dais in a near faint, ecstasy raising a rosy blush in her cheeks and across the tops of her large and heaving breasts.

Thump.

Mica moved closer to his angel and felt his heart beating wildly against his ribs. Her hand was so warm, almost *hot* to the touch.

. . . it had been so long . . . so very, very long since he felt warm flesh against his . . . .

"Of COURSE you expect that's what The Lord is going to do, because you're nothing but SELFISH, ARROGANT, CONCEITED CHILDREN!"

Thump, thump, someone in the congregation thumped.

"But that's all right, Brothers and Sisters, because The Lord knows that . . . He may not be happy about it, but He knows and understands. Now, that's fine and dandy if you want to remain children, but even the kindest father has a limit to his patience . . . and we all know what can and has happened when our Heavenly Father loses HIS patience, now don't we?"

Thump.

"That's right, we know. But let me tell you, Brothers and Sisters, that it's not too late to get back in The Lord's good graces before that final roll of the dice. Because He knows how weak you are . . . He knows and He doesn't care."

Releasing her hand, Mica slipped the gown from his hot angel's shoulders and felt himself shudder as it fell to the cold marble floor, exposing perfection he knew hadn't been seen since Eve. A murmur rippled up from the assembly when she leaned forward and pushed open Mica's ecumenical robes to reveal another miracle – his clothing was gone and he was as naked as Adam.

Pure and innocent in their nakedness, Mica slid his hands around the firm, twin globes of her ass and she responded. Sighing softly, she reached out and cupped her hands around his massive shaft, her fingers barely touching as she guided it toward the mound of golden-tufted curls between her legs.

"Oh yes, Lord. Yes," Mica groaned as he hoisted her, gently and slowly, onto his consecrated rod of salvation. "Oh God. Oh God. Oh God."

And her moist warmth folded around him, accepting his offer.

And God saw that it was good.

Good? Hell, it was fucking GREAT!

"Praise The Lord! Hallelujah!"

Thump. Thump.

"Yes! That's RIGHT, my wayward brethren. He DOESN'T care . . . what you've done or how pitiful and childish you are in His eyes, because He loves you. He loves you more than anyone has EVER loved you!"

"Yes! Oh yes, Lord. Love me! LOVE me!"

THUMP!

"He let His only son, that we know of, die for that love, and He will die for you forever because He wants you, all of you, right there next to Him and the Holy Ghost in His Father's Holy Kingdom of EVERLASTING LIGHT!"

Mica could feel his gonads swelling with the holy seed of truth and love and – "YES, LORD!"

Breasts squashed almost flat against his massive chest, his reincarnated Eve rode him like one of the Four Horsemen . . . pulling him in deeper and deeper with each thrust as they plumbed the depths of his words against the pulpit's springy surface. He was so hard now he could have used himself to chisel the Pharaoh's tomb out of the living rock and saved all those Israelites a whole lot of work.

"OH MY GOD, YES!"

THUMP! THUMP! THUMP!

Mica!

"That's RIGHT, Lord! Do you hear them, Lord? NOW they understand! NOW they know what to do! Listen to them, Lord, listen and forgive them their childish trespasses as they have forgiven themselves trying to make a 5-10 split. FORGIVE THEM, LORD! Say Hallelujah!"

"HALLELUJAH, LORD! Oh, God. I'm coming. OH LORD, I'M C-C-COMING. I'M COMMMM–IIINNNNGGGGG!"

Thumpthumpthumpthumpthump**THUMPTHUMP THUMPTHUMP!!!!!**

Mica! Turn off that damned radio before I come out there and rip off your fucking head!!!

Mica was sitting up in bed and reaching for the blaring clock-radio before his eyes were open.

"That's right, my Brothers and Sisters," Brother Beezer said, his rich baritone voice echoing in the darkened room, "the Lord wants you to know that He loves you in spite of all your faults. But do *you* want to love the Lord back in return?"

The muffled voices of the live radio audience answered in the affirmative. Loudly.

Dam–MIT!

"Well, Brothers and Sisters, I'm glad to hear it, but it's going to take hard work . . . not just faith and hope. It's going to take a study manual so you'll always know you're on the right track. Because none of us wants to go astray again . . . do we?"

"Nooooooo!"

Aurgh!

"Of course not. So for that peace of mind and life everlasting, just send in $39.95 – plus shipping and handling – and I'll send you the only guide you'll ever need, my own personally autographed book, 'Fleeced by the Lord, My Shepherd.' Make your checks payable to *Brother Beezer's Daily Sunrise Service, Amen* and begin learning how to climb back up into God's lap. All major credit cards and Food Stamps accepted. Once again, that address is –"

MICA!

Awake (and uncome), Mica accidentally hit the control lever to ALARM instead of OFF, and the room suddenly filled with the sounds of an electronic cat being skinned alive. The shock and rush of adrenaline didn't help his co-ordination much, but he finally remembered how to turn the radio off. The silence that followed, however, was brief . . . filled almost instantly by the sound of a coffin lid raising.

Slowly.

Although their bedroom was perpetually hidden from the bright desert sun during the daylight hours (and their neighbor's 5000-watt security light at night) by triple-thick insulated drapes, Mica had no trouble seeing her or the look on her face. Laser surgery had corrected his vision to better than the 20-20 he'd been born with.

Allison was still the most beautiful soulless, accursed, damned creature he'd ever been willing to give up everything (short of his life) for. The same. Always the same.

Even with the occasional minor variation.

For fun. And/or profit.

When they'd first come to Las Vegas, Mica hardly ever saw her as "Allison" . . . or, rather, as the physical image he'd known as Allison back in Hollywood. She said it was for their own protection – going incognito, like changing his name and giving up the "wild-eyed prophet" look for something that blended in better with the pressed chinos and polo-shirt crowd. Even though he still sometimes jumped when he saw his "yuppidized" reflection in the bathroom mirror (the only one she allowed in the house since she never needed to use any of the facilities therein), Mica had agreed with her. The Hollywood police had to still be looking for them, sending out APBs along with their descriptions to any and all law enforcement units within broadcast range: "Be on the lookout for Caucasian male, medium height, early thirties – longish-hair Messiah Freak and his stunningly gorgeous red-haired, undead female companion. Caution, female is dangerous."

And how, Mica thought.

Of course, he had to admit he enjoyed those first few months – Allison meeting him at the bus terminal and walking back through the sultry desert night, hand-in-hand . . . she as sultry and dark as the night. Raven d'Nuit. God, he'd loved watching her do it . . . transform herself from the raven-haired showgirl to whatever woman he wanted. Nordic goddess? Country fresh farm girl with freckles and pig-tails and not much else? Love-starved coed in peek-a-boo baby-dolls?

Or sometimes, if they were feeling nostalgic, she'd become Allison in clinging red satin. Or just fur.

Mica's dream-inspired erection reasserted itself, the tip of his penis spurting out a single crystal tear at the memory. She was so fucking beautiful that he forgot . . . always forgot.

Until they made love and cold, hard reality destroyed the lovely illusion.

His erection deflated with an almost audible thud. It'd been like sticking his dick into a snowbank . . . with the exception that a snowbank would probably have been a lot more co-operative.

Been.

Past tense.

Thank God.

Sort of.

About the time he was beginning to realize that he might have made a mistake, Allison had decided – quite firmly – that she'd had it with "trying to be his fantasy play thing" and started "wearing" night-length cotton nightshirts to "bed".

Eight months . . . and the honeymoon was over.

Eight months of dreaming about hot sex and warm flesh and waking up to ice-cold stares and kisses (whenever he could stomach it) that tasted like rotted meat.

Gee, thanks. I'll have to remember to pick up some mouthwash on the way home tonight.

Mica flinched at the sound of her voice inside his head and jerked his legs up to his chest, protecting as many vital organs as he could. He kept forgetting she could read his mind.

Really? And here I thought you kept forgetting things on purpose.

He wrapped both arms around his legs and tried to chuckle. She liked it when he laughed at her jokes – whether they were funny or not – but Allison didn't seem to notice. She was still glaring at him from her coffin at the foot of the bed – one lock of her autumn-bright hair (the gloom dulling the color to that of old blood) falling over her shoulder, the wrinkles across the front of her nightshirt all but obscuring *Garfield's* haughty sneer.

"What?" he asked, knowing the instant the word left his mouth that he really shouldn't have done that. "Good joke. Hah, hah."

Allison's eyes narrowed, meaning that he missed the point completely.

What did I tell you?

"About what?"

This time her sigh was audible . . . and rattled the window glass behind the shades.

About Brother-fucking-Beezer and his Sucking Sunrise Service. Ring any bells yet?

Mica almost gave himself a concussion against the headboard as he lunged for the clock-radio. "Sorry! I – I thought I'd turned it to contemporary rock. I didn't mean to wake you. Go back to sleep."

Her glare intensified.

I don't sleep.

"Oh. Yeah. Sorry, I–"

Forgot. I know. "You say that every morning, Mica."

"Yeah," he said again. "Sorry."

Allison looked up, her gaze stopping just short of Heaven, and slowly levitated out of the cream-colored coffin. The stunt had impressed Mica a lot more before he saw the *Masked Magician* do much the same thing on a TV special.

Which is why I don't watch TV.

Shit! Mica let his mind go blank – not a particularly hard thing to do even before he'd started doing it on purpose – and twiddled a knob on the radio.

"There," he said, giving the black plastic case a gentle pat, "all done. It shouldn't bother you again."

"You know," Allison said as she came down for a landing, "I keep offering to help take you out of the 9-to-5 grind. Just say the word and you could sleep all day and party all night."

One bite, Mica, that's all it would take. A little pain, little light-headedness and bingo . . . you're one with the eternal. I thought that's what you always wanted.

He'd been listening to the same thing every morning for the last eight months. It was like being stuck in the continuous re-run of a very bad horror movie. God, he hated her sometimes.

Feeling is mutual, honey.

OH SHIT!

"Sometimes," he shouted. "I said sometimes. Look, Allison, you know I didn't mean it. It's just – Awk!"

His throat suddenly closed as if an invisible hand had tightened around it.

"Shh," Allison said. "I don't want to talk right now, okay?"

Turning, she walked to the bedroom door and opened it. She was half-way through when she stopped and turned around, smiling at him over one shoulder.

"Oops."

The invisible hand around Mica's throat let go. He took a long, sobbing breath.

"Sorry," she said. "I forgot."

Mica waited until the sound of her footsteps had been swallowed by the bungalow's post-atomic era stucco walls, before flinging the sheets aside and getting out of bed. Shoulders back and head held high, he stuck out his tongue.

I heard that.

He pulled his tongue back in so quickly it snagged against the edges of his bottom teeth. The pain made his eyes water.

"D'aaam," he muttered, fanning the injury with one hand.

Exactly, pal, his disembodied voice answered. *Damn.*

"Stop it, Allison."

Her chuckle echoed inside his head. *Make me.*

Okay. Ignoring the pain, Mica closed his eyes and went on automatic pilot.

"And out of the ground Jehovah God formed every beast of the field, and every bird of the heavens; and brought them to man to see what he would call them: and whatsoever man called the living creature, that was the name thereof. And the man gave names to all cattle, and to the birds of Heaven, and to every beast of the field.'"

Mica.

Rolling his shoulders, he smiled and leapt from Genesis to Corinthians –

"'The glory of this world hath blinded the minds of the unbelieving, that the light of the gospel of the glory of Christ, who is the image of God, should not dawn upon them.'"

– to Peter –

"'Concerning which salvation the prophets sought and searched diligently, who prophesied of the grace that should come unto you, searching what manner of time the Spirit of God which was in them did point unto when it testified beforehand the sufferings of Christ and the glory which should follow . . . "

Mica opened his eyes and listened, but not for her voice – he'd learned, through trial and a lot of error, that she couldn't read his mind when he recited gospel. He was listening to the words that still came so easily to him, even though . . . even though he'd betrayed their meaning forever.

Eight months and counting.

Tick. Tick. Tick.

Forgive me, Lord? Jesus, had he always begged like that? But even as the words came and went, Mica knew the Lord wasn't listening . . . not to his words, anyway. Regardless of the promises Brother Beezer made in his book.

Mica licked his lips and let more words come. John's this time. 5:12 –

"'He that hath the Son hath life; he that hath not the Son of God hath not life.'"

And, finally, a few words of his own.

"Damn you, Allison."

Sitting on the bottom step of the basement/bomb shelter, Allison stared up at the reinforced concrete monument to one family's faith in their fellow man and followed the sound of Mica's path from the bedroom to bathroom with her eyes. The kiln-dry floorboards creaked so badly she had no doubt she would have been able to hear him even without (vampire) bat-like hearing.

The creaking stopped a yard to the right of the staircase and Allison closed her eyes, knowing what was to come next. And it did – in a hollow-sounding gush of water against water that finally ended in a parody of raindrops on porcelain roses.

And these are a few of my favorite things.

The toilet flushed and kept flowing until Mica jiggled the handle the required sixteen times. Each jiggle grating another layer off the inside of Allison's skull.

. . . thirteen . . . fourteen . . . fifteen . . . sixteen . . . *clunk.*

They needed to move. Or she needed to move. Soon. Alone.

Funny how that word used to scare her – when she was alive. Being alone. Dying alone. Now it seemed that was all she thought about . . . being alone. Being dead and alone. Free. Unfortunately, the price of freedom had gone up exponentially since she made that little decision about exchanging wrinkles for eternal damnation. To the world she might look like the perfect example of an independent woman of the new millennium – free (there was that word again) to come and go and do whatever she pleases.

But that was as much an illusion as she was.

A vampire was about the least free creature on the planet, imprisoned by nearly everything the living took for granted: daylight, finding satin sheets that fit a coffin-sized mattress, food (no Drive-Thru blood banks yet), and trying to maintain a working relationship with a human being who pissed and ate

and snored and belched and kept quoting the "Good Book"...
...without killing him.

It was hard being dead.

Allison puffed a sleep-tangled curl out of her eyes and immediately felt her hair smooth out into thick, sleek waves. A thought later and her nightshirt transformed into a pair of butt-clenching cut-offs and a skimpy halter top. Okay, so maybe being dead did have a few advantages over the living.

But it still sucked for the most part.

Which reminded her –

Her stomach was just thinking about growling in anticipation of breakfast when she heard Mica hawking up a juicy double-lunger of phlegm and depositing it – with a loud *splat* – into the john. And flush.

Rattle, rattle. ... seven ... eight ... nine ... ten ...

Growling, Allison clawed two sets of furrows into the step she was sitting on. If there was one thing, and *only* one thing she learned from Luci and the girls back at the *Fur Pit,* it was that a vampire needed to have a Watcher.

And Mica, O Joy of Joys, was hers.

For a while yet, anyway.

She'd met a number of possible Watcher replacements she thought she could work with – probably more than she could handle if she wanted to reveal her true nature to any of Las Vegas' growing Goth community. Any of them might be an improvement over her current "insignificant other." At least they'd keep about the same hours and she wouldn't have to worry about being wakened each morning to Brother Beezer.

Allison had noticed them her first night on the town – the pale, wan youngsters dressed in black despite the hot desert nights. Children playing make-believe ... hovering just outside the throbbing glare of the casino lights, lingering in the shadows, waiting to be noticed and then laughing so they could expose their glued-on fangs.

Ooo, scary. Vampires in Las Vegas, what a thought.

The only drawback Allison could think of about taking a Goth as a Watcher was that she'd never know (until it was too late) when the kid would decide to impress his friends and use her for "Show and Tell."

"Serious, dude, she's a real vampire. Lookit my neck."

"So? We all bite. That doesn't prove anything."

"Oh yeah? Well, just look what happens when I expose her to sunlight, dude."

Allison shook the image out of her head. No, Mica wasn't perfect, but he'd do. For a while. Yet.

Unless he *really* pissed her off.

Dusting off the seat of her shorts as she stood up, and adding just a bit more bounce to her T & A, Allison walked across the deep pile Persian rug that covered the floor of the bomb shelter from wall to wall. Like Mica, the little bungalow in its middle-class neighborhood would also do for a while . . . as long as she had E-Bay and the Internet.

It was amazing the things a dead woman could buy without having to leave the confines of her well-appointed crypt.

Settling back into the azure-blue velvet cushions of the carved "Lion's Throne" chair, Allison flexed her fingers and leaned her elbows against the edge of the Louis XV desk as she quickly keyed in her password.

"You have mail," an electronically feminine voice chirped happily.

"Thank you," Allison answered and chewed a little skin off her bottom lip as an appetizer while she waited. It was either an answer on the Ming vase she'd bid on, or the newest Peter Straub novel she'd pre-ordered.

The screen suddenly filled with the image of a rose carved

out of pink and green jade. It was the on-screen logo for a Thai auction house she dealt with on a more-or-less regular basis.

Dearest Miss: Have just acquired White Jade Burial Suit
Ch'ing Dynasty
Would you be interested? Price $28,000.00 + s/h.

Allison sat back, pouting. Well, it wasn't the Straub novel, but a jade burial suit might be fun to have.

"Hmm, let me think," she said out loud, her voice absorbed instantly by the thick rug and tapestry wall hangings that shared the wall space with the floor-to-ceiling bookcases (filled with first and rare editions), the big-screen TV and video library, and her framed posters. "Where would I put it?"

She looked around her "office" and frowned. *Where indeed?* Of course she could always move the life-sized replica King Tut sarcophagus CD cabinet upstairs, but the neighborhood wasn't *that* good and she'd hate to have to kill someone over the theft of a few tunes. For other reasons-yes. But not over music . . . she wasn't a complete monster, after all.

Besides, did she really *need* a burial suit? She already had her coffin all nice and cozy upstairs and couldn't really picture herself wearing white jade in public.

Except maybe at Halloween.

Hmm.

"So what do you think, boys?" she asked the gilt-framed photos that filled the desk between the computer screen and Tiffany lamp. "Should I get it? It's only 28-thou."

Gary Oldman, Antonio Banderas, Brad Pitt and Tom Cruise seemed cautious, but she could tell by the gleam in Christopher Lee's red-rimmed eyes that he thought it was a good idea. Allison always did feel a special bond with old Chris. He just looked like the kind of guy who knew what was important in an after-life.

"Okay, you're the boss."

Leaning forward, she clicked the ACCEPTED box, typed in her password and ident number and waited the thirty seconds for the company to make the necessary transaction from her VISA account. It was extravagant, but what the hell. Mica – burdened as he was with life, liberty and the constant pursuit of self-righteousness – wouldn't take any of her money, despite the fact that she made almost three times as much as a "first tier dancer" for the Follies Bergere as he did working as a Justice of the Peace.

That's why they still lived in a rental – because he wanted to pay for it without her help. He had, however, *allowed* her to buy the Mylar-lined drapes for the house.

"Chauvinistic air-breather," she said as the screen went blank, then glowed pale lavender.

Success! Congratulations on your purchase.
Order will be shipped within ten days time.
Rush Order – Yes? No?

Allison clicked *Yes* just for the hell of it. Well, why not . . . it might be worth a chuckle of two to put it on and go out for Chinese.

A dancing green dragon, the company's mascot, twirled and twisted above the red *PROCESSING* icon. A moment later the little dragon stopped dancing and blew her a kiss.

SUCCESS!
Your Rush Order will arrive between 36 and 48 hours of today's date.
An additional $2500.00 has been added to your charge.
May the suit bring you years of pleasure.

"I can guarantee it, pal," she said and returned the computer to SLEEP mode. "More years than you can guess. And now – breakfast."

Reaching under the desk, Allison opened the dorm-sized refrigerator and pulled out one of the plastic packs. A bright orange "Bio-Hazard" sticker partially covered the *University of*

Las Vegas Medical Center label, and the blood inside was the consistency of a slushy Italian Ice.

"Ah," she said, holding the bag up to the light, "September . . . a very good month."

Her fangs pierced the bag without conscious effort and her eyes fluttered in ecstasy when the first sweet, cold spurts hit her tongue. Not as good as fresh hemoglobin, of course, but the 64 units of contaminated blood had been too good of a bargain to pass up. Allison caught the story on the Ten o'clock News one night just as the "dinner" break began. So, while the other girls in the chorus line were slurping down *Slim-Fast* shakes or running out for a quick bite, she was lap-dancing her way into the heart, mind and circulatory system of the university's Hazardous Materials janitor.

He'd been an added bonus. AB-negative. *Yum.*

Smacking her lips, she tossed the depleted bag into the antique elephant's foot waste-paper basket opposite the desk and snagged another from the fridge. It was like eating potato chips – you just couldn't stop after only one. Besides, the Hepatitis C added a nice kick to the iced hemoglobin. Like mixing a drop of tabasco sauce into a Bloody Mary.

The thought of real food made her a little queasy – all that chewing and swallowing and . . . eliminating. Ugh.

Allison tossed the bag without bothering to suck it down to the last dregs and hurriedly punched in a number on her speaker phone. She needed to get her mind off solid food by-products and fast.

The phone on the other end rang five times before a breathless voice answered.

"Vict'm fer Vict'ms. How kin ah hep y'all?"

Allison smiled at the vintage Scarlet O'Hara accent. "I thought we were supposed to answer by the second ring, Jan. What if this had been a real call?"

"Oh, honey, ah a'ways have *9-1-* punched in an' my little ol' finga just a'hoverin' above t'other *1*, so iffen y'all had been a real damsel in distress the po'lee'd a'ready be on their way rat now. I may be slow as mo'lasses in Jan'wary, but I know my business."

The woman chuckled and Allison joined her. Jan was a real sweetheart, an ex-Mrs. Macon County (GA) Tractor Pull first place runner-up. Unfortunately, her coming in second hadn't been an option for Jan's (now ex- and imprisoned) husband. He hadn't even waited until they left the Fair Grounds to show his disappointment in her failure to win the brand-new set of radial tires that went along with the title, rhinestone tiara and complimentary biscuit-and-gravy breakfast at the local *Bob Evans*. He'd laid her face open with a crescent wrench right there in front of the Grandstands while their four kids, and the rest of the town, watched.

Jan liked to say that aside from getting the bastard put away for the rest of his life, her near-death experience got her picture, bruised and bandaged (and not the photo of the newest queen of tractor competition) on the front page of the local paper.

She said it made her feel just like a movie star – The Frankenstein Monster.

Jan could laugh at it now, because it was over. She'd lived. She was a survivor of domestic violence. Just like the other women who volunteered at the crisis line.

Just like Allison.

Except for the surviving part. Her abuser had actually killed her . . . not that she could actually put that down on her volunteer form.

But being dead, notwithstanding, she was as much a victim as the others. A man had abused her, made her a victim and she wasn't going to let that happen to any other woman if she could help it.

And she could. And had.

Some men just didn't deserve to live.

"So," Allison said, "where is everybody? I thought there was supposed to be at least three of you guys at the center at all times."

"Plus our b'loved sup'visor, Didi, best not t'forget her." Jan's voice suddenly dropped to a whisper. "Why? Y'all thinkin' bout comin' in for a shift?"

The hope in Jan's voice was so strong it almost curdled the blood in Allison's belly. The one thing the center prided itself on was its record of getting "women out of the shadows of their past and into the bright sunlight of a day life" . . . which was horribly counterproductive for a vampire. A reasonable lie – that her abusive relationship had left her with trauma-induced agoraphobia – had bought her sympathy and an "At Home" study course. The day she "graduated" a bouquet of sun-lilies arrived at her front door, signed by Jan and a dozen other women Allison only recognized by their voices.

"No." She lowered her voice. "I – I can't. Maybe . . . one day, but not now."

"Aw, honey, now don't get upset. Y'all are doin' a won'ful job."

Allison leaned back in the chair and put her feet up on the desk. *I know.* "So . . . where is everyone?"

"Whale, Evie's gone t'get coffee n'do-nuts, an' Margarita's . . . whale y'all know Margarita's in a fam'ly way, so she's back in the little girl's room rat now. You comin' on?"

"Yeah, plug in my line. And you all had better send over one of those do-nuts, you hear?"

Jan's purring chuckle started up again. "Aftah all this tam y'all are still talkin' like a damned Yankee. It's y'all and y'hear . . . hear?"

After six months Allison still couldn't hear the difference. "Yes'sum."

"That's bettah. Okay, y'all are plugged in. Take care now, y'hear?"

Allison smiled as she broke the connection and waited for her first victim of the day.

It wasn't a long wait.

She tapped the speaker button before the ring could echo off the concrete walls.

"Victim for Victims," she said with just enough perkiness to not sound threatening. "How may I help you?"

The line was silent – which Allison expected. Unless under immediate danger of physical abuse (or directly afterwards), there was always a moment of silence while the caller realized she was, in fact, a victim. As per her training, Allison was to offer "gentle encouragement to facilitate communication and ascertain the nature of the trauma that initiated the call," while always "maintaining a positive, supportive and non-judgmental demeanor."

Which she always did . . . for as long as she could.

Unless the situation called for something a little stronger.

Puffing hair out of her eyes, Allison picked up one of the *Victim for Victims* yellow pencils (a dozen of which arrived each month along with a stack of yellow *Victim for Victims* note pads and file reports forms – also yellow) and began twirling it around her fingers like a tiny baton.

When another thirty seconds on her internal clock had elapsed, she licked the last traces of packaged blood off her lips and began her "gentle encouragements to facilitate communications."

Part I.

"You've already done that hardest part," she said. "You called for help, so tell me what I can do, okay?"

The woman on the phone sighed. Softly.

But it was enough.

So much for gentle, supportive and non-judgmental. Part II, comin' up.

"Shit. Noreen, is this you?"

Noreen was a perpetual victim — twenty-four, a high-school dropout with five kids all under the age of eight, and a hubby whose hobbies included keeping her pregnant, gambling, and beating the shit out of her every time he lost the house money.

And he was a lousy gambler, even by Vegas standards.

Allison reached over and grabbed that month's log book, flipping through the pages. Part of her duties was to list each of her calls, with as much information as she could get from the victim. With the lists, according to theory, Social Services would be able to keep better track of the women and their families and get them into a safer environment.

Worst case scenario, the police would have hard evidence in a murder trial.

Noreen's name appeared at least three times on each page, if not more. And it was only two weeks into the new month.

"Oh. H-hi, Allison."

The training manual strongly "suggested" that volunteers not give out their names for their own protection. You never knew when some psycho scumbag abuser would take it into his head to come after the person who was trying to help. There'd already been one such incident — a *V for V* volunteer had been beaten up and raped by a man whose wife had finally left him — and from that moment on, Allison *always* made sure her callers knew her name.

It was like fishing—you throw out enough bait and sooner or later, you'll pull in a shark.

Her stomach grumbled.

Noreen tried to chuckle and failed miserably.

"I thought if I called early you'd . . . Don't you ever sleep?"

"No. Never. I gave it up for Lent." She sniffled. "Are you still at home?" *Home* being a single-wide trailer in one of the outlying districts the Chamber of Commerce never mentioned in its tourist brochures.

"Yeah."

Allison made note of it, as she was required, then snapped the pencil in half. She grabbed another out of the yellow *Victim for Victims* happy face mug and began twirling it again. It was a nervous habit that hadn't died just because she did.

"I thought you promised me that you were going to pack up the kids and get out of there the *last* time he used your face as a punching bag."

"Oh . . . he didn't beat me up this time."

This time. Allison stopped twirling the pencil. "He didn't, Noreen? Really?"

A child suddenly screamed in the background and Allison tensed until she heard *"I'm gonna tell momma if you don't give it back – MOM!"*

"'Cuse me a second, Allison, okay?" Soft static whispered over the line as Noreen cupped her hand over the mouthpiece. "Hush now. Momma's on the phone. Tommy, you give Casey back her doll right now and eat your oatmeal. Tommy, can you hear me?

"Sorry, Allison. Kids . . . you know."

No, she didn't. "Noreen, he didn't hit you?"

"Oh, well yeah, but it's only a black eye – you can hardly notice it much."

"Noreen."

"I know." Noreen sighed. "It's just that this morning I saw Tommy beating up on Casey and when I told him to stop he . . . he called me a really, really bad name and told me to go to hell just like his daddy does."

Allison added the names of *Tommy* and *Casey* beneath their mother's. Tommy was five, Casey three and the only girl. Another victim and abuser in the makings. *Shit.*

"Noreen, you have to get out of there for the sake of your kids." *Pause.* "Don't you understand what's going to happen if you don't?" *Pause, two, three.* "In another couple of years Casey's going to be calling this same number . . . if she's still alive."

"That's an awful thing to say, Allison."

"It's an awful situation you and your kids are in, Noreen!"

"Well . . . I don't think Casey will be calling. She doesn't know her numbers yet."

Paaaaaaaaaaaauuuuuuuuuuuuuussssssssssssseeeeeeee. Allison hadn't thought it possible, being dead and all, but the conversation was giving her a massive headache.

"Why'd you call, Noreen?"

"Oh, yeah. Well, see. "Buddy-Jim, *senior.*" you know, my husband?"

"Uh-huh."

"Well, he took the money I had put away for a new pair of glasses for Buddy-Jim *junior*, you know, my eldest, and . . . he said it was a sure thing and that he only lost because I'd hidden the money in the first place. So now he wants me to work the Strip. Hustling, you know, until I make enough to pay him back. And I . . . I was just wondering if you guys had the name of someone who wouldn't mind watching the kids tonight. Buddy-Jim's got a chance to get into this really hot game, so he won't be able to. Watch the kids I mean."

"While you're off whoring to replace the money he took?"

"Uh-huh."

The second pencil snapped in two.

"And you just called because you need a baby-sitter?"

"Yeah. You guys do such good work and all, I figured you'd know someone." When Allison didn't say anything, Noreen hurriedly added. "Well, it's not like I want to. It's just until I make enough to pay him back."

"For the money you were saving to buy your son a new pair of glasses."

"Yeah. Buddy-Jim *junior* really needs a new pair."

Screw the manual. "ARE YOU FUCKING NUTS?" *Pause, three, four.* "Look, Noreen, here's what you're going to do. Pack up the kids and get the hell out of there. Now."

"I can't. Buddy-Jim junior and the twins are in school right now."

Allison shook her head and ground the broken pencil into a powder between her fingers.

"Get them. Call a cab, go get the kids out of school and get to a safe house."

"Huh?"

"Never mind. I'll call the cab and give the driver the address of the school and a place where Buddy-Jim senior can't find you."

"Oh, no . . . Buddy-Jim'll be mad. He'll get home and see we're gone and figured I left with the kids. You really don't know what he's like when he's mad, Allison. It's really scary. He can really turn into a monster."

That makes two of us. "Don't worry, Noreen. I'll – I'll have someone stop by and talk to him. Where's he work?"

Noreen's voice dropped into a low, terrified whimper. "Oh, God, don't do that. One time a person from Child Welfare went over to the garage to talk to him and . . . it wasn't good, Allison. It really wasn't and he was so mad when he got home. . . ."

"It'll be okay this time, I promise. Just tell me."

"No."

"Noreen, I'm trying to help you."

"NO!"

Allison sat back and watched the dust from the pulverized wood and lead drift down through the Tiffany lamp's multi-colored glow as she concentrated — felt whatever passed for her non-existent soul reach through the phone lines and wrap itself around the frightened woman's mind. She didn't like to use this particular talent on anyone but Mica, but since the calls were regularly monitored for "quality control," it was better if some questions weren't vocalized.

If the supervisor listened in now, she'd only hear Noreen talking to herself and probably wonder how it was that poor Allison always seemed to get the nut cases.

Noreen, can you hear me?

"Y-yeah."

Good. Now listen, you don't have to be afraid anymore. But you're going to have to help me help you, okay?

"Okay, sure."

You're a good mom, Noreen. You proved that by calling — now I want you to continue proving it. Tell me where Buddy-Jim works and I promise he won't ever hurt you or your kids ever again.

"No! Oh God, no. Buddy-Jim *likes* me and the kids so he always pulls his punches . . . but he won't care what happens to a stranger. I —"

Shh.

Allison suppressed the fear center in the woman's brain and instantly shared the feeling of calm that raced through their connective beings.

Would it be so bad if Buddy-Jim never came home?

"No," Noreen sighed. "It'd be heaven."

Well, I wouldn't go as far as that. Tell me where he works.

"You — you won't hurt him, will you? I mean, he's not a bad man . . . not really."

He won't feel a thing, Noreen. And then, for her listening public – "I know, Noreen, no one is completely bad. Tell you what – let me give you the name and address of the optometrist who helps us out from time to time. I'll call and set up an appointment for you and you take Buddy-Jim, junior, there right after school, okay?"

"Um – yeah, okay."

"Good. And don't you worry, everything's going to be fine."

I promise. You understand, Noreen?

"Yeah." The fear in her voice was gone. She understood. "Thanks, Allison."

"Don't mention it." *To anyone. Ever.* "Now, jot this down–" *And tell me where he works.* "– and we're all set."

Addresses were exchanged and jotted down. *This,* was the real perk she got for volunteering her time and talent. Helping out left a real sweet taste in her mouth.

Or soon would.

Yummy, yum, yum!

CHAPTER 2

Mica stared at his reflection in the bathroom mirror and tried to see if there was anything left of the real Mica . . . the *real* Milo Poke left behind the clean-shaven face and bleached-blond, salon-styled hair. He knew "he" was in there . . . somewhere . . . and looking for him had become as much a part of Mica's morning ritual as brushing his teeth and wondering how the Lord had let him get into this mess in the first place.

Because he knew it wasn't his fault. He'd never believed in "free will" and never would . . . so it really bothered him that the Lord had allowed all this to happen to him.

"If there's a lesson here, Lord," Mica said, pulling down the bottom lid of his left eye *(No, no Milo there.)*, "would You mind speeding things up?"

But the Lord, as had been His practice over the last few months, remained silent. Mica would have been surprised by anything else, but he did add a "praise Thy name" just for old time's sake.

And watched his reflection yawn.

Mica let go of his eyelid and leaned his knuckles against the sink's cool porcelain, just staring at the face that stared back at him. *Hey, Milo – All the – all the outs in free. Come on, boy, come out and say howdy. I know you're still in there.*

Aren't you?

The man in the mirror shrugged again and sighed. Going, going . . . a little more each day until he'd wake up one morning and be . . . gone. It was almost as if Allison had been feeding on his soul instead of his blood. Along with his youth and vitality.

What do you mean "almost?"

His reflection was frowning at him, the slight wrinkles that had been barely visible back in Hollywood now grown to full-fledged crows feet. God, he was getting old – turning into an old man he wouldn't recognize any more than he did the suntanned, surfer-haired middle-management type.

Getting older, day by day.

While she stayed young and vibrant . . . night by night.

In a couple of decades people would start to tell him what a lovely *daughter* he had.

Then great-granddaughter and then great-*great*-granddaughter (if he was lucky). And then she'd bury his decimated remains and move in with the first poor shmuck she could lay her fangs on.

All while God watched and did absolutely nothing.

"It's not fair," he told the Lord by way of the yuppie in the mirror. "I did everything You've ever asked of me and more." *Much more.* "I've been on Your side from the very start . . . gave up whatever happiness I might have found in the arms of a living woman because of my love for YOU. And this is how You repay me? By letting me walk into all this shit without even giving me a sign? What kind of a fucking, two-bit God are –"

Oops.

His reflection stared back at him in shock and he finally saw a little bit of himself in those wide, fear-rimmed eyes.

"Ohmygod, God, I'm so sorry. I didn't mean that. You understand . . . I know You do. It's just that . . . I've really been under a lot of pressure lately. You know that, too, of course, since You *are* fucking omniscient and able to see the fall of a single, insignificant sparrow even if You happened to miss the fall of one of Your own sons!"

The look of horror on his reflection hadn't lessened to any great degree. *Well, screw you, too, you wussy.* And that's when he heard it – the soft giggling drifting up through the stained linoleum beneath his feet. *Shit! It was that bitch again!*

What?

His reflection had the nerve to look smug.

"Um – 'And . . . and the Lord said unto Adam –' ah . . . 'behold for I have created for thee this day a workmate . . . crafted by My hand from thine own rib so that she shall always be a part of thee and thou shall have dominion over her.' Yeah, right."

Mica joined his reflection in shaking their heads. Man having dominion over a woman . . . well, it was a wonderful theory, but the ancient Biblical prophets hadn't known Allison. He'd had his chance once but blew it and spared her unnatural life.

Maybe God wasn't the only one to blame after all.

"You're not going to wear that shirt again, are you?"

Mica's reflection literally jumped out of its skin when he turned around, his hands clutching the front of the flamingo-pink and black, 1950s era satin bowling shirt he'd bought for a dollar at *Goodwill*. Leaning back against the vanity, Mica swallowed hard and looked down at the floor – *Impossible! I just heard her down there.* – before hauling his gaze up to meet hers.

Allison leaned back against the door-frame, arms crossed under her breasts and a thin smile on her lips. The same kind of smile an over-indulgent owner would give a pet who'd just piddled on the rug.

He gave the linoleum one more look before patting the wrinkles out of his shirt.

"I– I didn't hear you come upstairs."

"I can be very quiet when I want to," she said, innocently. "Now, why don't you go put on one of those nice polo shirts we got at Lord & Taylor?"

"But I like this shirt."

Allison shook her head, her fiery hair shimmering in the light of the single 75-watt bulb as she pushed away from the door and walked toward him. She didn't hurry, she didn't have to – time would always be on her side.

"I know," she said, pressing the ends of the black-piped collar down against his clavicle. Mica shivered as the coldness of her touch seeped through the satin. "But the fact is you've already worn it to work this week. Everyone will think we're poor."

"But–"

Allison shook her head and his mouth slammed shut. "No buts. We may be living in middle-class paradise, but we don't have to dress like it. So, go change. For me. Okay?"

Mica wouldn't have answered even if he could, not with her fangs in such close proximity to his jugular . . . but he just couldn't keep himself from thinking.

(Which, of course, was the Lord's fault. *Free will, my ass!*)

During their first months in Vegas, Allison had seemed relatively content with their incognito lifestyle. To a point. And then one morning he woke to the sounds of knocking and opened the front door to the first, of many, UPS deliveries.

Allison had as much aversion to starting a savings account as she had for garlic bread.

"Why shouldn't I spend my money? Hell, it's not like I'm going to have to worry about retiring. I scrimped and saved my whole life and what did it ever get me? Two weeks, every other year

because that's all I could afford, at a spa on Catalina Island. Shit, I couldn't even afford to go to the casino there more than once. I'm dead now . . . I can buy everything I ever wanted."

Just about.

She had made one minor concession – she'd allowed him to furnish the ground floor of their "happy little love nest" using his money and taste. The results looked a lot like a combination of a scaled-back version of the Playboy Mansion (by way of K-Mart and Goodwill) and his old trailer back in Mrs. B's yard.

It was homey and cozy and comfortable . . . and Allison hated it.

She made up for it, however.

They really didn't need a car – Mica had a friend who picked him up for work and he enjoyed taking public transport or the free tour bus if he wanted to go anyplace special, and Allison could run, if she'd wanted to, from the center of town to Boulder City without conscious effort – but she bought a car, a classic 70's black Mustang convertible (with custom tuck-and-roll crimson leather upholstery).

She really didn't *need* to go shopping . . . at least not for herself, having the ability to change whatever she was wearing (right down to skin level) at will . . . but she *loved* to go shopping. For him. She'd allowed him to furnish the bungalow (a point she never failed to bring up when it suited her), but she wasn't about to let him shame her in public.

Bowling shirts notwithstanding. When he could get away with it.

Which wasn't that often.

So they went shopping – at all the trendier/priced-for-tourist shopping centers around town: Fashion Show Mall, Tower Shops, Gold Key Shops, Sahara Pavilions, The Boulevard Mall, gaze Gallerie, and every single store in the Forum Shops at Caesar's Palace where she'd make him try on one outfit after another like he was just some life-sized fashion doll.

Allison suddenly leaned back, her eyes going wide with surprise.

"What?"

"*What* what?"

She leaned close enough for him to smell the stench of copper and rotted fish rising from her lips. His stomach gave one shudder and collapsed into his lower gastrointestinal track.

"You're comparing yourself to a Ken doll?"

"I – *eek!*"

Her hand had grabbed his crotch so quickly that he barely had time to scream.

"Well, you got a point, I guess," she said, squeezing him like a ripe peach, "Neither of you seem to have any balls. Now, like I said, why don't you change. Now."

Mica nodded – once she released his package and thus allowed the flow of blood to return to his upper brain – and then *(finally)* the Lord took pity on him.

A car horn's rendition of the first seven notes of *"Love Me Tender"* reverberated through the bungalow's thin walls. Allison's nose twitched.

"Alvis is here," Mica yelled. "Gotta go."

Growling softly in her throat, Allison backed up, giving him a clear escape route. "I still think you should change."

Mica suddenly wasn't completely sure if she meant the shirt or what the shirt covered, and didn't have the nerve to ask. Instead he mumbled "no time" and bolted through the drape-dark shadows for the front door.

The bright, hot desert morning blasted its greetings and immediately began lapping up the fear sweat on his face. Living in the desert was a whole like lot living with a vampire – both had a craving for bodily fluids.

The car horn tooted again *(. . . love me tender, love me true . . .)* and Mica waved in the general direction of the curb, still blinded by the searing light.

"Hey, Alvis."

"Hey, son. You're lookin' mighty good this fine mornin'. And do ah see your sweet lady standin' back there?"

Mica felt the bleached and stylishly short hair rise on the back of his neck as he turned around. She was standing just behind the golden wash of sunlight – Raven in hair and figure but still all Allison around the scowl.

"Hey, there, sweet lady," Alvis called.

Allison/Raven sneezed.

"Hi," she answered, sniffing. "I'll be late tonight. We're rehearsing a new number. Don't wait up."

"I won't," Mica promised – not that he ever waited up for her. "Okay. See you later."

"Yeah. Later."

For appearances sake and nothing else, he stepped back into the shadows to kiss her good-bye. A quick peck on the cheek, which was all he could handle on an empty stomach. Mica could hear Alvis's groaning pity above the 1959 pink Cadillac Eldorado convertible's throaty purr. The still desert air was a great sound conductor.

Which was unfortunate.

"Son," Mica's best friend in Vegas yelled from the street, "ah seen elderly maiden aunts kiss with more passion. Ya want me t'come up there and show yah how it's done? What'cha say, Raven, mah raven-haired beauty?"

Before she could answer, Alvis sent her one via air mail.

And the next minute, Mica found himself standing on the cracked concrete front step, squinting into the sun, sweat already gathering under his arms and in the recesses of his boxer shorts, as the door slammed shut behind him. He didn't hear any cursing or screams of pain, so he figured she must have been able to close (and lock) the door without coming in contact with any stray sunbeams. But he did hear her sneeze.

"You know," Mica said as he walked across the lime-green gravel a previous owner had put down in lieu of a front lawn, "you keep teasing her like that and she won't let me ride with you anymore."

Letting go of the tire-sized white steering wheel, the man who had taken first place in every state-wide *Elvis Impersonator/Over 40 Class* competition pulled off his mirrored wrap-around sunglasses and hung his head in shame. One long sigh later, he turned his head and gazed up at Mica, azure-blue sincerity oozing from beneath thick black lashes.

"Ah know, but ah just can't seem to help mahself. Specially when ah see yah two actin' like some ol' married couple right outta a Ted Turner classic movie. Mah Lord, son . . . what yah got is a woman who needs some lovin'. Ah could tell by the way she was a'lookin' at yah that she wants yah, boy. She wants yah *bad*."

Mica felt himself tremble at the words, then realized it was just the ground shaking beneath his feet as Alvis gunned the Caddie's motor in an attempt to drown out the peal of his baritone chuckles.

"Sorry," Alvis said, still laughing as he lifted the hem of the *Viva La$ Vega$* muscle tee to wipe a tear from his eye. "Don't mind me, ah'm just teasin'."

There was a damp spot on the tee-shirt, just above the silk-screened image of the *real* Elvis Aaron Presley . . . almost like a halo. It wasn't hard to see why Alvis had beaten out all would-be Kings. Even though he was fit and trim and probably in better shape than the real Elvis ever had been in his life, it wasn't hard to see the resemblance between the two. They had the same eyes, the same golden tan, the same white mutton-chop sideburns and coal-black pompadour.

And the same adventurous nature when it came to culinary experiments.

Mica mentally burped, remembering the special order bacon-sausage-and nutter-butter pizza Alvis had gotten him to try. *And You didn't stop me that time EITHER, Lord.*

The only difference between Alvis and The Once and Only King was that he, Alvis, couldn't remember lyrics to save his life. As long as there was a karaoke-type prompter in front of him, no other impersonator stood a chance and for those few moments it was almost as if The King had lived beyond that terrible August night in 1977.

On his own . . . only the Lord knew what words would come out of his mouth.

That same mouth was still working its way around a smile when Alvis slipped the sun-glasses back on. "Yah know that, don't cha?"

"Yeah," Mica said as he popped open the passenger-side door and slid inside. "I know."

"Yah sure? Yah look a might peaked. Yah eat yet?"

"No, not yet."

Alvis tsk-tsked and shook his head. "That ain't right. Yah want me t'have a little talk with your lady?"

"NO!" The Caddie shimmied when Alvis jumped. "Sorry."

"Low blood sugar," the older man mumbled while Mica fished his own pair of aviator sunglasses out of his breast pocket and slipped them on. Tossing one arm back over the bench seat, the other over the door frame, he leaned back and smiled. Whereas he always felt self-conscious driving with Allison, Mica felt right at home in the salmon pink Caddie with the customized *ME L-VIS* license plates.

In fact, he felt 100% better just being in the car and with

his friend under the bright desert sky.

"Maybe you're right. So, you hungry?"

Alvis grinned from ear-to-ear and patted the washboard plane of his belly.

"Ah'm wastin' away, son," he said as the car pulled away from the curb. "Just a'wastin' away."

Mica's chuckle was lost beneath another horn solo – *". . . love me tender . . ."*

❖

". . . love me long."

Allison stopped at the top of the basement stairs and felt her body cringe. She hated that song. Had hated it the first time she heard it and would *always* hate it. For all eternity. She also hadn't cared too much for the man/singer/icon of the trailer parks.

All that hype and for what? A fat old man who'd drank too much and ate too much and died on the john. Okay, so the guy could sing . . . big, hairy deal. There were a whole lot of people who could sing. So why the near-god-like status of this one lone Tennessean?

Besides, there was something about Mica's friend that – "Ah-CHOO!"– she just didn't like. Elvis Impersonator or not. For all she knew the man could be the reason behind Mica's here-to nonexistent backbone. She still couldn't believe he'd actually walked out of the house wearing that god-(*sniff*)-awful bowling shirt after she'd specifically told him to change.

Yeah . . . it had to be the friend. Good ol' Alvis.

SNEEZE-RING!

Allison wiped her nose and stared at the back of her hand. That was the first time she'd ever rang. She was still staring at her hand when the office phone rang again.

"Oh."

Dead or not, it was nice to be needed.

All but flying down the stairs (even with all her practicing, she still hadn't figured out how to transform from woman to bat), Allison flung herself into her chair and hit the speaker button before the third ring ended. Another advantage to being dead was that she never sounded out of breath.

"Victim for Victims," she said gently, as the manual suggested. *I swear if this is Noreen again I'm going to come out there and–* "How may I help you?"

"Um. Well, I – ah. I'm not sure, actually."

The voice was soft and cultured (definitely not Noreen), troubled but coherent. A big plus.

"It's all right," Allison told the woman, "take your time. Are you hurt?"

"What? Oh, no, of course not. *I'm* not hurt."

"You're not?"

"No, why do you ask?"

The woman sounded confused by the question – which made two of them. Allison sat back and rubbed the center of her chest where she'd felt the stake that had gone through Luci's heart. True, it'd been a while, but the memory of the pain was still there. Those kinds of things just don't go away. If the woman had been hurt, in anyway, she should have remembered it.

"Because this is a crisis line for violence against women and you called."

When the line went silent, Allison reached over and initiated the (only slightly illegal for public use) phone trace that an admiring fan on the police force had given her. Allison never told Mica about it . . . or her "friend in blue." What her Breather didn't know wouldn't hurt her.

The small black box's first amber light blinked on. One digit down, six more to go . . . if the woman was calling from within the local area code. All Allison had to do now was keep her on the phone for a while longer.

"Ma'am, it's all right." Allison smiled as two more lights blinked on. "You can tell me anything. What happened?"

"I gave blood," the woman said, "but it didn't hurt."

Allison pulled her knees up to her chest when her belly started grumbling. "No, it usually doesn't but . . ." Light number four blinked on. ". . . ma'am, this is a help line for women, men, too, sometimes, who are or have been abused. Giving blood isn't considered abuse unless – Did someone force you to give blood? Were you held down against your will and have your veins opened and –"

She had to stop and swallow, but the woman didn't seem to notice how juicy her words had gotten.

"Of course not," she said. "I gave it freely in order to make good on the discount offer."

Huh?

"It's just that, well, I'm concerned about the young man involved. I think I may have beaten him a little too hard. Now, the management assured me that he was fine, but I'm not totally convinced." The woman lowered her voice. "And, of course, I wouldn't wish to be involved in any sort of lawsuit so it might come to light that the young man was injured. I do have my family and reputation to consider. I'm sure you understand."

Not at all. "Ah, so why did you call?"

"Well, the management gave me this number to call if I felt like I needed to talk to someone about . . . what happened."

The rest of the amber lights came on, as did a tiny car icon – indicating a mobile phone. The woman could be calling from anywhere.

"I see." Allison switched off the tracer and picked up a pencil. "So, let me get this straight. You beat up a man and got our number from his pimp, right?"

"Good God no! What sort of woman do you take me for?"

Allison flinched. "I'm not sure, but I don't think you're the kind of woman who needs any service I can offer. Although I do strongly suggest you get an HIV test if you fucked the guy as well as beat him up. Thanks for calling."

She was about to hang up when the woman broke into violent sobs.

"Oh God, oh God, I don't – I don't know why I did that. I – Oh GOD."

AH-CHOO! Allisons nose kicked into high gear with a stacatto series of sneezes. That the mere mention of ... of "Him", the mere thought of something sacred immediately sent her into hay fever hell was just one more of the many, *many* things she was still getting used to. About being dead, that is. Oh, and being a vampire, too.

Her nose finally took a rest. "Shh," Allison pleaded, "it's okay. Just tell me what happened. You were hurt, weren't you?"

"N-no," the woman sniffed, "I wasn't. But . . . I don't know what happened to me. I was out here to give a speech at the international business management seminar out at the convention center and . . . well, I saw this woman I'd known for years and she just seemed so . . . different. Vital and sure of herself – completely unlike the mousy little ex-secretary type I thought I knew."

Allison's concern about the woman diminished a bit. In life she'd been a mousy little secretary. Type A-positive, now just ex.

"I asked her about it, of course and she was the one who told me about this place. This . . . *dude* ranch out near Henderson. She actually raved about it. Said it changed her entire outlook on life and how she dealt with people. She said the experience showed her how much of a victim she'd been all these years . . . and how she'd allowed that to happen.

"Believe me, I understood that completely. It's hard enough to be a woman in today's business world and it's even harder if you're strong and capable and want the same respect and dignity that is afforded men. I know . . . I've been abused by the system my entire adult life. As my friend had . . . until now, it seemed. Naturally when she suggested we go out there I couldn't say no. Her transformation was absolutely phenomenal."

"So you went and . . . beat up some guy?"

The woman's bitch boss demeanor faltered again. "Y-yes."

"Why?"

"Because that's what you do there. From what I gathered it's an . . . S&M sort of club designed for women who feel they've been abused by the system . . . and men in general. It's supposed to be only recreational, but – but I may have beaten this man too hard."

The woman suddenly laughed. Allison grabbed the handset and held it to her ear, focusing all her attention on the sounds coming through the line. It wouldn't be the first time a battered woman had called while her attacker was with her – forcing her to make the call for help just so he could have an audience.

Allison burped, quietly, remembering the last time that happened.

And licked her lips.

"What's the matter? Are you in trouble? Is the man still there?"

"No . . . no it's – it's not that . . . it's –" Allison had to move the phone away from her ear when the laughter became hysterical. "Oh my God – I liked it. I mean I liked it so much. All these years of having to fight the system just because I'm a woman. Being held back while I watch men with less talent and brains move up the corporate ladder ahead of me. It was so good to hit back . . . to make a man pay for everything I've been through. I just wanted . . . I wanted to . . . I – Oh my God. I wanted to kill him."

Reasonable, Allison thought, even though she kept the opinion to herself – especially if her supervisor was listening in. "But you didn't and I'm sure he's all right."

"I don't know. I really hit him hard."

"And you paid for this?"

"Yes, but got the discount rate because I donated a pint of blood. They're very big on giving back to the community."

"I can see that." Running her tongue over her teeth, Allison pulled up her note pad. "And what did you say the name of this place was?"

"The Stud Farm," the woman, voice flat, no trace of the emotion that had her in tears only a moment before. "Out near Henderson. Straight down 525, just past the Horizon Ridge Parkway. It's very secluded. Take the first exit and bear to the right. It's about two or three miles out in the desert but you'll have to look carefully for the sign post. It's small and you can miss it easily."

"*The Stud Farm*, got it." *Why does that name sound familiar?*

Allison wrote down the name and town but wondered why the hell the woman was giving her directions as if she was going to jump in her car and go out there. She might stretch the rules a bit now and then, when it came to giving out her name to clients or killing a chronic abuser, but she'd be damned (*again*) if she'd jump in the car and waste her gas scouting out alternative lifestyle clubs . . . no matter how interesting they sounded.

"Well, thanks for calling. I'll give the information to my supervisor and –"

"No! *You* have to do this!"

Rule Number One in the training manual: Never argue with a crazy person. "All right," she said, "*I'll* look into it personally. How's that?"

The woman's voice softened. "Good. Yes, thank you. Thank you."

Allison scribbled the time, date and *Stud Farm – question mark, question mark, question mark* into her log and tossed the pencil aside.

"No problem. Now, just for my own files – do you know the man's name?"

"Um . . . I'm not sure, but I think it was Lance . . . or maybe Rod. I-I'm not sure any more."

The place was sounding better and better. "Don't worry about it. I'll make sure I find out if the man's been hurt. Do you think you need any trauma counseling? I can put you in touch with a number of reputable psychologists in your hometown, if you'd like."

"For what?"

"Pardon me?"

The aloof, indignant tone returned to the woman's voice. "Why would *I* need to see a psychologist?"

"Well, sometimes a person in your situation experiences post-traumatic symptoms."

"What the hell are you talking about?" the woman demanded. "And how did you get my private number?"

Allison pulled the phone away from her ear and stared at it. No, it was still a phone.

"What?" she asked after deciding she wasn't the one hearing things. "You called me."

"Why would I call you? I don't even know who you are."

"Wh–" The line went dead.

Allison listened to the peaceful static for a few seconds before hanging up. Then keyed up the lunar calendar on her computer. Nope, the full moon was still a week away . . . so she had no idea what had prompted the call.

Unless it was the slickest advertising campaign in history. Which, considering Las Vegas had been known to outshine even her old stomping grounds of Hollywood when it came to publicity stunts, might not be such a far-fetched idea.

Allison drew a circle around the name. *The Stud Farm*. "I don't think I've ever been down to Henderson . . . ."

RING!

"Victim for Victims," she said, using the speaker option again. "How may I–"

"That God-damned bastard hit me with a belt and threaten to knock my teeth down my throat if I didn't hand over my welfare check when he got back from shooting pool with his loser friends. I want his boney ass in jail!"

Ah, straight forward and direct.

Allison smiled. This one sounded like something she could sink her teeth into.

Her belly grumbled.

CHAPTER 3

Mica leaned back against the seat and closed his eyes, letting the morning wind run its hot fingers through his cowlick. He used to enjoy the feeling a lot more when his hair was longer and still the natural, dead-mouse brown he'd been born with. Maybe there was something in the "Sunshine Glow #42" dye the salon used that had desensitized his scalp.

And then probably went right on to seep into the pores of his skull until it reached his brain. He couldn't really remember the last time he truly felt "alive." Of course, living in sin with an animated corpse – and a bossy one at that – might have had more to do with it than the dye that was probably just giving him brain cancer.

Which was another thing he was upset with the Lord about.

Mica sighed loudly, knowing that the sound would be covered by the wind and Alvis (attempts of) singing along (somewhat) with the *Blue Hawaii* soundtrack blaring from the CD player hidden inside the Caddie's glove compartment – hidden from view because Alvis wanted to keep his "Pink Lady" as seemingly pure as the day she'd rolled off the showroom floor, at least to all outward appearances.

Alvis hinted that he'd fix up the Caddie in other ways, but never really said how . . . and, to be honest, Mica didn't care enough to ask. He didn't care if the Caddie could fly as long as it got them to work on time. If the man wanted to spend all his hard-earned cash on an old car, Mica wasn't about to lecture his friend on the sins of Pride and Detroit Idolatry.

Especially since he had a few sins of his own that the Lord didn't seem to be in much of a hurry to absolve.

"'. . . but ah can't help trawlin' for love . . . with . . . yooooooouuuuuu.' Yah sleepin'?"

Mica opened his eyes and watched the puffy green-tinted clouds, street lights and telephone lines sweep past overhead for a moment. The morning was so fresh and bright – the kind of morning he remembered when he was a kid back in Tulsa. Getting up early, before his folks were awake, so he could be the first one to see God rise in the east. And God could see him.

"Milo! Get back inside this house and put on some clothes this instant! How many times do I have to tell you the neighbors don't need to see your goodies!"

Mica heard the vinyl upholstery against his neck give him a wet-kiss as he turned his head.

"Just day-dreaming," he said, pushing himself back up into a full sitting position. The back of his bowling shirt was soaked through with sweat and clinging to his skin even though he hadn't been in the car more than ten minutes. The desert heat, like the ever-expanding multi-million-dollar "theme" casinos, was merciless.

"Dreamin's for the night," Alvis bellowed over the whine of steel guitars coming from the speakers and the roar of an out-of-state Winnebago passing on their left. "'Cept if yah see an especially fine lookin' woman walkin' down the street. Then a little dreamin's okay. Well, for me . . . you're taken."

"Not yet," Mica mumbled, "but she would if she could."

"Pardon?"

"Nothing," he said, changing the subject but pointing

through the windshield to a fenced-off corner where a construction crew was busy as ants. A pink-and-white banner tied to the fence fluttered in the wind. *Watch for the GRAND OPENING of the Pink Flamingo Family Fun Center and Casino/Loose Slots/AC.* "That used to be a really nice used book store. Urban renewal. You'd think Vegas'd have enough casinos by now."

Alvis smiled around whatever lyrics he'd just sung to "Rock-A-Hula Baby" and leaned forward to watch the Caddie's back fins in the rear-view mirror as he swung into a sharp right turn onto 1st Street.

"Oh, little brother, who can say what's enough? Ah mean, one man might think havin' a casino on every block might be a bit extravagant, while another man might see it as a monument t'free enterprise and the pursuit of happiness. Me, ah like havin' a lot of casinos around. Casinos have lots a'bright lights . . . and if there's one thing the unfriendly aliens don't like it's bright light, that's why the lights a'ways go out when they're around. And that's why ah like Vegas . . . aside from getting mah career back on track. Those nasty aliens try to turn off the lights here and they'd be facin' the wraith of about a million gamblin' fanatics. Course, that don't apply t'mah little alien buddies – they like the bright lights but their ships, bein' star-drive n'all, do tend t'mess up TV reception when they're in town . . . so they don't visit as much as they'd like."

"Uh-huh," Mica said. He'd heard the story before. Many times before. Besides being the Top Rated Elvis Impersonator in the state, Alvis Ambrose was a non-registered "Alien Abductee." Non-registered because, he said, it wasn't anyone's business but his, and his alien buddies, what had happened inside that star-drive ship all those years ago. And, the Lord knows, Mica wasn't about to ask. Just the mental image of Alvis being anally probed had put him off his food for a week.

"Yeah," Alvis said, nodding like Mica understood, "they're a sensitive bunch, mah little friends are. Not many people know that bout them, either . . . but they'd hate it if folks got mad at them.

"Whoops – look out . . . there he is!"

Mica sat up straighter, reflecting Alvis' ear-to-ear grin.

"All this reminiscin' bout mah little pals almost made me miss him. Yah ready?"

"Yup."

"All woke up?"

"And all shook up."

"Huh?"

Mica waved the question away. Not that his friend would have heard his answer anyway.

Letting out a Rebel Yell that turned heads and undoubtedly caused a few hearts to skip a beat, Alvis slowed the Caddie well below the posted speed while Mica grabbed the top of the windshield and pulled himself into a more-or-less standing position. Together, they raised their right arms in a stiff, forty-five degree wave and shouted up to the man who would always be the symbol of Las Vegas and all it stood for.

"HOWDY PARTNER!"

Mica held his breath, feeling the hot, exhaust-scented air ruffle the damp out of his shirt while their voices echoed down the neon-flecked canyon of old Downtown. A moment passed, then another, and then the slow drawl of the original rootin'-tootin', Stetson-wearin' Cowboy answered back.

"How - dee pard – ner."

Mica whooped and slid back down the back of the seat as Alvis urged the Caddie up to the speed limit and sped away. Famed in picture and postcard, the Cowboy Sign had always been the first thing Mica thought of, on those rare occasions in his youth when he even thought about Las Vegas at all. That and Ann-Margret, of course.

Back then, the glittering town (and Ann-Margret) had been just another thing he could dream about but never have. Now he and Cowboy Bob (as he'd secretly christened him one night) were old friends.

And one day, Ann-Margret might just show up and say "hi."

It had been the landmark that led Mica to his spot in front of the bus depot. Had called him from his self-imposed three-week isolation. Convinced that every police cruiser in town had his picture taped to their dashboards, right above the pump-action shotgun, Mica hadn't gone farther than the corner mini-Mart/video store/loose slots/AC.

Then one night, while Allison, nee Raven, was strutting her stuff under the bright lights, he'd grabbed his bible, a clean pair of underwear and the wad of twenties one of Allison's "dinner companions" had given her as a tip, stuffed them into the Army-Surplus duffle bag that Gypsy had given him *(May his soul find peace)* and headed for the first Greyhound Bus back to California. His plan — as far as he'd thought it out on two six-packs — was simple: He'd go back to Hollywood, confess that it was all Allison's fault, and stand proud on a "Not Guilty by Reasons of Mental Incompetence" plea.

There was no doubt that his plan would work. After all . . . it *almost* worked when they booked him for Mrs. B's murder.

Mica had been a full block away when he heard it.

"How-dee pard-ner."

Not exactly the Voice From Above that he'd expected, but Mica took it as a Sign anyway and followed it until he was directly beneath the neon-outlined Messenger. Mica looked up and the Cowboy looked down upon him and waved, his smile ever bright as it welcomed him . . . and the newly arrived tourists.

The cross-shaped scar on Mica's forehead had itched like a million demons as he dropped his bag and lifted his arms in prayer. He'd preached for three full hours before the transit cops suggested he move along. When, an hour later, the transit cops made a stronger suggestion to "get the fuck out of here," Mica had blessed them and left with a promise to return to save their souls.

He hadn't even noticed the duffle bag was missing until he was half-way home. It was gone when he got back to the depot, but the Cowboy was still there and still smiling. Mica came back every night since to preach and get run off . . . until Allison showed up the night one of the transit cops had done more than threaten to "give him a little English lesson."

When Mica came back the next night, there was a new transit cop who didn't mind if he preached or not, just as long as he didn't harass anyone.

Mica never asked what happened to the cop who'd sucker-punched him in the gut. He really didn't want to know.

Besides, it wasn't his fault. It was the Lord's. Again.

Mica jumped when Alvis slapped him on the leg.

"Ah do love this place," Alvis said, lifting his hand to wave to a limo driver who looked like a young Frank Sinatra. "Have ever since ah came here back in '64. Made *Viva Las Vegas* that year, you know. Knew this was a hunkah-hunkah burnin' kinda place even back then. Ah remember tellin' mah momma that when ah got home . . . ah told her Las Vegas was gonna be real good t'her little boy. And it was."

Alvis nodded his head, the smile on his face going a little sad.

"Then the aliens came and everyone thought ah was dead. Don't really regret it much and ah wouldn't of traded all them experiences ah had for nothin'. . . but that don't mean ah can't make a comeback now, does it? Funny how things turn out, isn't it." He sighed as the CD stopped. "Mind changin' that? Ah feel in the mood for a little golden oldies."

Mica scooted forward to the edge of the seat, but still had to lean almost in half in order to open the glove compartment and turn off the CD player. A dozen CD cases, mostly remastered classic Elvis hits with a few Madonna and Willie Nelsons tossed in for good measure, were tucked into the recessed shelves beneath the player.

"Anything in particular?" he asked, fingering the neat rows. "I see *Elvis' Gold Record* volumes 3 and 5."

"Hmm," Alvis said, smacking his lips as though he was already tasting the music, "both are pretty good, but see if yah can find *Elvis '56*, will yah?"

"Feeling nostalgic?"

"Yeah, a bit . . . talkin' about bein' abducted always does that t'me. Can yah just imagine where ah'd be t'day if ah hadn't left?"

Mica kept quiet as he slid the old CD into its slot and pulled out the requested '56 digital recording. Alvis was a gentle man and a kind man, even if he didn't have that firm a grasp on reality. Thinking he was The King was one thing, but believing in aliens went beyond all logic and reason. There was no aliens or "outer space" – there was only Heaven.

"Got it," he said, holding the case up for Alvis to see. "Any special requests?"

"No, just start at the beginnin'."

Smiling, Mica slid the disk in and tossed the case onto the seat next to him. Two seconds of lead and the first rock-a-billy classic blasted him back into the vinyl's sultry embrace.

"Oh YEAH! Whoah," Alvis said as he began keeping time (more or less) against the top of the steering wheel with his right hand. "That's what ah'm talkin' about. Man, just listen to that sound. Ah had it even back then, can't say ah didn't. Course, these songs'r from back before mah glory years . . . 1969 to 1976 when ah was playin' to more'n 1500 sellout crowds on The Strip. Man, it didn't get any better'n that.

"Join me?"

Having tried to sing with Alvis on more than one occasion, Mica shook his head. "Not when I can listen. It's all yours."

Alvis cleared his throat and lifted his face higher into the morning light – " . . . down at the end of Loser Street called Heartburn Hotel. Ah'm so loaded . . . ah'm so loaded . . . ah'm so loaded ah could fly."

Mica smiled. *Sounds like a good idea to me.*

❖

"Only fifteen left, ladies . . . and gentlemen, wouldn't *your* lady look absolutely stunning in this four-piece ensemble in eye-catching cerulean and pomegranate?"

"Eye-numbing's more like it," Allison mumbled at the big-screen TV while two anemic-looking models showed off the shirt (blue), shell (pink), bolero jacket (blue with pink buttons) and hat (pink with blue polka-dots – ugh). "What kind of living woman would wear something like that?"

"All for only $59.95," the announcer added cheerfully and the *Item Sale* indicator at the top, left-hand corner of the screen dropped from fifteen to four. The perky blond pitch-woman turned toward the camera and beamed. *Well, there's your answer,* her look said.

Allison ignored the look and sank her fangs into her sixth bag of frozen plasma.

The phone hadn't rung in over ten minutes (the last call from a woman who wondered if her husband's indifference to her creative endeavors constituted mental abuse – which Allison assured her it did), and the *QVC* channel's gold jewelry auction wouldn't be starting for another five minutes.

She was bored and overeating – just like when she was

alive. Only now it was blood and not junk food. Higher in protein and no fat. She was actually eating better now that she was dead than when she was alive.

"And now," the *Home Shopping Network's* hostess gushed, "our next item is absolutely breathtaking! A brilliant, baguette-cut tourmaline set in 16-karat Thai gold priced at *only* $98.25." A dainty hand, dominated by a massive ring, filled the screen. "Isn't it beautiful?"

"No," Allison answered.

"And as you can tell by the depth of color, it would make a wonderful accessory to the last item shown – which was the four-piece outfit that still can be purchased if you call our operators right now. Better hurry . . . in fact, order both. Order both RIGHT NOW!"

Allison wished she still could feel the need to yawn. Instead, she sank her fangs deeper into the liquid substitute for chili-cheese *Fritos* and started channel surfing even though she knew the morning lineup by heart (non-beating though it was). Kiddie shows, home improvement shows, talk shows (in both English and Spanish). Weather and shopping. Nature and bass fishing. Blah, blah, blah, yawn, yawn, yawn.

It almost made her wish she was dead. Really dead.

Allison paused in mid-surf to watch some naturalist try to untangle himself from a spider monkey that seemed to be taking an unnatural interest in the man's ear, when the phone rang.

Finally!

"Vithum fa Vithums – thit!" She forgot her fangs were still imbedded in the IV bag.

"Sorry," she said once her fangs were returned to their locked and upright positions, "let's try this again. Victim for Victims, how may I help you?"

There was no pause, no preliminary sigh. "I think I hurt

someone."

Allison turned off the TV. She'd never talked to an abuser before . . . over the phone.

"A child?"

"Of course not. It was a man." There was a slightly familiar indignant ring to the woman's voice. She sounded young, mid-twenties if Allison had to guess. Another guess would be well educated.

"Sorry, but I had to ask. Not all victims are adults."

"I know. But this one was."

Allison picked one of the pens she snagged from the club and jotted down the time in her log. All of her *V for V's* pencils were scattered (in piles) across the top of her desk. For a dead woman, she still had a bit of a temper.

"Okay. Do you feel like talking about it?"

"No," the woman said, "but I will. I suppose I'm a bit on edge because I've never done anything like this before."

"I understand. Did this man try to attack you? Were you defending yourself? Did you feel your life was in danger?"

"No, he was tied up. I was perfectly safe."

A prickly feeling of deja-vu began to slither up Allison's spine. "Uh-huh."

"And even though I know this place specialized in this sort of . . . activity and the proprietor assured me that the man in question hadn't been harmed, I can't – I'm afraid I can't get over the feeling that I may have caused him serious injury. I did whip him rather hard across the genitalia."

Ouch! "Why?"

"Because I was upset that I didn't get the promotion I was promised and needed to work out my frustrations. Why do you ask? You wouldn't have even thought about that if I'd been a *man*, would you?"

"No, of course not. Look, I'm a woman, too –" *Technically.*

"— so just calm down, okay?"

"Yes," the woman said, "sorry."

"No problem, so did you beat up your boss?"

"And throw twenty-seven months of hard work down the toilet? No, haven't you been listening? I beat up a complete stranger."

A complete stranger. The flesh along Allison's back tensed. "Where?"

"It's called *The Stud Farm,* just south of —"

"Henderson," Allison added. *Damn, they must be running a special this week.*

"Oh, then you know the place."

"No, but I'm starting to wonder how I missed it." Hah hah . . . not funny, girl. Not at all. "Do you know the man's name?"

"Willie or Cane or . . . it really didn't matter. If I'd known his name, the illusion wouldn't have worked. He was offered to me as Slave No. 4."

"Slave?"

"You would have liked him," the woman continued, a soft giggle breaking the surface tension of her voice. "He was very accommodating."

Allison moved back from the speaker phone as if she half-expected it to jump up and bite her. This whole thing about the *Stud Farm* was beginning to freak her out . . . and that was not an easy task to accomplish.

"If you were so concerned that you'd hurt this man," she said, "then why didn't you call the police?"

The woman suddenly laughed and Allison, despite being dead and a paid-in-full member of an internationally recognized order of monsters, jumped. The pen snapped in half and dribbled a teaspoon of blue-black ink onto the log book.

"Because I have an important meeting back in Chicago

that I don't plan to miss," the woman said.

"Then why did you call?"

"You're a help line," the woman chuckled. "Go help yourself to some fun."

Click.

Allison stared at the phone for a moment then pounded the top of her desk with both fists. *Shit!* She hadn't even thought to trace the call. That bitch could already be at the airport and –

So? the less emotional side of her brain asked.

"Yeah," Allison said out loud, "so what? The woman's a nut . . . just like –" *The other one who called this morning about the Stud Farm.* "Why is that so familiar?"

When neither side of her brain came up with an answer, Allison shrugged and was about to switch the TV back on (in hopes of finding a matching lavender-gold nipple ring to go with the set of earrings she'd already ordered) when she noticed the blob of ink on the log book. It wasn't a large blob . . . until she'd tried to clean it by laying a sheet of notepaper over it and pressing the book closed.

Then the blot looked like two butterflies fucking.

She wondered what Rorschach would have though about that.

However, she knew *exactly* what the wonderful people at the *Victim for Victims* home office would think about her sending in a log book that looked less than professional. They'd revoke her volunteer status . . . and cast her aside, forcing her to help without the benefit of their training manual and home video library.

Sob.

If that was the only reason, Allison wouldn't care, but knowing a little about how the world worked (even in a 98% volunteer organization) she didn't want her actions (or lack of them) to reflect on the call center.

Allison extended the nail on her right index finger until it was the size and shape of a scalpel, then carefully cut out the page and the one that preceded it. The notepaper hadn't been all that effective as blotting material which meant she had to rewrite both pages.

It felt too much like homework when she started, but halfway down the first page – which showed calls over a three-week run – things started to get a bit more interesting.

Okay, a *lot* more interesting.

As was her custom (and that of the other volunteers even though it wasn't strictly approved of by the powers-that-be), Allison denoted her "questionable" calls with a tiny version of *Mr. Peanut* in the far-right margin. She'd only had two on the ink-stained page, both of those from that morning, both connected to the *Stud Farm*. The previous page had seven smiling *Mr. Peanuts*, spaced at irregular intervals.

The page before that, ten. The page before that, eight.

Allison flipped the log book open to the first page and slowly went over the last four months of recorded calls. The log-book was meant to hold upwards to two-years worth of calls, depending on how bad an area the call center was in. Allison, since she was only part-time, had only filled up fifty-three pages in eight months – but on each of those pages there were at least a half-dozen smiling nuts in the margins. Each on the lines in which she'd written *Stud Farm*.

Dammit.

That's probably why the name sounded so familiar, she'd been writing it down for months and never made the connection. Even when she'd been alive, her memory wasn't all that good (there was still a woolen jumper and silk blouse waiting for her at a Hollywood dry cleaners that she'd never picked up), but the calls had been spaced too far apart for her to notice.

Except for today.

Two women had gone out of their way to make sure she noticed.

Allison picked up the phone and quickly punched in the number.

❖

"Stud Farm," a masculine voice purred. "How may I service you?"

The greeting was so similar to the one she'd been trained to give on the crisis line, that it caught Allison off guard and she verbally stumbled, canceling any hopes she had to sound professional.

"D'um."

The man's purr deepened into a laugh. "It's all right, little sister, don't be nervous."

Little sister? Nervous? I'll show him nervous.

"Um, no, I'm not. I'm – ah, calling for a friend."

"Of course you are." The condescending tone vibrated through the phone line.

Bastard.

"Sorry," he said, "I didn't mean to sound patronizing, I do apologize. I just meant that all of us need friends or we'd be alone in the world and at the mercy of those who might wish us harm." The lion-like drone was back. "And the world is such a hard and cruel place as it is. Don't you agree?"

Allison felt her head nod slowly up and down . . . right before she took back control and shook it. Hard, from left to right.

"What are you talking about?"

"Nothing important," he said. She could hear the sound of his tongue moving across his lips as he licked them and had to force herself not to do the same. "I'm sorry, I interrupted you. Forgive me, mistress."

Well, okay – mistress was better than little sister at any rate. The man on the line chuckled for some reason. "Like I said, I'm calling for a friend of mine who'd . . . who was at your establishment earlier today."

"And did she enjoy herself?"

"That's just it," Allison said, feeling that the conversational lead had finally returned to her, "she seemed convinced that she might have gotten carried away and hurt someone."

"Oh," the man said, "I see."

"So I was wondering if you could . . . check and see if he was. Hurt, I mean."

The man's voice lowered to a whisper. "If he was, I'm sure he deserved it. Men can be very naughty sometimes and need to be spanked. You know that, don't you? Wouldn't you like that? To hurt a man for all the hurt men have caused you? I know you would. And so do you."

Allison eased her back against the chair and let her fangs slip down just enough to dimple her bottom lip but not so long as they'd get in the way. "Look, asshole, I'm not calling for a cheap thrill."

"Of course not. But we are reasonably priced and do accept all major credit cards."

"Fine," Allison said, her fangs drawing twin drops of the blood she'd had for breakfast, "I'll just turn this over to the authorities in Henderson and let them deal with it."

"With what, mistress? They wouldn't find a thing."

Of course not, Allison thought, places like the *Stud Farm* could pack up and move faster than Bedouins in a sand-storm.

"Then let me speak to the manager . . . and don't try telling me that's you. I'm not in the mood to play games."

"Oh, but I think you are, little sister."

"AND STOP CALLING ME THAT!"

"Sorry, mistress. And I'm sorry that I can't get you the manager. He's – engaged at the moment."

Shit. "Alright, then will *you* please find out if this man is hurt?"

"I suppose I could. If that's your desire."

Allison stopped herself from ripping the phone out of the wall socket and throwing it across the room. Again. She'd already replaced it twice. So far.

AUGH!

"I do," she said, maintaining her composure.

"Do you remember the man's name?"

"My *friend* wasn't sure, but *she* said he was Slave Number 4."

"Oh," the man said, "then I can personally assuage your *friend's* distress. Slave Number 4 is perfectly all right."

"Oh?"

"Of course, mistress. I'm Slave Number 4, but you can call me Willie. Little sister."

"Fuck you."

"If that's your wish, but usually our clients just like to beat the hell out of us. Like your friend did."

"She didn't beat you *hard* enough."

"Yes, mistress."

"Asshole."

"Yes, mistress."

"Oh . . . go . . . fuck yourself!"

"I'll give you my best effort, mistress."

Allison slammed the handset down hard enough to rattle the Tiffany lamp and knock Antonio right onto his gilt-edged face. Up until the last few moments she'd never saw the fascination with being a Dominatix . . . now she was being to understand. Oh yeah, some men needed to be beaten over and over again.

"Jerk!"

The phone rang and she jumped.

"Victim for Victims," she growled. "How can *I* help you?"

"Well, my boyfriend and I had an argument and he slapped me . . . so I ran over his motorcycle with my truck."

"Was he on it?"

"Um, no."

"Oh," Allison said. "Too bad, better luck next time."

CHAPTER 4

The *Desert Rose Budget Wedding Chapel & Casino (Non-denominational/Loose Slots/ AC)* shared a parking lot near the Downtown Transportation Center with *Wa-He-Ho Sing's Micro Sake Brewery & Casino (Loose Slots/AC)* and *Dunkernfield's Discount Drugs & Deli (Loose Slots/AC)*. The Chapel's nearest competitor in the instant matrimony game was the County Courthouse – which had no real ambience to speak of – and with the fact that the sake "pub" a mere stagger of only twenty-five feet away, the *Rose*, as Mica liked to call it, had the advantage of being closer than either the more often photographed and publicized *Little Chapel of the Flowers* and *Little White Chapel Drive Through*.

The other wedding chapels were all along The Strip . . . much too far for inebriated young love to travel without a police escort.

Location, location, location.

"Whoa, howdy, son," Alvis said as he parked the Caddie in the employee lot behind the chapel's service entrance. "Ah can tell you honestly that mah belly thinks mah throat has been cut from ear to ear. C'mon over here and help me out . . . ah don't think ah got the strength t'walk all the way to the buffet line mahself."

Mica hurried around the car while Alvis slumped behind the wheel, the back of one hand pressed dramatically against his forehead.

"Hurry," he gasped, "ah'm fading fast."

"Hold on," Mica shouted over the rumble of morning traffic on Casino Center Blvd. behind them. "Just hold on a little longer. I'm coming – oomph!"

Alvis spilled out of the car and into Mica's waiting (but unsteady) arms the moment the driver's side door opened. Early-morning gamblers, newlywed wannabes, hung-over sake tasters all stared, gawk-eyed, at the sight of his 5'10", scrawny, bleached-blond frame valiantly struggling to keep a 6'1", muscle-bound Elvis impersonator upright and steady as they lurched toward the kitchen entrance.

When they got to the door, they turned and bowed.

"Thank yah," Alvis said as he tossed an arm around Mica's neck and forced him down for a second bow, "thank yah verrah much. And mah friend Johnny here thanks yah, too. Don't cha, Johnny."

That was Mica's cue to smile and wave. *Johnny*, he reminded himself again just like he did every morning. *I'm Johnny. Here in Vegas I'm Johnny Nil . . . says so on my drivers license and social security card. J.W. Nil on the VISA and Lord & Taylors card. Library card to John W (for Walker) Nil – Nil, for nothing.*

A cipher, Allison's living fashion doll.

Johnny Nil when he was out in public, Brother John when he was within the air-conditioned, rose-pink and white, glass-fronted wedding chapel.

Mica Poke, R.I.P. Gone, but not forgotten.

"Hey, Johnny? Yah okay, man?" Alvis was asking when Mica blinked him back into focus. "Yah went all pale'n peekie lookin'."

"What? Yeah, I'm fine." But he could tell his friend wasn't buying it, quickly added– "Maybe just a little hungry."

"Ah knew it."

Reversing their roles from a moment earlier, Alvis pushed his sunglasses up into his pompadour and threw a well-muscled arm around Mica's shoulders, dragging him through the kitchen to the steam tables in the casino's "All You Can Eat for $5.00" Rose Garden Restaurant and Lounge. Alvis never bothered with the salad bar unless it was to sneer at the mounds of leafy greens and glistening cherry tomatoes as he hurried past on his way to the dessert counter.

The room, despite its name and the garlands of plastic roses that decorated the tables and cash register, always reminded Mica of a high-school cafeteria. Formica tables set up to accommodate parties of two to twenty, plastic self-serve trays, silverware in perforated bins next to the stacks of trays; napkin dispensers on the tables, salt and pepper in little packets. Even the food had the same, prepared in bulk taste to it.

The only up side was that he, as a full-time employee, got to eat there for free.

It wasn't much of a perk, but it was the only one.

"Here," Alvis said as he shoved a tray and plate into Mica's hands. "Now start pilin' it on or ah'll do it mahself."

Mica ladled a slotted-spoon size glob of scrambled eggs onto a warm plate before setting it down on the tray and quickly moving onto the next row of steamed delicacies.

"That better not be all," Alvis said, his own plate already half buried beneath biscuts-gravy'n grits. "Yah want some help?"

"Nope," Mica said and quickly dumped another spoonful of something onto the plate next to the eggs. The last time Alvis had *helped* him fill a plate, Mica almost got a hernia walking to a table. Mica tossed on a few soggy strips of bacon over the eggs

P. D. Cacek

for good measure.

"Aw, c'mon, Johnny," Alvis said, taking excessively full advantage of the free food benefits. "Yah're a growin' boy. Here."

A slab of fried grits, slathered with chunky peanut-butter landed next to the eggs before Mica could move out of range. Alvis smacked his lips and winked.

"That's good eatin', son."

Mica was just as glad he still had his sunglasses on, otherwise his culinary-challenged friend might have been hurt by the look in his eyes. It still amazed Mica that Alvis could eat what he did (and in the quantity that he did) and hadn't yet slipped into the "Fat Elvis" slot in competition. The man had to work out.

Alvis added a slice of peanut-buttered grits to his mound-o-food.

"Hmm, don't it just make your tummy jump up n'say howdy? Women like men with a little meat on their bones. Ain't that right, B'linda?"

Belinda, the Grand Dame of the steam-table-brigade twittered and winked at Mica through the wisps of humid air.

"He's right, Johnny," she said. "Loving a man who's too skinny can leave bruises. Here, baby, have some of my special sausages . . . and give your lady a little something to sink her teeth into tonight."

Mica's appetite disappeared. Along with a good portion of his self-control. His hands began trembling so hard the fried grits slid off the plate and onto the tray.

Of course, both Belinda and Alvis misinterpreted the action.

"Boy's thinkin' about it," Alvis chuckled and tried to add another sausage to Mica's plate.

"N-no thanks," Mica said quickly, "I – I'm . . . one's plenty

66

for right now, thanks."

Belinda shrugged at him through the swirling mist. "Man doesn't know what he's missing."

"Well, ah do!" Alvis said, thrusting his brimming plate toward her under the glass sneeze-shield. "Ah'll take his portion long with mah own, if yah'd be so kind. Yah steam the best sausage o'anyone ah know, B'linda, mah love."

Belinda sighed, whirling away the steam that covered her face. Only for a moment, but it was enough. Mica's hands jerked again. Belinda was a woman of inner beauty – but that was all.

"Sweet talkin' fool," she grumbled at Alvis at the same time she tonged four dripping sausages onto his plate.

"No, now ah'm as serious as rain. Johnny, don't ah a'ways say how beautiful ah think our B'linda is?"

Mica nodded and two more sausages ended up on Alvis's plate.

"Truth be told, B'linda, ah think yah're even prettier than Jocelyn Lane . . . mah lovely co-star in the 1965 cinema hit, *'Tickle Me.'*"

Mica agreed with the critics that the movie was probably the weakest of all of Elvis's pictures, but that didn't seem to bother Belinda. She giggled and clicked her tongs together like castanets when Alvis began singing the movie's only memorable song to her – "Ah'm Yours."

A soup bowl filled with sausages and apple sauce immediately made its way to Alvis's tray.

"Now move along," Belinda said as she picked up the empty bin and headed for the kitchen. "You're holding up the line."

"Yessum," Alvis said and winked Mica toward a small table near the back of the dining room even though it was almost empty. Only about a hundred people were taking advantage of the buffet and, of those, most seemed content with black coffee and dry toast.

"Got enough sausage there?" Mica asked when they sat down.

"For this trip," Alvis said as he inhaled. "Ah a'ways thought this must be what Heaven smells like, yah know? Boy, ah remembah sittin' in mah mama's kitchen, watchin' her cook and stabbin' one of them sausages right outta the fryin' pan. Like to burn off mah tongue more'n once, but, man, there wasn't nothin' better than bitin' inta that sweet chuck o'pig. Don'cha think this is what Heaven smells like, Johnny?"

Mica scooped a single bud of eggs onto his spoon and shrugged. *Maybe that's why the Lord hasn't been around much lately – He's too busy cooking.*

"Yeah," he said, swallowing the eggs without tasting, "this is probably exactly what Heaven smells like."

❖

Mica was slowly sipping his second cup of coffee and watching while Alvis plowed through this third helping of peach-cobbler, when the manager's voice directly asked for them over the loudspeaker.

"Call for C.L. Two pair in hand and one awaiting shuffle. Budget on cut, special order with poi on deck."

Translation: There were three couples waiting to be married in the Rose's "Chapel of Love" – the first two going with the $29.95 "No Frills/Basic Wedding" plan while the third couple had sprung for the $50.00 "Hawaiian Fantasy Special" which included silk commemorative leis (pink for her, blue for him . . . or any combination thereof), one each, BRIDE and GROOM one-size-fits-all (usually) t-shirts, music, a coupon good for $25.00 in chips (one coupon per couple) and one glass of house champagne or beer.

Non-alcoholic beverages for only $1.25 extra.

Mica had the advantage of already looking at Alvis when Alvis raised his eyes to meet his. Both of them lifted their right hands, balled into fists.

"One. Two. Three. Shoot!"

Mica shot out two fingers, Alvis an open hand.

Scissors cut paper.

Alvis sighed and pushed the (small) uneaten portion of cobbler away. He looked like he was about to cry.

"Mah turn t'play preacher, ah guess," he said, eyeing the last spoonful.

Mica couldn't stand it.

"What are you talking about? I lost." Mica held up his two fingers, opening and closing them twice in front of Alvis's nose. "These are baby scissors, they wouldn't even cut air. Tell you what, I'll do the budgets and you can come in for the big show stopper, how's that?"

Alvis frowned, struggling to be magnanimous, so Mica sweetened the deal.

"So why don't you grab another cobbler or something and –" He smiled as his friend scooped up the remaining mouthful and bolted for the dessert tables. "See you down there in about twenty minutes, okay?"

Alvis waved without turning around as Mica stood up and gently pushed his way through the meandering lines of half-asleep, hung-over gamblers looking for places to collapse into. No one noticed him or answered his apologies when he accidentally bumped into them. No one knew he existed at all. Even the couples who stood before him, hand-in-hand and heart-in-heart would probably be hard put to describe him or pick him out of a line-up.

Should such an event become necessary.

As much as he hated his current "life choice," Mica had to admit he loved living in Las Vegas.

Las Vegas sucked more than she did.

It wasn't a new observation for Allison, but one that kept coming to mind as she leaned back against the faux-marble column and watched a Roman Centurion mug for the camera, one bronze arm around a blue-haired woman in zebra-striped Bermuda shorts and "I LOVE NANA" t-shirt while a bald man captured the moment for posterity.

A real *Kodak* moment, that.

Across the "Open Air Marketplace," a young and scantily clad slave girl was performing more or less the same ritual with two men who could have been her great-great-grandfathers while a third escapee from the Geriatric Ward took a video.

Allison folded her arms over her breasts and watched a crowd begin to gather as the animatronic gods and goddesses at the Atlantis fountain began their snipping.

It was the third "show" she'd seen after deciding she needed to take a break. The conversation she'd had with "Willie," Slave # 4, had affected her more than she thought – although she hadn't realized just how much until she heard herself telling one woman (whose husband had forgotten their anniversary) to "beat the jerk severely about the head and shoulders until he stopped twitching."

The woman had hung up and Allison called in to tell the center she was taking the rest of the day off.

Without the phone calls, however, she had nothing to concentrate on except the memory of Slave-boy Willie calling her "little sister," and, after a very short while, even the televised jewelry bargains hadn't been able to hold her interest. There was only one thing to do, but since suicide wasn't an option, she wiggled into a thick coat of SP 98 ("– greaseless, odorless and now with Aloe!" – $15.98 per bottle +$2.00 s/h from *AlbinosRUs.com*) and headed for her favorite place to catch a quick bite, The Forum Shops at *Caesars Palace.*

Safe in her pre-vampiric disguise – hair limp, bust-line a whopping 34-B, body unaltered, unembellished and revoltingly unexceptional – Allison could wander around and window shop, or just sit back and watch the crowd.

It was the only place in Vegas where she could watch the "sky" overhead slowly shift from daybreak to dusk and back again without making a mad dash for her coffin. Sometimes it was just nice to play tourist.

The man who was that shift's "Caesar" winked at her as he walked by. He was very handsome, very regal and proud as befit the role; the type of man who was used to getting whatever he wanted from a woman with minimal effort. Probably the same type of man who worked at *The Stud Farm.* Yeah, just that type.

Allison mimed a yawn and grinned at the look of shock in the man's eyes. *No rending unto Caesar today, guy. And you don't know how lucky you are.* She just wanted to be left alone.

"Hey, pretty lady."

So much for that thought. Allison turned her head slowly to behold Geek I and Geek II.

"Pretty lady like you shouldn't be standing all by herself looking glum," Geek I said.

"Chum," Geek II added, laughing uproariously at his own wit. "Get it, glum, chum. It rhymes."

Allison just stared at them.

"Is this a boss place or what?" Geek I asked, thrusting a red-and-white striped bag toward her. "Here, have a piece. It's rock candy, all natural . . .none of that artificial coloring. You know, sweets to the . . . um, pretty lady, like they say."

Allison wondered if there was anyone who said it besides these two. When she didn't move toward the bag of candy, Geek II took a piece for her and popped it noisily into his mouth, crunching and spraying her with little shards of sugar as he talked.

"I'm Andy and this is Alex and . . . Hi. You're a tourist, too, huh? You look like a tourist . . . no tan and everyone who lives here, like, has a tan. Have you ever noticed that? Boy, talk about skin cancer central, huh? Well, anyway Alex and I work at the same Internet company and we decided to just take a mini-mid-week holiday, you know . . . get in on the special air fares and we just got back from our tenth visit to *Star Trek: The Experience* over at the Hilton . . . we're not staying at the Hilton, of course. Have you seen it?"

"The Hilton?" Allison asked.

"No," Geek I, Alex, chirped in. "The Enterprise. I mean, jeeze if you haven't seen it you really need to go check it out. It's awesome. You wanna go with us? I mean, it's been over an hour and I could use another dose. I mean this place is cool and everything, but you see one animated statue you seen 'em all. Right? Besides, if you haven't tasted *Glop on a Stick* you haven't lived."

Allison was suddenly very glad she'd managed to do just that. "Glop?"

"It's really just a corn dog," Andy explained. "So, you wanna come with us? I mean, we don't *have* to go there."

"Hey!" Alex whined.

"No, really. I mean *we* can always go back to see it . . . Alex and me, if you know of something else all of us can do that's just as much fun." He lifted one eyebrow and leered at her. Either that, or he had gas. "You know?"

Oh boy, did she know. Running a hand through her hair – that immediately curled down to the small of her back like spun copper, Allison pretended to take a deep breath which inflated more than her emaciated lungs. And their dual, spontaneous erections saluted the effort.

They were ideal slave material . . . without the attitude.

"Well, I was gonna go over to the *Adventuredome*, you know – "

"Oh man, yeah!" Andy shouted, spraying sweet spittle into her left eye. He didn't notice. "Yeah, they got a double-loop, double-corkscrew indoor coaster that's supposed to be awesome."

Allison fluttered the spit out of her eye with her lashes. "That's what I heard. But . . . I didn't want to go there all by myself. Some of those rides look pretty scary and I'd need someone to hold onto."

And they rose like fish to a worm.

"Well, you got us now!"

Both of them offered her an arm – and glared daggers at each other. It was all so cute she wanted to throw up. Allison giggled, girlishly (or as best as she could remember) and stepped in between them, linking her arms with theirs. They shuddered as if they'd just come in contact with a high-voltage wire and the musky scent of semen filled the air. Fortunately, for the other tourists in the immediate area, Alex and Andy – the Geek Twins – were wearing their oversized, button-down, short-sleeve dress shirts untucked.

"Great," Allison said, giving each of their arms a little squeeze. "I'm Al . . . Allie, by the way."

"Cool, like *Ally McBeal!* And, boy, you really are cool. Your skin is freezing. See, Alex, that's why I won't let you turn on the air-conditioning back in the room. It drastically lowers the body core temperature."

Alex nodded and managed to *accidentally* brush his hand across Allison's breast as he snagged another piece of rock candy. "Yeah, well I know a great way of raising body temperature."

"Oh," Allison said.

"Yeah. Laser Tag. I hear the one they got at the

Adventuredome is really great. Just awesome. Don't you worry, Miss Ally McPretty —" His high-pitched giggle made three roving Centurions reach for their rubber short-swords. "We'll warm her up, right Andy?"

"Right," Andy answered back as they marched, in step, toward the exit. "You haven't lived until you've partied with us! You'll think you've died and gone to Disneyworld!"

"Awesome," she said.

CHAPTER 5

The first two wedding ceremonies went without a hitch —
except for the couples, of course. A joke. Hah, hah. Neither
couple laughed.

Wedding No. 1 set a new land speed record, with the couple
in question each holding a plastic *winnings* bucket full of nickels
and demanding every couple of seconds that Mica hurry it up
because they were on a hot streak and didn't want it to cool. The
whole thing, from the reciting of vows to Mica's "By the powers
vested in me by the State of Nevada" and final proclamation that
they were man and wife, took all of ten minutes. Mica had
timed it on the $500 *Rolex* Allison said she "found" one night
while she was driving around.

Lord, how dumb does she think I am?

Don't answer that, Lord.

The new couple was so happy that before they left for
another go at the slot machines, they each scooped out a handful
of nickels from their respective buckets and poured them into
Mica's hands.

The tip came to $1.55.

Watch over them, Lord . . . they know not what they're doing.

The second wedding involved cell-phones and a conference
call and netted him a good tax tip . . . but nothing he could put

in the bank.

And Mica didn't hold out too much hope of padding his income from the young couple currently standing before him. He could tell by the bright and shining and frightened look in their eyes that the almost newlyweds had probably spent all of their combined allowances on the "Hawaiian Special."

Not that he blamed them. After all, what could compare with plastic leis and the sound of tropical bird calls and ocean waves from the chapel's P.A. system. It was pure Vegas magic.

Dressed in the drab brown robe and cowl that constituted his "Brother John, the Marryin' Monk" costume, Mica patiently waited while the runaway teen couple recited bad poetry and promised undying love to each other that would "endure beyond the grave."

His stomach clenched a bit when he heard that, but since he hadn't even bothered asking for their proof of age or parental consent forms, he didn't think he had the right to warn them about making that kind of commitment.

Besides, he thought, looking down at those innocent young faces, that's what the Lord is supposed to do.

Whenever He gets around to it.

"– because you're the best thing that has ever happened to me and I want to be the best thing that's ever happened to you. You give me hope and happiness and . . . ah, oh yeah . . . and a reason to go on even when the going gets rough."

The bride-to-be, looking radiant in her white maternity dress and pink BRIDE t-shirt, blushed while she recited the vows they had written and continued to blush when she turned back to face that altar. The boy, wearing his blue GROOM t-shirt over a dress shirt and tie, looked a little less radiant and wasn't blushing at all.

They were both so cute and so fucking much in love it almost made Mica physically ill.

Which, naturally was the Lord's fault. Who else? Who else let him eat so much knowing what he was about to face. Not him. He wasn't omnipotent, God-dammit!

This is really wearing thin, Lord.

Mica licked his lips and placed one hand over the two leis that covered the rose-colored bible resting in his other hand. The boy had confessed to him, during one of his intended's bathroom breaks, that after getting a full tank of gas and paying for the wedding he didn't have any money left over for rings and asked Mica's opinion on what he should do. The boy had wanted everything to be perfect . . . as much as possible. *God, to be that young and innocent again.*

Mica told the kid not to worry, that a lei was as good as a ring in Las Vegas (especially in Las Vegas) and would make a suitable token of their love and commitment. He also went against company policy and personally redeemed their $25.00 chip coupon for gas money back home to Barstow. The newlyweds were too young to get into the casino anyway.

He kept the free drink voucher for the same reason.

"All right," he said, looking down at them. "Are we ready?"

They smiled back and nodded, their joy brighter than the rose-colored neon lights that shined down upon them. Mica could almost remember that feeling – back when he saw the Lord's handiwork in everything.

Before the Lord had stopped taking his calls.

It just wasn't right. He'd done all the Lord had asked of him . . . with one minor exception which wasn't even his fault.

You could do it, Lord. You could take away my sins as easily as You could wink out a star . . . so why don't You? What are You waiting for?

The young GROOM cleared his throat.

Christmas? What do You want from me? I already said I

know what I'm doing is wrong. What more can You ask of me? I was wrong, Lord.

"Um, excuse me?"

I was wrong and You were right . . . I shouldn't have started living with a dead woman, I know. It was wrong. Is that what You want to hear? Well, You're fucking omniscient so You already KNEW that, didn't You?

"Uh, sir?"

Okay, but You have to take some of the blame for that, too. You don't have one Commandment that says 'Thou Shalt Not Fuck a Dead Person' . . . so if we're REALLY going to lay blame then –

"Sir?"

Mica blinked. "What?"

Both the BRIDE and GROOM looked a little less brilliant than they had a moment before.

"I – We're ready, sir."

"Oh. Yeah. Okay . . ." Mica took a deep breath and pressed his hand down on the leis. The plastic crumpled against his palm as a shadowy form waved to him from the other side of the chapel's rose-colored-glass wall. "Then by the powers invested to me by the state licencing board of Nevada and the Desert Rose Wedding Chapel and Casino –"

He nodded to the shadow behind the glass as he walked around the pulpit to stand in front of the young couple. The pre-recorded tropical paradise was momentarily drowned out by the rush of gambling sounds that filled the chapel when the door opened. Mica raised his voice until the soundproof door swung shut.

"I now pronounce you man–" He dropped one of the leis over the boy's head. "– and wife." The second over the girl's. "You may now kiss the bride."

The moment their lips touched, Alvis clicked on the portable electronic microphone he was carrying and began singing his rendition of "The Hawaiian Wedding Song" as he hip-swiveled up the chapel's narrow central aisle.

"Th-is is the mo-ment . . . ah-of sweets and blenders . . ."

Hair teased and lacquered in place and wearing a near-exact copy (cut loose so his muscles wouldn't be too obvious) of The King's white sequined jumpsuit, Alvis stopped swiveling when he got up to the young couple and, taking one of the (slightly) more expensive silk leis from the dozen he wore around his neck, slipped it over the blushing bride's head as he continued to sing only for them. It was all part of their "Hawaiian Wedding Special" package deal.

A tear glistened and fell, hugging the curve of the bride's cheek.

Mica brushed imaginary dust off the Bible while the young couple listened in rapt attention. When Alvis finished – " . . . the crowds of Hawaii smile on this our wed-ding day . . . " they applauded politely.

"Thank yah, thank yah verrah much," he said, dipping his head modestly. "Now, ah'm not supposed t'do this, but yah're such a lovely lookin' couple, ah'm gonna give yah yah're first weddin' gift. Name a song and ah'll sing it, free a'charge."

This was also included in the package, but usually the couple never got that far down in the contractual fine prints to know it. Besides, as Alvis liked to say, everyone likes to think they're getting something for nothing.

"Really?" the BRIDE asked.

"Word'a honor."

"Cool!" After a brief discussion with his new wife, the boy turned back to Alvis and said – "You know any *Bon Jovi?*"

Alvis looked at Mica. Mica shrugged and looked down at the Bible.

"Let us pray?" he suggested.

There is nothing so terrifying as a vampire, moving unnoticed, among the living.

For the vampire.

Arms filled with a lavender-and-white panda bear, orange-foam lizard on a stick and jumbo-sized bag of Kettle Corn, Allison looked out from under the oversized brim of her oversized foam cowboy hat and wondered what the hell had possessed her to suggest they come to the five full acres of climate-controlled mayhem.

She hadn't even liked Disneyland all that much when she was alive.

Her "dates," on the other hand, were having a ball. Having paid for three full-size prices ($16.95 for those 48" and taller), they were, by gum, going to get their money's worth. With or without her.

Mostly without.

The first ride few rides had been okay. She'd even enjoyed the feeling of flying she got on the double-loop, double corkscrew roller coaster . . . and then they'd dragged her onto the water flume ride with its climactic 60-foot free fall (thinking it cute the way she kicked and screamed and fought). But there'd been a reason behind her struggles: In some of her home study courses on vampirism (movies) she'd noted that running water, regardless of depth, was generally considered a pretty effective way of destroying the undead. And she didn't want to be the first vampire in history to discover that some third-rate screenwriter had gotten one fact right.

The drenching at the end of the 60-foot plunge didn't exactly destroy her, but it did make her toss up three of the four pints of blood she'd had for breakfast that morning. Andy, or was it Alex, clicked his tongue knowingly as he watched her empty the contents of her stomach into a clown-headed trash container and commented that she really shouldn't drink so much fruit punch . . . as it was a known fact that Red Dye No. 40 could be just as hazardous as Red Dye No. 2.

He'd read all about it in an on-line conspiracy site.

"The truth really is out there," he'd told her.

And she almost told him a little truth of her own. But didn't. There were just too many people around. Unfortunately.

Soon, she promised her stomach when the "boys" came bounding through the crowd at her. Andy was munching on a corn-dog. Her stomach rumbled. *Very, very soon.*

"Man," Alex said as he re-established claim on the panda and Kettle Corn, "you sure you don't feel up for another ride? This place is awesome. You hungry?"

Allison shook her head and handed Andy back his foam lizard and hat. "A little, but I can wait."

"Yeah, you should," Andy said, sucking the last inch of corn-dog into his mouth. "This doesn't compare to *Glop-on-a-Stick*. You wanna stick around some more or head over to the *Hilton*? I'll spring for some *real* food at Quark's place on the Promenade."

Allison nodded like she knew what he was talking about. "Is it crowded there?"

"Oh man yeah! There's probably a lot more people there than here. And in costume. You'll love it. Wanna go?"

Alex had answered for Andy, not that there was all that much difference. They were a near perfect mix-and-match set, almost indistinguishable from one another – other than blood type. She'd smelled it on their breaths, Alex was B- and Andy was O+. Her stomach roared but still wasn't loud enough to be heard over the ambient noise level.

"I'm sure I would, but . . ." She leaned in closer and tipped her head to its most beguiling angle (at least according to some of her dining companions). "What I'd really like is to go someplace a little more . . . private."

She batted her lashes. And they missed it completely.

"You wanna go home?" Andy said, heart-broken. "But I thought we were going to see the *Enterprise*?"

Allison closed her eyes. And screamed. Silently. To herself.

AHHHHHHHH!

"Headache?"

She opened one eye. The fearless duo looked concerned.

"You know," Alex said, taking control, "flourescent lighting can do that to people who have high I.Qs. I remember I was at a convention one time and got this massive headache because of the flourescent lighting. They produce this high frequency hum that can really disrupt the natural synapses of the brain. You want some Ibuprofen? I've got Ibuprofen caplets, 200 milli-grams each. And they're coated."

Allison closed her eye.

AHHHHHHHH!

"Oh, good going, moron," Andy hissed, "now look what you've done. And for your information there is no scientific proof that people with higher I.Qs are bothered any more by flourescent lights than people with normal intelligence. I never get headaches and my I.Q is two points higher than yours. Besides, you're not helping Ally McPretty feel any better by yakking at her." Allison felt a gentle tap on her shoulder. "I have some *Extra-Strength Excedrin*, 500-milli-grams per tablet, if you think that will help."

"Thanks," she said, smiling weakly as she opened her eyes, "but I'll be all right. I'm just feeling a little . . . anxious. You know what I mean?"

Alex nodded. "You want to go catch the show over at The Midway?"

"No, I – I'd like to do something that requires a little more

. . . movement."

"Skee-ball!"

AHHHHHHHH–.

"No," Andy said. "Laser tag!"

–AHHHHHHHH– "Oh! What a great idea! And it's dark inside those places, right?"

Andy, having won the round, winked at her. "Oh yeah, it's real dark in there . . . so you can make sure when your laser hits your opponent."

"But," Alex said, not wanting to be outdone, "it's not so dark so you'll fall on your face or –"

Shut up.

"Trip or anything," Andy continued, picking up where his rival left off. "So you don't have to worry about–"

You, too, Allison said, then clapped her hands together to break their momentary paralysis and giggled. They both snapped out of it looking like they were the sole reason for her merriment.

"So, what do you say?" Allison asked as they walked arm-in-arm-in-arm toward the line of people waiting to play laser tag. "Winner gets to pick dinner?"

"Deal," Andy said. "And you're going to love *Glop-on-a-Stick.*"

"Pretty sure of yourself, aren't you?"

"I don't like to lose, Ally McPretty."

"Neither do I."

"Hey," Alex said, jerking his chin toward the arcade's entrance. "Where'd all the people go? There was a line here about a mile long a second ago."

Allison shrugged. "Maybe they all decided to do something else. First one out is a Deviled Egg."

"Rotten egg," Alex corrected.

"You eat what you like," she said, smiling up at him, "and

I'll eat what I like."

❖

They agreed to play "Boys against the Girl" – her choice, but which she instantly regretted when Andy scored two direct hits on her within fifteen seconds of their walking into the "battlefield": A murky, warehouse-sized room illuminated by black-lights and filled with various flourescent-edged obstacles that could be hidden behind or, as in Allison's case, fallen over. Great night-vision didn't mean much when it was constantly being ruined by sudden slashes of laser light.

Zap. Ping.

Another "hit" registered on Allison's vest harness and she turned, laser gun up and ready and smashed the side of her helmet against a non-flourescent-edged obstacle.

"I told you I don't like to lose," Andy shouted as he disappeared around a flourescent barrier. "Got er, got er! I got Ally McPretty!"

And somewhere to her left Alex whooped. "Only thirteen more hits to go. We're coming for you All-eeeey."

Zap, zap – ping, ping!

Hits number three and four registered as Allison's breasts got tangled against the harness straps. *Shit, she hated wearing real clothes. It felt like she was wearing a straitjacket!* Shoving her breasts out of the way, Allison turned and fired. And missed by a mile.

"Hah!" He confirmed. "Missed by a mile!" *Zap.*

Ping.

Zap.

Allison ducked and saw the red beam of light hit the swinging neon-outlined pendulum above her head. Damn, those boys were good . . . but it wasn't her fault! She was dead, goddammit, not used to wearing anything but fabricated illusions and here she was strapped into a plastic and velcro contraption that restricted her movements and a head-piece that –

Zap. Ping.

"Shit!"

"Now, now," Andy's voice chastised her from the darkness, "that's not a very nice thing for a lady to say."

Who said I was a lady?

"Huh?" Andy stuck his head out from around a barrel-shaped divider, the green "target" lights on his helmet giving his face a lovely carrion look.

Allison shot six times in rapid succession – *zap zap zap zap zap zap*

Ping. Ping. Ping. Ping. Ping.

Miss.

Then fired again. Nothing happened.

"Gotta remember to recharge, Ally McPretty," Alex said, suddenly standing directly in front of her, laser gun drawn and aimed at the flourescent X over her – *gulp* – heart. "But since you're empty, I'll be nice and won't take the easy hits."

"Thank you." Allison held up her hands, the empty laser pistol dangling from one finger. "Where do I recharge?"

His smile glowed blue under the black-lights. It matched his eyes and socks. "At one of the recharge stations. All you have to do is stick the tip of your blaster into the center of the bulls-eyes and shove."

Hmm? "I have to do what again?"

Alex rolled his glowing eyes, shaking his head as if suddenly realizing she was "just a girl" after all.

"You stick the tip of your gun into the center of the bulls-eye and . . . Um-a, um-a, um-a."

Allison had stood up while he was explaining the procedure again, her shorts and top disappearing along the way. The only thing she was wearing was the harness and helmet . .

. and lots and lots of skin tinted pale red *(her favorite color)* by her slowly throbbing target lights.

"Show me," she said, parting her legs as she took the barrel of his light pistol and manually lowered it toward its intended target. "Show me how you stick it in and . . . shove."

Allison had put Alex at about thirty to thirty-five, old enough, she thought, to have seen at least one naked woman in his life. She was wrong.

Alex dropped the gun and screamed.

"What's the matter?" Andy's voice called out. "Alex? Alex, answer me."

But Alex was too busy screaming as he plowed over (or through) a number of barriers on his way to the illuminated red *EXIT* sign. When Andy finally decided his friend's sudden departure wasn't just a ploy to get him out into the open, Alex was already fifty yards away from the building – running hard with at least two security guards and one teenaged laser tag employee in close pursuit. *"Hey, pal . . . come back here with that equipment! It's not yours!"*

"Oh my–"

Allison pouted and shrugged, making sure her nipples were hard and her harness-bound breasts quivered just enough to keep Andy's attention. She'd already let one potential nosh get away, she wasn't about to lose this one.

"Shh," she said even though they were still the only players inside the building. "It's okay."

Andy's glowing gaze dropped to her equally glowing breasts. The string of drool easing down his chin gleamed like crystal when he nodded. "Okay."

"I think I scared Alex," Allison said as she unhooked the seatbelt-like clamp at her waist.

"Alex can be a real dork. No, don't." Her hands stopped. "Leave it on."

She snapped the harness back in place.

"Oh yeah. Oh yeah." Sticking the laser pistol down behind the target grid on his chest, Andy took a deep breath and reached out toward her breasts. And kept reaching. Moving slower than a snail on a 90-degree incline. "Oh yeah. Oh yeah."

Oh fuck it.

Allison grabbed his hands and mashed them against her breasts. And a change suddenly came over her little Geek-boy.

"OH YEAH!"

Releasing her breasts, and with all the subtlety of a hydraulic shovel going after a particularly stubborn boulder, Randy-Andy grabbed her pussy. Then her ass. Then her pussy and breasts. Then her pussy and ass and back to her pussy. Ass, breasts, pussy, pussy, ass, ass, ass. PUSSY!

Not that she minded being mauled, it reminded her of those wonderful first groping sessions she had back in junior high school, but he was moving so fast she couldn't get a decent bead on his jugular.

Somehow he managed to slip a finger directly into her pussy. "Oh MAN!"

"I beg your pardon."

Pulling herself off the non-distinguishing digit, Allison grabbed a handful of harness and dragged him over to a four-foot wide, raised platform near the center of the room. It was wide enough for someone to stand on and use as an observation stage, but well enough hidden that it made it hard to see. Very hard. There was only a thin flourescent-orange strip marking the top edges to keep living people from bumping into it.

Allison had bumped into it.

Twice.

But it was flat and steady and that's all she cared about at the moment.

A quick flick of the wrist and Randy-Andy was likewise flat on his back. Well, mostly flat.

"You watch a lot of TV, Andy?"

"Uh-huh." Andy's eyes widened as she neatly tore open his chinos and boxers without first bothering to use the zipper. His cock leapt out at her faster than a little alien popping out of a chest. It was a fitting image, she thought.

"Well then, you control the horizontal . . . I'll control the vertical."

Andy's mouth moved, but nothing except a soft whimper escaped his lips as Allison let her fangs slowly extend. To his credit, though, his penis not only stayed erect, but seemed to get harder.

Jeeze, what a pervert.

"Oh, man," his voice, when he finally found it, was quivering. "Are they . . . real?"

"Touch them," Allison said, "and find out for yourself."

He did, jamming the pad of one thumb against the tip and yelping softly when it pierced the flesh. The rich warm scent was too much for her. Allison swiped the drop of blood clean with her touch and then pulled his thumb into her mouth, sucking contentedly. They shuddered in unison.

"Oh. Wow. This is so bitchin'. Ally McPretty's a *Vampire D* fan."

"Mumph?"

"Shit, my Anime club's not going to believe this. All of us have been trying to get . . . you know women interested in joining, but you're the first, you know, woman I've met who's really into it." He started fumbling with his pants, but instead of his penis, he pulled out a small, use once and develop, disposable camera. "Can I take your picture for my web site?"

His thumb slipped out of Allison's mouth as she backed up. "What?"

Andy followed her up, his penis leading the way. "No really, it'll be great. You'll probably get about a million hits a day."

"Yeah? Well, do you think your little computer friends would like to see a picture of THIS?"

She backed up another step and . . . "demonized" herself – turning her skin a bright fire engine red at the same time she reformed her hair into realistic ebony horns. She completed the "ensemble" with a trident-tipped tail and rudimentary wings. It wasn't any more difficult than when she'd turned "furry" back in Hollywood, but the effect – judging by the fountain of cum that spurted from him – seemed to be a bit more dramatic.

"Oh. Wow. Man. Oh."

Allison bowed.

"This is almost better than anything I've seen in animation."

Almost? Allison felt her wings sag back into her shoulder blades. She'd just shown him something few living men ever got a chance to see – and he thought it was *almost* as good as watching cartoons.

He snapped a picture.

"Fuck you."

"Oh yeah!" Andy lay back down on the platform, camera at the ready. "Fuck me . . . like that. Do it like that, like *Vampire D*, okay?"

"My pleasure," Allison growled. Gripping his cock, she shoved it up inside her and smiled at the sound he made when he discovered vampires (*A, B, C* or *D*) didn't come equipped with body heat or lubrication.

He did manage to get off two more shots, *flash, flash* (but no *ping, pings*) before she leaned forward and sank her teeth into his neck.

Unfortunately, she'd only gotten two mouthfuls into the

first pint when a family of tourists, each sporting matching *Caesar's Palace*-logo t-shirts and flourescent yellow laser gear, walked in. Noticed what was going on. And screamed. In unison.

Allison slowly raised her head and thought of the best way to handle the situation. But since there really wasn't one, she opened her mouth and started screaming, too.

When in Rome, as they say. It seemed appropriate.

Mica finished his cup of coffee and reached for the table carafe only to discover he'd finished that as well. Without Alvis to act as observer and co-consumer, he'd managed to down the ten-cup pot without even noticing. Boredom always did that to him – made him lose track of time.

Setting the empty carafe back on the table, he toyed with the remaining half of his ham-cheese-baloney-fried egg-and bacon sandwich. Even though it was his lunch hour, he wasn't particularly hungry. His belly was still pretty full from breakfast and his feet were damp from having stood for a full thirty-five minutes in the casino's reflection pool with a Cowboy and his "Little Filly" while a small herd of their closest friends and relatives serenaded the couple with a medley of Country-Western songs.

Alvis had offered to help, only to wander off in a sulk when it became apparent that the group liked Willie Nelson more than they liked The King. The last time Mica'd seen him, Alvis was singing "Chunk-ah, Chunk-ah, Burnin' Love" to an outlaw biker couple who had roared in on matching Harleys.

Mica poked the sandwich again – the management didn't like to see their employees sitting in the dining area unless they at least pretended to be eating – then pushed the plate aside and reached for his empty cup until he remembered why it was empty.

"Shit."

"Here," a soft voice said from above, "I was just bringing this to you."

Lord? Mica looked up into a pair of doe-soft eyes. Hair that was the color of warm honey shimmered around the heart-shaped face and fell gently over tanned shoulders. She was wearing a low-cut, lime-green sun-dress. An unusual color, he thought, for an angel.

As was the fact that she was holding a coffee carafe in one hand and empty cup in another. But that didn't matter. Nothing mattered, not the coffee or the sandwich or Alvis's hurt feelings or the tour group of octogenarian gamblers from Sun City who were arguing loudly at one another over their early-early-bird dinner specials.

Even the ambient sin of Las Vegas lifted slightly when she spoke again.

"Mind if I join you?" she asked, tossing the strap of her shoulder bag over the back of the chair opposite him and sitting down without waiting for an answer. As if anyone could have said *no, go away, I don't feel like company right now* to such a creature of light.

And she was all light – the complete and opposite of the daughter of darkness living in his basement.

Lord? This is a sign, isn't it? You've sent this angel of light to let me know You've not forgotten me. Haven't You?

"I hope you don't think I'm being too forward," the angel said as she filled both their cups then added two packets of artificial sweetener to hers. "I mean about my coming over. You are a man of the cloth and all . . . but I noticed you were out of coffee and, well, you looked like you could use another cup."

Mica smiled and pulled his damp, sandal-clad foot further back under his chair. It was a sign. The Lord knew how much he liked coffee.

"Yes, thank you, it's very nice of you. And I don't think you're being forward at all. The Lord sent you."

Her golden-brown lashes fluttered slightly above her gray-green eyes, but a tiny blush rose along her throat.

"That's a way of looking at it, I guess," she twittered, then added another packet of sweetener to her coffee after taking a quick sip. "Seeing as God's everywhere and all. My name's Angela, by the way."

Angela. Angel. *Yes, Lord! Yes, YES!*

It was all Mica could do to keep from grabbing her hand and pulling her to the floor so they could thank the Lord for finally recognizing he'd already suffered more than Job.

A whole *hell* of a lot more.

"That's right," he said. "You're right. And thank you . . . for the coffee. My name's –"

"Brother John. Yeah, I know." She reached out and shook his hand. Her skin was warm and soft.

"You know me?"

"Well, I've listened to you sometimes, you know, you and the other guys when you're standing up there marrying people. I mean . . . Well, not when *you're* marrying someone but –" She giggled. It was a good sound for her. "Oh, you know what I mean."

He knew. God, yes, he knew. And she knew him . . . it *was* a miracle.

Welcome back, Lord. Good goin' man.

"It's just that I know how hard being a member of the clergy is. I used to date this priest and he always looked like he was one cup short of a full pot, if you know what I mean."

Mica's cup got half-way to his mouth and stopped. "You dated a priest?"

She fluffed her hair and shrugged. "He wasn't a very good

priest, but I got to where I just loved to watch wedding ceremonies . . . and funerals. But mostly weddings. That's why I always try to stop by here on my way to work. See if I can catch a wedding. I hate to say it, but . . . well, it makes me a little horny. You know, just thinking about what's going to happen next."

She giggled and Mica smiled and only managed to slop about a quarter of the coffee down the front of his robes before he could stop his hands from shaking.

"Oh, you spilled," she said, as if he hadn't noticed the burning sensation, and pulled a napkin from the table dispenser. Standing up, breasts straining the seams of the thin cotton, jiggling with each tiny movement, she leaned over the table and dabbed the napkin against his chest. The folds covering his lap twitched, begging like a dog for a little of the attention.

"'And the Lord sent down His Angel. . . .' Are those real?"

Her hand stopped in mid-dab. "Huh?"

It took longer than he thought it would before he could drag his eyes out of her cleavage and up to her eyes.

"Nothing," Mica said. "Sorry. Just thinking out loud. Sorry."

"Oh, okay." She dabbed his robe one more time and sat down. Taking her breasts with her. "I don't think it'll stain, but you'll probably want to soak it in cold water when you get home, just to make sure. Or have your . . . wife do it."

There was a light in her eyes Mica hadn't noticed before. "I'm not married."

"Oh?" The light brightened. "Girlfriend?"

Allison? A girlfriend? "Hell, no!"

"Oh."

Angela leaned forward again as she picked up her cup, elbows on the table, arms pressed   against the sides of her breasts.

"Well," she said. "Well, well. How did you escape?"

Escape? Mica slid his chair away from the table. "I – I – "

But she was already on her feet, frowning prettily at the thin gold watch around her wrist.

"Darn, gotta go to work." Sighing, Angela opened her purse and pulled out a small white business card. "It's really too bad, you know . . . our conversation was just starting to get interesting. Here –" She flicked the card against Mica's nose, laughing, before handing it to him. "– that's my cell phone number. Call me any time."

Mica looked at the card – *Angela Chaney/Licensed Physical Therapist* along with a local phone number – and felt his heart (among other things) wilt in despair. A "Physical Therapist". Wow. And "Licensed." Golly gee-whiz. It didn't bother him (much) that his "angel" was human . . . in fact, that part was fine, and he really didn't care (much) what she did for a living as long as she was – living. Breathing.

"Oh," he said, "you're a hooker."

Mica saw the blow coming, but couldn't get out of the way fast enough. Even with the background drone of conversation and sounds of gambling that drifted in from the casino, the open-handed slap against cheek was loud enough to startle the covey of senior citizens to their feet.

"WHAT?" Angela shouted at him as if daring him to repeat himself.

Which, unfortunately for his other cheek, he did.

SMACK!

"A hooker?" she screamed. "I'm a God-damned Physical Therapist, you sack of shit! How dare you."

Purse flying as she turned and head held high, Angela snatched back her card and marched out of the dining room, stopping only long enough to hand her card to one of the old men whose spine resembled a question mark and offer Mica one last withering glare.

"I hope to God you break something and try to find a better therapist. Because you won't. Ever!"

Sitting there, cheeks throbbing, Mica poured himself another cup of coffee and swallowed it as loudly as he could . . . but it was no use.

He could still hear God laughing at him.

Life just wasn't fair sometimes.

Especially when the dealer was using a marked deck.

Allison felt the wind tug at her hair (momentarily short and dishwater blond) as she walked slowly through the late afternoon shadows to her car.

Behind her, people were still milling around the *Adventuredome's* front doors, watching the paramedics load Andy – disposable camera still in hand and gauze bandage at his throat – into the ambulance and waiting for the police to give the "All Clear" so they could go back and resume the arduous task of having fun.

The *All Clear* was needed, of course, because a "rabid dog had attacked one man and then gone after a family visiting from Provo."

The rabid dog hadn't really been her idea. It'd been the image she'd seen in the youngest child's mind, but it seemed like a good idea so she went with it . . . one all purpose mental suggestion to the family and Andy and she calmly walked away in her nondescript summer clothes and sensible shoes.

She'd even taken pity on Alex, poor little Alex, when she found him – cowering neck-deep in plastic balls – and erased the mental image of her naked. Replacing it with a mental image of Andy naked.

He was still screaming when the paramedics strapped him

onto a gurney. Poor, poor Alex.

Gary Oldman would be proud of her.

Smiling as she kicked an empty beer can away from the Mustang's front tire, Allison heard a cheer and glanced back just in time to see the police finally give up their search for the imaginary dog and wave people back into the building. About time, too, she thought, it was starting to get dark.

A vague feeling of unease . . . of urgency shifted over her skin. She was supposed to do something . . . something that she promised . . . someone . . . she'd do . . . .

What was it?

Allison leaned back against the driver's side door, thinking as she looked up. The western sky above the mountains was still bright and even though, according to the tingling sensation on her skin, there was still an hour or two of daylight left, she was in no danger of suddenly finding herself turned into a sentient pile of ash. No, that wasn't it. In fact, this was her favorite time of day . . . always had been. The sun was low, night was coming and she didn't have to be at work until –

"Shit!"

She remembered.

Cursing the two sheet-covered mounds of meat as they were being lifted into the ambulance, Allison climbed into the Mustang and had the engine growling before she got the door closed all the way. Despite what Luci had tried to tell her, all those months ago back in L. A., about a vampire not being able to take on the attributes (or deficiencies) of their victims (like thinking she was drunk after draining Big Mike, the Hollywood Fur-Pit's original, 100-proof Watcher), Allison knew better. From first-hand experience.

Now, granted that it might be different with other vampires – depending on a number of variables and the fact that vampires were notoriously unreliable when it came to telling the truth – but whenever she "supped" with a drunk, she felt tipsy afterwards. If her dinner companion took drugs, she flew right along beside him. A winner who'd just hit a jack-pot in the casino made her feel buoyant inside, as if her newly acquired blood was laced with little helium bubbles. A loser produced feelings of angst and worry . . . and she tried to avoid Mormons entirely – they were a pretty tasteless bunch.

The few slurps of Andy's blood had made her want to just veg out in front of a computer and put her brain on hold. And almost made her forget a previous and very important appointment she'd promised to keep.

Her brain still felt a bit sluggish as she tried to calculate the best route without running into rush hour traffic. *Damn it! That's the last time I pick up geek fast-food for lunch.*

"Now," she muttered, "what to wear? He's probably used to trailer-trash strippers so why not give him what he wants?"

Eyes shifting to bright, *empty* pools of indigo-blue, Allison burnished her blond curls to golden ringlets and changed her sensible linen outfit to one that would cause insensibility – a spandex sarong with fish-net stockings, "fuck me" sandals, and an off-the-shoulder gauze blouse that left little doubt of the braless wonders beneath.

But, just in case, she swelled her bust-line into a matched pair of 44-Ds.

Oh yeah, Buddy-Jim, Sr. was gonna like what she was packing.

Yes, sir.

CHAPTER 6

Allison decided she probably could have picked Buddy-Jim, Sr. out of the crowd at the *$tumble On Inn* (Loo$e lot/AC) even without help from the harried waitress. Buddy-Jim, Sr. was the loudest, the angriest, and the one wearing the most beers down the front of his grease-stained work shirt.

A real charmer and, according to himself, an expert on women.

". . . can you believe it, bitch had the nerve to try'n say no to me. *Me,* God-dammit, on account of the damn kids being asleep and she's still angry at me – hah, now there's a laugh, huh . . . her being mad at me – for taking my own money. Shit, you believe that shit? Well, anyway, I let that part pass, cause that's the kind of man I am . . . but I tell her, like I'm telling you right now, that no kid of mine is gonna wear glasses like some fucking four-eyed freak. Hell, I used to beat kids like that up all the time.

"Shit . . . I still do!"

Buddy-Jim, Sr. stopped to catch his breath and marinate more of his shirt, laughing at the fact that he, a man in his mid-twenties, still liked to beat up kids. Whadda man.

"So where was I? Oh yeah . . . so anyway I tell her my son ain't gonna wear glasses and I don't care if he can't see a fucking train coming at him head on. Besides, he sees the TV just fine. Got me one of those big screens and believe me, that kid can see great. But you think that fucking cunt I married listens? Hell no. She goes on and on and on about it while I'm trying to get friendly, you know? I swear that bitch is just too fucking stupid for words sometimes. So I give it to her –"

Another voice mumbled something too low for Allison to hear, but Buddy-Jim, Sr. heard it all right. And brayed like a jack-ass with a mouthful of thistles.

"No! That's not what I meant, you son-of-a-bitch . . . at least not right then. No, I mean I give her a nice little tap, a real light one across the face to shut her up and teach her a little manners . . . show her I ain't in the mood to play that game, so what does she do? Fuck if she doesn't threaten to call the cops on me. Me! Shit, like a woman's gonna threaten me in my own fucking trailer when I'm the one who has to go out every morning and work my dick off just to support her fat ass and those snot-nose little bastards? Fuck that . . . so I did . . . dragged her into the kid's room and did it to her right there on the floor so the kids could see and start learning about life. Just like my daddy showed me.

"It really was something to see, too. Her trying to be so quiet and telling the kids to 'go back to sleep' and 'close your eyes,' and 'don't look' at the same time she's telling me 'no, stop it, please stop it.' Shit. Like a man can stop when he's right in the middle of things, right? Shit. Well, I tell you . . . a couple of these –"

Buddy-Jim, Sr. hauled back and fired two quick upper-cuts toward the water stains on the ceiling.

"– and she got real co-operative fast, if you know what I mean. Hey, honey . . . bring me another long-neck and here's a little something for your trouble." He pulled a wad of crumpled dollar bills from his breast pocket and shoved them down the front of the waitress's blouse – after helping himself to a feel of the merchandise. "Compliments of my son, Buddy-Jim, Jr."

If looks could kill, pal, Allison thought. Oh yeah, he was every woman's dream. She could see why Noreen stayed with him.

"So," she said, "I guess that makes you Buddy-Jim, Sr.?"

He, along with a couple dozen of his good buddies, looked up at her and smiled like hungry foxes. Allison smiled back like a defenseless little chicken.

And ruffled her feathers – just enough to keep the foxes happy.

"That's my name, honey-pie, don't wear it out."

Oh, and clever, too. She giggled.

It was working out better than she'd hoped. Originally, she planned to catch him just as he was getting off work, but street repairs along the usually less-traveled residential roads put a major crimp in her time-table. Buddy-Jim, Sr., she was told by the owner of the gas station where he worked, had taken off early *("slacking son-of-a-bitch")* . . . but was there anything he could do for her.

Pant, pant.

Finding out where Buddy-Jim, Sr. liked to go to unwind after a day of scraping bugs off windshields was the easy part. Convincing the station owner she really didn't want to fuck him in the backseat of his brand new pick-up truck took a little more time. He just wasn't a man who took "no" for an answer.

May he rest in peace.

Allison burped at the memory and batted her lashes. "You're funny, Buddy-Jim, Sr."

And apparently he thought so, too, because he stood right up and laughed in her face. *Nummy – beer and Cheese-Whiz . . . the breakfast, lunch and dinner of champions.* Allison tightened her pectoral muscles, simulating a deep breath that both lifted and pressed her breasts against the near-transparent gauze of her blouse.

She let the sheer material slip off one shoulder.

"Well, you're about the prettiest thing to walk in here without police protection in a long time. You know that?"

Allison giggled. "Not yet."

"So, you know my name," Buddy-Jim, Sr. said, "but I don't know yours and I don't think that's fair."

Shit, she was getting tired of giggling. "Guess," she said.

"Well, let's see." Leering, he shifted his weight back on one steel-toe booted foot and reached under her sarong and ran one finger up the inside of her thigh. Allison made her eyes go wide and angled her hips forward so he'd have no trouble discovering she wasn't wearing panties.

"Oh, honey." Buddy-Jim Sr. smiled as he slipped his finger up past the second joint, "you been sitting on a piece of ice?"

"Something like that. I think I had the air-conditioning on too high in the car."

Allison shivered and tightened her vaginal muscles around his probing digit. "So, can you guess my name?"

"Who the fuck cares?" He pulled his finger out in order to take her arm. "Now, why don't we go someplace less crowded, like the pool room in back, so I can warm you up."

One of the men sitting at the table stood up and sucker-punched the air. "Yeah, and I call sloppy seconds."

Buddy-Jim, Sr. backhanded him over the top of the table without loosening the grip on Allison's arm.

"Nobody's gettin' anything off this but me. We all agreed to that?"

There were a few mutters of discontentment from the herd, but no one else stood up to challenge the claim. She'd definitely have to remember to come back when she had a little more time. Maybe buy a few rounds of drinks . . . for herself.

She quieted her belly when Buddy-Jim, Sr. turned around to smirk at her.

"So, you wanna go into the back or what?"

Allison reached down and brushed the hard bulge in the front of his jeans with her fingers, whispering as if she was afraid the other men might hear.

"You have a car?" she asked, "cause I know this place out in the desert . . .not real far from here that we can . . ." It wasn't hard for freshly digested blood to produce a glowing blush. It seemed very natural, in fact. "If it's really good, you know, I can get pretty loud."

His hand tightened on her arm and he seemed very surprised when she didn't react.

"Oh, you'll get loud, baby, I promise, you'll break the fucking sound barrier. Okay, let's go . . . . Uh, what did you say your name was?"

"I didn't," she said, giggling. *Shit, I hate that sound.* "But it's . . . Titania."

"Great name." Winking, Buddy-Jim, Sr. released her arm (since it didn't seem to be getting the desired results) and shoved his hand under her blouse – much to the obnoxious delight of his buddies. "Okay, TIT-anya and me are gonna take a little drive. If that bitch I married calls tell her to have em spread wide and waitin' for me when I get home . . . whenever that is. C'mon, Tit-anya, let's go."

Allison melted into his embrace as they stumbled from the bar and into his primarily gray-primer Chevy quarter-ton and tried to remember not to put up any resistance to his do-it-yourself gynecological examination.

She even batted her lashes at him when he accidentally ripped her blouse off as he helped her into the cab.

Buddy-Jim, Sr. or B.S. as he said he liked to be called, was already sweating by the time he climbed in behind the welded-chain steering wheel.

"Yeah, you just lean back and let me see that little pussy while we're driving. Oh, yeah . . . whoo! Oh, hey, I forgot to ask. . . . you're not thinking of making me pay for any of this, are you?"

Allison spread her legs as wide as the confines of the cab would allow.

"Maybe," she sighed, "but not in money."

❖

Allison licked her fingers clean and grimaced. He left a bad taste in her mouth and gut and mind . . . she just couldn't stop thinking about their last minutes together.

They hadn't been parked in the empty little stretch of desert she liked to think of as her own private "Picnic Grounds," for more than a minute when he'd punched her in the mouth. No prelude, no reason, just one fast shot right in the teeth. It could have been bad if she'd had her fangs down at the time, considering she didn't have any idea if fangs could be grown back or not. But she bit him out of habit. And all that hot, angry blood started to flow. She couldn't help herself, despite the taste – she sank her teeth in deeper and held on when he jerked back, tumbling out of the cab on top of her.

Allison let go when they hit the ground and started to roll away. Slowly, playing possum until he was back on his feet. Foot. One, the other cocked and aimed at her head.

"Fucking bitch!" he'd yelled. "Bite me, will you? I'm fucking going to kill you. But first I'm gonna fuck you six ways to Sunday so you better spread em and spread em wide. Here, let me help you."

He kicked and she caught. And the next minute he was on the ground and she was straddling his chest.

"What the –"

His last words.

"Tell you what, B.S., how bout we spread this instead. Take a deep breath."

Using her fingers like a trowel, Allison pierced Buddy-Jim, Sr.'s neck just below the Adam's Apple and slid her hand inside. He did take that breath when he felt the pain and that was good, since he wouldn't be getting another.

His head came off a bit on the ragged side, but she was still able to balance it on a sandstone boulder so he could watch while she cradled his body in her arms and drained it. The large quality of beer he'd consumed gave her a light buzz . . . and gas.

Burp!

"Whoops," Allison told his head as she tossed his body over her shoulder, then tapped her blood-smeared chest. "Sorry. That wasn't very lady-like was it? But I guess you've probably already figured out I'm not much of a lady, didn't you?"

His eyes followed her as she squatted down in front of him, continuing their downward path until they were starting at her exposed crotch. Allison shifted her weight and closed her knees.

"A bastard right to the end, huh? Well, why not . . . death doesn't change anything. Believe me, I know."

Smacking her lips at the taste of yet another belch, Allison reached out and patted his cheek gently, being careful not to dislodge him from his rock.

"You know, it's really too bad – I mean that you're such . . . excuse me, that you *were* such a bastard. You weren't a bad *looking* guy, just a bad guy. Were you always like this? I mean, if your folks had given you that shiny red fire truck you wanted for Christmas would you have turned out to be such a misogynistic asshole?"

His mouth twitched.

"Oh, sorry, that's right, you can't really answer me, can you? Pretty cool, though, huh? Being dead and still being able to hear and see . . . for another couple of seconds at least. I remember it was kind of a cool feeling in the beginning, but then you realize that everything you were and hoped to be one day is all over and what you see – or don't see in my case – is what you got. Forever and ever."

Buddy-Jim Sr.'s left eyelid was beginning to droop. Allison snapped her fingers in front of his nose and he blinked.

"See, you just proved a theory – doctors think that hearing is the last function to go. Isn't that nice? With any luck you'll be able to hear the coyotes and worms chowing down on your face and brains. Neat, huh?"

Allison waved her hand slowly in front of his eyes. They moved, but not as quickly as only a second before.

"Getting hard to see? Well, I'll make this quick. If you haven't figured it all out yet, which I somehow doubt, I'm Noreen's crisis center advocate."

A lie, but just a little one. The skin around Buddy-Jim Sr.'s eyes wrinkled.

"After some of the stories she told me about your abuse, I just had to find out for myself and, after seeing you in action, I can honestly say I had no alternative. My initial decision to kill has been justified.

"May you rot in Hell for all eternity."

His eyes turned in toward his nose and glazed over. Allison wrapped her knuckles against the top of his skull.

"Buddy-Jim? Oh, B.S., are you still in there?"

She tapped harder and his head rolled off the rock and landed nose-first on a red-ant mound.

"As much as I'd like to let them munch away –"

Grabbing the head by its thatch of greasy brown hair, Allison carried it back to the truck and set it down on the tailgate while she searched through the rusted chains, rusted tools, empty beer cans, broken jacks, and spent shot-gun shells for anything she could use as a shovel.

She found a shovel. With a broken handle.

"Damn," she told his head, "and I just had my nails done. Okay, any particular place you'd like to be planted? Hmm? Oh, you're going to leave it up to me. Well, let's see."

Hands on hips, Allison scanned the patch of desert sage and scrub and frowned. There were at least a dozen . . . maybe fifteen ex-abusers scattered (literally) in about a thirty-yard radius. Another half-dozen or so and she'd have to find a new spot.

But that was the nice thing about living in the middle of a natural litter-box — there were so many places you could dump crap.

❖

Allison drove the truck back to town wearing the same outfit and body style she'd left in. It'd make it easier for the police, when and if they started an investigation into Buddy-Jim Sr.'s disappearance, to only have one woman to look for. And she always wanted to make things easier for the police — as long as they never found her.

Somebody at the bar would remember the over-stacked blond in a sarong Buddy-Jim Sr. had left with, the same way a different somebody inside the all night convenience store/gas station would remember seeing a similar over-stacked blond in a sarong pull in and then hurry away down the street without even coming in for a pack of smokes or six-pack.

It would all be very suspicious.

Allison just hoped Noreen wasn't an over-stacked blond who had a penchant for sarongs.

Two blocks away from The Strip, the over-stacked blond in the sarong stepped into the shadows next to an ATM and Raven d'Nuit stepped out, wearing a silver lame cat-suit that almost caused two major traffic accidents.

It was nice to have things back to normal.

❖

Mica declined Alvis's dinner invitation at the free buffet in favor of feeling sorry for himself and a long, aimless walk home.

It was just punishment, he decided, for having jumped to a wrongful conclusion about physical therapists.

Even if it was the Lord who'd really been responsible for him doing that.

Mica wore the collar of his bowling shirt up against the back of his neck despite the heat, because that was the kind of mood he was in . . . a mood that required mist and fog and a bone-numbing drizzle that went right down to a man's soul. Unfortunately, he was in the middle of the desert and the only chills he felt in the otherwise 98-degree night were whenever a casino door opened.

He just couldn't work up a real feeling of melancholy.

And *that* most certainly was the Lord's fault.

So why don't you just go home and have a beer? The Lord asked. *What do you hope to accomplish? Getting blisters isn't like being visited by a plague of boils, you know.*

"Blisters will do for now," Mica answered back.

And then what? You plan to walk in front of a bus?

Now there's an idea. Thanks for the suggestion.

Oh, now don't start blaming ME for all this again. But seriously, turn right here and go home. I know you've got a "Hungry Man Turkey Dinner" in the back of the freezer. Mmm-mmm. Num-num-good.

Mica ignored the suggestion and watched his feet continue to take him straight off the curb and onto the next block without stopping. From somewhere just ahead, he could hear The Cowboy, howdy-ing a whole new batch of pard-ners.

Left! Turn left! MY, don't you ever listen?

Mica turned left then, just to avoid any more arguments with the omnipresence. The sound of a car horn followed by a gush of hot wind whirled past him.

That was too close, kid.

"Why don't You just go back to ignoring me?" he asked and startled a tiny woman in a *Disco Granny* sweatshirt.

"I–I'm sorry, I didn't see you."

Mica hunched his shoulders and quickened his pace.

Think you can outrun ME, Mica? Go home.

Leave me alone. Again. Please.

But I never left you, Mica. Do you know where you are?

Las Vegas, Nevada.

Hah, hah . . . funny man. Stop for a minute, will you?

No.

I SAID STOP!

And Mica's feet stopped so suddenly the rest of him almost landed on the concrete.

Thank you. Okay, look where you are.

Mica looked up and felt himself stagger back a step. He was standing directly across the street from the Greyhound Bus Terminal.

"Oh shit, Lord."

Watch it, kid.

He'd decided to skip his nightly preaching session to the newly arrived, as a punishment for his wicked thoughts . . . and delusions. He knew that it wasn't the Lord who had just spoken to him. The Lord had abandoned him in the desert – just like He had His own Son *(Say Hallelu– yeah, whatever)* – with the exception that Jesus, being nearly as celestially psychic as His Dad, knew He'd get out alive and well and have the whole thing written down in a best-selling book.

It just wasn't fair how God played favorites like that.

The light at the corner turned green, welcoming him to cross and Mica felt the rush of the crowd – coming and going – as he stood there. And watched the lights change twice more before he let himself be dragged across the street. The pair of transit cops saw him, but only one waved and pointed to the spot just outside their assigned jurisdiction. The other cop just gave him a steel-eyed glare and mouthed, *no trouble.*

Mica shook his head, *no trouble*, and went to his designated spot between the *Keep Our City Clean* trash basket and row of coin-operated newspaper boxes. Taking the small, butt-molded Bible out of his back pocket, he stepped back out of the way of a boisterous gang of young people and settled back to watch for a moment.

The scene never changed.

Gamblers arrived, boisterous and optimistic, their bravado filling the sultry night air around them like a mist as they shoved their way across Main Street to heed the siren's call of the casinos. The losers truded slowly toward the cheapest fare back home, wherever home was, with their tails between their legs. Soon-to-be and the newly wed-on-a-budget nodded and smiled at the very start of their lives together, pimps and hookers, cabbies and tour guides waited along the outermost ring for whatever service they might offer.

Mica stood alone, off to one side. The Lord's Own.

Once removed.

Pressing the Bible against his chest, Mica looked up past the stylized neon-outlined Greyhound and took a deep breath.

"Father? Why have You forsaken me?"

A car backfired, but Mica didn't take that as an answer.

"Okay then," he said, "have it Your own way. 'In the beginning, there was nothing . . . a void and then God said, 'Let there be light,' and there was light' . . . and God saw through the light and into the future and it was all shit. Nothing but shit as far as the eye of the Lord could see."

"Hey! What kind of talk is that?"

A hand, the size of a football, suddenly came at him out of a billowing cloud of blue and yellow and knocked him back into the trash barrel.

"You think it's clever talking about the Lord God like that?"

Mica blinked at the powerful woman in muumuu and flowered straw hat. The string of puka shells resting on the massive shelf of her breasts rose and fell with each angry pant.

"You keep it up and the Lord's going to squeeze off your head like this."

She snapped her fingers and Mica jumped.

"That's right," she said, her Bronx accent ruining the full effect of her *Hilo Hattie* disguise. "You should jump because the Lord, my God, is a vengeful God and doesn't like skinny assholes dissing Him. Amen."

Mica's mouth answered for him, "amen," while he was busy trying to get the transit cops' attention. The cops were watching, all right, and smiling. One of the cops even waved.

Bastard.

"I– I wasn't dissing the Lord," Mica stammered. "I was . . . I've just had a bad day. Sorry."

The apology seemed to placate the transplanted New York wahine. A bit. At least the heaving of puka shells seemed to lessen.

"Well, okay. I guess everyone's entitled to a bad day now and then, but–" She fastened a look on Mica that made his ass suck in a few inches of underwear. "Don't you do it again."

"I won't," he promised and meant it . . . at the moment. "Here."

Without thinking (or remembering he and the woman were in full view of the transit cops), Mica reached into the

front pants pocket and pulled out the first few bills he felt.
Tips. He didn't have to worry about the denominations, they
were all ones.

The woman didn't seem shocked and the cops didn't seem
to care when she took the bills and somehow managed to find
room between the massive folds of her breasts. Mica expected
the offer of a hand-job at least, but instead got a not-so-gentle
cheek pinch.

"It's just like Brother Beezer says in his book," the woman
said, adding a bit more pressure to Mica's cheek to make sure he
was paying attention. "Chapter Three.   'There's good in
everybody if you're willing to go look for it like the Lord looks
for it in ourselves – long and hard but with faith.' This money's
going straight to Brother Beezer. You know Our Lord's favorite
son?"

Favorite son? Now that hurt, it really did. "Brother Beezer?"

The woman closed her eyes and covered her money-laden
breasts with both hands.

"Oh yes," she cooed, "you've heard him, haven't you?
You've heard him talk of the Life Everlasting and glory to come
in that wonderful voice of his?"

"Yeah."

"Isn't it inspiring to hear him? My husband and I just lay
there in bed, side by side with the dogs, and listen to every word
Brother Beezer says. Do you and *your* beloved one do that?"

Mica felt the blush start down around his toes and was
happy his little patch of Main Street wasn't all that brightly lit.

"Um, no."

The woman opened her eyes, anger brimming just beneath
the surface. "And why not?"

"Well, my . . . the woman I'm with doesn't care too much
for evangelical messages first thing in the morning."

"Oh," she said. "Then get rid of the slut."

"What?"

"It's like Brother Beezer said in Chapter 15 – 'Put Satan and his minions behind you and run like hell.' You can't be in love with this . . . woman, can you?"

"Well, no," Mica said, the honesty feeling so good on his tongue that he repeated it. "No, I don't love her, but . . . it's a very complicated relationship. The Lord has turned his back on me."

"Because of her, " the woman said, with a note of finality in her voice. "So buy yourself a blow-up sex doll and throw the hump you're living with out on her blasphemous ass. And the Lord will forgive you . . . like Brother Beezer says, because the Lord is all about forgiving, son, remember that."

"Yeah," Mica said, "He is, isn't He?"

"But only if you do something about it. The Lord doesn't like whiners who say they're going to do something and then just sit around waiting for the Lord to do it for them. I know . . . because I was just like you – a sniveling little whiner who thought God owed me something instead of the other way around. But that was before I found Brother Beezer. Did you hear all of his sermon this morning?"

Ashamed, tears whelming, Mica shook his head and slipped the Bible back into his pocket where it belonged. He'd been kidding himself all these months . . . years. He wasn't a real preacher, not like Brother Beezer. If he was, the Lord would have seen to it that he had an early morning radio show, too.

"No. The woman I . . . She made me turn it off."

"The bitch. Well, don't you worry, because I found you."

It was almost imperceptible, but Mica thought he noticed a increase in the size of the woman's bust as it swelled with pride.

"I'm a member of the *Beezer Brigade*, a Block Captain, and

this morning Brother Beezer told all us captains to go out and search the town for lost lambs and invite them to the revival meeting he's having right now out in the parking lot of the *Wet n'Wild Water Park*. I had Bingo and my kick-boxing classes today, so I got kind of a late start . . . but that didn't matter, did it? Because I found you, didn't I? So, would you come with me and let our dear Brother help you get back into God's good graces and put a little meat on that backbone of yours?"

Mica's feet, poor soles that they were, began moving on their own even while his brain, the real whiner of the organization, forced words into his mouth.

"I can't . . . the woman I live with . . ."

"Is a whore and evil unto the eyes of the Lord, regardless if you married her or not."

"I didn't."

"Well, there you go." Smiling, the woman tucked Mica's arm in hers and began dragging him down the street. "As Brother Beezer has written in Pamphlet 14: 'It is only when our souls are at their weakest and most fragile point, that the Lord All Mighty swoops them up with His great Heavenly thongs so He may beat and pound and temper them once more in His celestial forge until they come out as strong and hard as – "

"Mica."

The woman lifted one fuzzy-gray eyebrow and shushed him. "Brother Beezer wrote 'steel' . . . as strong and hard as steel. Period."

Mica didn't say another word until they got within eye-shot of the giant canvas circus tent that had covered most of the water park's southernmost parking lot.

It was the first tent revival he'd been to in almost twenty-two years, but just seeing it and hearing the frenzied singing and shouts of praise that drifted from it, he felt just like a kid again.

An innocent child.

"Praise the Lord," he gasped.

And that was all his self-appointed shepherdess needed to hear.

Deep in the throes of spiritual ecstasy, she pulled them both to a stop and lifted their hands – Mica's clenched firmly in hers – toward a heavenly night sky bespeckled with stars and bisected by one of the *Luxor's* green lasers.

"Yes, Lord . . . did you hear that? I have found my lost lamb, Lord, and I thank You in the name of Your mouthpiece here on Earth, Brother Rudolpho Beezer. Amen. For as Brother Beezer tells us, You love Your lost lambs the most and never, never turn Your back on them. Only man turns his back on the lost lambs because he's a weak and puling creature no *much* better than the dirt beneath the feet of the first man . . . which You then breathed life into Lord. Which was really cool, Lord."

Smiling, the woman lowered their hands and pulled Mica into a suffocating hug. "Come on, Lamb . . . let us march forward singing Brother Beezer's theme song!"

Mica had a little trouble singing while trying to stay in step with the cadence set by the tune of the *Battle Hymn of the Republic*, but he managed as well as he could.

"Oh, my eyes have seen the glory of Brother Beezer's plan,

He will stop the fall of all our souls and give them room to stand.

He will bring us back into God's grace and spread joy across this land,

May his tracts go world wide soon!"

God, it felt good to be back in line for Heaven.

Even if he wasn't the leader.

Oh Lord. Heaven was a whole lot closer than Mica ever suspected.

A chorus of beautiful women, clothed only in shimmering,

translucent robes and what God had blessed them with, sang like the Seraphim and Cherubim they were made up to represent while Brother Beezer, resplendent in his white satin "plantation suit," shouted praise and blessings over the impassioned congregation, and a man dressed as Jesus (in non-translucent robes) hung suspended on a clear Lucite cross, waved and blew kisses.

It was everything Mica had ever wanted in Heaven . . . or a church. His own church, the one he dreamt of every morning. Before Allison told him to shut off the damn radio.

Mica reached up and wiped a bead of sweat from the cross-shaped scar on his forehead. It really was all Allison's fault. He'd known it, but having a complete stranger in a muumuu tell him the same thing made a bigger impression on him. And his soul.

But did You have to wait so long, Lord?

The Lord still didn't answer him, but this time Mica understood the reason behind the silence – God was watching the show just like everyone else.

Okay, Lord, get back to me when You can. I'll be here.

"And what do we have here, Sister?"

Mica jerked, slamming his spine into the metal back of the folding chair he was sitting in when he noticed Brother Beezer's golden "Direct Line To God" microphone less than an inch from his nose. The matching gold portable amplifier hung from Brother Beezer's white, patent-leather belt with the 14-carat gold JESUS SAVES belt buckle.

He – Brother Beezer, not Jesus – had descended from the stage to walk among the first row of the faithful.

Praise be.

"We have a lost little lamb, Brother," Mica's muumuu-clad guardian angel shouted into the microphone as she pulled it toward her. Her position as a Block Captain had allowed her and her lamb (him) a front row seat to the holiest of holies. "I found him alone and lost and blaspheming out in front of the Greyhound Bus terminal. Poor lamb."

And a thousand voices filled the tent with their echoes, "poor lamb," while the choir raised their hands above their heads in worship.

It was a nice effect.

Mica noticed that the flying-Jesus thought so, too. There was a definite infusion of holy spirit beneath those homespun robes.

"Yes," Brother Beezer shouted into the mike when he was finally able to wrestle it away from the woman, "here is a poor lamb – praise the Lord God All Mighty and His Heavenly Hosts, Amen! A lost lamb who is even now trying to hide the mark of Cain upon him."

"Hal –le –"

"What?" Mica yelped as he was pulled to his feet and spun around to face the audience.

"–lujah!"

"Why the scar, Brother," Brother Beezer explained to those who might not have had a clear view of the video monitors placed around the tent. "The scar upon the very flesh of your forehead that is a mockery of that most holiest of symbols. Say Amen!"

"AMEN!"

"It's not!" Mica shouted back, only to be hissed and booed at. "It *is* a cross. Put there by the Hand of God himself!"

"PRAISE!"

"Now, now," Brother Beezer said, calming the audience, "don't go challenging the Lord's work or one of His own chosen few here on earth. That scar may look like a cross to you, but only because your eyes are still blind to the Holy Truth. Your mind is still closed to the Holy Word. But that's all right, because that's why *I'm* here. To show you and tell you . . . all of you what the Lord wants you to know. And that cross on your head, Brother, is nothing more than a mark against Him. For it is, oh my Brothers and Sisters, the same sort of mark that Our Lord placed upon the head of Cain after he slew his brother, Abel."

The tent compressed slightly as the air was sucked from it and into the lungs of the faithful.

"GASP!"

"But fear not for him, brethren," Brother Beezer continued, "for I can save him. Do you believe?"

"WE BELIEVE!"

"Are you sure?"

"YES, LORD!"

"Then let us pray —"

Mica. "— for this poor unfortunate man's soul—"

Mica, do you hear ME?

Lord? "—who didn't even know how lost he was until he came to me. For I shall save him, Brothers and Sisters. I shall—

Yes, Mica. Now . . . how about taking this jerk out for ME?

You got it, Lord. "—because that's what the Lord wants me to do! Halleluj— AAAAAAAAAAAAAAAAAA!"

The congregation didn't have time to gasp again and the choir went into anaphylactic shock when Mica grabbed the front of Brother Beezer's shirt front and dragged him back onto the stage. In the front row, his muumuu'd patron swooned against a heavier-set woman in capri-pants and a *Brother Beezer for President* middy-blouse.

"First off," Mica shouted into the mike still gripped in the shorter man's hand, "the mark on my forehead *is* a cross that Jesus Christ himself put there."

"GASP?"

Upon hearing this, his unconscious Block Captain

regained consciousness and clasped her meaty hands over her puka shells. It was a miracle, the first that would be remembered and retold of that night.

"That's right, Jesus Christ came down from Heaven and gave me this scar after my own daddy tried to kill me."

Muffled whispers of *hallelujah* and *praise the Lord our God* began drifting up from the sea of shining faces. It was almost exactly like he'd dreamed it . . . except for the squirming man in white satin. Mica took the microphone and dropped the man. And there were sounds of applause.

"*This,*" he said, facing the cameras and pointing to the scar, "is my covenant with the Lord as much as the rainbow was Noah's and the Ark was Moses . . . es. The Son placed this upon my head with His Own Hand when I thought my life was at the lowest depth it could possibly reach. But I was wrong. That wasn't the lowest."

"We – we hear you, Brother," Brother Beezer said as he got back to his feet and tried to take back control of the mike, "and we'll pray for you and your delusions. For all of us know the . . . the pain and loss that comes from falling . . . yes, falling away from the Lord's Holy light. As I have written in Pamphlet Number 43, 'Being the Lord's Best Friend,' – 'Only by suffering and accepting that for which we suffer can we truly begin to understand God's holy plans for–"

Brother Beezer wasn't even able to get another surround-sound squeal out before Mica strong-armed him into the floating Jesus & Cross. The momentum carried both man and cross directly into the center of the choir . . . which the man didn't seem to mind all that much.

Mica didn't wait to see where Brother Beezer finally ended up. Turning back to the congregation, almost as large as the one in his dream, he took a deep breath and smiled down upon them.

"I was lost and foundering and thought God *had* turned his back on me . . . and I was really bummed out about it. I thought I'd fucked up good, but I was wrong, because now I know that the Lord was always right next to me . . . watching me and waiting for me to figure that out. It was a test. A test of His love for me, not the other way around . . . a test to see if I was strong enough to accept His love unconditionally. And do you want to know the answer?"

The congregation, even those who looked like they spent their days tossing drunks out of Biker Bars, leaned forward, waiting in breathless anticipation.

"The answer was yes, I am strong enough to accept His love unconditionally."

"PRAISE THE LORD!"

"WAY TO GO, GOD!"

"And all because I was brought here tonight by this woman —" Mica smiled down at the woman who, filled with holy pride, swelled out her muumuu to double its original size. "She didn't know it at the time, but she was holding up a mirror . . . a mirror that was empty because, up until a moment ago, I had no reflection. My soul had been taken from me."

"TESTIFY! TESTIFY!"

"But my soul is back now, right Lord?" *Right as rain, Mica.* "And see, the Lord knew this had happened and so He just stepped back to let me try and deal with it myself. The Lord is a clean God so He really didn't want to get His hands dirty and let me sink deeper and deeper down the crapper until I didn't think even a divine plunger could get me out.

"So that's why — blind and helpless and reeking of supernatural decay and pussy juice — I allowed myself to come before this man."

"AMEN!"

Brother Beezer, having scrambled back onto the stage from

wherever it was that he fell, held out his arms to the crowd, welcoming back their adoration.

For a moment.

"This false prophet!"

"HUH?"

"He doesn't know what the Lord wants because he doesn't hear the Lord. I do! And the Lord has made it clear to me that if any of us want to get anywhere in this life we'd better stop thinking we have free will and just fall in line and do what God wants us to do. Because if we don't, God will turn His back and walk away and no amount of donations and pamphlets will get you into Heaven then. Isn't that right, Lord?"

You're bettin' 100, Mica.

"Thank you, Lord!"

Mica felt God's love seep back into him as he gazed down at the wide-eyed stares and gaping mouths of the faithful. The woman in the muumuu had passed out again, but that was okay, she probably needed the rest. Tossing the microphone up to the floating Jesus, he spread his arms wide and lifted his chin to the center of the big top.

"I FORGIVE YOU LORD! DO YOU HEAR THAT? I FORGIVE YOU FOR BEING AS SHITTY TO ME AS WE ARE TO OUR FELLOW MAN! I AM MICA! Let us pray, 'The Lord is my shepherd, I shall not want."

Half-way through the psalm, and with tears of joy streaming down his face, Mica felt the warm love sink deeper into his body and spurt out into his jockey shorts. A moment later he got cold-cocked from behind *(Lord? Is that You?)* and was carried out of the tent – by the arms and legs – to be tossed, with pomp and circumstance and benedictions (that smelled like beer) into an industrial-sized dumpster somewhere out behind the tent.

But that didn't matter. Neither did tearing his bowling

shirt on the edge of the dumpster as he crawled out.

Mica forgave the Lord for that, too, because, after all it was the Lord's fault. Not his, never his.

"I'm back, Lord. I'm back."

Say hallelujah. . . now, about Allison . . .

Oh God, Allison. He forgot all about that.

Mica looked up when he heard the Lord chuckle.

"Shit."

Allison made her final turn-wiggle-grind-grind and paused for the full count — two, three, four — arching her back to emphasize her bare, glitter-dusted breasts, before striking the famous and oft-photographed Follies pose: Right arm up, angled just slightly in front of the massive feathered head-dress, left arm bent at the waist, fingertips almost touching the rhinestone-covered front of the G-string thong . . . smile wide enough to reflect the barrage of camera flashes back at the audience.

Poor jerks, she thought to all the shutter-bugs who hoped to capture her bare likeness in photos they could show around the water-cooler. What they didn't know, and wouldn't until they got their pictures back from their local Wal-Mart, was that vampires just weren't very photogenic.

When the fanfare of trumpets and strings sounded again, their exit cue, Allison turned in perfect step with the rest of the troop and, waving and winking with equally rehearsed precision, strutted her stuff off stage. She stopped smiling, waving, and strutting the moment she got behind the side curtain.

Along with the rest of the company.

Being a Las Vegas showgirl might seem glamorous and exciting to the never-ending parade of tourists, but "seeming" was not "being" . . . and there were very few dancers who still dreamed about going solo and becoming a star. Most of the showgirls Allison knew preferred a steady paycheck and the anonymity of being a small part of a much bigger whole. She certainly did. Her one shot at stardom at Luci's back in Hollywood had been more than enough for her.

Besides, being just another boob in the crowd hadn't deprived her of anything. She made good money that allowed her to buy whatever her dead little heart desired . . . and she ate regularly.

Sometimes more than regularly.

Allison stepped back out of the way, and pressed her hand against the quarter-sized rhinestone in her bellybutton. Old B.S.'s blood was still fighting with Andy the geek's hemoglobin and that was really pissing her off.

She burped, but that didn't make her feel any better. *Beer and gummy worms.* Yuck. *God-damned, woman-hating, browbeating son-of-a—*

"Hey, Raven?"

Allison turned her head slowly. "Yeah, Tony?"

Tony was a full-time stage hand and free-lance appropriations' agent. You needed something – pills, booze, a "date", an abortion, someone who broke kneecaps, the best deal on a house . . . social security cards and other forms of I.D. if a new identity was in order – Tony was who you went to first. "Raven" was one of his best and most loyal customers.

"Got a minute?" he asked and nodded his head slowly toward the hall leading to the dressing rooms. Allison glanced at the two old men tottering nearby and snorted. Neither of them looked like they would have had more than a half-pint of blood between them.

"So?" she asked.

Tony looked a little surprised. Usually she would have jumped at his invitation to introduce her to "a couple of live ones just dying to meet you" (although he'd never figured out why she'd laugh whenever he said that), but tonight she just didn't feel like being some dried-up Sugar Daddy's sweet little girl.

Allison scratched her belly, ignoring the ants-crawling sensation as the gaping wounds closed. Being dead meant never having to say "tummy tuck."

"So?" Tony lowered his voice as if either of the two geriatric-ward Lotharios could have actually heard anything they were saying. "Honey, these guys got money and are looking for ways to spend it. See the short, bald one over there?"

"You'll have to be more specific."

"Okay, the short, bald one in blue . . . he owns a golf course in Palm Springs. A whole fucking golf course."

"I don't play golf."

"Other guy's a mulit-multi-millionaire in pharmaceuticals. You gonna tell me you never get sick?"

"Not for about eight months now," Allison said, shaking the feathers in her headdress. "Must be all this good desert air."

"Raven, honey . . ."

She stopped him with a (comparatively) gentle tap against the breastbone. It was to his credit, and that of his daily workout routine, that he only stumbled back a few inches.

"Thanks, but no thanks, Tony," she said. "Why don't you see if one of the other girls is interested?"

"But they asked for you, Rave. They *specifically* asked for you. I mean, they each handed me a hundred just to get them backstage. Hey, what harm's it gonna do, right? You smile, let em pinch a cheek or two, have some good eats and we both walk away winners. What'cha say? You gonna be a pal or what?"

Allison looked over at the two old codgers and smiled. They immediately began to primp and straightened into the stance of men only half their ages . . . which would have still put them around 70. Shaking her head, she turned around and chuckled as she lifted Tony off the ground and hurled him back into the curtain lines.

Buddy-Jim, Sr.'s blood seemed to think that was real funny. Allison didn't.

Hands clamped over her mouth to stop the laughter, she watched Tony try to untangle himself from the ropes without bringing any of the curtains and backdrops crashing to the stage floor.

"Raven!"

"I'm so sorry, Tony," Allison said from behind her hands. "I'm . . . just not feeling myself tonight."

❖

The Lord hadn't said much on the walk home, but He'd been a good listener.

However, standing there at the edge of the gravel front lawn, its normal lime-green tint gone a soft, putrid-yellow beneath the sodium street lamp behind him, Mica wouldn't have minded a little two-way conversation.

Before he spoke with Allison . . . to tell her it was all over between them, that after eight months of living in necrophilic-sin it was time for him to move on and move out and lift his face up to the sun, for the Lord was back in his life and —

"You *are* back. Right, Lord?"

The Lord remained silent, but Mica could tell He was there.

"Okay, but You know she's really going to be pissed off. I'm supposed to watch over her and . . . other stuff."

He didn't know if the Lord could read minds as well as a vampire, so he tried not to think of any of the *other stuff* he'd done for Allison. Besides, that was all over with. Just the thought of slipping his cock into her cold, hard flesh made him want to —

"RETCH!"

Mica spit and wiped his mouth off against the back of his hand. He'd gotten a little vomit on one shoe, but it was barely noticeable among the other stains he'd gotten in the dumpster.

"Sorry, Lord," he said, "must have been something I ate. Okay, here We go."

Straightening his shoulders, Mica pulled his house keys out of his pants — along with a blackened banana peel — and marched up to the house.

"'Verily, verily I say unto you,'" he said as he opened the front door to utter and terrible darkness. *She could be anywhere — watching him at the very moment. She didn't need lights — she was darkness itself.* His stomach gurgled threateningly. "Um — 'I say unto you, if ye shall ask anything of the Father, He will give it you in My Name'."

Mica stepped over the threshold and turned on the 60-watt hall light.

"Allison? Are you home?"

The latch sounded much louder than usual when he closed the door, but he didn't let that stop him.

"Allison? We need to talk."

The living room, where she sometimes liked to read fashion magazines in the dark before crawling into her coffin, was empty. Oh, that's right . . . she said she'd be home late and not to wait up for her. He'd have to talk to her in the morning.

"Well, darn. But You saw me, Lord. You saw how I was all ready to tell her. First thing in the morning, You'll see. I'll leave her a note telling her we have to talk when I get home and that she better be here. Right, Lord?"

The Lord still didn't say anything, but Mica knew He was proud of him. Who wouldn't be, after all . . . he was Mica.

❖

The clock-radio went off at its usual time.

"No more mis-ter NICE GUY . . . no more mis-ter CLEEE-EEE-EEEN!"

Shit! MICA!

Mica almost dislocated his shoulder before he managed to turn down the volume.

TURN THE DAMN THING OFF!

He did and glared at her coffin. It was over. How could he even think about staying with a woman, dead or alive, who didn't even like Pat Boone?

"Sorry," he said.

Ah-CHOO!

Mica smiled. "Bless you."

CHAPTER 7

"Ah-choo! Dammit."

Either one of her last meals (probably B.S.) had been coming down with a viral infection or she'd suddenly become allergic to the 100% real silk lining in her casket. *If* the dead could become allergic to anything, that is. But whatever it was, the early morning sneezing fit that had started when the alarm had gone off and lasted until Mica *(ah-choo)* had finally left with his Elvis-*(ah-choo)*-impersonator friend, Alvis *(AH-CHOOOOOOO!)* had left her feeling a little irritable.

Sniff.

Allison reached up to rub her nose and banged her elbow into the coffin's side. The resulting hollow echo vibrated ice-picks through her brain. The buzz she'd gotten from Buddy-Jim, Sr. had devolved into a bit of a hang-over.

The bastard . . . no, bastards, she thought, and added the manufacturers of her special order "Sleeping Beauty Model" coffin. She'd paid almost as much to have the damned thing customized — top-notch stereo sound system with convenient over-head CD mount, coiled-spring mattress, and *supposedly* extra-thick side padding — as she did for her Faberge egg.

Allison thumped the side panel again and winced at the sound. It was obvious that someone had skimped on the extra-thick padding . . . but, after all, who was ever going to find out? The dearly departed usually aren't in any condition to complain or ask for their money back.

And she wouldn't either, complain or ask for her money back, that is. She'd just have Mica track them down for her and –

"Ah-choo . . . damn!"

Allison kicked open the lid and was already shuffling toward the basement in a facsimile of the ratty old bathrobe and pink bunny slippers that had been her "self-pitying" outfit. There was only one thing she wanted to do.

"Victim for Victims," a voice Allison didn't immediately recognize said. "How may I help –"

"Supervisor, please."

"Um . . . one minute please."

The musical selection when she was put on hold, *Having my Baby*, didn't help improve her mood . . . although it did strengthen her resolve. She was going to quit. Period. No one was going to talk her out of it. It's not like she got paid or anything. And this way she could spend her time doing what she wanted to do.

Whatever that was.

Pulling a non-*V for V* pencil from the holder, Allison snapped it in half, then into quarters, and then into eights. She was just about to try for sixteenths when the music went off and the all-too-chipper voice of her supervisor answered.

"Gerri," she said before the woman could ask how she could help her, "this is Allison. I quit."

"Okay."

"I mean it, Gerri."

"I know," Gerri said, "you mean it every time you quit. How many times has it been?"

Allison sprinkled pencil dust off her fingers.

"So, you're taking the day off?" Allison heard the rustle of paper in the background. "Oh . . . the tally sheet shows you went off early yesterday, too. Are you having your monthlies? Tell you what, take the rest of the week off and live on *Midol* and bourbon. That usually does it for me."

"Believe me, Gerri . . . I'm way beyond *Midol* and bourbon. I quit."

"Gee, you don't sound that old? Must have had an early menopause, huh? Lucky you."

Allison pulled the phone away from her ear and stared at it. Gerri kept right on talking – unaware that anything had changed.

"– an appointment with the City Council in about fifteen minutes about putting on a carnival to get the public more aware of domestic violence. Have a good rest. Bye."

"Wait a minute, I – Shit."

She punched *Redial* hard enough to drive the button all the way down into the plastic housing. Well, she was thinking about getting a new phone anyway.

"Vict'm fer Vict'ms. How kin ah hep y'all?"

"I'm going to kill her, Jan."

Jan laughed softly as if she didn't want to be heard. "Gerri, right? Yeah, she said y'all was goin' through the change or sum'min. Y'all okay?"

"I've already changed as much as I'm ever going to, Jan," Allison growled.

"Okay."

"Look, Jan, I'm sorry I snapped, but I've made up my mind – I'm quitting the help line."

"Okay."

"What's going on down there? Is 'okay' today's secret password?"

"Aw, no, honey, but y'all is a'ways quittin'. Least once a month." Every word out of Jan's mouth dripped with molasses.

"Guess that's why Gerri thought you were still havin' PMS an' the likes. I know I wanna quit every twenty-eight days or so."

"Yeah, okay," Allison said, stopping the woman before she got off on another tangent, "but I mean it this time, Jan, I —"

Too late. "Oh, y'all's gonna love this. Got me a call this mornin', first thing, from one'a our repeat'rs. Y'know . . . Noreen Hetrick."

"Oh?" Allison smiled for the first time that morning and patted her belly. "Yeah, I got a call from her yesterday. Did anything happen? Is she okay?"

It might have just been that she knew what happened and that Noreen was, finally, okay, but the last two questions came off sounding pretty phony . . . even for her.

"Well, yeah, I guess. Well, Noreen she calls and is cryin' t'beat th'band. Course, I immediately pull up her file and see she's called an' talk'd t'most of us at one time or a'nuther . . . so I figger that sum-sack husband a'hers been beatin' on her, y'know? Well, y'all coulda knock me over with a turkey, cause this gal is cryin' and all worried cause the bastard didn't come home all night. And she tells me he *a'ways* comes home t'her and the kids . . . even if it's just t'whomp on her. Then . . . on and this is the best part . . . she asks me if I might know how she could call up t'hep t'try and find him.

"Can y'all believe that? This bastard beats her reg'lar and she's worried when he don't come home t'do it! Ain't that sum'min?"

"Yeah," she agreed, "it's something all right. She didn't go to the Safe House, did she?"

More paper rustled. "Guess not," Jan said, "phone number's the same as every other time she called. Why, y'all tell her t'high-tail it over there?"

"It doesn't matter. Bye, Jan."

"Okay, y'all take care now, hear. See y'all in a week."

Allison tossed the handset down and slumped back into the chair. Noreen hadn't packed up her kids to somewhere safe, like she promised she would. Noreen had stayed in her little trailer, like a good wifey, and waited all night for her abusing asshole of a husband to come home so he could beat on her.

Some people didn't even deserve to die.

"You know something, Antonio," she said to his framed picture, "the living deserve each other. They're useless. They ought to be herded into pens for their own protection. They should be. . . ."

She smiled down at her note pad and the phone number that was written there.

"The living need to be beaten regularly," she whispered as the phone on the other end was picked up.

"*The Stud Farm*," a low voice purred from the speakers. "How may I service you?"

❖

It wasn't exactly what she expected.

Although never having been to an S&M/Bondage & Domination "club," she really didn't know *what* to expect. Something along the lines of *Luci's Fur-Pit* back in Hollywood . . . flashy – with neon (naturally) – and palm trees or, in keeping with the Las Vegas tradition for themed amusements, something in the motif of a riding stable. Yeah, a riding stable would have worked . . . and it wouldn't have had to be an Upper-Middle Class riding stable where the girls all own their own horses and wear English riding breeches and attitude. It could have looked like one of the quaint little stables her father used to take her to in Griffith Park.

It wouldn't have taken much.

A few bales of hay, a couple of plastic horses tied to a hitching post; a split-rail fence.

Something with just a little glitz, if not glamour.

Or at least fresh paint.

This can't be the place.

Allison leaned forward, resting her arms on the top of the steering wheel, and double-checked the words burned into the wooden arch above the entrance to the property.

THE STUD FARM

Yep, this was the place: A metal Quonset hut surrounded by desert on three sides and a fenced-in parking lot on the other. A parking lot that seemed to be extraordinarily crowded for 8 o'clock in the morning in the middle of a work week.

"Maybe today's 'Free Whip Day,'" she said to herself as she watched a woman in a business-suit and high-heels set the alarm on a silver Mercedes and march purposely toward the building. "Or she's the accountant or. . . . something."

Again . . . something, that was as far as her imagination could go. *Something* obviously was happening inside the Quonset hut S&M parlor, but Allison – *femme fatal* that she literally was – couldn't come up with anything beyond a flashback of Rosie O'Donnell and Dan Ackroyd in the black leather costumes they wore in a movie.

Yikes.

The miserable truth was that, up until she died and began her career first as a furry stripper and now a hot showgirl, her life had been pretty boring. She'd fall asleep watching late-night soft core, blushed at the really "juicy" parts of modern Romance novels, and had never even been invited to a naughty lingerie party.

As Allison pulled the Mustang into a slot between a gleaming Lexus and dust-rusted military jeep, she suddenly realized that dying really had been the best thing that ever happened to her.

Grumbling to herself, she changed from the O'Donnell-inspired outfit to a more conservative silk pants suit and reduced the size of her bust-line by a full cup size. If the *something* going on inside the building did involve whips, she wanted an unrestricted swing zone. She remembered her junior-high softball coach telling her that little piece of wisdom on the first day back from summer vacation . . . when everyone in her Phys. Ed class, except Allison, had "blossomed" into A-cup womanhood.

She kept her hair red, because it looked better with the dove-gray silk, but sucked it into a tight bun at the back of her neck. That way, if *nothing* was going on inside the building, she could say she was a Real Estate agent who'd lost her way and was only asking for directions.

Or maybe she'd just put a scare into everyone and say she was a Vice Cop.

Allison chuckled as she crossed the parking lot. Now *that* could be funny.

The door slid open when she was still a few yards away and an electronic voice – male, naturally – invited her in. From the outside the building might look like a refugee from World War II, but inside . . . .

Allison smiled as she stepped into the soft darkness.

Inside was really *something.*

Mica felt better than he had in eight months. Maybe longer.

And he wanted everyone to share in his happiness and to know that God was back in his good graces.

Especially those dearly beloved couples who came before him that morning.

As a general rule (and one that Mica promised to uphold on his job application), unless otherwise designated by the couple and the amount of extras they were willing to pay for, the standard wedding ceremony ran ten minutes. Fifteen if the names were hard to pronounce.

Mica's first ceremony lasted forty-five minutes and had more couples circling the lobby outside the chapel than La Guardia had planes in the air. It was a beautiful thing and the Lord was pleased.

The *Desert Rose's* day manager, however, wasn't. Mica could tell from the way the veins were sticking out in the man's temples as he pounded on the glass wall and pointed to the door – which Mica had taken the liberty to lock so the Lord's attention wouldn't be diverted from the service.

Mica did wave to his employer every few minutes, however, just to let him know everything was okay. Perfectly okay and only getting better. He'd made up his mind on the drive into work that morning, while Alvis butchered "But I Can't Help Crawling to Love in You."– he was going to go home for lunch and tell Allison it was all over. And forgive her while he sent her on her way.

Pausing to catch his breath, Mica looked down at the foot-long piece of wooden dowel that rested comfortably on the pulpit's top shelf next to the stack of *Desert Rose* wedding certificates. He'd whittled a point on it during his first coffee break, making sure it was sharp enough so it'd slip in nice and easy. Soulless demon though she was, he didn't want her to suffer any more than she had to.

Until she reached for redemption through the flames of Hell, of course.

And then it would be up to the Lord and not him.

"For the Lord knows what's in your hearts and minds and if it's only a carnal desire that's wrong unto His eyes and you'd both better make amends right now," he warned the dazed couple standing before him. "For I am . . . Brother John and I'm here to tell you, as one who knows the Lord's mind, that He won't take kindly to impure thoughts about lust. No, sir, and you can believe me about that. The Lord doesn't want His name linked up with anyone who's only out for a good time. Therefore, since neither of you have turned into a pillar of salt, I will assume you're both God-fearing and pure of heart with only love in your minds for one another. But woe be unto you both if you're lying to the Lord . . . especially you —"

Mica checked the name on the license.

"Steve. For it's up to the man to make sure he's being truthful, for the Lord God made man in His own image because He knew that women are weak in mind and spirit and easily swayed to the dark side."

"What?" The woman (Amanda) shouted. "You can't say something like that!"

"See there, Steve," Mica said, picking up the dowel and pointing it at the woman. "She's fighting against the Lord already."

"I am not!"

"Shh," Steve said, "it's okay, honey."

"No it's not! Didn't you hear what he just said about women?"

"Yeah, but you and I know that's not true, right sweetie-pea?"

Mica tapped the dowel lightly against the top of the pulpit like a teacher calling a class back to order. And it worked. The arguing couple looked up at him in utter silence.

"I don't lie, Amanda, for the Lord gets really pissed off when people do that. 'By oppression and judgement he was taken away: And as his generation, who did reason? For he was cut off out of the land of the living. For the transgression of My people that had become one.' Isaiah 53:8. See?"

The couple was silent. Mica took that as a good sign and waved to his employer. The man's face definitely seemed a shade or two darker than it had a moment before — but that could have just been a trick of the light that was caused when the glass around the dead-bolt shattered.

And a tide of voices and gambling sounds challenged the peaceful little world of love he'd tried to create. Oh well.

Mica shrugged his apologies to Steve and his shrew-to-be and placed his hand, still holding the dowel, over the open Bible. At the far end of chapel, Alvis was struggling with their boss. It was obvious both of them wanted to come in and share in the joyous moment. Mica never felt more proud.

"Okay, then," he told the couple. "Steve, do you take this . . . woman?"

"Um."

"And Amanda, do you promise to obey Steve for as long as you live?"

"WHAT?"

Alvis was suddenly at his side, his big hand covering Mica's and half the Bible.

"Then in accordance with the laws governin' this fair state a Nevada, ah now pronounce you man n' wife. Yah may kiss the bride, yah lucky so-n-so."

The couple were too stunned to move and Mica couldn't blame them. After all, they'd come to be married by a simple man of God and ended up with Elvis in a blue suede jumpsuit. It had to be a little unnerving to say the least.

"Cuse us a minute?" Alvis asked as he grabbed Mica's arm and began dragging him toward the door behind the floral display table. The door led to a service hall that ran the entire length of the building — from the registration desk to kitchen — used mostly to deliver champagne or kosher wine as required, or when local crime bosses found it necessary to leave their weddings of momentary convenience in a hurry.

Mica and Alvis only used the hallway if the route from chapel to buffet tables was too crowded.

"But I'm not finished," Mica protested. "And it's too early for lunch, isn't it?"

Alvis gave him a look that said it was *never* too early for lunch, but nodded in agreement nevertheless.

"Ah know, but the boss-man wants yah t'take a little break. He also wanted me t'remind yah that he don't pay us per word."

Mica shook his head as Alvis opened the exit door. "But I was only doing what the Lord wanted me to do."

"Amen t'that, but ah lived long enough t'know that sometimes what the Lord wants ain't what an employer wants. Go take a break, Johnny. 'Sides, most of them couples waitin' t'be hitched are goin' for the *Viva Las Vegas* special. And we gotta give the audience what it wants, right?"

Mica couldn't argue with that, although he did offer to officiate for the couples who wanted a non-traditional Vegas wedding.

"That's good of you, but Darth Vader's comin' in as back-up. Poor guy needs the extra money . . . he and his missus just had twins a while back. So don't worry bout it."

He slapped Mica on the shoulder to hurry him along, plucking the dowel from his hand as he went sailing past.

"Nice stick."

"It's for . . . Raven," he said, taking it back and slipping it under the rope belt at his waist. "I'm carving it for her. It's going to be a . . . stake. You know, for the garden?"

Alvis winked. "Well, it's a good'en. Now, go on and rest. It's all covered."

"But the Lord really likes what I'm doing here."

"An' so do ah. But, like mah mama always said, the good Lord takes care of em that takes care of themselves. So go take care of yerself, Johnny. Sides, don't yah think the Lord'd have better places t'be than in this place?"

Mica stared at the limerick someone had scratched into the

industrial-green paint on the back of the door as it closed –

"There once was an old whore named Pluckett" . . . . and shook his head sadly.

"The Lord's everywhere."

And a small voice answered, "Amen."

The girl stepped back into the shadows of a portable freezer when Mica turned. He couldn't see her very well, it was too dark – he could just make out the faintest outline of incredibly long legs and a tight little body wrapped in something pale and diaphanous. Her face was equally pale, framed by blackness deeper than the night . . . her eyes were dark as well, large and dark, but with an illumination that came from within. She didn't look real. A ghost? Maybe. He'd heard that Las Vegas was crawling with restless spirits of murdered gangsters *(no, she didn't look like a gangster)*, suicidal showgirls *(could be, she was beautiful enough)*, jilted lovers *(maybe – her eyes were so sad)*, busted gamblers, depressed losers and even the ghost of the real Elvis was supposed to wander around . . . although Alvis always argued that was impossible, since he was still alive. Alvis, that is.

The girl sighed and her outline seemed to fade. Mica had never believed in ghosts until that moment.

Vampires, hell yes . . . they were real, but never ghosts.

"Don't go," he pleaded. "I believe in you."

The girl's form brightened as she stepped out of the shadows and pulled the voluminous gauze shawl tighter around herself. If she was a ghost, Mica was going to run right out an buy a Qui-Ja board.

"I know I'm not supposed to be back here," she said and let the shawl drop to her shoulders – revealing the plunging neckline of her micro-mini, white sharkskin halter-dress.

"No," he said, "you're not. Are you another physical therapist?"

She smiled, brushing back a thick curl of blue-black hair that had escaped the thick braid at the back of her neck. She looked so young, not much more older than he'd been when he left home on that ill-fated bus ride to Hollywood – eighteen, no more than nineteen – which was remarkable given her career choice.

"In a way, I guess," she said. "I'm a hooker."

Mica nodded. He was really batting a thousand when it came to guessing occupations.

"Oh. Sorry."

"I'm not," she said. Tying the shawl around her tiny waist as a make-shift skirt, the girl began fiddling with the red scruncy tie. "I make good money and get to meet a lot of . . . interesting people and I'm not ashamed of what I'm doing. Not at all. I – I'm —"

She took a deep breath and looked straight into Mica's soul as tears filled her eyes.

"That's a lie," she whispered. "I hate what I'm doing. I wish I was dead, Father."

That was the second time in two days that a beautiful woman had mistaken him for a man of the cloth, but this time, unlike the last, he wasn't going to correct her.

"It's all right . . . my child."

"NO IT'S NOT!" Her voice filled the corridor like thunder. "GOD HATES ME!"

Mica caught her just as she collapsed, cradling her in his arms as she wept against his chest. He could feel her breath against his throat, hot and wet.

"No, he doesn't," he said and angled his lower body away from hers. He didn't want her to get the wrong impression . . . that he only thought of her as a whore. "God doesn't hate anyone."

The girl looked up, tears streaming from her red-rimmed

eyes and wiped her nose across the front of his robe. She was so beautiful in her agony.

"Y-yes he does," she said, her voice almost too soft now. Mica had to pull her closer in order to hear. "God hates me. I heard what you said . . . in there, about how God hates liars. You were pretty loud and I heard you all the way in the kitchen. I was giving one of the dishwashers a blow job."

Mica tightened his grip and glared in the direction of the kitchen. "Which one? You tell me which one and I'll get him fired."

"No, it wasn't his fault, he didn't do anything wrong. But while I was . . . doing it, you know, I heard what you said and I knew why God never talks to me anymore. It's because I've lied to him and me about what I am. I'm a WHORE!"

"Shh." He could tell by the tiny catches in her throat that she'd started crying again. "You're wrong. God doesn't hate you, He just likes to . . . play games with us once and a while. And sometimes He likes to pretend He's not around, you know, just to teach us a lesson. But He's there . . . and I'm sure He doesn't hate you for being – you know."

The girl wiggled out of Mica's *brotherly* embrace just far enough so she could meet his eyes.

"You're nice, but I know God hates me. I'm a whore and I always have been a whore and I al-always and . . . WAAAAAAAAAhhhhhhhhhhhhhhhhh!"

Mica had never heard anyone, outside of prime-time melodramas and on *The Jerry Springer Show*, make that kind of sound. Or at that volume and pitch. It had literally thrown him back against the chapel door with the force of a Class 5 tornado, and since she was still locked in his arms, the impact against his spine doubled.

"–aaaaaahhhhhhhhhhhh–"

"Hey, what's goin' on in there?"

Alvis? Mica shook his head, trying to clear it, but only made the ringing in his ears worse. Of course, it might have helped if the girl had stopped yelling.

"–aaaaaaahhhhhhhhhhh–"

The door jerked him forward into her and when she pushed him back, his elbow slammed into the knob and depressed the lock.

"Hey!" *A different voice, definitely not Alvis this time – not that the girl noticed.*

"–aaaaaaahhhhhhhhhhh–"

"Open this door!" The new voice ordered. "Do you hear me? This is Chapel Security."

Uh-oh.

Mica pushed the girl off him at the same time something hard and heavy hit the door behind him.

"–aaaaaaahhhhhhh——"

"I repeat – this is Chapel Security! OPEN THE DOOR OR WE'LL BREAK IT DOWN. NOW!"

"–hhhhh-Shit!" Three heavy thuds filled the sudden silence. "Come on, let's get out of here."

For someone who'd been hysterical only a moment before, the girl was surprisingly adaptable. Grabbing Mica's hand, she pulled him away from the door just as another thud splintered the wood around the knob. She seemed very familiar with the layout of the passageway, weaving and darting around storage boxes and serving carts without slowing down; her shawl fluttering around her hips like misplaced wings. Fortunately, there wasn't much time for Mica to dwell on the subject of her hips or her working knowledge of the best escape route. It was all he could do to keep up and not get his legs tangled up in his robes.

If fact, it wasn't until both of them were outside and halfway across the brew pub's section of parking lot, that Mica managed to gather his thoughts together – and realize he was about to die of heat stroke. The robes worked great against the near-arctic chill of the *Rose's* air-conditioning, but it was literally hell out beneath the noon-day sun.

"I –" was all he got out before melting into a puddle on the scorching blacktop.

She was stronger than she looked – all muscle beneath the warm skin, skimpy clothes, and mascara-racoon mask. Her little hands caught him under the arms on the way down and helped him, gently, back to his feet.

"Jesus!" she gasped, panting, the cinnamon-tinted edge of her areola playing hide-and-seek with him each time she took a breath. "Jesus, are you all right?"

"I'm not Jesus," he wheezed and that made her laugh.

"I know. You're the Preacher Man." Satisfied that Mica could stand on his own, for a moment at least, she quickly unwrapped the shawl and brought it up to cover her head. Even with the red eyes and smeared makeup, the resemblance to Mary, the Lord's Own Mom, was remarkable. "I used to hear you, you know, out in front of the bus station?"

"U-u-u—" Mica took a deep breath, staggered a bit, and tried again. "Used? To?"

"Yeah," she said and dropped her head in shame, and that one action spoke louder than her tears and cries had. She was a whore and therefore didn't think herself worthy to hear the words of God.

Lord, You and me really need to talk about this.

Mica reached out and lifted her chin. She looked sad, but she wasn't crying anymore.

"Anyway," she continued, "I thought I recognized your voice today and then when you came out into the hall I – I just wanted to say thanks for all the other times I heard you. It made things easier. I'm sorry I got so emotional."

Her gratitude seized Mica by the balls and squeezed until he thought his head was going to explode. Tears blinded his laser-restored vision as he looked up into the white-hot sky and smiled. This was just like when Mary Magdalen came to Jesus . . . could there *be* any clearer sign? The Lord had chosen and finally made His choice known – he, Mica, was the True Voice of The Word . . . not Brother Butt-head-Beezer.

He winked out a tear. *Thanks, Lord.*

There were still tears in his eyes when he looked down and silently blessed her.

"You okay?" she asked.

"Perfect. The Lord is with you . . . um – What's your name?"

"Elena. Elena Valdez."

Not Mary, but it would do. "The Lord is with you, Elena."

Elena cocked her head to one side and Mica felt himself fall into the bottomless brown-black pools of her eyes.

"You know, when you say it like that, I almost believe you."

"Believe me, you can believe . . . me. Sorry, that sounded funny."

"It sounded wonderful," she said and smiled. "You know, I usually don't work the chapels . . . it's not the best place to get a . . . date, you know, unless the new bride is really lousy in bed. And–" Her smile fell. "That's not the whole truth. I work all the wedding chapels except this one. I hate the *Desert Rose*, no offense. But this guy I knew, the dishwasher, offered me a hundred-dollar chip if I'd do him with whipped cream and butterscotch pudding while his friend video-taped it. He said he was going to send the tape to an ex-girlfriend and tell her he was a porn star or something. I wouldn't have come back, but I needed the money. I'm sorry if I got you into trouble, Preacher Man."

Mica crossed his hands in front of him. He *really* liked

butterscotch pudding.

"Came back?" he said after a moment. "You worked . . . you were an employee at the *Rose*?"

A small quiver touched her full, sensuous bottom lip. "No. I was going to get married there. I gotta go now, thanks again, Preacher Man."

She turned to leave.

"No! I mean, my name's M– John."

Elena stopped, glancing back at him from around the edge of the shawl. "Thank you, John. I'm glad we finally met."

And she turned and began walking away, head down, the weight of her sin making her wobble on the stiletto heels of her sandals.

Lord, You can't do this. You can't just bring this poor creature to me and then let her go away. I know I'm supposed to help her . . . but how? Lord, I'm not joking . . . Lord, are You listening? DO SOMETHING!

And the Lord was listening and did something.

Mica's stomach grumbled so loud Elena heard it and turned around.

Thank You, – urp – *Lord.*

"Lunch!" Mica said walking up to her and pointing in the direction opposite the *Desert Rose* and its free-to-employees buffet. He didn't think he'd be able to concentrate if there was butterscotch pudding anywhere in sight. "Look, the deli's right here. The food's great and the prices are reasonable and. . . ." *Okay, Mica, you can stop the commercial now. Right, Lord.* "So, how about it? Will you have lunch with me?"

Elena smiled and, if it was possible, the sun brightened in the sky.

"You think we're dressed okay? I mean, you and me . . . like this. You look like St. Fiacre."

Mica nodded. "Who?"

Shaking her head, she linked her arm in his and led them toward the restaurant. "He was an Irish monk who set up a retreat in France. He was supposed to be a good man . . . like all the saints, except he wouldn't allow women to worship at his church because he was afraid of being tempted by them. Silly to think about that nowadays, isn't it, but I guess that's why they made him the Patron Saint of people suffering from venereal disease. I did a report on him in the eighth grade and Sister Mary-Mary said it was the best paper she'd ever —"

Elena stopped just before they got to the entrance and took a deep breath.

"I'm sorry, I shouldn't have gone on like that. That girl, the one I was, doesn't exist anymore. She died eight months ago."

Eight months . . . that was *way* too much of a coincidence.

"Don't say that!" Grabbing her arms, Mica spun her around to face him. "Don't ever say anything that stupid again, okay? You aren't dead – you're alive and warm and breathing and . . . real. Here, see for yourself."

He turned her back around until they could both see her reflection in the glass door. Elena yelped.

"Ohmygod!" She gaped at the dark smudges under her eyes. "I look like the Bride of Frankenstein! Why didn't you tell me I look awful?"

"You don't," Mica told her reflection. "You're beautiful."

Elena's reflection shook its head. "And you've been out in the sun way too long, John. Come on, you get us a table while I go to the little girl's room and repair the damages. All I need's about five minutes and I'll show you how good I really can look. Mirrors are our friends."

Mica didn't realize how long he'd missed hearing something like that until she'd said it.

CHAPTER 8

Thirty-five pairs of female eyes, in all shapes and sizes, watched Allison as she entered and walked to the reception desk. Tucked into a niche next to an unmarked door and closed off from the room by a sliding window of frosted glass, the desk reminded Allison of the one in her dentist's office.

Hell, the whole waiting room reminded her of her dentist's office.

Three times the size, of course.

The walls were (if memory served her right) a soft sunrise peach, the upholstered chairs and couches off-white and the lush carpeting a deep burnt-orange. Low tables, antique-white and covered with every kind of magazine imaginable (except *S&M Monthly*, which disappointed Allison) were within easy reach. The lighting was recessed, the hanging silk plants well dusted. Hotel-benign prints were artistically arranged and the soft music that drifted on the air-conditioned breeze was decidedly New Age-plus.

A phone rang as Allison reached the desk and a shadow moved behind the frosted glass. *Stud Farm*, a man's voice said. *How may I service you? Yes, mistress. Of course, Mistress. Your reservation for a three way for this evening at 8 pm has been recorded. Yes, Mistress . . . I was very slow and I should be punished.*

Thank you, Mistress. I look forward to your strong hand.

Allison was giggling when the frosted window slid open and a Greek God wearing a thick black-leather dog collar and . . . nothing else that she could see from the waist up . . . handed her a clipboard and pen. The sheaf of papers beneath the clip looked like standard "New Patient" information and release forms. She was a bit disappointed, figuring an S&M joint would at least have a pretty cool logo – like a pair of cat-o-nine-tails crossed above an naked ass.

"Sorry," he said and Allison stopped giggling. "We've come to believe that subtle is always best." He winked at her. "Greetings, little sister."

And the bronze man with golden curls and azure eyes went from Greek God status to jerk. She didn't even rate one lousy "mistress."

"What did you just call me?"

But the big jerk just smiled – and the room was suddenly filled with the sound of lust and longing. Allison pivoted on her heels and glared the supposed aggressive females into embarrassed silence. A gentle nudge against her back turned her back around.

"Just fill out the forms," he said, glancing down at the clipboard as if she'd forgotten all about it, "it's for insurance purposes only, of course. None of the information written here will ever be made public." He winked at her and lowered his voice. "I have to say that to everyone, no offense intended."

He winked again and Allison didn't know whether to be insulted or honored that he was treating her like they were old friends. She made her decision, however, when he pulled the clipboard back as she reached for it and inked something out.

"Sorry," Jerk-boy said, handing it back. "That item doesn't count for you. Bring the completed forms with you when your name is called. You'll find a table just inside that door." He jerked a thumb to the door next to his cubicle. "Just leave the clipboard and pen there. We're happy you're here."

He blew her a kiss and closed the window. Allison could still see his grin through the frosted glass.

"Hey," she said, pulling the window back open, "I didn't give you my name."

He wasn't there.

Allison leaned forward over the narrow counter and looked inside the small, efficient office. It looked like a standard office -- desk, chair, multi-line phone, computer for billing, secure cash drawer, filing cabinets, copy of *People* magazine – nothing out of the ordinary. Nothing at all.

Except it was empty.

Allison had seen receptionists disappear before, but not as quickly as that.

"Jerk must work part time for Siegfried and Roy," she mumbled to herself, but made sure it was loud enough to be overheard by every woman in the waiting room.

A few of the women looked shocked by her "private thoughts," most seemed to take it as a personal insult. Allison ignored both ends of the emotional spectrum as she walked to an empty chair in the very middle of the room. If any of the women wanted to start something she'd be more than willing to finish it, but right now she had forms to fill out.

Making herself comfortable, Allison picked up the pen and tapped it against the first form. Frowned long and hard at the item that had been crossed out.

Blood type.

Why would he have crossed that out?

Better yet, why was it on the form in the first place?

Questions, questions, everywhere . . . and not an answer in sight.

Yet.

The first page, other than the request for a blood type, was pretty typical: Name, address, age (reduced by five years . . . which was also typical, for her, regardless of her non-living condition), e-mail address, marital status, blah, blah, blah, yaddah, yaddah, yaddah.

Page two: Basic health questions. Allergies, no. Heart problems, no. Asthma, no. High blood pressure? Low blood pressure? Blood clots? No, no, no. Back injury or recent surgery, no. Dizziness, migraines, epilepsy, inner-ear infection, diabetes, hypoglycemia, emphysema, arthritis, hives, glaucoma, periodic black outs, menopause, menstrual cramps, PMS, low potassium, high potassium, pregnancy, ulcers, hemorrhoids, urinary tract infection, drug addiction.

No, no, no, no, no, no, no, no, no, nononononononononononononono!

Allison finished checking off the last *NO* box and leaned back. It was sad really. Except for being dead, she was in pretty good shape.

The door next to the receptionist's desk opened and two women left, one young, one middle aged. The door closed. A name was called (not hers) over the intercom and the door opened again. Three new arrivals entered and waved at a woman across the room. Five minutes passed and two more women left this time, giggling and joking with each other like old friends. Allison finished two more pages of forms, listening to the comings and goings.

It'd been like that since she'd arrived. Women coming and women going. Doors opening and closing on the average of once every five minutes. Allison gave up watching after about thirty minutes.

"I'm very disappointed," a voice said and that, at least, got her attention.

Looking up, Allison watched a gray-haired matron in a wheel-chair being pushed by a very humbled-looking receptionist/jerk. He winked at her when he saw her watching – *Asshole!* – and blew her another kiss.

"Did you hear me?"

The woman didn't give him time to answer. Swinging her handbag over her head, she caught him against the chin. A number of women applauded, a few whistled. Allison jumped.

The receptionist, in his collar and black leather bikini briefs, looked suitably chastised.

"Yes, Mistress," he said, hunching his shoulders as he knelt in front of the wheel-chair. "Forgive me, Mistress."

The old woman smiled. "Well, I'll think about it. Now, about my disappointment. Tell whoever's in charge of supplies that I don't like those new kid-skin floggers. They're much too soft. What's the use of something that soft? When I hit a man, I want him to know it. Do you understand?"

The receptionist rubbed his chin where the purse had hit him. "I understand, Mistress, and I'll let the Slave-Master know of your displeasure. I am sorry, Mistress."

Smiling, the woman patted his head, then sank her thin fingers into his thick curls and jerked his head up. There was a small bandage on the back of her hand.

"See that you do, Lance. Or else I'll pick you next time."

Lance cowered like a beaten dog. More women applauded. Allison went back to filling out the forms. He was faking it.

"Now, slave, wheel me to the door, I've got baking to do. I promised my Bingo club I'd bring the cookies tonight. Oh, and tell Willie he was right . . . the back of the hand is a lot more comfortable. See you next week."

"Until then, Mistress. And may all your numbers come up tonight."

The old woman giggled like a school girl as he held the

door open for her. Two new women entered and Lance greeted them in humble supplication.

Allison flipped to the sixth and final page.

And licked her lips.

Hmm.

DOMINATION TOY LIST

Dearest Mistress, we are here only to serve you and your desires. Do not be ashamed or embarrassed to answer the following as your heart, soul and mind dictate. We are yours to command and correct. Do with us as you will. We desire only to bend to your will and fulfill your most secret longings.

Your answers and desires will not be revealed to anyone. We ask only that you share them here so that we may better serve you. When completed, please do not forget to sign your name and today's date at the bottom of the final page . . . along with the method of payment you wish to use.

We are your slaves, first and foremost. Our bodies are yours to dominate. Our spirits are yours to break. How may we service you (please answer below):

What followed weren't questions, exactly, but three columns of items that could be checked off. It was like ordering from a menu in a Chinese restaurant. Everything looked *so* good. She had a choice of whips, riding crops and canes (or all of the above) in a variety of styles, diameters and textures and flexibility. Did she want her slave clothed, unclothed, or gagged and butt-plugged (yuck!)? She could also order branding irons, scalding water or ice cubes . . . but those items required at least a half-hour to prepare.

And did she have a specific body type in mind for her slave? *Please describe on lines provided.* Allison described Mica.

Since there didn't seem to be a limit to how many things she could select, she checked off everything except the hot-saltwater enema (that just sounded too messy), signed and put down her VISA number.

No price was listed, but she figured whatever it cost she was damn well going to get her money's worth.

❖

Mica stabbed a catsup-soaked French fry onto his fork and popped it into his mouth, grinning across the table as Elena took a sip of lemonade. It was so good to see a woman drink something besides blood. The wooden dowel sat on the table between them, the point facing toward the window. He'd forgotten all about it until they sat down and almost punctured a lung. His sudden scream of pain had made most of the customers and wait-staff jump, but she just sat there, reading the menu and asking what kind of soup they had. Any other woman would have asked him what the hell that was – like their waitress had – but not her. She accepted him . . . and his stake.

And that's how Mica knew the Lord had brought Elena into his life to fulfill something beyond his spiritual needs.

Thank you, Lord.

She smiled at him and picked up her Patty-Melt. "This is really great, John, thanks again for inviting me. I don't know what I'd be doing right now . . . except maybe the rest of the kitchen staff."

The fry stopped halfway down his windpipe and had to be helped along with a coughing spasm. When he finally managed to swallow, Mica's throat felt like it'd been scalded with acid.

Okay Lord, we still have a little work to do here.

"You okay?" she asked. "You went purple even before you started choking."

"Fine," Mica gasped. "Really. Glad you're enjoying . . . lunch."

"I am. And I'm also glad I'm not back there, you know. I really hate that place. Oh, I'm sorry, I know you work there and everything. It's just. . . ."

Elena sighed and looked away. It was about the tenth time she'd done that since they sat down to eat. Every time she'd start to talk about why she hated the *Desert Rose*, she'd sigh and turn away. Mica had let it pass before, but now it was getting late and his lunch hour was almost up.

"Did something bad happen to you at the *Rose?*"

"There? No, nothing bad happened to me there."

Elena dropped her sandwich back to the plate and hunched forward, staring at it. She looked so lost, so alone. Setting the fork aside, Mica reached across the table and took her hand. His elbow bumped the stake and rolled it off the table. He let it go, he could always make another one. Allison was already dead, her final release could wait for a day or two, it wasn't like the Lord had given him a specific time . . . and besides, right now, Elena needed all his attention.

"Look," Mica said, "you don't have to tell me. I'm sorry I asked."

But she shook her head and laced her fingers between his, holding on tight.

"No, it's okay." Elena took a deep breath and Mica crossed his legs under the table so he wouldn't be distracted from what she had to say. "Then you'll know why God hates me."

"Elena —"

"Shh," she said and leaned forward to touch the cross on his forehead with her free hand. Mica tried not to stare at her breasts as they surged forward . . . and failed miserably. He wanted to close his eyes when he felt her finger touch him, but kept them open and reproached himself thoroughly for having enjoyed the way her breasts jiggled when she yelped and pulled away.

"Ouch!" She said, shaking her finger (which made her breasts jiggle even more). "Got a shock. Must have been static electricity. You really are blessed . . . aren't you?"

Mica lifted his chin proudly.

"Yes, I am Mica . . . like 'mica', strong in the Lord's blessing." When she didn't answer, he sat back and smiled. "You were going to tell me what happened at the *Rose*?"

"Huh? Oh. Oh, yeah."

She cleared her throat and let go of his hand. Mica understood. It would have been hard trying to hold his hand and the glass of lemonade the way she was trembling. *Poor little thing.*

"Anyway . . . My boyfriend, C.J. and I had been in love for a long time. Almost a year. We really loved each other, you know, from the start, so when he showed me the brochures he got from Triple A and told me to pick out which wedding chapel I wanted to get married at, I knew it was for real, that we were going to run-away together and get married. I picked the *Desert Rose* because I've always liked roses. He said he'd take care of all the arrangements . . . he even said he'd book a honeymoon suite at *New York, New York* because we saw the new *Godzilla* movie on our first date. It was so romantic."

Elena took a long sip of lemonade.

"And I believed him. I thought he really loved me. That was on a Thursday night, I remember that because I'd gone over to his house to help him study for a make-up algebra test he had that Friday. We didn't study much. After I picked out the chapel and everything he said he was scared . . . that he didn't know if I loved him as much as he loved me and that there was only one way I could prove it to him."

Mica heard their waitress groan as she walked past.

"You mean?" he asked

And Elena nodded. "Yeah, the only way I could prove to him that I loved him was to pull down my panties and spread my legs."

Mica pressed his thighs tighter together, but that still didn't stop his penis from twitching in righteous anger when he thought of her . . . with her panties down around one ankle . . . her hot little pussy opened wide.

His hand was shaking almost as much as hers as he reached for his glass of ice water. *Damn, Lord . . . how could You have let that happen to her?*

"Yeah, I know," she said, shrugging, "but I was just this stupid little virgin and I let him do me. Five times. Two in front, two in back and once in the mouth. He tasted awful, like he never washed, but I did it because I loved him. I loved him so much I was walking bow-legged the next morning when he dropped me off at the Greyhound bus station and gave me money to buy a one-way ticket to Las Vegas. He told me he'd drive out after he finished taking his test, so no one would be suspicious. I was a straight-A student, so no one even thought about looking for me, I guess. I was so stupid."

"You weren't stupid," Mica said and heard their waitress snort as she passed their table going in the opposite direction. "You were just naive. Your boyfriend didn't show up, did he?"

Elena shook her head and exchanged the lemonade for her sandwich. Her bad experience hadn't hurt her appetite any.

"No," she said, swallowing before she continued, "but it was worse than that. He knew I'd be here . . . at the *Desert Rose*, I mean, so he had them page me, you know, over the loud speakers so everyone could watch me run over to one of those courtesy phones you have in the lobby. You know, the pink ones?"

Mica knew. He used those phones every time Allison

called to tell him she was going to be late and not to wait up for her. "Go on."

"Well, so I'm running to the phone all happy and smiling, and carrying this bouquet of silk roses I bought at the gift shop. You know the ones they sell? They're kind of expensive and it took the last of my baby-sitting money to buy them, but they were for my wedding . . . so I didn't care. Besides, once my boyfriend got there, we were going to live happily ever after, so it didn't matter how much I spent on flowers, right?"

"You know," Mica said, trying to be helpful, "the kiosk in the bus terminal sells real flowers for about half the pri– sorry. Please go on."

Elena took another bite, swallowed.

"Anyway, I answer the phone and he starts laughing at me. Told me I was pretty stupid for a straight-A student if I thought he was going to give up playing football and a good paying job at his daddy's Dairy Queen franchise to marry someone who'd let a guy fuck her the way he fucked me. He said he got the brochures from his brother who'd done the same thing to his girlfriend. He said it was even funnier, because he told his brother he could get me to go all the way to Las Vegas. They even bet on it. $25.00, the same amount I paid for the bouquet."

She shrugged and finished her sandwich. Her eyes were dry, Mica's were burning.

"But why didn't you go home after that?"

Another shrug. "Couldn't. After C.J. hung up, I called home, collect, and talked to my mom. I was about to tell her everything when she told me that C.J. had already told everybody at school that I was a whore and had done it with the whole football team. Varsity and juniors, both. The Mother Superior called my dad at work and told him . . . and he called my mom and told her that if he ever saw me again he'd kill me.

So I figured it was safer for me to stay here.

"I made back the twenty-five dollars the first night . . . out behind the bus terminal. That's when I first heard you, John, and that's where I always take my tricks. Just so I can hear you while I'm . . . you know. Even though I know God hates me, listening to your voice while I'm getting it up the ass, makes me remember back to when I was pure. So . . . you still think God doesn't hate me?"

When Mica didn't answer, Elena sighed and looked out the window.

"It's okay, John. Really, it is. God can hate me all he wants . . . as long as you don't."

"Never!"

And she smiled then, her supple skin crinkling around her eyes. "Then everything's okay. Really. Um, John?"

She wanted . . . something from him, Mica could tell it from her tone. "Yes?"

"I know you've already done so much for me. Bought me lunch and all, but. . . ."

"Yes! Anything. Just tell me what you want."

"Dessert?"

"Huh?"

"I know," she said, blushing, "but I have a real sweet tooth. Do you think we could get some?"

"Sure." Lifting one hand, Mica signaled their snorting waitress over. "I just love to watch you eat."

CHAPTER 9

They didn't call her name like they had everyone else. Lance, undoubtedly trying to make up for not giving her the proper respect earlier, came over and personally escorted her – and the late-thirties psychologist she'd gotten chummy with – to the changing area.

"A pleasure as always to see you again, Mistress," he groveled to the woman, who had literally been boiling over like a pot of oatmeal while she broadened Allison's knowledge of the joys of bondage and domination, then suddenly leaned back on her three-inch leopard-print stilettos and glared Lance into a quivering puddle of fear.

It was awe-inspiring to see the 6-foot plus man tremble before the 5-foot in heels woman.

Allison finally understood why the women in the waiting room had applauded.

"You dare speak to me without permission?" the woman asked and the icy tone almost made Allison want to shiver.

"I'm sorry, Mistress. It won't happen a –"

"Silence!"

Allison saw the slap coming and stepped out of the way. She gave it a thumb's up.

"Nice one."

"A bit off center," the woman said, rubbing her hand. Her palm was already pinking up, but Lance's face remained its same bronze perfection. The guy either sanded off his beard or the constant beatings had really toughened him up. "I pulled back at the last moment. You just can't get a decent arc in street clothes."

"Yeah," Allison agreed, then backhanded their toadying slave boy across the narrow hallway and into the drinking fountain between the *Mistresses Room* and *Maintenance.* "That's why I always wear silk."

Lance might have skin like granite, but she could tell from the shock in his eyes and the way he was touching the pale outline of her knuckles on the point of his chin that he felt it, all right. Unfortunately, so did she. It was only the fact that she didn't have a pulse that kept her hand, wrist and forearm from throbbing, but it still felt as though she'd just tried to punch her way out of lead-lined safe.

"Wow," the leopard-print lady said. "That was totally awesome. You've got to show me that move. Come on, you can do that while we change. And *you*–" She glared at their hobbled escort and he shrank. "You're disgusting, you wussy. Leave us, before I sic her on you again."

"Yes, Mistress," Lance said, bowing low as he scurried away. "Thank you, Mistress. Right away, Mistress."

He looked up, however, and winked at Allison before disappearing through the waiting room door.

"I'll see *you* later. Mistress"

There was something in the way he said it that made Allison want to run after him and finish whatever job she'd started, but the woman latched onto her arm and hauled her like a stubborn sack of potatoes toward the door of the Changing Room.

"No!" Allison yelled. "Wait!"

But it was already too late. The door swung open and all Allison could do was try her damnest to sidestep out of the line of reflective fire. You put women and clothes in a room together and what you got were mirrors, mirrors everywhere . . . and nowhere for a little vampire to hide. That was the reason she always arrived at the *Tropicana* early and was already out in the wings when the rest of the dancers were getting into costume.

Being early not only got her a good reputation at the casino, but saved a whole lot in explanations.

But that was there and this was here . . . and unfortunately the only place she found to hide in such short notice was behind the smaller woman.

"Are you all right?" the psychologist inside the dominatrix asked as she turned to look down at Allison.

"I'm just shy," Allison whispered, "and I hate the way I look. You just toss me something and I'll go change in the bathroom."

"Not on your life. Now stand up and be proud of who you are. You're a beautiful young woman who's fed up with having to contend with a life dominated by men and you want to change that, don't you?"

"Well," Allison said, "I suppose so."

"Of course you do! That's the reason you came out here to the belly-button of nowhere to face your demons . . . and beat the shit out of them. It's a hard thing to accept, I know, and society may look at you like some kind of monster –"

Oh, now that's going to be traumatic.

"– but you've already taken the first step."

Allison brushed her hair out of her eyes. "Did you ever help write a crisis center training manual?"

"Hundreds of them, baby," the woman said and grabbed Allison's arms. "Now stand up and let's get this show on the road."

"No! Really, I think I made a mistake and I should be go—"

The little leopard woman had incredible upper body strength (probably from administering all those beatings she was just talking about) and yanked Allison to her feet. A good head taller, Allison had a clear view of the room. It was larger than the *Tropicana's* dressing room and filled with rack upon rack of clothing in basic black (leather, vinyl, velvet, suede, and plastic) and silver (studs, chains and zippers). The two far walls were decorated in floor-to-ceiling gym lockers — empty ones open, those in use closed — just like a high school gym. Low, wooden benches were spaced at regular intervals in front of the lockers.

Shit, it was like high school. There weren't even any windows.

No windows and only two doors — the one behind Allison marked EXIT, the one at the opposite side of the room, marked STABLE. There was one other exception that made the dressing room unique.

"—ing now. Oh. No mirrors?" She kept her eyes wide and hoped she sounded genuinely surprised . . . considering she really was. "How are we supposed to see ourselves without mirrors?"

"We aren't."

Patting Allison on the shoulder as if standing up had been a major huddle, the woman left her and headed for the first rack of black corsets, chaps and/or demi-bras . . . it was hard to tell what some of the things were since she'd never studied the *Fredrick's of Hollywood* catalogs all that closely.

"And that's what makes this place a very healthy emotional and psychological cleansing experience."

"Okay," Allison said and watched the woman go through the first rack without finding anything to her liking.

She hit pay-dirt halfway through the second rack. Tossing

a black, patent-leather, steel-studded Valkyrie bra onto one of the benches in front of an empty locker, the psychologist and advocate of healthy emotional cleansing, slipped out of pelt and into hide.

Allison didn't think the bra went with the white satin garter-belt and men's jockey shorts she was already wearing, or that the spider-web lace camisole and leather head-band really worked as an ensemble . . . but what did she know from S&M fashion?

Not a hell of a lot.

"Now, let me ask you this," the woman said as she finished the whole outfit off with a wide motorcycle belt hung with scalps. "When was the last time you looked in a mirror and liked what you saw?"

"Oh, a little less than a year ago," Allison answered honestly.

"Exactly. Nine times out of ten when a woman looks in a mirror she's not going to like what she sees . . . even if she's drop-dead gorgeous. She won't see the perky breasts or long legs or high cheekbones – she'll only concentrate on the flaws. And if a woman has to try on clothing . . . my God, I'm surprised there not a higher percentage of suicides in store dressing rooms than anywhere else. But not here."

The woman lifted her arms out to her side and turned slowly.

"There are no mirrors because this way we can *imagine* what we look like and not have to face the devastating reality of what we *really* look like. For instance, right now I mentally see myself as a hot, sexy bitch with an attitude. I don't care how I look, because I can't see myself.

"Now, be honest . . . how do *I* look?"

Allison wished the EXIT door was just a little closer. "You look – hot."

"Liar," the woman laughed, "but I'll accept that from one hot, sexy bitch to another. And you've proven another point. Women won't generally hurt each others feelings . . . unless they're rivals or real bitches . . . and they especially won't hurt a stranger. So, without mirrors and kind, if not utterly false, compliments, we can indulge in the fantasy that we're beautiful and powerful . . . and then go out and show it. It's all part of the illusion."

"But what about the . . . beatings? Are those part of the illusion, too?"

"Oh, hell no," the woman said, stroking one of the scalps that hung from her belt. "Those are real."

"And it doesn't bother you that you're hurting them?"

The woman looked at Allison as though she'd just fallen off a turnip truck and sighed. It was a very sad sound.

"Oh, honey, you definitely need to get out more. There are people in this world who are true masochists. They not only like being hurt, but they get off on it because they can convert the sensation of pain into pleasure. These guys love it. If they didn't, do you honestly think this place would have stayed in business for more than a week?"

"I guess you're right," Allison said, "but I've never *beaten* a man before."

Hit, killed, ripped off their heads, drained them of blood, yes . . . but never beaten them.

Intentionally.

"Then I envy you. The first time's always the hottest. So, what are you waiting for? Don't be shy, remember, no mirrors – only our own self image. Now, pick out something you'd never think of wearing in a million years and let's get go break us some studs. Yee-HAH!"

Uh-huh.

Allison looked at the rack of costumes and slowly began

walking toward them, fumbling with the buttons on her silk blouse. It'd been a while since she'd had to do anything as mundane as actually *taking off* and *putting on* real clothes and the prospect didn't sound appealing.

She lifted a pair of black leather, crotchless panties off the rack. There was a small tag safety-pinned around the neck of the wire hanger: *Sanitized for your protection.*

How nice, she wouldn't get cooties.

"Oh, yeah . . . you *go*, girl! Yeah! Well, I'd love to stay and watch what you come up with, but I'm not a voyeur. So." Flexing the muscles in her shoulders, the woman crossed the room and opened the door marked STABLE. "See you later, sweet potater. God, I hope I get a screamer. There's nothing like disciplining a good screamer to let you know you're really accomplishing something."

Allison nodded and waved bye-bye, then hung up the panties and mentally got undressed. It was so much easier than having to worry about buttons and zippers for hell's sake. Naked and still standing in front of the costumes, Allison was about to conjure herself up a little something in leather-and-lace (traditional, but not gaudy) when the hall door opened and two just-barely twenty-ones exploded into the room beneath a torrent of giggles, twitters, snickers and other assorted "girly" sounds.

The sounds increased exponentially when they saw her standing there as God – or the Devil – had created her.

"Hi," Allison said and grabbed the first two things off the rack that her hands touched. She didn't even look at her selection until she was standing in front of the lockers, choosing one of the closed ones so the Giggle Twins would think her clothes were already inside. And even then, it took a moment to sort out what went where and what the hell it was.

A pair of black vinyl gauntlets and matching zipper-front

corset dangled from one hanger, a pierced black leather garter-belt and fishnet stockings hung from the other. No panties or bra, but what the hell . . . black and red went so well together.

Allison fluffed her pubic hair and tried to remember how to put stockings on without getting her toes stuck.

Or falling on her ass.

More than once.

Not that the newcomers were paying all that much attention to her. Stripped down to white cotton panties, suntanned arms covering their perk little breasts, the gigglers were huddled close together in front of the first rack – daring each other.

"Go on and pick something. It was your idea to come out here."

"No way. I just told you what a girl at work said about this place. You wanted to come so you pick something."

"Way. Besides I drove, so you pick first."

"You."

"No, you."

"You."

Giggle.

"You!"

"No. You!"

Giggle, giggle.

"Na-uh. You!"

Both of you pick something NOW, dammit!

Like Allison before them, the girls grabbed things at random and seemed equally shocked by their selections.

"Good choices," she told them as they stumbled past her to their lockers. "You'll both be the life of the party."

They nodded and stumbled on. Allison would have loved to just sit back and watch them struggle into the leather harnesses, push-up bras and one-piece nylon cat-suits, but she was having her own troubles trying to remember how hook-and-eyes worked. It was amazing how many tiny details one forgets after dying – like shoving and hauling and maneuvering quantities of flesh.

Allison grunted as her one of the garter belt's elastic straps got away form her. *Shit!* Dressing was *so* much easier when all you had to do was think and –

"Wait a minute."

Something was wrong.

Frowning, Allison looked down and ran her hands slowly down the corset's shiny contours, following the inverted heart-shape from her bare breasts to the edge of the garter belt and down to the lips of her vulva.

Terribly, terribly wrong.

Her inner flesh was cold and hard, like it was supposed to be, but when Allison slipped her fingers in deeper and felt –

Dammit, that was it!

She could feel.

Allison bent down to examine the situation closer and yelped in pain when she pinched her clitoris. *OW!* It was so weird . . . it was as if wearing real clothes, instead of the ones she fashioned herself, had somehow short-circuited her nervous system and gave her back a little of the feeling she'd lost when she died.

"Weird," she muttered to herself and then noticed how quiet it was in the room.

The two girls were staring at her – mouths open, eyes wide.

"Oh, this?" Allison asked, pointing to her crotch as she straightened up. "I'm doing an in-depth, hidden camera investigation for an upcoming 'Reality TV' series. Well, gotta go."

Allison wasn't surprised to hear the gathering up of clothing and the whispered *"I knew we shouldn't have come"* accusations as the STABLE door closed behind her. What she was surprised at was the black wrought-iron spiral staircase that led down into a murky basement room. Leaning over the handrail, Allison tried to make out details, but couldn't see past the flicking electric "torch" that illuminated the bottom-most stair.

Well, she didn't think there'd be a real stable, anyway.

She realized when she was half-way down the stairs that she'd forgotten all about shoes. Oh well, a little error, easily corrected. Spit-polished thigh-high boots with three inch Cuban heels suddenly appeared . . . and just as suddenly disappeared again.

Her legs had gone numb the moment the boots materialized.

"Better a bare-foot dominatrix," she said and wiggled her toes inside the scratchy cotton netting, "then a numb one, I always say."

Giggling at the pins-and-needles sensation that coursed up from the souls of her feet, Allison skipped all the way down the stairs.

Wheeee—whoa!

"You've got to be kidding."

It wasn't a basement, it was in a small subterranean cavern . . . and there was no STABLE in sight.

Although there was a horse. Sort of.

Illuminated by the small torch, the "Bucking Bronco" waited upon its stand with the patience of a stone saint. It was painted gold with a silver mane and tail and had a *real* English saddle strapped to its back. It was beautiful, Allison had to admit that, and looked to be in much better condition than any of its relatives she'd seen out in front of supermarkets and discount stores . . . but it was still a kiddie ride and beating it would probably not give her the spiritual satisfaction or emotional cleansing her friend, the psychotic psychologist, said it would.

Walking up to it she slapped the painted pony across the flank. It thumped hollowly.

"What a rip-off."

"Hey, watch it, darlin'," the mechanical horse said, one marble eye rolling back to look at her.

Allison jerked her hand away, then laughed. "You . . . talking to me?"

"Do you see anyone else standing here?" A smile tugged at the corners of the mouth. The animatronics must have cost a small fortune, but it was still just a toy. She smacked it again and heard a grunt as she walked away. "Lookin' for something?"

"Yeah," she said, "all those nice, juicy slaves I'm supposed to be able to whup into shape. Shit, anyone ever sue your ass?"

"Now, why would anyone wanna sue me? I'm just a poor lit'l pony and every lit'l girl's fantasy."

"Bull-shit."

"Think back t'when you were lit'l, sweet thing. Didn't you climb up on a pony like me and pretend you were ridin' the range? It's true and you know it. Just like it's true that inside every grown-up woman is a lit'l girl just wantin' another ride." The horse winked at her. "So, why don't you just settle your fine lit'l self right down on my saddle and we can start negotiatin'."

"Negotiating?" Allison asked, squinting into the shadows to try and locate the horse's human counterpart. "For what?"

"For what kinda stud you wanna try and break. What? You think this was it? Oh, baby, I'm just the Head Wrangler."

A rock fell somewhere farther down the cavern and Allison tensed. There were no sounds after that, but she stood motionless for a good minute just to make sure – no one could hurt her, but she still didn't like being snuck up on.

"Then there really are studs?" she asked, returning only a small portion of her attention to the hobby-horse. Someone was watching, she could feel eyes on her and it made her newly resensitized skin crawl. "Besides you, I mean."

"As many as you think you can handle, darlin'. For a price."

Okay, maybe it wasn't a rip-off after all.

"I see."

With a nonchalant toss of her head, Allison walked back to the smart-mouthed kiddie ride and swung a leg over the saddle . . .and the minute she did, the horse began a slow and steady gallop to a music box rendition of *"Achy-Breaky Heart"*. The hydriodic lift was glass smooth, the only shudder coming from Allison each time her clitoris bumped against the saddle horn.

None of the hobby-horses she rode as a kid ever felt like this.

Allison closed her eyes and scooted in closer to the horn. *Man, just think of all that money I've been wasting on precious gems and antiques when all I really needed was a pair of 501s and one of these. I could really continue to die happily.*

"That's right, darlin', just enjoy Ol' Faithful like your daddy tells you."

"Ummm." *My what?*

"That's right, sweet lips, you just ride and relax. Right now's when I usually make my sales pitch, but I don't think that'll be necessary . . . do you?"

My daddy? Allison opened her eyes and pushed back from the horn.

"Oh, darlin', weren't you havin' a good time?"

"Pitch away, daddy," she growled at the horse. "I don't want to be treated any differently from your usual clients."

"Even if you are."

Allison folded her arms across her chest and stood up,

completely out of range. The horse stopped and looked up at her.

"Damn, woman, you are stubborn'r than a mule in a cotton patch."

"I'll take that as a compliment. How much?"

"Well, my studs are the finest around. Real champions, every last one of em. You wouldn't believe how long it took for me to find em all. Now some of em are just green broke and need a firm hand sometimes. Course, these cost a bit more."

"How much more?"

"Well," the horse said, clicking its wooden teeth, "there's the equipment and harnessin' fee. Ride's clocked in at an hour – same as all the regular ridin' stables with four-legged studs. Mine only got three legs . . . if you catch my drift."

The chuckle vibrated against Allison's thighs. She yawned to show how little it meant.

"How much?"

"Regular's a thousand. Green broke can go up to twenty-five."

Her feigned yawn lengthened into a shocked gasp.

"Twenty-five hundred?"

"Twenty-five thousand. Honey, you wouldn't believe how rich some of my ladies are. And how much they're willin' to spend whoppin' prime ass."

"Twenty-five thousand dollars to hit someone? Are you fucking nuts?"

The horse rolled its eye away from her. "Damn me, if that ain't a bitch. Livin' or dead don't make no difference. You tell a woman the price of a thing and she's gonna try and break your balls over it. I'm disappointed in you, darlin', I thought you'd of learned something by now."

A small red light suddenly came on above a narrow fissure in the cavern wall, illuminating a tall, pale man wearing jeans and a western-style shirt. His eyes looked gray under the light, but she knew they were green as grass.

"Hey, darlin'," he said, smiling at her. "Long time no see. I was wonderin' how long it'd take before you showed up."

Allison felt her still heart tremble.

Seth.

"Are you okay, John?"

Mica blinked the sudden fog out of his eyes and smiled as Elena's face swam back into focus. "Yeah . . . I'm fine."

It had taken most of his powers of persuasion and a few well-placed psycho-babble terms he'd learned from late-night infomercials, but he'd managed to get her inside the lobby of the *Desert Rose* . . . only to be squashed into a narrow alcove between the public phones and gift shop by gawking tourists and seasoned paparazzi.

He'd forgotten, in spite of the rock-a-billy music blaring out over the parking lot and the worn red carpet in front of the main doors, that today was the beginning of the annual "King of Las Vegas Elvis Impersonator" competition . . . and that *Rose* was sponsoring the first round of the contest. Mica had seen Alvis, along with six other competitors – three fat and three pre-fat, a good balance – striking poses in front of the chapel wall and waved. Alvis had shot a quick "hi" back and nodded behind his wrap-around shades. He was in his favorite powder-blue, rhinestone-dusted, bell-bottomed jumpsuit with matching half-cape and three-inch high stand-up collar.

Mica had to admit the outfit looked a lot better on him than the other bell-bottom, half-caped, rhinestone-glittered jumpsuits with stand-up collar looked on any of the other men who would be the King.

He'd been just about to suggest to Elena that they slip away and find someplace less crowded to continue their conversation (and feeding . . . she'd ordered an egg-cream after the sundae), when his whole body suddenly jerked as if he'd stepped on a high-voltage cable and he almost passed out.

"Are you sure?" Elena asked, standing on tip-toe so she could press her lips against his forehead. Mica almost passed out again. Her lips were so warm. *Oh, Lord.*

"Well, it doesn't feel like you have a fever," she said, backing away, "but you did go all pale and wonky for a minute."

Mica nodded and clasped his hands in front of him. Hard.

"Wonky?" He liked the way the word felt against his tongue. "Yeah, I guess I was a little wonky, but I'm okay now. I really should have changed before going outside. Sack-cloth really isn't the right kind of material for the desert . . . unless you're the Lord, of course."

"That's what I thought – so why don't you change and then we can split? You know," she dabbed his cheek with the edge of her shawl, "to someplace a little less crowded."

God it was a tempting offer. *Just like You knew it'd be, right Lord?*

"You don't know how much I'd love to go someplace," Mica said, "but with Alvis in the competition, it's just me and Darth Vader left to handle the weddings. Although no one seems to think about marriage when there's this many Elvises around."

Elena's big eyes grew bigger as she pressed against him in order to look over her shoulder.

"Wow. You know one of them?"

Mica puffed out his chest to give her a better hand hold. "Yeah. Alvis is my best friend. He's the one in the blue jumpsuit."

"Him?"

"No, the thinner one in the middle, without the corset."

"Oh. Him."

"No, the white guy. Third one in on the left."

"Oh! Gee, I never knew Elvis was a body builder." She waved and Alvis waved back, then raised an eyebrow at Mica who didn't do anything in return. "You know, I really love these impersonators. They're, like, keeping a part of history alive, you know . . . and they're really generous. Darn!"

Before Mica could ask her how she knew about their generous nature, Elena scooped a tiny pager out from between her cleavage and completely derailed his train of thought.

"I have to make a call. Be right back."

Mica watched the hem of her shawl flutter behind her like wings as she wiggled through the dozen or so people standing between her and the phones. Wings of an angel. A fallen angel.

His fallen angel.

The foggy . . . wonky feeling swept over Mica again when she turned and smiled just as the crowd closed between them, but it wasn't the same as before. The first time felt liked someone had kicked his nuts into the top of his skull . . . this time there was no pain, just an emptiness he knew wouldn't go away until she returned.

Elena. Just thinking her name instantly made him feel better. Allison's name never did that.

Bad move – his stomach tightened. He shouldn't have thought of Allison.

Mica frowned and looked up at the rose-colored ceiling tiles.

"What?" he asked, daring the Lord to answer.

But the Lord had the good sense to stay quiet which was probably for the best, since Mica didn't feel like getting into a knock-down, drag-out with the All Mighty . . . especially not in front of Elena.

"Was it important?" Mica asked as she squeezed in next to

him. "The call, I mean."

"Just a client," she said, smiling. "I told him I'd be busy all day. Do you mind if I just hang out with you? I mean, no funny stuff or anything."

She suddenly looked down, a faint blush deepening the color in her cheeks to cinnamon.

"Unless you want to, you know."

"No," he said. "I – I –" *Love you, Elena. I know it's sudden and you're a whore and that I've just forgiven the Lord for being a jerk, but I love you. Come with me and be my love and all that. I love you, Elena. I love you. "*– think hanging out . . . with you, is fine. I mean I'd love to . . . um, but – ah–"

The blush had faded by the time she looked up. "Hey, don't worry about it. Just didn't want you to think I didn't find you attractive or anything." She leaned against him, her breath tickling his chin. "Because I do."

Mica's knees suddenly got a major case of the wonkies. "Oh?"

"Yeah," she said, hip pressing hard against the wonkied bulge in the front of his robe. "Only thing is that this guy offered me two hundred dollars and . . . well, I really could've used the money. I still try to send a little something home each month, you know, to help out."

Oh, Lord – how could You have let this happen to her?

"I– I'll give you the two hundred."

Elena's eyes began to sparkle. "Really? Wow, that would be great."

It would be.

"Okay, you stay here and I'll be right back. There's an ATM machine in the casino. Don't leave."

She shook her head. "I'll never leave you, John."

Heart pounding and cock playing backup rhythm, Mica pushed his way through the crowd currently enjoying an acappella rendition of *"In the Getto"* by all the Elvises . . . except Alvis, who was singing, "With a Gecko," and tried to think of what he was going to say to Allison when she noticed two-hundred dollars was missing from their joint account.

She usually didn't care how much he spent or what he spent it on – as long as he had a receipt she could show her accountant. Allison could be very anal for a dead woman.

Maybe he could get Elena to write him out a receipt for services rendered. *Oh, Lord.*

CHAPTER 10

Allison could hear every dead nerve in her body crackle like static as she stepped away from the mechanical horse. Seth just smiled, tiny wrinkles puckering the skin around his bottle-green eyes. It was the same smile, the same little wrinkles . . . the same God-damned good looks and boyish charms that had first attracted her – like an idiot moth to a flame – to him.

Shit.

Although the loss of her soul had somehow eliminated her ability to dream, she'd still been able to envision what would happen if they ever again crossed paths. A sudden attack. Bones breaking. Long bamboo stakes and a barbecue pit played major roles, as did dismemberment and decapitation. Not in that order. Those fantasies had kept her happy all through those long, lonely months.

Reality was a real bitch by comparison.

The only thing that broke was one of her nails, when she balled her hands into fists as he leaned down to kiss her cheek.

"How you been, darlin'?"

"You fucking bastard. Stay away from me!"

But neither of them moved.

"C'mon, sweet thing, is that anyway to talk to your Maker? Dead all this time and you still haven't learned any manners."

He shook his head, clicking his tongue against his fangs. "We're gonna have to work on that, pun'kin."

"Try it, asshole."

Seth backed up, feigning shock. "My, my, such language. But if memory serves me right, I did prove it to you. A couple'll times. And you loved it." He cleared his throat and her voice came pouring out of his throat. "'Oh, God. Oh, yes. Do it! Do it to me harder!' 'Kill me . . . kill me.'"

Was that what she sounded like? "Fuck you."

"Exactly what I had in mind, darlin'."

His clothes vanished as he reached down, sliding his hand slowly over the rock-hard abs to a massive cock that seemed a whole lot bigger than Allison remembered.

Oh baby, gimme!

Well, he thought at her, laughing. *It's nice to know some parts of me are still appreciated.*

Allison manually hauled her gaze up to his eyes. She'd been solo for so long she forgot mental telepathy worked both ways.

And that's why I'm glad you finally decided to show up, baby. You need me.

What are you talking about? I don't need you any more now than I did . . . when you fucking walked out on me!

Seth grimaced. "Damn, baby, take it down a notch. You don't have to shout." *Now, where was I? Oh yeah . . . right here.*

Smiling, he rubbed his cock until the flesh stiffened and a single drop of blood oozed from the pale lavender tip. Allison folded her arms across her chest and snorted. Why did men – living and dead -- always think it came down to this.

"Wow," she said without any enthusiasm whatsoever. "That's really something. Yah, man. Mmm, gotta get me some of that."

Seth had the strangest look on his face. So did his penis. "What?"

Allison fluttered her lashes at him and walked back to the mechanical horse. He followed — just like she'd hoped he would. Thank God men were predictable even after they were dead.

"Ah-choo." Allison rubbed her nose then leaned forward, running her hands over the horse's back from saddle horn to tail. "Yes, sir. What a cock."

Seth didn't bless her. "What the hell are you goin' on about, woman?"

Allison patted the horse's rump. "Just admiring the equipment."

"Well, stop admirin' it and hop on."

"I got a better idea."

Putting all her weight behind it, Allison snapped off the horse's silver tail and plunged it, pointy-end first, into the center of Seth's pale chest. Blood the color of mud gushed out, spraying her arm and chest. His blood was cold, icing over immediately as she backed away, hands pressed over her silent heart . . . waiting for the conjoined pain to strike.

And waited.

And waited some more.

It seemed to be taking an awfully long time. Allison remembered feeling the pain almost immediately when Luci and the other fem-vamps were staked. In fact, Seth didn't seem to feel it either. He stood there, hands on hips, and stared down at the tail protruding from his chest with a baffled look on his face.

Maybe I didn't jam it in far enough.

"Excuse me." Leaning forward, Allison pushed the tail in deeper.

Seth burped.

"Could I ask you a question," she said.

"Sure."

"Why aren't you dead or, at the very least, writhing on the floor in agony?"

He chuckled and the tail wobbled up and down. "You are the sweetest lit'l thing, ain't cha? First off, honey, I'm already dead . . . just like you. Second, this ol' thing is fiberglass and that don't even give our kind heartburn."

"Oh."

Satisfied that he'd explained one point in the Meaning of Death, Seth extracted the tail and tossed it over one shoulder.

"Didn't you know that, baby?" he asked as the wound sucked the escaped blood back into itself and closed.

"How the hell was I supposed to?" Allison screamed at him, claws extended but never reaching their intended mark. He caught her hands as easily as a kid catching bees in a jar. "You never told me anything about being a vampire, remember?"

Seth let go of her hands and lowered his head in shame. "I know . . . I was a real bastard back then."

"Then?"

"Yeah, but I can change."

I can change – the appeal of every abusing husband right before Allison had turned into an ex-abuser. And worm food.

"Like hell you can," Allison screamed at him. "We're dead . . . we *can't* change!"

"Oh, that's right," Seth said. "Well, then, I guess we'd just better enjoy what we got."

He came in low and fast and grabbed her shoulders, pulling her down, belly first over Ol' Faithful's back. Hand against the back of her neck, Seth held her down, struggling, as he walked around to her side of the horse . . . and spread her legs. The tip of his penis, hard where living flesh was soft, slide down the crack of her ass as he leaned forward, over her.

The fiberglass horse creaked ominously under their

combined weight.

"Get *off* me!"

"Don't you mean, get you off?" Seth's fingers found the bottom edge of the corset and followed it down to the garter belt.

"Nice choice." He snapped one of the straps holding the stocking in place. It didn't hurt, but Allison jumped. She'd felt it . . . and not just a dull sensation of something hitting her skin. She *felt* each ripple of the gathered satin the same way she felt his fingers slip into her vagina. He was so cold. Freezing.

Allison had forgotten how good cold could feel.

98.6-degrees was the perfect temperature for blood, but when it came wrapped in bulgy, bumping flesh and stuffed up into your private parts, it was like getting humped by a lukewarm tampon. Barely noticeable at the best of times, just plain annoying at the worst.

She was just as glad Mica had stopped wanting sex. He'd been annoying.

But this . . . Allison had to stop herself from pushing back.

"No," she said and began reciting the liturgy of commands listed in one of the *Victim for Victims* 'Preventative Measures' brochures. "Stop. Don't. Fire."

Seth stopped moving.

"What are you doin'?"

"Calling for help."

"Oh, baby, you and me don't need help. Now just relax and enjoy it . . . you know it's only good with your own kind."

She was about to remind him that she didn't know squat when he grabbed her hips and pulled her all the way down over his cock. Allison didn't know which one of them had groaned the loudest, the echos in the cavern were deceptive. He was slower after that, pulling out almost all the way and then slipping in a fraction of an inch at a time . . . and being that he was almost a good ten-inches, Allison was about ready to beg before he was half-way back inside her. Then just as she could feel the tip of his penis mold itself to the wall of her uterus, he'd start back out.

In.

Out.

In.

Out.

And he wouldn't let her speed things along. Seth's hands were like vice-grips. He was in control and just wanted to make sure she knew it.

God-damned bastard.

"You been needin' this ride for a long time, darlin'," he said. "I know, I been keepin' tabs on you. You been givin' it away when they should be beggin' for it."

Allison couldn't move her body, but she could damn well tighten up. And she did. Which brought things to a grinding halt.

"Damn woman – open up!"

She tightened her grip on the situation as she looked back at him over one shoulder. Given where she had him and what she had him by, Seth suddenly didn't seem so intimidating.

"What did you just say?"

"I said, open up. You havin' a little trouble hearin', baby? Cause if you are, I can help."

He lifted one hand off her hip and balled it into a classic *'do as I say or you'll get this'* fist. Oh right. Allison brought another dozen foot-pounds per inch of pressure to bear on the situation.

And watched his pale face get even paler as his arm, hand still clenched, shot straight out in front of him.

"You're threatening me," she asked. "Put down your hand . . . you look like a really bad Adolph Hitler Impersonator."

Seth lowered his arm faster than Allison could follow and only knew it was down when she felt its gentle caresses against her back.

"I appreciate you bein' upset and all . . . bout me having left you back there in that motel room, but all that's changed now. That's why I kept tabs on you and sent you all those subtle invitations."

Allison frowned. At both ends. *Fuck!* "Invitations?"

"Yeah. I left a few suggestions – sort of hypnotic-like . . . you know the kind of stuff those magicians do. They tell people they're a chicken and give em a special word and then wake em up and a couple of days or weeks later somebody says that word and the person suddenly starts behavin' like a chicken. It's a real hoot."

"Or cluck," Allison added and felt his forced laughter squirt up into her like a cold sitz bath. He was rambling and she knew from experience that when a man started rambling, he was lying.

She compressed his penis down to the size of a pencil. *Now he can apply for that government job he's always wanted.*

"The women who called me at the crisis line?"

"Yeah, pretty cute, weren't they, sweet lips?" He said – *hah, hah, some joke.* "But damn, pun'kin, you sure took your time. I been trying t'get you out here since I smelled you on the wind, honey. Gotta admit I couldn't figure out what you were doin' at first . . . I mean you didn't even feed off those women. Then my boys an' me started sniffin' some pretty ripe smells comin' in from the desert. You been busy, sweetheart, no doubt about that. Makin' the world a better place, huh?"

Sweetheart. Baby. Darlin'. Pun'kin. Sweet thing. Sweet LIPS. Honey. He didn't remember her or her name. She was just one of shit-knows how many women he'd turned and left behind.

Allison grinned at him over her shoulder and expelled him

like a particularly hard turd.

The comparison wasn't that far fetched.

Caught by surprise, Seth reeled backwards, windmilling his arms to keep upright. Watching him struggle to regain his dignity and balance would have been funny any other time.

"Who am I?"

Seth stopped against the far wall. Casually dusting himself off, he walked back toward her — but was careful to keep Ol' Faithful between them.

Names are for the livin', baby, same as faces. Thought you'd at least figure that part out . . . same as how we can only really feel things when we're with our own kind. Like one of our own dyin'– "– or lovin'. Honey, you just got a little taste of what it can be like between us."

"So you don't care who I am or where you left me?"

Seth shook his head. His penis had recovered nicely from its forced confinement and had regained it previous girth.

"That's right, dar'lin, I don't. You were just one of . . . hell, I don't think there's a number for the amount of women I've done this to. I'm a real bastard."

"MY NAME'S ALLISON!"

Seth nodded and began stroking his penis. "Nice t'meet you again, Allison."

"You are a bastard."

He nodded. "Yeah."

"God-damned, fucking, misogynistic asshole."

"That I am."

"You're worse than all the living shit-heels I hear about every fucking day!"

"Yes'sum."

"You need to be taken out and . . . and. . . ."

"Horsewhipped?"

"Yeah! Horsewhipped until you're nothing but a pile of

bones!"

"Well," he said and handed her something, "that might be a little much to ask for, but I think we can start with this."

Allison didn't know how or where he'd gotten the braided-leather riding crop -- *maybe he was working the nightclub magic scene* – and she didn't care. The crop looked expensive, just like the kind the rich Brentwood girls used when they took their riding lessons . . . while she rode by in cheap jeans and dime-store cowboy boots.

Rich little bitches who'd grown up to be rich middle-aged bitches.

Just like the ones in the waiting room. The ones waiting to see Seth.

Allison slipped her hand into the thin loop handle and slapped it against the mechanical horse's rump.

"Hey!" Ol' Faithful whined. "What did I ever do to you?"

Seth was smirking when she looked up.

The sound the crop made when it struck his face wasn't that different from when it hit the fiberglass. Allison was a little disappointed by that, and the fact that not so much as a welt appeared on his all-too-solid flesh. But at least he'd stopped smiling.

He backed up when Allison raised the crop again. *Hey, this is something new.*

"I'm– I'm sorry, Mistress," he said, eyes downcast.

Wow. She hit him again, hard enough to make the joint in her shoulder pop. He cringed and fell to one knee. *Oh yeah, this is what it's all about.*

Allison snapped the whip and watched her Maker cower. *Yes, yes, yes.*

"You left me alone," she said, tapping out each syllable against the side of his face.

"Yes, Mistress."

"Without any idea of what being a vampire really meant."
Tappidy-tap-tap-tap.

"Yes, Mistress."

"And you didn't care." *Tap. Tap. Tap. Tap. Tap.*

"No, Mistress."

"I didn't think so." *SLASH!*

Seth caught her arm on the back-stroke. "Okay, that'll do. I think you got the general idea of why this place is so popular with the ladies."

Allison tried to pull her arm away and heard the joint pop again.

"What the hell are you talking about?"

"Just this, sweet thing," he said, walking her back to the hobby horse. "You were ready to rip me a new one with that lit'l ol' whip, weren't you? Why?"

"Because you're a fucking asshole."

Seth's fangs glistened in the torchlight when he smiled. "Well, that's a matter of opinion, but I can see why you might have thought that. Anyway, it's that feelin' of rage we're exploitin' for fun and . . .about an average of a hundred and eighty gallons of blood per week. One voluntary unit at a time, of course."

The whip dangled like an afterthought from Allison's wrist. "How?"

"As part of our on-goin' charity efforts. A pint of blood, freely given afterwards and the price drops down to $25.00. Come on, darlin', you were alive once, that's a sweet deal. And, unlike you, we don't have to worry about coverin' our tracks . . . or the remains.

"So, you want in, baby?" Seth asked as he spun her around and leaned her over the saddle. "T'make up for lost time, I mean."

You God-damned bastard! I don't want anything to do with

— Oooo!

Seth's cock slammed into her from behind.

Feels good, don't it? This is how it can be for always. You just gotta quit pretendin' to be human. Whadda ya say, sweet lips?

Fuck you!

Thought that's what I was doin'. He shifted his weight and began humping her like an ice-cold oil derrick.

"My name's Allison," she said and brought the riding crop round in a sweeping arch that cut through the air and landed with a sizzle against his ass.

"Yes, Mistress. Of course, Mistress. Whatever you want, Mistress."

Damn, but she could get used to this.

WHACK!

Elena's large eyes widened almost to the point of popping out of her head when she saw Ben Franklin, in triplicate, grinning up at her. But the shock only lasted a minute. Less. Mica barely had time to register the snatch-and-grab before the bills were safely tucked down into her cleavage.

It took a little more time for Mica to pull his eyes out of the same crevasse. But when he did, the shock was gone from Elena's eyes and they'd taken on a soft gentleness that made his heart ache.

Along with other anatomical bits and pieces.

"I only said two-hundred," she said, although Mica noticed she wasn't reaching down the front of her dress to pull out the extra bill, "so I guess I sort of owe you . . . something, don't I?"

"No!" Mica shouted, then quickly lowered his voice when he noticed a few of the wait staff shift their attentions from watching the commotion in the lobby to him. He hadn't wanted to go back into the dining room, it felt like he'd spent more than enough time there, but it was the only place he could think of – besides the chapel, which she vehemently refused to go into – where they could be relatively alone.

And where Elena could get another piece of pie.

She had one hell of an appetite for someone as thin as she was.

"I mean," Mica said when he was able to, "all I want to do is talk. Nothing else. I swear."

"Nothing?" The look in her eyes had changed again – the soft innocence was replaced by something that increased the ache in his lower parts a thousand fold. "You're going to be pretty hoarse if you talk *this* much."

Her fingers caressed the swell of her breasts that left a trail of goose-bumps on both their skins. She giggled.

"But that's okay, because I like talking to you, John . . . you make me laugh."

"And you make me –" Mica's mouth took off running before his brain even knew it was gone. It wasn't pretty when they met up, but at least his brain managed to stop his mouth before it made a complete fool of itself. "– hot. In here?"

Well, *almost* managed to stop his mouth. Elena giggled.

"Are you hot in here?" he asked, as nonchalantly as was humanly possible at that moment. "I think they always keep the dining room hot."

Elena shrugged her shawl off her shoulders and onto the back of her chair. "I dunno. I'm always hot."

Oh, baby, are you ever!

Mica fingered the cross-scar on his forehead and hoped that would be enough to remind his brain just whose side it was on.

"Oh. Um, so . . . what kind of pie would you like?"

She leaned back in her chair, fingers still playing with her cleavage, and smiled.

"Surprise me," she said.

And Mica's brain deserted as he walked to the dessert table. *Oh yeah, baby. Uh-HUH! I would LOVE to surprise you. Oh man . . . just let me get my hands on that pie of yours and I'll pile on the whipped cream so high you won't be able to pee without coming for a month.*

"Would you like whipped cream?"

Elena thought a moment then wrinkled up her nose and shook her head. "Do they have hot apple pie? You know, like at *McDonald's*?"

Oh, yeah . . . you want it hot, don't you. Hot and steaming and dripping with juice. I bet your pie's already juicy, isn't it? I bet if I slipped my hand up under your skirt my fingers'd get waterlogged it's so wet. I bet —

"I'll — check," he said and thanked the Lord again for the masking power of loose-fitting robes. *I'm trying, Lord . . . You know I'm trying. It's just that it's been so long since I felt.*

Mica's sandaled foot slipped on a dollop of custard the floor-mop missed which caused him to hip-check the table's metal edge. The pain was more than enough for him to know that the Lord knew *exactly* how hard he was trying.

He latched onto the first two plates his hands came in contact with.

"'My little children, these things I write unto you that ye may not sin, and if any man sins we have an advocate with the Father, Jesus Christ, the Righteous.'"

"Amen," the blowsy bleached blond (two shades lighter than his dye job) working the table asked. "That'll be $1.50, employee discount. You want me to put that on your tab?"

Mica nodded and stumbled away without looking down at the plates until he got to the table and then — *Oh Lord!* Both pieces were cherry — his all time favorite — not apple. He couldn't go back, he'd look like a fool . . . besides, Elena was watching. Her eyes were bright and she'd tucked a paper napkin into the point of the plunging neckline.

There was nothing he could do but continue forward and throw himself *(all over her)* on her tender mercies.

"I –" He began to confess. "The apple pie looked kind of grungy so I got this instead. You're not allergic to cherries are you?"

Elena's grin stretched from ear to ear as she grabbed one of the plates and fingered a cherry into her mouth. A look of rapture spread over her face as she crushed the fruit to pulp between her molars.

"You know," she said, digging into the pie in earnest with her fork, "I almost called you back and said I changed my mind . . . that what I *really* wanted was cherry. Cherry pie is my absolute all time favorite."

Mica felt his heart start pumping again as he watched her fork in another mouthful.

"Yeah. Mine, too," he said and crossed his fingers before asking the next question. "Coffee?"

Elena looked up and tongued a drop of cherry jelly out of the corner of her mouth.

"You read my mind. Two creams, one sugar."

Mica uncrossed his fingers. That was just the way he liked it. If he needed a stronger sign – *not that he did* – it came by way of Alvis and his lyrical disability.

"Don't wanna sheep in clover,

"Don't wanna old soft shoe.

"Want you, kid, just you, miss –

"My good luck charm, through n' through."

Mica thought the real Elvis might be doing a little spinning in his grave at the new interpretation of his classic, *Good Luck Charm*, but then again he might not. Elvis understood the Lord's work as well as he understood true love, so maybe he'd just let it pass. Mica hoped so, because this was the strongest sign he'd gotten yet.

He and Elena were meant for each other.

Praise the Lord.

Meanwhile, back at the ranch . . . .

"Still don't have it all figured out, do you, pun'kin?"

Seth was still having problems remembering her name, but Allison was beyond caring at this point. Dressed again in his "aw shucks ma'am, t'weren't nothing" cowboy outfit, she watched him watching her mentally slip into something a little more dominating — a black vinyl cat-suit with peek-a-boo openings at nipples, crotch and ass, and thigh-high boots. With tiny golden spurs dangling from the stiletto-heels and a leather bull whip wrapped twice around her waist . . . in keeping with the stud farm theme.

Bits and pieces of her *real* costume were scattered on the floor around Ol' Faithful. Despite having probably seen and heard a good number of things, there seemed to be a look of shock in the mechanical horse's eye. *Poor baby,* Allison thought and patted his tailless rump gently as she bent to retrieve what might have either been her garter belt or part of her corset. It was hard to tell after the shredding it got.

Man-made fibers were fine except that they were too confining and constrictive and . . . and brought back too many memories of what it was like being alive. The dead weren't supposed to have memories like that — they were supposed to go on and on for all eternity and —

Shit.

Besides, she might not be able to do anything about being

able to "feel" only the touch of another vampire, but she'd be damned *(like she already wasn't)* if she was going to let herself get all sentimental over Calvin Klein.

Allison ripped the offending remnant into smaller bits. Seth just kept on watching. He hadn't minded her wanton destruction of one of his obviously expensive costumes; in fact, he hadn't seemed to mind *anything* she'd done to him.

And that just pissed her off.

Still mad, huh?

He winked at her when she looked up. Dammit, he could read her thoughts even when they were nothing more than free-floating emotions.

Y'know, this is why I don't like workin' with women. You just love hanging onto a grudge, don't you? Haven't you figured it out, baby – grudges are for the livin' . . . we're all done with that kinda shit.

"Really?" Allison shook her hair out until it flowed like a river of blood down her back. "Well, maybe if you'd given me the damn vampire training manual I'd know that."

Grudges and harpin' . . . shit.

"But of course, that never crossed your dead fucking mind, did it?"

Seth just kept looking at her, but at least that damned smile was gone.

"I had to figure out how to survive all by myself."

Givin' out piss-poor advice to piss-poor women durin' the day –

"It's good advice."

– and killin' off what's been pissin' on them at night.

"Those men deserved it."

And why's that, sweet lips?

"Allison."

Seth's smooth brow wrinkled. "Pardon?"

"My fucking name's Allison, you festering son-of-a-bitch.

I know it's probably not important to you, having gotten what you wanted, but it matters to *me!* I'm somebody, dammit. My name's Allison and you will acknowledge that I exist!"

Seth burst out laughing. "You aren't serious. Sheeee-it, baby . . . cuse me, sheee-it, *Allison*, but let me explain a lit'l something to you. You don't exist, I don't exist, my boys don't exist . . . we are all members of a non-existent club. We're not even shadows of what we once were. Hell, baby, what we were, with or without a name, is gone to dust."

He walked over to her and slapped her on the rear hard enough to bring tears to her eyes. If she were still able to cry.

"What we are is what you see . . . nothin' else."

He lifted his hand and Allison tensed, hating herself. They hadn't been together for more than twenty minutes and here she was acting just like the women who call her every fucking morning. She'd been abused and here she was . . . waiting for the next blow

"Naw, honey, I wouldn't hurt you. Sides, it'd be a plumb waste of time. We can regenerate ourselves easier than changin' clothes, dependin' on what happened to us, a'course. It's all trial and error. What don't kill us means we get to do it one more day. Hell, sugar, most of what we're supposed t'do was made up by writers anyway. I wandered around for almost ninety years before I figured out I didn't have to wear my Colonial Militia uniform. Good thing, too. It was pretty much in tatters by the time I traded it in for a butternut uniform. Pickin's were good back then, let me tell you. So you see, you already know more'n I did when I first got turned. It's just trial and error."

He leaned forward and kissed her, filling her mouth with his tongue. "Taste that?"

Allison pulled away and swiped her lips clean with one hand. Seth chuckled like back-up sewage.

"I always fall for the hard-ass bitches," he said. "Serious —

what did you taste?"

"Rot."

"Besides that."

"Slime. Putrefaction."

He rolled his eyes. "Don't. You wanted a lesson about bein' a vampire, so stop bein' such a cunt and tell me what you taste."

She could have done without that particular designation – *living or dead, men always resorted to name calling* – but smacked her tongue against the roof of her mouth. And shrugged.

"Nothing."

Seth nodded and crossed his arms over the faux pearl buttons on his faux linen shirt.

"Okay. Now, what do you smell?" He held up a finger. "And don't go for the cute answers this time, all right? We got better things to do than stand here and play games."

Allison *really* wanted to ask him what he had in mind, but decided to play along . . . for a while longer, at least. Breathing had become a forgotten art, but she'd learned *(by trial and error)* that she could taste smells on her tongue much like a snake could. Most smells left a bad taste in her mouth and this time wasn't any better.

"Moss, dirt . . . lubricating oil in the gear box. Old sweat and pussy juice."

"Breathers?"

Allison smacked her lips again. "Yeah. Rust. That's what they taste like. Just more rust."

"Anything else?"

She shook her head.

Seth lowered his arms and took a step back. "Smell me again."

Shit.

Just do it, baby.

"You're a pervert."

"Aw, c'mon. Humor your Maker. Smell me . . . but turn round in a circle again so you can sort my scent from all the others. Go on. Do it!"

She hated herself for doing it, but hands on hips and fingers tapping out an angry beat, Allison made a slow, 360-degree turn, tasting all the smells there were to taste. Cavern — water, mold, first-rain tang. Ol' Faithful — musk, dead fish *(ah, estrogen)*, caster beans. *Yuck!* Seth — nothing *(one point for our side)*. Scattered clothes — detergent and lemons. Back to Seth.

"Still nothing. So what *are* you supposed to smell like?"

"That's just it, darlin'," Seth said. "Nothin'. With all the millions of smells and scents in the world, you catch a whiff of absolutely nothin' and you know one of us is around. That's how I knew one o'my own was in town. I was walkin' along The Strip and caught this sweet band of nothin' on the night wind. Followed it right into the *Tropicana*. And there you were, up there in the bright lights, shaking your money-maker t'beat the band."

"You're shitting me."

"Would I do such a thing, pun . . . Allison. Hell no, I watched you up on that stage and I watched you when you picked up that jerk-wad after you left. Damn but you did a number on him, shit, baby. We're vampires, not fuckin' werewolves. You don't have't rip a man a whole new set of openin's, you know."

Allison leaned back against the hobby horse, arms across her breasts, and tried to figure out which of her many late-night dinner dates Seth was referring to. Luck had really been with her over the last couple of months, as far as wife-beating bastards went.

"Some men deserve to die as painfully as possible," she said. *Present company not excluded, of course.*

Seth only chuckled. "Cause they beat up on women. Yeah, I know."

"How?"

"I got my ways, honey . . . and I got my spies. But shit, baby, workin's for mere mortals. We're better'n that."

Allison stood up and watched him back up – hands raised in front of him like he half-expected to be attacked, but with the stupid, shit-eating grin still plastered on his lips.

"Whoa there, little filly."

"Whoa nothing! You bitch at me about working but –" Allison jerked a thumb back toward the ceiling of the cavern. "– what do you call *that* up there?"

"What? *The Stud Farm?* Hell, baby, that ain't work . . . that's fun'n games. Lemme show you."

In a snatch-and-grab that would have made the late Ted Bundy proud, Seth tossed Allison over one shoulder and literally spirited her into the narrow tunnel he'd been hiding in when she first entered the cavern. It wasn't the most comfortable ride she'd ever had, but, fortunately, it was relatively short.

And ended, abruptly, at the crumbling edge of a stalagmite-laced grotto some fifty or sixty feet below. The cavern was decorated in a combination of modern Marquis de Sade and vintage Lone Ranger – torture devices that she'd only seen before in Roger Corman movies were draped with bridles, saddles and coiled rope. Sprinkled among the display racks of whips, pinchers, knives and chains, plastic steer skulls and tumbleweeds shimmered in the light from a dozen flickering torches. The only thing missing was a cast of writhing souls.

Even for the lowest budget Hollywood B-epic, it was the most disturbing sight Allison had even seen.

"Welcome to the Stable, sweetheart," Seth said and stepped back from the edge just far enough so he could drop Allison down in his place.

And she forgot she was dead. Again.

"SHIT!"

"Easy, honey-pie," Seth whispered as he took her arm. "Don't tell me you still haven't learned to fly."

"Fly?"

His wide, toothy smile should have given her a hint of what he had planned. Should have, but didn't. In fact, Allison was about to ask when Seth stepped out into thin-air . . . and pulled her along with him. It seemed to take a very long time before her stiletto heels hit the well-swept cavern floor, longer still for her eyeballs to stop jiggling in their sockets and –

A flicker of motion . . . a shift in the air, like a heat mirage, over by one of the man-sized wagon wheels caught her eye. Then another, in front of the pillory strung with barb-wire and another . . . no, a lot more flickering over by the rack and St. Andrew's Cross and . . .

A blur suddenly fused into a shape – a man, naked except for a thick dog-collar and studded jock-strap. Their eyes met for only a second, less, but he winked at her just as he disappeared.

"What the hell?"

Seth reached up from behind her and pressed a hand over her eyes. "You're still thinkin' like a breather, darlin'. You're dead, start lookin' at the world in that way."

"How can I see it any other way, you fucking asshole? I *am* dead."

His chuckle hurt her ear. "Yeah, you are, but there's some part of you that's still not convinced. Oh, you drink blood and stay out of the sunlight, but you still act like you're alive . . . like anytime you want to you can change your mind and go back to what you were. Well, I'm here t'tell you, baby, that ain't ever gonna happen. We're dead and gone, baby-cakes. Ashes to ashes and all that shit. Accept that and look what happens."

Seth's hand dropped away and Allison blinked. "Oh."

She was surrounded by ghosts. The ghosts of a dozen leather and vinyl encased women – whipping, flogging, paddling and generally beating the crap out of five men who kept disappearing and reappearing, first here and the next minute, there. Allison leaned back against her Maker as she watched one man, the man who'd winked at her, pop in and out of existence in front of four different women – none of which seemed to notice that he wasn't their constant plaything. They weren't ghosts, of course, the women were real. Allison could taste blood on her tongue, but the men . . . the men left nothing in their supersonic wake.

"The men are vampires."

Seth patted her on the back. "That'a girl, knew you'd figure it out. Those are my boys, all right."

"The woman are . . ."

"Customers."

"But why is everyone moving so fast?"

"Gotta think of my overhead, baby. In real time, a full S&M session'd be about forty minutes long, from gettin' into costume t' payin' the bill . . . plus the time it takes for them t'donate blood. If they want to, of course."

"Yeah, right."

Allison shook off his hand and stepped directly into the path of a beautiful black woman in full dominatrix garb. The woman passed through her without so much as a shudder, leaving only an aftertaste of her excitement and warmth against Allison's skin.

"Look baby, I don't care what you believe, but if I want to show a profit on this place and keep me and the boys in blood, I gotta fudge with the laws of nature a mite. Besides, time's a human construct, honey. We speed things up so everybody gets what they want and can still make it home in time to pick up the kids and cook dinner."

"Einstein would be thrilled," she muttered.

"He was," Seth said, pointing to a man who was happily keeping three women fully occupied. "Still is, as far as I know."

"Shit. So when did you decide that it was okay to be around your own kind? You told me there was safety in numbers and that number was —"

"One. Yeah, I know, but I'm a vampire of the new millennium. We may not be able to change on the outside, but we can still change on the inside. You don't and you wind up sucking nothing but air. Or work for some crisis line."

Allison elbowed him in the gut as hard as she could — and came away with a sore elbow.

Seth didn't seem to notice either.

"Now, you see that skinny drink of water over there?" Seth pointed to the man with a satanic looking Van Dyke beard who was simultaneously getting flogged with a cat-of-nine-tales by a large blond and having his scrotum threatened with red-hot pincers by a tiny brunette. "He was an accountant up in a backwater town in New Jersey before he met up with me. The whole time management concept was his. See, if I hadn't changed I'd still be picking up miserable women in bars."

Allison would have liked to have booted him into the middle of the next eternity, but if the throbbing in her elbow was any indication, she didn't want to impede her ability to run — should it be called for — so she just place-kicked a basketball-sized chunk of limestone across the cavern. It detonated next to the western-style version of a St. Andrew's Cross where a manacled black man was being whipped by two women, neither of whom seemed to realize she was sharing.

The man looked up and blew Allison a kiss.

"You like him?" Seth asked. "That's Shaft. I found him

about the same time I found you . . . he was one mean mother when he was alive, but he's good as gold now. He's a natural-born submissive, but fast as lightning."

Allison nodded and tensed her shoulders as Seth moved in close. He was right about vampires not having a scent, but his particular brand of nothingness had a rankness to it that made her want to gag.

"Time and space, babe," he said, watching Shaft move in stop-action quickness from one beating to the next, "we just ain't part of that scene anymore and the minute a Breather steps into our circle, the same rules apply. Take all these ladies for instance, these lovely little walking blood banks think them and their 'stud' are the only ones down here – that's what makes them so uninhibited. They can whomp away in ignorant bliss while my boys zip around like horseflies at a rodeo."

Allison smiled at a bronze-skinned Native American stud in full war paint who was alternating between a flogging, a caning, and a quick once-over on the rack. She had to admit it really looked like fun . . . a whole lot of fun.

"Who's that?" she asked.

"Slave #1 – Rod, to you. Yeah, pure blood Lakhota. You want him?"

Allison turned away and tried to find a section of the cavern that wasn't in use. That proved to be impossible. Every square inch of space was a blur of movement. *Dammit.*

"You didn't answer me, honey. You wanna try puttin' the spurs t'him?"

She walked through a half-dozen beatings before Seth caught up with her. "What's the matter, sweet-lips?"

"Why are you telling me all this?" she asked. "I didn't come here to listen to you."

Seth chucked her gently under the chin. "Then why did you come out here? To bust a stud or two?"

"So what?"

"So nothin' – you go ahead and pick one out. Get it all out of your system . . . and then you and I'll have us a little talk."

"About what?"

"About you leavin' the wonderful world of Breathers behind and come here t'be with your own kind. I could use a good woman t'run things."

She laughed without humor.

"I'm serious. I'm thinkin' of expandin' . . . and I think that pretty little face of yours'll have men pourin' in through those doors."

"To beat up on your guys? Why would a man want to do that?"

Now it was Seth's turn to laugh. "Hell, you give a man a willin' victim and he'll take it every time. Sides, I'm sure you know a couple'll breathin' women who'd like a little immortality. They can't get hurt doin' this . . . we're quick healers y'know. It's all in the blood."

It took a moment for the meaning to sink in. "You want me to . . . turn women into vampires so men can beat them?"

"Well, hell, honey, it's not like they're gonna feel it. Besides, you should know more'n enough from that help line you volunteer for. See, female blood's good, but I've always found that testosterone gives it a much better flavor." Seth ran his fingers slowly over her breasts and Allison shuddered. Shit, it felt so damned good. "Whadda ya say?"

"Can I think about it?"

He pinched her nipple hard enough to pop it. "Sure. You got time, baby . . . all the time in the world. I won't pressure you. Don't have to. I'm just offerin' this to you as a courtesy, us havin' once been so close and all. You don't want the job, no problem . . . I got me a whole herd t'pick from right here."

She nodded and pushed his hand away. A cold fire raged

in her crushed nipple, but it was nothing to the fire she felt in her belly. If she told him to take his offer and go fuck himself with it, he'd just turn another woman to head up his new "mare" section. If she said yes . . . she'd be no better than him.

And she *was* better. Shit, she was a fucking saint compared to him.

Allison rubbed the sneeze out of her nose before it could escape and felt his eyes as she walked over and picked up a thin bamboo cane. It whistled through the air when she tested it. A living man . . . or woman . . . wouldn't be able to stand more than one lashing with something like this. A vampire might last for hours. Days even.

"Well, I'd hate to think I came out all this way for nothing and I do have a couple of hours to kill before I have to be at the club."

You still playin' breather? Fuck the club.

She smiled and slashed the air. "Can't just walk out without giving them my notice, can I? I'm not that kind of vampire. Besides, I might be able to talk some of the girls into . . . a new career."

Seth's laugh sounded funny coming from directly inside her head. *Oh, yeah, that's my girl. So, which of my studs would you like?*

Allison looked up into those dead green eyes and smiled. "You. Stud. Me . . . Mistress."

. . . tick . . . tick . . .

CHAPTER 11

. . . tick.

❖

"I can't imagine where she is," Mica told Alvis as he watched his friend work the styling gel into his pompadour. "It's not like her to miss a show, especially not a new number. Raven really likes performing."

"Well, mebbe she got stuck in traffic. Yah know how bad the Strip gets on Fridays, or mebbe that sweet lit'l lady of yours just decided t'take the night off and treat herself t'a lit'l shoppin'. Yah know how the ladies like t'pick up things."

Mica knew and that's what he was afraid of. Allison had a set routine and never broke it — that he knew of. She was supposed to be at the nightclub so he could tell her the lie he made up about losing big on a sure thing and having to take out the money to cover it. It wasn't the greatest lie, but considering where they lived, it would work.

He hoped.

"Sides," Alvis said, winking at Mica from the mirror, "Everyone's entitl'd to a break now'n then, right? Just like yah with that pretty lit'l honey ah seen yah talkin' to all afternoon. It's just a break. Right?"

A fiery blush instantly heated Mica's cheeks and nose . . . the flames of moral outrage that his friend could think his relationship – concern for Elena could be anything else.

"It's not like that, Alvis. We were just talking."

"Ain't that what ah just said, Johnny?"

Mica looked at their reflections in the glass, then turned and walked away. He hadn't liked what he'd seen.

"Oh, c'mon now, don't be like that," Alvis shouted after him as he swivelled his make-up chair around. The sound made the fashionable short hairs on the back of Mica's neck stand up on end. "Yah know ah was only fun'n yah. Ah know that lit'l gal of yours means the world t'yah, same as yah mean to . . . Oh. Trouble in paradise?"

Alvis had sung the last question, but Mica didn't know if that was because it was part of an Elvis song or if his friend was just trying to lighten the mood. It didn't work, but Mica turned around and smiled.

"Some," he said without going into any of the gory details. "Al – Raven and I are just from two different worlds. I really thought it could work out but you know how it goes."

"Ah do indeed," Alvis said, "and ah'm truly sorry t'hear it. How long y'two been together?"

"Feels like an eternity."

The big man grunted thoughtfully. "Yeah, been there. Well, people change, yah know."

"I know, Alvis," Mica said, "but that's the whole problem. She hasn't changed and she never will. She can't."

"Hey, now. That's not like you t'be so neg-a-tive, Johnny. Besides, she might just surprise you one day."

Mica leaned back against the dressing room door and shook his head. He'd changed out of his robes once his shift was over, becoming just plain Johnny Nil – collector of second-hand bowling shirts and sinners. Amen.

"Believe me, Alvis," he said, "it'd take a miracle."

"Yeah, seems like that sometimes, don't it? But ah know what yore sayin' . . . believe me, man, ah do. Yah fall in love with a lit'l gal and think it's a'ways gonna be roses and soft summer nights, and then you find out her transfer t'the third moon o'Jupiter just come in and she don't want yore sorry ass taggin' along cause her career comes first. Ah, Sskkielletka."

"Bless you."

"Thank yah, but that was her name. Sskkielletka, mah lit'l star voyager. First time ah looked inta them silver-almond eyes o'hers ah thought it would last forever. Never did consider the fact that she might have other plans, but a man don't think of them things when he's in love, does he?"

Mica rubbed the scar-cross on his forehead. Alvis had mentally left the building.

"No," he said, "no he doesn't."

With a soul-grinding sigh, the big man pulled the face towel out from the sequined collar of his jumpsuit and stood up. His broken heart over his lost alien love not stopping him from giving his reflection a final going-over.

"Yeah. Well, ah am sorry t'hear about yore troubles, but it might just be for the best, y'know? Don't take offense, but it does seem like little Miss out there may be kinda sweet on yah."

Mica's hand dropped slowly to the pocket of his jeans. "I'm just helping her find her way back to the Lord, Alvis. Nothing else."

"Well, then ah wish yah both all the strength that the good Lord can bestow, for ah know how long and rocky the road back can be."

Clasping his hands around the towel, Alvis closed his eyes and sang two full stanzas of *Amazing Grace*. Without adaptation. When he finished, he sighed and opened his eyes. There were tears in both his and Mica's.

"It is too bad these competitions don't go in for the sweet

stuff," Alvis said, "but ah'm sure the Lord understands and forgives us our hip swivels and pelvis thrusts. Much like He forgives us our bird-doggin' after all that original and reasonably priced sin, which is a blessin', Johnny. His forgiveness, not our hound-doggin'. Cause if He didn't forgive that, we'd all of us be out of jobs. Speakin' o'which . . . yah gonna watch the show?"

Mica nodded as he walked over to the water-cooler in the corner and helped himself to a dixie-cup full of tepid, fluoridated water. Talking about Allison had really given him a bad case of dry mouth.

"Wouldn't miss it," he said, crushing the paper cup as Alvis' lucky make-up towel came sailing his way.

"Then let's go," Alvis said as he slipped on his silver-rimmed shades. "The King has returned."

"Long live the King. Amen."

Towel over one shoulder, Mica opened the dressing room door and then followed his friend's glittering path to the casino's dime-sized stage. The rest of the impersonators were already waiting in the wings, indulging in a little last minute primping and fussing with the help of hand-held mirrors, their official numbered signs fluttering in the air-conditioned breeze as they moved. Mica kept his eyes lowered, that many rhinestones in such a confined space could easily knock a man's vision out for hours.

"Now, that's what ah like t'see," Alvis said, nudging Mica gently in the ribs. "New faces and old clothes."

Mica glanced up to where Alvis was pointing and chuckled. There was no danger of going blind here. The skinny kid with the crew cut and baggy suit looked like he'd just stepped out of a *Happy Days* repeat – early, *early* Elvis right down to the wide-eyed, "Wow, is this really happening" enthusiasm.

It was sweet.

"What do you think he'll sing?" Mica asked, watching while one of the fat Elvises in sparkling red, white and blue helped pin the number 9 to the hem of the kid's Eisenhower-cut jacket.

"Probably something from mah greaser days, fore ah went into the army," Alvis said, papa-proud. "Either *All Shook'em Up* or *Jailbait Rock*."

Mica didn't correct his friend. Alvis would be fine once he had a prompter in front of him.

"He even got mah look, don't he?"

"Yep."

"Right down t'the bargain basement suit. Ah had me one just like that."

"Yep."

"Doesn't stand a snowball's chance."

"Nope," Mica agreed, but that was all part of the fun.

❖

And games.

"Who's your mama?" *Whack.* "Come on, say it." *Whack.* "Tell me who your mama is."

"All right, dammit . . . *you're* my mama."

WHACK!

Seth pulled his hands out of the fur-lined handcuffs and spun around to face her.

What the hell was that for? I said you were my damned mama.

Allison pursed her lips and blew him a kiss.

But not fast enough. Baby. Besides, we're just playing, right?

Seth rubbed the bloodless welts on his ass. "Yeah, that's right. We're just playing."

She blew him another kiss and twirled the cane around her fingers like a baton. All around them the air flickered with the accelerated comings (sometimes literally) and goings of human women and their dead slave-boys. Occasionally a face or hand or bare butt would solidify in the quick-silver current and she'd react in proper dominatrix-style.

It hadn't taken long for Allison to come to understand the pull of the place. There really was something therapeutic about beating something . . . even if they didn't bleed. What was even better was that after the first dozen or so blows, it became pretty clear that pain – real honest to you-know-who pain – was just one more sensation a vampire could feel only when inflicted by one of their own kind.

Death was suddenly looking better to her.

"So I take it you're still considering my offer?" Seth said, fanning the wounds on his rear as they slowly healed.

Allison walked away, humming and slashing the air, and whatever materialized in front of her, with the cane; playing indifferent about the offer even though she hadn't been able to stop thinking about it since Seth (the bastard) brought it up. Of course she'd never consider turning battered women into battered vampires, but the thought of taking the farm over after she killed him, had its appeal. Or she could tell him thanks, but no thanks, kill him (that didn't change) and then continue doing what she was doing – playing the happy housewife and crisis center volunteer exotic dancer.

Shit.

Neither (except for the part about killing Seth) was how she'd envisioned spending her life. But, of course, she hadn't actually pictured herself being dead and still having to worry about it, either.

She stopped feeling so good.

"So?"

Allison tossed the cane over one shoulder and turned around to look at him. His butt looked healed and he didn't look any more pissed than usual. Cool. The tune she'd been humming, *Daydream Believer* had done its job – Seth hadn't been able to read her thoughts.

"You going to answer me?" he asked.

"Oh," she said as if she'd forgotten, "about your offer? Well . . . I think I need just a little more time. And maybe a little more incentive."

She walked over to a wall display of hanging (and well hung) dildos and other strap-on riding devices. Some of the women, Allison noted, were definitely of a masculine bent. A few of the items, like the yard-long, glow-in-the-dark "Mastodon," seemed very popular, but she didn't want to kill Seth just yet and she sure as hell didn't want any possibility of him enjoying any part of his demise, so she selected a sedate little foot-long number and strapped it on.

Without mirrors Allison could only look down at it . . . but she liked being an "outie."

A whole lot more than Seth was going to.

"Okay, slave, bend over and touch your toes," she told him. "Mama needs to take your temperature."

Shit.

"Nope, and I'm just as glad. It could get messy."

Using her thumbs, Allison spread his icy butt cheeks and placed the tip of the hard rubber against his ass. She could feel him tremble. Cool.

What?

"Sorry, wasn't talking to you . . . but now that you mention it, we could use a little music in here. If I decide to accept your offer, I want this place laid out with the best sound system blood money can buy."

"We already have one," Seth said from somewhere down around her ankles. "It's just playing too fast for you to hear it. Stop thinkin' like a Breather, God-dammit."

"Oh." Allison thrust her newfound manhood into her old

Maker's ass and stopped thinking all together.

Damn, she could hear it. The Stones doing *Time Is On My Side*.

Oh, yes it is.

The kid with the crew-cut sang *Blue Suede Shoes*, with a Minnesotan-Norwegian twang and went home with a lovely consolation prize.

Alvis Ambrose, the reigning monarch of Elvis Impersonations, sang his signature *Viva, Las Vegas*, and came in Third.

It was an emotional blow from which Mica feared his friend would never recover.

"But . . . but ah'm Elvis," Alvis said, gripping one of the tiny handles on the Third-Place loving cup tight enough to crush the imitation metal. "Ah *am*."

Mica nodded and pushed the bottle of beer closer to his friend. He'd been saying the same thing, over and over for the three hours since the competition ended and the winner, a retired proctologist from Monticello, Mississippi, walked away with the grand prize and a chance to go on to the next round of competition. Thank yah, thank yah, verrah much.

Alvis grabbed Mica's hand before he had a chance to pull away.

"But ah really am Elvis, Johnny. Really." There were tears in the man's bright blue eyes. *Oh Lord.*

"I know, Alvis," Mica said, glancing at his watch as he pulled his hand free. It'd only been five minutes since the last time he'd called the bungalow to hear his own voice telling him to leave a message at the sound of the beep and he'd get back to him. Again. He'd been calling the house since eleven-thirty, right after the *Tropicana's* backstage manager had finally convinced him that "Raven" wasn't there, hadn't shown up, and would be canned the minute she stepped into the building for bailing on the show without explanation. Thank you and don't call again. "I know, man. I know."

It hadn't been a very good evening for anyone in their little group with the possible exception of Elena.

She was having a ball.

Dressed in a rose-colored *"Love that is as enduring as a ROSE in the DESERT"* terry-cloth short set she bought at the gift shop, Elena smiled at him from around the straw of her Cherry-Coke-and-rum. With her vinyl dress and shawl stuffed inside an oversized canvas tote, she looked like just like an average, innocent tourist out on the town.

Mica liked that look on her.

"You want to call again?" she asked as he reached for his beer. She'd been so understanding – not at all like Allison would be. At least, not like Mica thought Allison would be.

"No."

"Well, maybe your friend did take the night off. Like me."

She giggled and Mica felt his stomach tighten.

"Yeah," he said. "Maybe. She does love the night life."

"Then you don't have to worry about her, right?"

He looked up to watch Elena suck the juice out of the maraschino cherry that had decorated the top of her Coke. Pink tongue, white teeth, red lips, red cherry.

"Huh?"

Elena pulled the cherry off its stem and chewed it slowly. "I said then you don't have to worry about her . . . but you do, right?"

"Yeah. Silly, isn't it?"

"No." Elena wiped her fingers off on one of the *Annual Elvis Competition* cocktail napkins and took his hand. Her fingers were cool when they first touched him, but warmed up quickly. She was so warm. "I think it's sweet. It just proves

P. D. Cacek

what a good man you are. A lot of guys I know wouldn't care enough to worry about anything but themselves. But you . . . you're really different, John."

"I could be better."

She shrugged but didn't let go of his hand. "Everyone could be better, I guess. But I still think you're pretty neat."

Mica gave her hand a gentle squeeze. She squeezed back. It was a magic moment . . . that ended all too quickly when Alvis covered both their hands with his one.

"It ain't right," he said. "It ain't. Ah'm the real Elvis. Ah'm the King and a'ways have been."

Mica looked at Elena and sighed. *Lord, if this was part of Your plan I think You have to work on Your timing a little more.*

"Maybe that's the reason," he said to his friend.

It took a moment, but the beer-blurred eyes finally met his. "What'cha talkin' 'bout, boy?"

Lord, I apologize about the timing comment . . . a little help here, okay?

"I mean – Well, I mean you've won every competition . . . up to now . . . for years, so maybe the judges just thought it was time for some new blood –"

This is helping, Lord?

"I mean –for a change of . . . face. You know, like the new Coke." Mica had no idea why he added that, since the new Coke didn't taste any different, that he could tell, from the Coke he drank as a kid. It had to be the Lord trying to help. "You know, same great look, different . . . You know what I mean."

The weight of Alvis's hand increased as he leaned toward Mica. "But ah'm Elvis."

"Yeah, you were . . . but now this new guy is."

"But he's seventy-five years ol' and fat. I don't look like that."

214

"No," Elena said, flashing him an innocent smile, "but he sounded pretty good. I mean not as good as the real Elvis, I guess."

Alvis lifted his hand off theirs and sat back, staring at the little trophy as if it was something he'd find in a gas station men's room.

"But ah'm Elvis." He closed his hand around the trophy and crushed it into a simulated-metal free-formed sculpture. "Yah don't understand, Johnny . . . ah really am Elvis Aron Presley."

Mica sighed long and hard– *Lord, help this poor man* – and unfortunately, Alvis heard it.

"Ah mean it," Alvis said louder than Mica had ever heard him off-mike. "AH AM ELVIS!"

Three of the other losing competitors, who'd been drowning their sorrows at the bar, turned around when they heard that and lifted their drinks.

"I am Elvis," the one in the middle shouted back.

"No, I am Elvis."

"No. I'm Spartacus . . . I mean Elvis!"

The bar crowd applauded and offered to buy them all, Alvis included, another round of $2.00 well drinks. The three losers instantly took the crowd up on their generous offer. Alvis stood up and tossed the broken trophy onto the table.

"Ah'm goin' home. See yah in the mornin', Johnny. Usual time." Smiling sadly, he picked up his sunglasses and put them on. "Glad t'have met yore acquaintance, miss. Vaya con Dios. Night, Johnny."

Elena sniffed loudly as the big, sad man walked away without so much as a single hip-swivel.

"God, that's heart-breaking, isn't it? I mean, winning this really meant something to him, didn't it?"

"Yeah," Mica said and wished he'd been kinder. Even if

Alvis was delusional, he still was a good, God-fearing man "But he'll be okay. I asked the Lord to help him come to term with losing."

Elena smiled at him as she dug another cherry out of her drink. "Guess you really are a preacher. Here, you want this?"

My cherry, Mica silently thought. He could feel the blush start up the back of his neck as he shook his head.

"No thanks, I'm good."

"You're more than just good, John," she said. "I knew that the minute I heard your voice this morning. I felt your goodness and then, when I looked into your eyes, I saw it, too. There's a light inside you that almost takes away all the darkness that I've been living in for so long now. When you look at me . . . you almost make me feel like I could be good again, in spite of everything I've done."

Mica's heart swelled with saintly pride and he was about to tell her that she was almost good enough to come back into the Lord's embrace . . . when he felt the ball of her foot gently press into his crotch, her bare toes kneading the shaft of his equally swollen cock. He looked down and saw that her toenails had been painted ebony black.

Um, Lord?

"Oh God . . . you're huge! I've never had a man this big before. Want to?"

Oh, Lord, where art thou?

"Because I do, John. I want to do it with you. God, I'm already wet and I want you, John. I want to feel your power inside me . . . taking away the darkness. Will you? Please?"

Mica's mind raced through all the scriptures, searching for the right passage to fill him *(like he wanted to fill her)* with the pure and sweet *(oh yeah, dripping sweet, like honey)* love that only could *(cum)* through the blessings of our Lord Jesus *(humping that hot, tight little pussy until she threw back her head and screamed–)*

"HALLELUJAH!"

Elena pulled her foot away so quickly Mica thought his cock must have tried to bite her. Silly thought. Sure was.

"Oh, God, John," Elena said as she quickly began gathering up her things, "I'm sorry, I didn't mean to insult you. It's just that . . . that . . . you're not like other men, John. You treated me the same way Jesus treated Mary Magdalene. She was a whore and our Lord didn't care. You didn't care about me, so I just thought . . . I mean–"

Her voice had gone child-soft again. "I thought that maybe it could be like that for us. You know? I'm so sorry . . . will you forgive me?"

And now the Bible verses filled his mind – only to be batted out of the cerebral ballpark by his massive libido.

"There's nothing to forgive," he said, pulling her to her feet as he stood up from the table. "I want to be with you, too."

"Really?"

"Yes. 'That ye may be filled unto all the fullness of God.'" Mica smiled. Then giggled. Then felt the heat of her body as he pulled her into his arms. "See, I never really believed Our Lord could be that close to Mary Magdalene and not do anything either. I mean, if you've ever seen *Jesus Christ, Superstar* you know something had to be going on."

Elena looked up into his eyes and shuddered in his sight.

The Lord's message *couldn't* be clearer. He may have been born Milo Franklin Poke, biological son of Curtis and Eloise, but today he was sure that he was God's second son, The Christ's Own Younger Brother.

And Jesus didn't like that one bit. In an atypical show of sibling rivalry, Mica's erection suddenly filled with something other than God's pure love. He never had to pee so bad in his life. Mica pushed her back and clamped both hands against the front of his pants. Elena looked a little confused.

"You okay, John?" she asked.

"Yeah. Sure. Uh, 'To forgive each other like He forgives us' . . OH! Gotta go. Sorry. I really want to . . . I –"

If he held it any longer he was going to burst.

"Be right back and I'll – I'll, OH LORD!"

Mica couldn't tell if the laughter that followed him out of the bar and across the lobby to the public restrooms was directed at him or the "Better Luck Next Year" conga line that had spontaneously formed . . . or where it came from – Heaven or earth. Not that it mattered much.

He'd really have to talk to Dad about this. Jesus was acting like a spoiled brat.

When Mica came out of the bathroom, Elena was gone.

The crowd was still laughing as he headed for the doors and the long, hot walk home. This was *not* how he'd wanted the evening to end. Not by a long shot.

Dammit.

It hadn't taken Allison long to figure out how to slip in and out of accelerated time, and once she did, it was like a brand-new toy – she kept playing with it. A second became an hour or a minute, it was all up to her. Voices and the snap of leather surrounded her like a hellish choir.

She wanted to see everything, be everywhere at once.

And she could.

"You promised it would be different!"

Huh? The familiar phrase yanked Allison out of fast-forward and into real time.

"You said you fucking loved me," a small blond woman screamed while her naked slave, # 5 (aka Cane, she was beginning to recognize faces) cowered before her, hands raised in supplication while she snapped riding crop against her vinyl motorcycle chaps. "You told me that if I just waited until your divorce became final, everything would be different. You fucking lied to me, you pussy-whipped bastard."

The little woman couldn't have been five-foot three without the two-inch platform work boots, but even Allison jumped when she swung the riding crop down against the man's back. His scream didn't sound very convincing.

"I never meant to hurt you, Mistress." His whimper didn't sound any more believable as his scream had. The first thing she was going to do when she took over, Allison decided, was to get the "boys" some theatrical training.

"Forgive you, you two-faced shit? Nev–"

Allison cringed when the crop lashed the man across the face. *Shit.*

Oh, please, little sister. You think one of them can hurt me? He gave her a big "Me Man, Me Macho" grin. *Be right back. I see two of my regulars need a little saddle–*

He winked out and winked back in without the blond even noticing.

"– ver. What do you think you are? God's gift to women?"

Allison sneezed and this time the woman jumped.

"Oh!" The blond dropped the riding crop and covered her mouth with both gloved hands. "I didn't know there was anyone . . . I thought . . . I thought he and I were alone and . . . Oh God – "

"I didn't mean to interrupt you," Allison said, wiping the sanctified tickle out of her nose. "Sorry. Please . . . go on."

Uh-oh, there's my one-thirty. Be right –

Allison ignored him. *–back. You think she's done?*

"May I?" Smiling, she picked up the riding crop and gave him one across the haunches. This time his scream sounded very real. He looked very surprised by the whole thing . . . as did his little blond Mistress.

"Here," Allison said, trying to hand the crop back. "Please, don't let me stop you."

The woman dropped her hands from her face, but shook her head. "I can't. I'm too embarrassed."

"Don't be. You were doing the right thing. A man lied to you and made you feel like you were the stupidest woman on earth because you believed him, right?"

The blond licked the black lipstick off her bottom lip and nodded.

"Yeah, I know . . . a man lied to me once, promised me things would be different and you know what – nothing was different. It was the same old shit, only now I know it was shit where before, I could pretend it was organic compost."

The woman smiled. "Yeah. They're all a bunch of liars, aren't they?"

"Yep and they deserve to be lied to and beaten up and have their heads torn off and their remains buried out . . . Ahem. Yeah, living or dead they're all pigs."

"Huh?"

"What? Oh, nothing . . . I was just thinking out loud. But this really is good therapy. I know – I'm a professional."

That was all it took. This time when Allison held out the crop, the girl took it.

"You're right, men are awful. Want to join me?"

"I'd love to."

Rolling the muscles in her shoulders to loosen them, Allison selected a suede-covered police baton from a nearby rack, then positioned herself next to the man's left haunch. Slave # 5 was cowering in earnest now.

This is just for fun, right, little sister?

Allison cracked the baton against an open palm in answer to his silent question.

"So, you want the front of back?"

"Front," the woman said, "I want to watch his eyes."

"Good choice," Allison said and positioned herself directly behind him. His ass dipped away from her like a frightened dog.

"Um," the trembling male vampire said, "I think your time's almost up, Mistress."

"Shut up, slave," she growled back, but still pushed back one gauntlet to check the diamond-encrusted watch on her wrist. "Darn, he's right. I guess we'd better hurry then, huh? After you."

"With pleasure."

If Seth and the "boys" were watching, they weren't being obvious about it. But she still hoped they were. And taking mental notes.

Um, you think we could talk about this, little sister?

The name's Allison, shit head. She kicked his legs apart. "Spread em wide, butt-boy. I want to see daylight at the end of this tunnel."

Groaning, he reached around and pulled his ass-cheeks apart.

And for some reason, Allison thought of Mica.

Mica felt his deflated, dejected and damp cock shudder inside his briefs and thought of Allison. Of course, that wasn't very hard to do when he saw the group of Goth kids loitering in the shadows just beyond the Amtrak station. Black clothes and pale faces – deep shadows under their eyes and blood-red lips. *Fucking stupid kids.* They wanted so much to be like Allison that it almost made him sick to his stomach.

It did make him sick to his heart.

Jesus may have played a dirty Big Brother trick on him, but Mica knew right then and there – while the wannabe blood suckers stared back at him as though he was a tourist – that his momentary lapse in the bar with Elena . . . hell, maybe even Alvis's crushing defeat had all been Allison's fault. The Lord could forgive, but He really hated having to keep forgiving the same sin over and over again.

Mica understood that now that he was part of the Family.

And these poor, deluded babies of the night, were going to be the first beneficiaries of this new knowledge.

"Thanks, Dad." As he walked toward the group Mica felt like a seventeen-year-old about to take the family car out for the first time. "I can handle it from here. For You have provided me a place among my enemies that I may pour down Our wrath upon their heads and turn them away from the darkness and back into Your everlasting light. Amen."

One of the Goth girls smiled at him. There was enough pierced jewelry in her ears and on her face that she made a soft jingle-bell sound when she turned her head to look back at her companions when Mica stopped in front of them and spread his arms.

A tall boy with long pale hair that hid most of his face stepped in front of the jingle-eared girl. The protective posture infuriated Mica. *Little bastard.*

"Good evening, sir," the boy said. "May we help you? Are you lost?"

"Lost? Me?" Mica forced himself to laugh and the Goths backed up as a single unit. "Am *I* lost? No child . . . you're lost. You and all the rest of your brand of freaks are lost from my Father's sight. You lost the True Way the minute you decided it would be *fun* to pretend you were one of the undead. Was it you? Are you the leader who corrupted these poor, dim-witted children? 'Through the one man's disobedience, the many were made sinners.' Romans 5:15-16."

"Actually, sir," the boy said, "it's Romans 5:*17 - 19.* But that's a hard one to remember."

The boy smiled and Mica was sure he could hear Jesus laughing.

"You fucking little freak!" Mica screamed at the boy. "Even the devil can cite scripture, but that doesn't mean my Dad's going to let him back into Heaven. So you all had better just listen to *me* if you want the Lord's forgiveness . . . because only I can give it."

Another girl, with less pierced-work, suddenly clapped her hands. "Are you Brother Beezer? God, my grandma listens to you every morning."

"NO, I'M FUCKING NOT FUCKING BROTHER FUCKING BEEZER! I am the way to your fucking salvation. Say FUCKING AMEN!"

The group backed up another step.

"Please sir," the boy leader said, "there's no need to use profanity. There are ladies present."

"Ladies? You call these whores of Satan ladies? Shit, you idiots really live in your own little world, don't you? But I'll tell you this, that world is going to be blown apart like Sodom and Gomorrah if you don't listen to me. You think it's cool to dress in black and pretend to drink blood? But let me tell you something, it's not cool . . . it's an abomination in the eyes of the Lord, my Father. It's eternal damnation . . . that's right . . . damned for all time. 'For ours is not a conflict with mere flesh and blood, but with the despotisms, the empires, the forces that control and govern this dark world, and the spiritual hosts of evil arrayed against us in the heavenly warfare.' Huh?"

The boy was motioning his group to retreat.

"Sir, please, we're not like that. We don't drink blood and we don't worship the devil. We believe in the dark beauty of a gothic past, that's all. And we really don't want any trouble, okay. So, if you'll please excuse us, we have to be heading home now."

"HOME? You're not going to have a *home* in the eternal here-after until you clean that make-up off your faces and start working on a tan! The Lord, my Father, doesn't want to look out from His Golden Throne Room and see a bunch of pasty-faced, dark-eyed angels flying around. Hell no, that's not what He wants at all. 'That through death He might bring to naught Him that had the authority of death, that is, the devil.' So all of you had better listen to me right now!"

Mica hadn't really intended to grab the front of the boy's black-mesh shirt. He'd just gotten carried away by the Spirit of the Lord. Which was how he almost got carried away by the city sanitation crew the next morning.

Who would have thought a Goth could be a champion kick-boxer.

Mica wouldn't have.

But he strongly suspected his Big Brother not only knew, but set the whole thing up.

Jesus.

CHAPTER 12

Tightening her grip on the baton, Allison lifted it to one shoulder in a stance that would have made Mark McGwier proud, and was just about to let it swing when –

Accelerated time screeched to a halt and snapped Allison back into minute-by-minute real time as if she'd been hooked to some gigantic bungee-cord.

Her bottom and the baton hit the cavern floor at the same mundane moment, giving her an ant's eye view of the changes that had occurred. A split second *(less)* the cavern was filled with the sounds and cloying, sweet-sour musk of women, the thick air rippling with time-lapse images superimposed one (or more) over another, the next . . . Allison was flat on her ass watching the males of her species stretch and yawn and scratch themselves just like . . . just like regular guys. Seth was dressed again, in work shirt and jeans – nothing fancy now that the living women were gone.

It was all too depressing for words, but that had never stopped her before.

"What happened?" she asked.

And Seth ignored her.

"Okay, boys, that's it. You all did great, as usual, so after you turn out the lights and flip over the welcome mat, go grab yourself a couple'll quarts."

"Seth."

He finally looked at her and winked. "Oh, and bring her a quart, too . . . on the house. Something in a nice '83. But next time, baby, you don't work, you don't eat."

Next time? Hah! "So, are you going to answer me or not?"

Seth raised one eyebrow.

"About what happened to everybody?"

"Well, I guess most of 'em went home t'sleep or make breakfast for the husband and kids. Local jurisdiction says we can't stay open 24-hours so we always close down at dawn and open up again at —"

"Dawn?" Allison felt a tremor bore into the small of her back as she stood up. "What the hell are you talking about? I couldn't — I mean, it's only been . . . a couple of hours since I . . . . How long have I been here?"

Seth's smile widened. "Real time or *our* time?"

"Shit. You mean it's morning?"

"You can't even tell that much? Damn me, girl, you can't even feel it when the sun's up? Don't you feel it pricklin' your skin all the way down t'the bone?"

Oh, so *that's* what it was. She'd always thought it was just some sort of death-onset rash.

"I missed work."

It was something she'd never done before in her life — or death — but the statement met with a hardy round of whoops, hollers, and applause.

Damn Seth, Willie, LITTLE Willie, Slave # 4 said, *she's funny!*

Yeah, guess we'll keep her.

Allison glared at him. *Go to hell.*

Have, did and probably do it again if I'm lucky. "Now, you just hush up that pretty mouth of yours for a minute while me and the men talk, okay?"

That did it. "All right, you chauvinistic bastard, you listen to me!" She took a step forward and stumbled over the hem of the high-necked, floor-length black velvet gown she was suddenly wearing. Which was a very neat trick . . . considering she hadn't created it. "What the fuck is this?"

"We really are gonna have t'do something about that mouth of yours, darlin'," Seth said as the other *men* murmured in agreement. "I may have t'put up with breathin' cunts t'pay the bills, but I won't have my women actin' like sluts. But not t'worry, baby, I'm sure with a lit'l trainin' you'll become a perfect lady. Now, turn around and show off that pretty dress like a good girl."

"Ex-fucking-cuse me?"

Seth snorted and the dress tightened, crushing flesh and bone with a level of pain Allison had never experienced before. And hoped to hell she never would again. Dying had been easy compared to this.

One snap of his fingers, however, and the pain – and dress – were gone. She stood there, naked and trembling while the male vampires laughed.

"First secret, baby, on bein' a vampire," Seth said, "never talk back t'your Maker when he isn't play-actin'. Now –" The velvet dress was back, swirling around her like a storm cloud. "Show us how nice you walk, baby-doll."

"I thought . . . I was your Mistress."

Only during business hours. Now walk.

An invisible hand shoved her across the room as the dead men applauded. When Allison looked back Seth was smiling that same, sweet little boy smile that had first caught her attention through the testosterone-smoky haze and come-on lines of the Country Western bar where they'd first met. Wrong – where she'd been trying to anesthesize her premature mid-life crisis and ended up being his mid-meal snack.

"You lied to me," she said, going back to old familiar ground. "You said it would be different."

The invisible hand slipped off her back. "Oh hell . . . are you startin' this again?"

"But you did."

"Stop." And every muscle in Allison's body froze. *Uh-oh.* There were apparently a LOT more secrets to being a vampire that he wasn't going to tell her. "I never lied to you or any woman, living or dead, about what I promise. I don't have to. Now, I didn't lie to you, did I?"

Allison's head shook from side to side without her consent. *La-da-dee-dah bastard, la-dah.*

"Same way I didn't lie to you now, right."

Up and down. *Yes, master.*

"See there, now aren't you glad we had this discussion? Cleared the air between us, didn't it?"

Nod. Nod. Nod.

"That's my girl," Seth said, motioning for her to turn and walk away. "Now you're learnin'."

But she didn't turn and didn't walk away even though her body wanted to. Desperately. *No.*

"Pardon?"

"Let." "Me." "Go."

"My, my. She's a real fighter, ain't she?" Seth was smiling, making a joke of her disobedience – all for show. Allison had never seen him angry until now . . . and she decided she really could have waited another millennium for that privilege. Color the tone of a bruised plum slowly seeped up into his cheeks. It really didn't do much for him.

Or her, for that matter.

"Well, if it's a fight she wants. . . ." He said, still smiling, still joking as he started toward her.

Oh God – "Choo!"

Mica. She hadn't thought about him – or their wonderful Vampire-to-Watcher mental bond – for minutes . . . or hours, depending on the whole time dilation thing. He'd rescue her. He had to. That's what always happened in the movies!

Allison to Mica . . . come in Mica! HELP! S.O.S. Follow the sound of my . . . thoughts and get your hairy ass over here. And bring stakes! Mica! Yo, can you hear me?

Seth stopped in front of her and tapped the side of his head. "Sorry," he said, "but we're about twenty-five feet underground right here and that sort of blocks things. So, who's this Mica character?"

Allison tried to back up but her feet were glued to the spot. So she did the next best thing. She smiled and batted her lashes.

"Oh, he's just my Breather. I was just going to tell him to pack up my things and bring them out here. I've made up my mind."

Seth nodded and her velvet gown disappeared. "That's why you told him t'bring stakes?"

"Sure . . . why, don't you eat meat?"   She managed to confuse him for about a split-second – real time. Then he leaned forward and pierced her right nipple with his fangs. Icy waves of pleasure/pain ricocheted through Allison's body as the five male vampires moved in to watch. "Bu-but I can always have him bring something else. Mica's okay . . . for a watcher."

Seth's tongue left a slime-trail from breast to neck and she felt the atrophied flesh around her making wound suddenly gap open like the mouths of hungry baby birds.

"I'm sure he is," he said, "but isn't it hard living with a preacher?"

Allison felt another wave of ice as their eyes met.

"I told you, sweet thing, I followed you. You don't think I know all about that cozy little bungalow and the man you're living with?" He slipped his fangs into the wound and shuddered as if he'd just climaxed. *I know everything about you and him, baby . . . but you don't have a clue about what he's doing right now, do you?*

"What the hell are you talking about?"

"Hush, lit'l baby and don't say a word . . ." Seth kissed her cheek and stepped back as his band of Merry Deadmen pranced up. "Papa and the boys are gonna give you the bird. Stretch 'er, boys."

They surrounded her with smiles on their faces that went from ear to ear . . . literally. Allison knew screaming was a rather gauche thing for a vampire to do, but she did it anyway – even a dead woman had her limits. And Allison's limit was being hog-tied, hand and foot, by writhing, maggot-white tongues the size and shape of fire-hoses.

Her screams, however, turned to words – mostly Anglo-Saxon in nature and content – when the tongues tightened their grips and hoisted her off the ground to hang, spread-eagled between them like a fly caught in a spider's web.

"You mother-fucking, shit-eating, pussy-whipped perverts . . . let me go! You can't treat me like this!"

"Of course we can," Seth said, motioning the two men tongue-tied to her legs to spread them wider, "since you're the only pussy we seem to have, right now. A poor little pussy who needs to be whipped into shape."

Allison stopped struggling. "You try it and I'll rip your fucking head off."

"I do believe you'd try," he said, running a finger up her cunt from asshole to clit, "but I don't want to hurt you, honey . . . I just want t'give you a little tongue lashin' s'all. Rod, shut 'er up."

Another tongue wrapped itself over her mouth as Seth's

lower jaw broke away to reveal a tongue the color of oil.

That's what happens when they hang a man, he told her as his tongue uncoiled and slowly dropped toward her snatch. *My Maker turned me right there on the gallows tree. Remind me t'show you what I can do with my neck sometimes.*

Allison groaned as the tip of his tongue slipped between the folds of her vagina. Back when she was alive, it seemed that men were always in too much of a hurry to eat her . . . but that didn't seem to be a problem now.

Not now.

Time slowed down to a crawl.

And Mica crawled right along with it.

One agonizing step at a time.

If it hadn't been for his next-door neighbor who'd seen him slumped up against the *I-5/North* on-ramp sign and ladled him into her car, he would probably still be walking home.

And also wouldn't have noticed that Allison's black Mustang wasn't parked in its usual spot in the drive.

Fortunately, what his neighbor did notice was the missing car along with the bruises or bloodied nose, which saved him from having to lie about being mugged by a roving gang of bikers, and why he'd had to walk home. Mica had tried never to lie to his earthly father and he'd be damned (literally) if he'd lie to his Heavenly Father.

Besides, it just plain hurt to talk. Or think. Or move. So he did as little of all three as he limped across the barren front lawn. Especially the thinking part – he didn't want to think where Allison was or what she was doing. Or to whom.

All he wanted to do was take a couple of Codeine-laced Tylenol, washed down with a medicinal tequila chaser, and fall asleep.

An equal number of chasers later, Mica finally did fall

asleep and smiled as *the warm breeze rustled the tumbleweeds and the small wreath of pink roses and white carnations that Elena had selected for the cream-colored coffin . . . while a miniature neon "Desert Rose" logo flashed tastefully above the imported teak-wood stake that protruded through a hole in the curved lid. It was a closed casket service because Mica knew how vain Allison was. But he forgave her for it. After all . . . she was at rest now.*

Finally at rest.

Walking to the edge of the grave, Mica nodded to Alvis, conservatively dressed in a black sequined jump-suit, who immediately nodded to a little green alien, in matching jump-suit, holding a CD boom box. When the music started, Alvis sang "It's Now or Never" as Elena began tossing daisy chains around the protruding stake. And won a blue-suede teddy bear with silver dollar eyes.

The audience, made up of Allison's victims, cheered and instantly ascended into Heaven while Mica and Elena consummated their joy as Jesus Christ sulked nearby.

He hit a spiritual jackpot as he came – lights flashed, Jesus wept, bells rang and –

Mica's body reminded him of what he'd done to it when he jerked awake and reached for the phone next to the couch. Oh Lord, did it remind him.

"Ow- 'Lo?"

"Um, Hi. Um."

The voice was soft and light and utterly feminine. Mica's body didn't take kindly to the sudden increase in blood pressure.

"Elena?"

"Um, no. Um, is . . . um, Raven there?"

Not Elena. "No."

"Oh. Um. I'm Bridget and – hi, um. I work with Raven at the Trop and . . . um. Anyway, I'm supposed to, um, tell her to come in as soon as she can and, um, pick up her severance check. She never came in last night and, um, we're supposed to give 24-hour notice if we're not going to be, um, coming in. The new routine was kind of, um, ruined. You know."

"She never showed up?"

"Um, no. Could you tell her I'm, um, sorry and everything and that I'll, um, call her later? Oh, and I think they're hiring over at, um, *Excalibur* for serving wenches. Um. Pay's okay. Do you think she'd mind becoming a blond? I think they're looking for a, um, blond."

Blond, brunette, red head . . . what was hair color to a vampire.

"No, I don't think she'd mind," Mica said. "I'll give her the messages. Thanks."

"Um–"

Mica broke the connection, waited five seconds and dialed *The Rose.* When a semi-familiar voice answered, he told them that he was taking a sick day and hung up with an air of smug, self-satisfaction. Allison had gotten fired for just taking off . . . without notice to anyone . . . but not him. Not the newly appointed Younger Son of God. Not –

If she didn't go to work then where the hell was she?

❖

Still spread-eagled and dangling above the cavern floor, Allison sank her teeth into the tongue covering her mouth and grinned as Rod or Willie or maybe dear old Lance screamed in pain.

Whoever's tongue that was instantly undid itself and slipped away . . . unfortunately, the other two that had been holding her arms did the same and Allison suddenly found her top half on the floor and her bottom half still elevated. And thoroughly engaged.

What the hell are you doing? Pick her up.

Hell no! The voice echoing inside her head sounded higher pitched. *I'm not getting any where near her.*

Fuck that shit. You never said anything about her being able to hurt us.

Allison lifted herself to her elbows and looked into Seth's eyes. "Oh? You mean you've been keeping secrets from your boys as well?"

The tongues wrapped around her ankles slipped away, all but unnoticed until her legs, still facing east and west, respectively, hit the cavern floor with a cloud of . . . nothing.

Shut up, darlin'.

"What secrets is she talking about, Seth?" Lance asked.

Allison opened her mouth in a tight little *O*. "You mean you really didn't tell them?"

"Tell us what?"

Seth ignored the question as he withdrew his tongue and Allison ignored the popping sound it made when it left. The "boys" however weren't ignoring the silent exchange between them.

Don't play with me, little girl he thought at her.

Me? Never. I'm just a weak dead woman and you're a big, strong dead man.

His tongue lashed out and caught Allison around the throat, pulling her forward on her knees until the tip of her nose nestled amid his wire-tangled mass of pubic hair. She clamped her lips together.

That's right, baby, I am. So can you guess what I want you to do right now?

To help her out, just in case she couldn't guess, Seth's penis sprang up like a semaphore and caught her under the chin. Head snapping back, Allison had no choice but to look up at him.

Her Maker.

Bullshit.

"Seth?" Shaft this time, Allison recognized the smoggy L.A. quality of his voice. "What's she talkin' about?"

"Nothin'. Our little lady's just tryin' to be funny. Ain't that right, pun'kin?"

"Yep, that's right. Just being funny . . . same way Seth's been about telling you that vampires can only feel another vampire. Ain't that a hoot? Hah. Hah."

Unfortunately, the "boys" seemed to think so, since they laughed at the thought. Seth gave her a smug grin and fingered his cock. *Well, what'cha waitin' for?*

Christmas? she thought and bit him.

Seth's bellow of pain was multiplied by five as the male vampires each fell to their knees, hand pressed firmly over the phantom pain in their groins. Allison could only imagine the sensation, since, even without the right equipment, her clitoris was burning as if it'd been bee stung.

She'd almost managed to get to her feet when Seth, obviously made of sterner and more petrified stuff, picked her up and threw her across the room – straight toward one of the few real wall mounted torches.

Fire, she knew from watching movies, was un-discriminatory when it came to monsters. It'd eat anything.

FUCK!

Not till I'm healed, baby! his mind shouted after her. *But I don't think you'll be in much shape.*

NO! NOT LIKE THIS!

And time listened and slowed. Allison watched the flames wave back and forth slowly in front of her as she turned in mid-air and latched onto the limestone wall below the torch with her toes. Seth may have made fun of her trying to educate herself by watching movies, but she'd like to have seen him scramble along the ceiling using nothing but her fingers and toes.

No, on second thought she really wouldn't. She much rather watch Frank Langella.

See you boys later, she mind-whispered to the shaken crew below, *Oh, and Seth, try not to go off half-cocked again. It's undignified.*

Allison's mind was so shocked by the language that followed that she almost stopped laughing.

❖

If his watch was right, he'd been asleep for five hours when the doorbell rang. If the stiffness in his muscles was a more accurate gauge, then he'd been unconscious for at least five years. And possibly buried and dug up at least once during that time.

He hurt. He hurt so bad as he pushed himself off the couch and limped, whimpering, to the front door, that he doubted his Brother, Jesus, had suffered more pain on the cross. The big wuss.

The door bell *ding-donged* three more times before Mica even reached the foyer. The visitor was getting impatient. It was probably his Good Samaritan neighbor. He knew it wasn't Allison — and that was the only reason he was still shuffling toward the front door and not beating a less-than-hasty retreat out a back window. Allison wouldn't have knocked, even if she wanted to "surprise" him after discovering yesterday's bank transaction — she simply would have kicked the door down.

She was a dead woman of action.

That had been one of the things he thought he loved about her.

"Dad, You really let me screw up on that one," he said, eyes raised to the cracks in the ceiling as his hand closed around the door-knob. "You should have handled it better."

The Lord his Father should have handled a *lot* of things better — including sending a little celestial warning about what bright desert sunlight can do to post-lasered optic nerves that had been tenderized by a fist.

"Shit!"

When the fire went off behind his eyes, Mica's first thought was that Allison had come back while he was sleeping and turned him into a vampire.

"Oh God, John, what happened? Are you okay?"

It took some heavy rubbing to clear out the tears, but when he finally was able to see he still staggered back. In awe. The setting sun had made a golden halo around her dark head and Madonna-blue tennis dress.

"John?"

Mica blinked and the air snatched the last of the tears from his eyes and ruffled the slip of paper in her hand.

"I – I hope you don't mind, but I went back to the *Desert Rose* this morning, you know, to apologize about running out on you last night . . . I, ah, just figured it was better if I left – you know, before anything happened and your friend, you know the Elvis guy, he said you called in sick this morning." Elena looked down at the paper. "He gave me your address and, um, said for me to give you this."

She leaned forward, across the threshold, and kissed him on the cheek without looking up. The moment her lips brushed his bruised flesh, Mica felt a healing warmth rush through him. *So warm.* She smelled like honey-suckles, sunlight and Kung Po Chicken.

"There," she said, meeting his eyes as she stepped back. "Now you can tell him I gave you his message. The poor guy still looks upset about last night. He wasn't even dressed right, you know? He was wearing a suit, like the kind my daddy wore to work. There wasn't even sequins on the lapels, you know? I . . . God, listen to me jabber. I do that when I'm nervous. But are you okay? Did you get mugged or . . . oh shit, did your –

friend do this to you?"

"No. I just – I just put my big mouth where someone else's foot was. A couple of times." He tried to smile and winced at the effort. "Besides, Al – Raven didn't even come home last night."

"So, you're alone?"

Mica grunted in the affirmative and watched while she stuffed the slip of paper into the small belly-bag she had slung low on one hip.

"So, you gonna invite me in or what?"

"What?"

Elena giggled at the same time she slid in under his left arm.

"You're funny, John. Here, lean on me, I'm a lot stronger than you think. Do you want me to call a doctor or anything?"

He mumbled a negative tone.

"You sure? Well, okay. Gosh, John it's dark in here, but I guess it keeps it cooler, huh? Is the bedroom back through here?"

Mica stumbled into the wall as he turned to look at her. And Elena laughed.

"No, silly, I just thought you'd be more comfortable in there. It's okay, really. You get comfortable and I'll go find the bathroom and get you a cold washcloth. I think you're getting a black eye and that's supposed to help. You want a couple of aspirin, too? Okay. I'll take care of everything John, don't worry."

Mica wasn't worried. He watched her undo her belly-bag and toss it onto the top of Allison's coffin, before scurrying away on her errand of mercy. It was nice not to worry. Sighing, Mica pulled the wrinkled bedspread up over his shoulders and turned onto his side. She was so cute, so helpful and she *tossed her belly-bag on top of Allison's coffin!*

"Fuck!"

Muscles screaming and trailing the bed-spread behind him like some color co-ordinated mummy, Mica was half off the bed and reaching for the belly-bag when Elena came back into the room – a bottle of straight Tylenol and the water-filled toothbrush tumbler in her hands.

"You don't have any washcloths, you know that? What are you doing, John?"

She seemed much more concerned that he was standing up than she was that there was a cream-colored coffin in the room.

"I can explain about . . . that," he said.

"That?" Elena looked at the coffin and shrugged. "Hey, John, it's okay, really. I know a lot of guys who are into . . . you know, play-acting. And you know, not one of them is a mortician."

Mica's hands balled into fists. *She saw the coffin and she has to die.* What? *What do you mean what? She saw the coffin and she has to die.* Why? *Because you're a Watcher, asshole, remember? And that's what Watchers do, they protect their vampires.*

My vampire? Watcher? Yeah, a Watcher, like Gypsy. God, what has she done to me?

"You okay, John?" Elena said, trailing the bottle of Tylenol over the coffin's polished surface as she walked toward him. "You got all wonky again."

She saw. She'll figure it out. Kill her like the good little Watcher you are. Go on, make Mama proud.

Mica raised his hands.

"John? It really is okay, if you want to use the coffin, I mean. I really don't mind playing dead."

The spread fell as he grabbed her shoulders. "No. I've been playing with the dead too long. I need to feel a living body in my arms."

"Okay," she said, "but first —"

She fed him two Tylenol, one at a time, then held the tumbler against his lips until he'd completely drained the peppermint-flavored water. Smiling, she put the cup and bottle down next to her belly-bag and stopped his hand when he tried to knock them off. *Her hand was so warm.*

"It's okay," Elena whispered, "leave them."

"But," the Watcher part of his brain said, "it'll stain."

"Leave it," she repeated and lifted the hand she held to cup her left breast. The firm flesh beneath the thin material was so hot it burned his palm. *Oh Dad.* "I'm alive, John. Can you feel my heart beating?"

"Shit, yeah."

"Your . . . friend doesn't deserve someone like you, John. You don't need a woman who likes to pretend she'd dead."

"She's not pretending."

Elena pressed his hand harder against her breast. "She's that frigid?"

"Petrified."

"I'm so sorry, John. But it's okay . . . I'm here now."

She reached around behind her and the tennis dress fell to the floor. She wasn't wearing any panties and the thought of her, standing on his front porch with the hot desert wind teasing the short skirt . . . lifting the hem so anyone, everyone could see . . .

Suddenly dizzy, Mica pitched forward and landed face-first against her breast. Her nipple hardened against his tongue and she moaned. Lacing her fingers into his too-short hair, Elena lifted herself onto her toes.

"Oh yes, John. You needed someone who's not afraid to be alive. I'm alive John. Feel me? Feel how alive I am."

His hands took the hint and glided down her *warm* little back to cup the firm globes of her ass. But they didn't stay there long. Following the line of her hips, his hands slid down her flat belly and softly, gently parted the soft tuft of hair. *Warmer . . . warmer . . . you're getting hot. Hotter. You're almost there. Getting hotter. YOU'RE BURNING UP!*

Mica's groan joined hers as he slipped two fingers into her. She was already dripping wet and ready. Wanting him. Wanting him inside her.

Thank You Father!

His cock was already testing the strength and durability of the jeans material when Elena pushed him down on the bed. His hands were shaking so hard he couldn't get his belt undone.

"Here," she said, "let me."

Her heat soaked into him as she undressed him, slowly reawakening every fiber of his body. He shivered each time her fingers caressed him, each time her warm, living flesh broke another chunk of ice off his soul.

Among other things.

"You don't have to worry, John," she said as she straddled him, pulling her lips wide to accommodate him. "I'm healthy. I always make my customers wear something . . . but not you . . . I want to feel you inside me, John. And I want you to feel me. Is that okay? Can I, John? Okay?"

Mica brushed the hair away from her face. She was still so much a child, asking permission to fuck him. He fell in love with her at that moment and realized that he'd never truly been in love before.

Ever.

"No," he said and soothed the worried look on her face as he reversed their positions, "let me."

As much as he wanted to plunge into her, Mica wanted to taste her more . . . and it was worth it. There was no rotten fish taste, no stench of decaying meat. Elena smelled like ivory soap and tasted like honey-cured ham – sweet and salty and warm.

Mmm, his favorite.

It'd been a while (longer than he liked to think about, actually), but he could tell by her squeals and shuddering spasms that Elena had already come once and was heading for number two.

"Put it in me!" She panted, grabbing a handful of his beach-boy bleached hair as a handle to drag him up into position. "PUT IT IN ME NOW! OH GOD, OH GOD, PUT IT IN. NOW!"

She said the sweetest things.

"Okay, baby," he whispered and only bit the inside of his cheek a little when her hand fell away and took a dozen strands with it. "Ouch. Okay."

Mica took a deep breath as he kneed her legs apart. *It's now or never, Mica.* Which he probably shouldn't have thought, since he found himself mentally listening to Alvis's rich baritone croon that exact song as he plunged into her.

Elena's scream of pleasure knocked the song right out of his head.

Lord! I mean Dad! This is . . . Mica . . . hard as . . . steel. OH LORD, thank You for showing me Your will. DAD! You are so good . . . and hot . . . and ohmyGOD, now I know this is right. This is good. I fell, Lord . . . Dad, but You picked me up and held me . . . tight, so fucking tight, that I knew I was . . . was coming to . . . You. I, Oh God . . . I'll get back to You in a minute, okay?

Then, setting a pace that would have driven a rabbit into coronary arrest, Mica slammed into her only to meet an equal force slamming back. The Lord, his Father's, message couldn't be any clearer – this was meant to be. Elena was to be his Eve on this, the first day of his rebirth.

As the true living Son of God.

"Say Hallelujah!"

"H-h-h-h-" Elena tried to say it, but couldn't seem keep

enough air in her lungs.

Mica forgave her and drove himself into her up to the hilt. Her legs wrapped around his spine and added another inch he didn't even know he had. She was helping now, grabbing onto his hips and helping as best she could.

Not that he needed it. The Holy Ghost was moving through him just fine, but, damn, it felt good.

"Oh, YES, Lord —" He knew his Dad didn't want him using the family name in vain. "I understand and accept Your offer. For I am MICA, Your ever-LOVING servant and son. SAY Amen and PRAISE Your name, oh Heavenly Savior and Father All Mighty, hallowed be THY name . . . Oooooooooooohhhhh GOD!"

That was another benefit of being the Lord's son — he couldn't remember ever coming harder or longer . . . or with more selfless clarity.

It felt as if his entire insides had shot out his cock and filled Elena with his mortal remains while the Lord refashioned him in His image.

"Well, well, well." A voice. An all too familiar voice said.

Both of them turned and Mica felt his entire sack do a quick one-eighty back into his pelvic girdle at the same time Elena screamed and buried her face against his chest.

Naked, bald and sunburned to the point of weeping blisters, Allison stood watching them from the doorway.

"Having fun, kiddies?" she asked.

CHAPTER 13

After a prolonged screaming fit, the little Chicana jumped out of the bed and moved like she had a lightning rod up her ass and a storm was a'comin'. It was an impressive sight to behold and if her hands hadn't been burned down to the nubs, Allison would have applauded the performance. Instead, she just tapped the unburned sole of one foot impatiently and watched the girl shimmy/squirm back into a tacky dress.

Guess I know why you didn't kill her, Watcher. If she'd had an eyebrow left, she would have raised it when Mica looked away, shame-faced. *I knew I should have replaced you. Breathers, shit, what a waste of air.*

"And here I thought you were just a passionless little prick. Guess all you needed was a different starter motor, huh?" She tried to smile and felt half her incinerated cheek fall off. The girl shrieked. "So, are you going to invite me to your party or no?"

The girl paled to white. Mica darkened to green.

"Stop it, Allison," he said when he could.

"Don't you mean Raven? Oh, and where are my manners?"

Walking stiff-legged to keep the bubbled flesh on the back of her legs and ass from going the way of her cheek, Allison hobbled up next to her coffin and held out her hand. What was left of her hand. She might let bygones be bygones and even forgive the fact that he hadn't killed the girl when she'd first seen the coffin, if only Mica, in all his shriveled naked glory, hadn't pulled the girl back behind him.

Protecting the little whore from her.

Allison lowered her hand. "I'm Raven d'Nuit. Ex-lover and soon to be ex-roomie."

Mica gagged when her left butt cheek hit the floor. "Jesus, Allison."

She sneezed and her right butt cheek joined its twin. Allison avoided rubbing her nose.

"Sorry," he said, "I didn't mean to . . . I'm sorry."

Allison wasn't sure if he was sorry about making her sneeze or about the girl or . . . . She picked up the toothbrush holder with her palms and glared at the pale blue ring it left behind on her coffin. She didn't care what he was sorry for, only that he sounded as though he was in as much pain as she felt.

Which wasn't very likely.

In her blind-panic to de-ass the *Stud Farm* (and Seth) she'd forgotten that her extra supply of sun-screen was in the Mustang's glove compartment. And that time had continued doing its "funny thing" while Seth and the boys worked her over.

It was the first time she'd seen daylight in almost a year – and the reunion wasn't a pleasant one even though the sun was almost set.

Trying to stick to the long, wind-blown shadows hadn't done much good. The blood-red orb had scalded her flesh almost down to the bone and instantly raised blood-filled blisters over the rest of her. It was final-stage skin cancer gone wild.

The sun-screen had stopped any further damage and the thick smoke that rose from the stubble field of her scalp did provide an adequate cover, should any of their more nosy

neighbors be watching, as she sprinted, smoldering and bare-
buck-naked, from the driveway to front door.

Without thinking, she rubbed her forehead and it came
away in pieces against the side of the toothbrush holder. *Shit.*
Mica made a wet little sound in the back of his throat and
closed his eyes. The girl, much to her credit, looked like she was
about to throw up, but kept her eyes open.

Allison tossed the crisped skin-covered tumbler to the bed
and watched Mica pull the girl away.

Yeah, just imagine the cooties you could get from that. She
looked pointedly at the dark-eyed senorita. *Or that.*

"Allison, for G–"

"Stop." She backed out of the room in a slow shuffle
because it took less muscles than turning around. "Look, I'm
going downstairs. You and Miss Tijuana here are welcome to
stay and fuck until your dick falls off, okay? I'm the open
minded sort, you know. A fact which, if I hadn't stopped you
from saying something, you would have found that out for
yourself."

"Jes–"

"Save it . . . okay? Oh, and it was nice meeting you, miss.
Please stop by again, the door is always open. Much like your
legs. Ta."

The girl mumbled something in Spanish as Allison
stumbled down the hall. The whole scene would have been
very moving, very dramatic . . . if both her breasts hadn't
decided to drop off. She left them there, smoldering enough to
set off the smoke detectors.

Even in death, life sucked.

And it just wasn't fair.

❖

"Oh God, John. Oh God, John. Oh God, John."
Elena kept repeating that as though she was counting off

Rosary beads. That and the occasional muffled sob had been the only things Mica had managed to get out of her while he hurriedly dressed and escorted her out of the house. There'd been a brief change in cadence – "Oh, God John. Oh, God John. Oh, God John." – when they found a steaming chunk-o-Allison on the front step. She didn't calm down or go silent until they reached the Bus Stop at the end of the block.

"I'll call you," Mica promised as the bus pulled up. "What's your number?"

Silence.

"No, better yet – you call me at the *Rose* and leave a message, okay?"

Silence.

"Okay. Just leave me a message when you're feeling better and tell me where I can meet you." Mica kissed her gently on the lips as the driver watched. "It's going to be okay, Elena, I swear on my Father. He's watching over us and He won't let anything happen. Not now."

Her big eyes blinked once. Slowly. Mica took it as a sign that she was listening.

"That's right," he said as if she'd been holding up her side of the conversation, "He won't let anything happen to us. And . . . um, about my friend . . . don't worry about how she looks. She's studying to be a Fire-Breather for *Cirque du Solie* and she's not real good at it yet. But she heals fast. Really."

Elena nodded. "Oh. God. John."

"Yo, buddy," the driver called out through the open doors. "I got a schedule to keep, y'know? Anybody getting on?"

Mica dug a wrinkled dollar out of his jeans and shoved it into Elena's hand as he pushed her on board.

"It's fine. Really. A little cold cream and she'll be as good as new. Get some rest and then call the *Rose*."

Elena's head was nodding as she shoved the dollar into the

fare box. But she looked a little less pale when she turned around.

"You're going to be okay, Elena. I – I love you."

"Wh-what did you say, John?"

"I said –"

The doors closed with a *whoosh* and Mica could hear the driver shouting – "Hey, lady . . . exact change." – as the bus pulled away.

"– I love you, Elena."

There. He said it. And it felt good. It felt right. After eight months of living in a nightmarish fantasy land, it felt great to finally say something *REAL*. Mica stood on the curb and waved the bus out of sight.

"I love you, Elena," he shouted to the vapor trail.

Well, whoop-de-do.

Mica turned around and saw his Brother, Jesus, leaning up against the street-lamp. The yellow sodium light hissed as it came on and cast a bilious glow down upon the Lord's First Born.

"What's your problem, Bro?"

Jesus shrugged one shoulder under his sack-cloth and pretended to clean his nails with one of the thorns from his crown. *You think it's going to be that easy? What about the other one?*

"What other one?"

For an answer, Jesus opened his mouth to reveal two, blood-tipped fangs.

"Oh, that other one."

When he walked past the street lamp, Jesus was gone.

"Hey, it's not going to be that bad, right Dad? I mean, with You by my side, there's nothing We can't do . . . and this is nothing. Not really. I mean, people break up every day, right? Besides, she knew it wasn't going to be a long-term commitment. How could it be? We're from two different worlds. I like anchovies on my pizza and she's dead. It could never work out. Right?"

Mica thought he heard both the Son and Holy Ghost giggle.

"I believe in the Father, Creator of Heaven and Earth and she's . . . dead. I know my place in Heaven is assured and she's . . . dead. I'll have an eternity of bliss and . . . Ah, the hell with it, Dad, You know what's going on. You always have. Even when You didn't say anything. Amen."

Mica took a deep breath of the clean desert night as he opened the front door. The dark, silent house was filled with a thin gray-white mist and the scent of rancid barbecue.

His stomach puckered up into a knot.

"Okay, Dad, here We go. Nothing can stop Us now."

He hoped.

❖

By the time he stopped pacing back and forth overhead and finally decided to face her, new skin was already beginning to form beneath the charred patches. And it itched like hell. The only other time Allison could remember feeling the same creeping, crawling burning tickle was when she and "Tricky-Ricky" Finn had discovered each other in a lovely patch of poison oak, one summer night at Camp Hi-Hill in the Sierra Madras mountains. Of course, then the itch had been localized to only her back, butt and the bottoms of both feet.

Allison peeled off a long strip of southern-fried flesh from her forearm and vigorously scratched the smooth white flesh underneath. As nice as the new skin looked, she doubted she'd recommend charring as a legitimate beauty aid.

When he reached the bottom step, Allison sneezed – as carefully as possible – and pulled a handmade Amish quilt around her. She was just a little embarrassed about the prepubescent size of her reforming breasts. He may have seen her beaten and bloodied, humiliated and nearly incinerated, but she was not about to let him see her flat-chested. Especially not now.

It was over and she was going to tell him that. Hail and farewell, O Breather Mine. It's been fun, a lot of laughs . . . so don't let the door hit you in the ass when you leave.

If I let you leave.

All the reconstruction had left her feeling drained to the point of being dizzy, even after having finished off the last of her tainted blood packs. Six quarts of the fresh stuff would really take the edge off right about –

"Ah-ch-IT!"

"Bles– sorry."

Allison grunted and leaned back against an antique Fainting Couch and modestly covered her legs. And sneezed. *Shit!* She glared him to a stop before he got any closer. Something was different about him. Something besides having just gotten laid.

"Have you been eating garlic bagels again, Milo?"

He seemed shocked that she'd use his real name, but recovered quickly and shook his head as he held up a white plastic shopping bag. "No. I, uh, I found something of yours on the . . . Do you need it?"

"No. Whatever it is will grow back, if it hasn't already." She nodded to the wastepaper basket next to her desk. "But thanks for asking."

"No problem." He didn't say anything until he dumped her body part. "Allison, last night –"

"Yeah, I should have called, but the show didn't go as well as we'd hoped so the director had us pull a couple of extra rehearsals. One of the girls, Bridget, has a place near-by so I just stayed there. We slept most of the day and then I forgot about sun-screen and . . . . "

What the hell am I doing? I don't need to explain anything to him. He's not my father. Fuck, he's not even a decent Watcher.

But for some reason, she still couldn't stop herself.

". . . it was a good thing Bridget went shopping or she would have seen me and −"

"Bridget called this morning. You were fired for not showing up last night. Sorry."

"Oh."

"So where were you?"

"Excuse me?"

He took a step closer and crossed his scrawny arms over the members of KISS on his T-shirt. Allison sneezed into the quilt. *Fuck, what the hell is going on?*

"I asked you where you were. And I think after all we've been through you owe me an answer."

Allison laughed and ran a hand through her Demi Moore *GI-Jane* buzz cut. "I don't owe you anything, Breather."

"The fuck you don't."

"Wow, the little mouse found himself a new set of balls? Or did humping little Miss Chili-Spice give you a death wish? Honey, I don't even owe you your life, so cut the attitude before I cut your throat."

His all-too-human face became unappetizingly pale, but he wasn't backing down and that bothered her a bit.

"I need to know where you were last night, Allison."

"Sure, why not. I was with . . ." *Shit, what do I call them?* ". . . friends."

"And how many of them are still alive?"

She smiled. It was so much easier not to have to lie. "Not a one."

Allison jumped, shedding another few layers of burned skin and body parts, when Mica suddenly lifted his hands toward the ceiling and invoked the name of . . . the guy upstairs.

Sort of.

"Oh Father, did you hear that? She killed them all. Please, Dad, oh Heavenly Host All Mighty, find those poor souls and take them into your light. Praise be thy–"

STOP IT!

He stumbled back a few feet as if she'd cold-cocked him, but he stopped.

"Don't do that again. Besides, I didn't kill anyone. They were dead a long time before I showed – oops."

I shouldn't have said that. Allison wondered what the penalty for divulging vampiric secrets was.

"Just forget what I said, okay?"

"Forget?" Mica backed up until he'd reached the basement stairs. "Are you telling me there are more of . . . *you* here in Las Vegas?"

"Shit, no."

"Liar. Oh, my God."

Ah-CHHHHHHOOOOOOOOO!

"Crap, you've got your freakin' faith back." *Ah-choo. Ah-choo. Ah-fuck.*

"You did this," he said, gripping the banister so hard Allison could hear the wood creak beneath his hands. "You brought the plague of death with you. Harlot of hell. God help us."

Sneeze. "Knock it off, they were here before we showed . . . . " *I've got to learn to shut up.*

"There are more of you? So that's why we came here, so you could be with your own kind?"

"If I wanted to be with my own kind I would have stayed in L.A. and hung out with lawyers."

They glared at each other until Mica broke the silence.

"Fuck you. I'm leaving."

"What?"

"I'm leaving you, you unholy bitch. I just came down here to tell you that."

"*You're* leaving *me?*" *No, that wasn't right.* She *was supposed to kick* him *out.* "What the hell are you talking about? You can't do that, you're my God–" *Ah-choo!* "– damned Watcher!"

"Then watch me do this."

The quilt slipped to the floor when Allison stood up. The bastard had actually turned his back on her and was walking up the stairs. Shit, the little bitch had given him balls after all.

Stop.

And he did, rather abruptly. "Let me go."

The words sounded too familiar – as did the situation. Allison released her control and watched him look at her over his shoulder.

"That's the only power you have over me, Allison. It's over. I'm leaving."

"Fine," she said, "go off to your little whore and let me know what growing old is like, okay?"

He walked up the rest of the stairs before stopping. "I know I should put you out of your misery and give your soul peace, but if you promise that you . . . and your kind won't bother me and Elena, then I won't bother you."

"I'm touched, Mica. Really."

"But if you come after us, I swear to God, my father, I will kill you. Goodbye."

It took almost all the strength Allison had, but she kept herself from sneezing . . . and only ruptured a minor organ doing so.

Following the sound of his footsteps with her eyes, she tracked him from basement to bedroom, and then from bedroom to living room. He stopped there to make a phone call – she could hear his muffled voice through the lathe-and-plaster-and cobwebs. He was calling someone, probably the little twitch. Even her Preacher Boy wouldn't be stupid enough to call the cops on her.

He couldn't. He was wanted in California just like her . . . and she somehow doubted that the Las Vegas police would be any more open to the idea of having vampires in their midst that the Hollywood police had been.

Besides, re-established zealot or not, Mica had himself a brand-new little honey and wouldn't want to take the chance of being separated from her for twenty-five to life.

He was moving again, from living room to front door. And from front door to out of her life.

Good riddance.

Bad rubbish.

And all that.

"Allison? There's one more thing I want to tell you." His voice already sounded too far away to answer. "God bless you, Allison."

She sneezed and blew her nose across the room where it crushed itself into a pulpy lump against the King Tut CD-case.

Upstairs someone chuckled just before the front door closed.

"Thith," she said.

Even though the sun was hidden behind the western mountains and the temperature had dropped a digit, it was still hot enough to soak Mica's T-shirt all the way through. He hadn't bothered to change out of his huarache sandals and into more substantial shoes before leaving the bungalow, and his toes were covered in an inch of warm dust by the time he trudged the quarter mile of dirt road from the Bus Stop to the front of Alvis's double-wide trailer. The swarm of moths that had been circling the porch light, momentarily broke formation when the two Army Surplus duffle bags that he'd packed with most of his earthly processions – consisting mainly of underwear and bowling shirts – hit the ground on either side of the smiling "thin Elvis" *Welcome* mat.

His shoulders felt like he'd been carrying anvils and he suddenly had a greater understanding of what Moses and the Israelites went through when they fled Egypt. He'd only packed enough stuff to show Allison he really meant it and planned, once he got to the *Rose* to ask Alvis to drive him back, for the other essentials, like the big-screen TV and bed.

It was a good plan, and would have worked perfectly . . . if Alvis had been there. When Mica started asking about his friend, the night manager pulled him aside and clapped him on the back like he was an old friend instead of a worthless employee.

"I sent your fucking friend home. To fucking rest, you know. I mean, shit, just between you and me, that fucking friend of yours has gone totally fucking ape-shit about losing the fucking contest, you know. I mean, I'm really fucking sorry it happened, we all are, but fuck me hard it's not like it only fucking happened to him. I mean, we've got to change all the fucking "Get married by the KING of the Elvis Impersonators" advertisements, right? Unless you think the new fucking winner is gonna want to fucking work here, which doesn't seem fucking likely. And I fucking told him that. And then you know what he fucking said? He starts fucking telling people about how he really fucking is Elvis and how these fucking little green men fucking kid-napped him. I mean, fuck! Pardon my language, but shit, you know what I'm fucking saying? Your fucking friend is a fucking genius. I told him to fucking go home early and get some fucking rest because I fucking want him early tomorrow so we can fucking fit him for a fucking space suit. This'll be bigger than anything any of the other fucking wedding

chapels got. I mean, fucking think about it — couples can fucking get married by a fucking alien abductee. It's fucking fantastic, isn't it?"

Mica might have thought so if he knew that Alvis would never have told anyone (besides his best friend Johnny) about being an abductee unless he was drunk or stoned or suffered a compete mental breakdown . . . and since Mica had never seen his friend score anything harder than beer, he knew there was something wrong.

And the worry didn't go away when he called Alvis's number and only got *"Ah-huh. Leave a message an' ah'll get back t'yah. Thank yah. Thank yah verah much."*

There was something terribly wrong with his friend.

Mica took a deep breath of the mimosa scented air and felt the hair stand up on his arms.

It was just too quiet, even for a barren plot of land stuck out in the middle of the desert. It took a moment, but he finally realized why — the trailer/mobile home's massive swamp cooler wasn't running.

There was nothing that Mica knew of that could survive the sweltering desert heat.

Nothing alive, that is.

Mica's stomach knotted itself into a tiny ball as the memory of his landlady in Hollywood — sweet Mrs. B and what she'd been turned into — came back to haunt him. He'd been responsible for that . . . just like he was responsible for whatever had happened to Alvis.

"God, Lord . . . Dad, she wouldn't have. Not to Alvis. I know she never really liked him, but . . . she wouldn't have. Would she?"

What do you think, Bro?

Jesus was standing at the far end of the trailer, the hem of His robe up around His waist as He peed into a sagebrush.

Hell, she stayed out all night, right, and then tried to lie about it, didn't she? Damn, boy, open your eyes and smell the pork roast. She came out here and partied hardy with Alvis so you could walk right into a trap.

"You think?"

Jesus shook off the last few drops of Holy Water and rolled His eyes. *Would I lie to you, little brother?*

Mica would have felt better if He hadn't started laughing as He ascended.

"Okay, here we go. I am Mica, my Father's man and I always have been!" He'd shouted the last few words and the silence that followed was deafening. If Alvis was still alive . . . and unchanged he would have come out to see what was going on. "Guess that's my answer. You ready, Dad?"

His Heavenly Father sent a sign that He was in the form of a tiny brown bat that swooped through the deepening twilight above Mica's upturned face and pooped right on the cross-shaped scar. It was the greatest sign of divine love that he had ever received.

Mica rubbed the warm, runny guano into his hair and smiled. "Thanks, Dad. Okay, here we go."

Legs shaking with fatigue (not fear) and the hairs prickling the back of his neck (with the Lord's Own Excitement), he looked through the shadows for anything that could be used as a weapon. Not that he questioned his Dad's protection or power, Lord knows he did, but a nice thick stake would go so *good* right about now.

Unfortunately, there seemed to be a decided lack of wood and wood by-products in Alvis's particular section of desert. The only thing Mica found was a thin, sun-bleached bamboo pole that was stuck into the ground next to a dead tomato plant. He didn't know if bamboo was considered wood or not and he really didn't much care. It felt like wood and that was enough for him.

The stick whistled through the air as he yanked it out of the ground. And that was a good sign, too.

"This should work," he said and took a couple of practice swings against another dead plant – beans he thought – and the dessicated tendrils exploded on contact. "Yeah. This'll do just fine."

The stick may not be big enough to send Alvis to eternal rest, but Mica sure as hell could switch the devil out of his friend's body. Oh yes, indeed.

"For I am Mica," he said, wiping some of the Holy Bat Doo that was still on his fingers onto the bamboo. "Strong as the stone that bears my name. Alvis is . . . was, and always will be my friend and I shall not fail him. He may have fallen into the pit, but with Your help he can be saved and brought back into the light."

"Ah-men."

Mica turned around slowly, both hands gripping the bamboo stick like it was a samurai sword. Alvis was standing in the open doorway of his trailer, bathed in the warm glow of the porch light as though nothing was wrong. Stark naked.

Except for a pair of oversized sunglasses.

It was not a pretty sight.

"Ah do appreciate yore prayers, Johnny," he said, "but yah don't haffa worry. Ah'm feelin' much better now."

Mica tightened his grip. "Yeah?"

"Yeah. Ah just been sittin' here thinkin' and ah think this was the Lord's way a'tellin' me it's time t'move on."

"Blasphemer. Don't you dare say my Father did this to you."

Alvis's eyebrows lifted above the rim of the sunglasses. "Ah didn't say he did, Johnny. Ah'm just sayin' that ah got me a little over ego-tized and the Lord swatted me down. And ah deserved it, Johnny, ah truly did."

The tip of the stick trembled as Mica walked toward the trailer. "No, Alvis, no one deserved what happened to you."

Alvis sighed and scratched his dangle-balls. "Wish ah could b'lieve that, Johnny, ah surely do. But ah did wrong by comin' back and tryin' t'pick up where ah left off. Ah shoulda been happy just t'let it pass, like all things must. But ah got greedy. Praise the Lord for His justice, Johnny – He's hard, but He's fair."

"Yeah," Mica said and Alvis nodded in agreement.

"Yeah. Ah wanted t'stay the King even though mah lit'l alien friends warned me that ah shouldn't. The past's the past, they said, and shouldn't be haul'd into the present. They kept sayin' how everyone knows ah'm dead . . . even those folks who keep seein' me pump gas and bus tables. They said ah should get on with mah life as it is now. But ah couldn't let it go . . . all the bright lights n'stuff."

Alvis leaned against the doorjamb and took a deep breath, his middle-aged man-breasts, though well defined, jiggling just a bit as they settled. Mica mentally picked a spot between them. It was going to be an upward thrust, difficult even if they'd been the same size, but if he got lucky, the bamboo stick would slide in fast and hit the heart before his poor, dead ex-friend knew what hit him.

Praise be.

"Ah wanted mah cake and to eat it, too, but like ah said, ah guess this is just the Lord's way a'tellin' me it's finally time. The King is dead, Johnny . . . long live th' new King."

Mica felt tears well up in his eyes as he looked up at his friend. Alvis, despite having been turned into an unholy, soulless atrocity to all that was good and pure, was telling him to stake him . . . to put him out of his potentially endless suffering.

"Amen, Alvis," Mica said as he lifted the stick. "Your suffering will be over soon."

"Huh?"

"It's okay," he promised. "Just close your eyes."

"Why?"

Mica swallowed the lump in his throat and lifted the bamboo into shoving position.

"So I can put you out of your misery."

Alvis caught the stick a half-inch away from his heart with one hand and pulled off his glasses with the other. There were tears in his eyes, too.

"Ah thought yah'd be different, Johnny, but ah guess mah mama, God bless er, was right after all. She said the minute yah stop bein' on top would be the minute yah'd find out who yer real friends were. And who yer real friends weren't. Ah thought yah were a friend, John. Ah didn't think yah'd forsake me just cause ah lost the competition."

Shaking his head sadly, Alvis slipped the glasses back on and let go of the stick as he stepped back into the trailer. *He's getting away.*

"DIE MONSTER!"

Shouting a combination Rebel yell/Lord's prayer at the top of his lungs, Mica charged into the dimly-lit trailer. And froze. Not literally, since the stuffy air inside the metal and press-board box felt like it was well into the three digits, but . . . stuck in mid-lunge.

"Lord, boy," Alvis said as he slipped into a black-silk kimono embroidered with silver flying saucers and little green men. "What happened to yer face? You get beat up?"

Mica could only shift his eyes around wildly and blink.

"Oh, sorry. Here, lemme fix that."

Alvis picked up a TV remote and clicked it. Mica collapsed into a heap on the avocado-green linoleum, the would-be stake snapping in half under him.

"Ah forgot t'turn off the defense grid cause ah didn't think ah'd need it. It only reacts when ah'm in danger. So why were yah gonna stick me with that?"

Mica groaned as he pushed himself up into a sitting position. It felt as if a million ants were crawling over his skin.

"Vampire."

"Say what?"

"You. Allison turned. Vampire. Must release your. Soul."

Alvis closed the kimono with a red satin tie and cinched it down. "Ah think yore still a might scrabbled up top. Come with me and ah'll fix yah right up."

Mica shook his head and tried to crawl back into the slightly less-muggy night, only to feel himself plucked from the floor and tossed over Alvis's broad shoulder like he was a dish-rag.

"N-n-n-no . . . Fa-fa-father help . . . me."

"Hush now, Johnny. Yah mighta hurt mah feelin' a bit, but that don't mean ah can't take care'a yah."

Oh Lord, help me! Help Your son. Father? Brother? MAMA!

"Stop yore squirmin'," Alvis told him as he swatted him lightly on the rump. "Ah'm likely t'add t'them bruises on yore face if ah drop yah."

As if he'd listen to a vampire. Squirming, kicking, wiggling . . . Mica latched onto every piece of Elvis memorabilia that looked sturdy enough to become a weapon or hand-hold. Lord knows there was enough of it scattered around the inside of the trailer, but nothing he could use to free himself from the merciless grip of the pompadoured dead man. Posters and old-fashioned LP albums covered the walls and ceiling. Elvis lamps and decanters and Valentine boxes littered the faux-fur couches and blue-suede carpet. Oversized cardboard cutouts of

The King stood silent guard at the windows and doors.

Mica did manage to grab a porcelain music box and was coming in with a wide, arching back-swing when his arm and shoulder froze.

"Ah told you, Johnny," Alvis said as he took the box and carefully set it on the lap of an *Official Elvis 'I Wanna Be Your Teddy Bear' Teddy Bear.* "Now, knock it off fore ah get mad and leave yah t'yore bruises."

"Alvis, it's not too late," Mica said when his arm was returned to him. "Please, let me kill you so your soul can be at rest."

Mica felt Alvis's shoulders tighten under his belly. "It was just a contest, son. Ah think ah will get over it without havin' to resort t'that."

"God, she must have just turned you. Listen, please . . . 'And you being dead through your trespasses and the uncircumcision of your flesh –'" *Not that I check, Dad.* "–'you did He make alive together with him.'Colossians 2:13."

Mica waited for Alvis to sneeze, just like Allison did when he started preaching and was a little disappointed when Alvis only belched. But he still took it as a good sign. *Maybe it was different for male vampires.*

"Yes, that's right, Alvis. Listen, 'Even dead through our trespasses made us alive together with Christ.'" *There You go, Bro.*

"Ephesians 2:5," Alvis answered. "Okay, your turn – 'For ours is not a conflict with mere flesh and blood, but with the despotism, the empires, the forces that control and govern this dark world, and the spiritual hosts of evil arrayed against us in the heavenly warfare.' Huh?"

Mica's mouth fell open. It wasn't possible . . . vampires couldn't do that. Could they?

"And here ah thought yah knew just bout every verse by

heart." Alvis chuckled and Mica's teeth clicked together from the ride. "Ephesuans 6:12. That was one of mah mama's favorites. Now, here's one yah'll get easy. 'For by grace have ye been saved through faith; and–"

"Stop it! Look, I'm sorry you're a vampire and I'm sorry your soul is now damned for all eternity, but you will NOT fuck around with the words of the Lord, my Father. Okay? I thought I'd be used to anything you blood suckers could do, but not this. This I won't stand for. Do you hear me?"

The sound of his voice was still echoing through the trailer when Alvis leaned forward and set him down. Mica squared his shoulders and felt about a tablespoon of courage begin trickling down the inside of his leg.

Alvis pulled off his glasses and tossed them aside. "Vam'par?"

"Uh, yeah." Mica tried to swallow only to find he was scared spitless. "I really am sorry Allison killed you and turned you into the living dead, but you know how women are. Now, if you have a nice solid piece of wood, a dowel or something like that, I can kill you and release your soul before the need to drink blood becomes overwhelming and you . . . you know. And I promise to put in a good word for you with my Dad. He'll understand, I'm sure."

"Um, Johnny?"

"Y-yeah?"

"Ah think there's a couple things yah need to know."

"Y-y-yeah?"

"First off, ah ain't a vam'par."

"No?"

"Not even a little. But ah think we really need t'talk bout summin'." Nodding his head as if he'd just answered a question, Alvis tossed an arm over Mica's shoulder and pulled him into the master bath's purple-and-black shower stall.

"Oh God, Alvis, no. I'm not like that!"

Hands clamped firmly over his ass-hole, Mica managed to recite almost two full (and quick) verses of *The Lord's Prayer* before a deep rumbling vibrated through the soles of his feet and the shower stall slowly descended beneath the floor boards.

The last thing Mica saw before the lights went out was Alvis winking at him.

"Yah ain't seen nuthin' yet."

And the night settled down to a dull roar.

CHAPTER 14

By midnight all of Allison's skin had grown back, although her eyebrows were still popping in – one at a time – and it was driving her nuts. So much so that she'd gotten into her "Private Reserve/Emergency Supply": Pig's blood mixed with everclear. She'd received it as a gift from one of her Goth admirers, a tall, soft-spoken young man who told her he'd created the drink for one of their Masquerades, then shyly admitted that no one'd had the nerve to try it.

Which was just as well, Allison decided as she poured another glass from the skull-shaped decanter. The blood had gone rancid and the grain alcohol had tripled in strength, and would have either killed a Breather outright, or rendered him blind.

The only thing it gave Allison was a bad case of hiccups.

But it did manage to take her mind off certain things, like wanting to scratch her newly-reformed, overly-sensitive new skin down to the bone.

Or pulling her hair out a strand at a time.

Or that she still didn't have enough energy reserve to fabricate silk lounging pajamas and had to settle for plain imaginary cotton.

So the evening wasn't a *total* loss.

–hic–

She'd counted 456,982,873,223,012 hiccups when the phone rang.

"Mi-*hic*-a. Figures the bas-*hic*-tard would call."

–hic–

Kicking aside pieces of furniture she'd destroyed earlier in the evening to avoid scratching, Allison walked into the living room and picked up the house phone.

"Lamia Pizza Parlor," she said cheerfully. "Free Bloody Ma-*hic*-ee with each delivery."

The deep, purring chuckle told her that it wasn't Mica.

"Y'all are just so funny."

"Jan?"

"Sure as rain, honey. So, how are things, sweetheart?"

Allison looked down at the phone. "Jan, how did you –*hic*– get this number? The crisis line is set up on my office –*hic*– line."

"Oh," the woman said, "we'all have our ways. But y'all didn't answer me, sugar – how are y'all?"

There was something about the woman's voice that made Allison want to swap her cotton jammies for an arctic snowsuit. "I'm –*hic*– okay."

"Y'all ain't busy?"

"No. –*hic*–"

"Well, that's real good, cause Seth thought y'all might be busy."

Allison's hiccups disappeared. "How do you know about Seth?"

"Well, shit, sugar, y'all think you were the onliest one worried bout gettin' older? Oh, and y'all might want t'turn around about now."

Mica's little whore waved at her from the hallway, a tiny clam-shell cell phone in her hand.

"Hey, Allison," she said into the phone. "Glad t'meet y'all."

Allison tossed the handset onto the couch. "You're Jan?"

"One of my various disguises," the girl said as she closed the cell phone and dropped it into a ratty croscheted purse. "Seth says he likes my southern accent. Oh, and that reminds me . . . "

The girl's hand disappeared into the purse and pulled out a small perfume atomizer. Smiling, she gave herself a couple of squirts as she closed the distance between them.

"This is from Seth. It's not his favorite, but it works."

Allison caught the scent on her tongue and crumbled to the floor. The last coherent thought she had before the girl bent down and gave her another squirt for good measure, was that the scent was faintly reminiscent of the super-deluxe garlic sauce she used to make every time she got dumped.

It was almost fitting, in a way.

Mica sipped slowly at the over-sugared ice tea, just as Alvis instructed him to. To steady him. And it was helping. A little. But not enough to steady him completely to the fact that the three-minute descent in the shower stall had brought him to a massive room that looked like a cross between Baron Frankenstein's laboratory and the control room from every cinematic space ship he'd ever seen.

Or read about in comic books.

But the room with all its flashing lights and whirring motors . . . and *things* that he had no description for, was still easier to accept than what Alvis – the man he knew as Alvis Ambrose, friend, fellow licenced Justice of the Peace for the State of Nevada, supposed alien abductee and, until recently, King of the Elvis Impersonators – told him.

That he was Elvis. The *real* Elvis Aron Presley.

And an alien abductee.

And no amount of iced-tea was going to steady him to that.

Elvis Aron Presley had not died on August 17, 1977, at the age of 42, while sitting on the john trying to squeeze off a loaf. A man named Alan Webster Curtis had died – on August 17, 1977, at the age of 42, of a massive heart attack when four aliens (*"They ain't green, Johnny, that's just Hollywood bunk. They're more greyish, like that writer fella said."*) suddenly materialized while he was sitting on the john trying to squeeze off a loaf and, telepathically, asked for autographs.

Thinking Alan Webster Curtis was the real Elvis Aron Presely.

It was an honest mistake.

Alan Webster Curtis was Elvis' secret body double, the man who waved and smiled and showed up for photo-ops and overindulged in peanut-butter and bacon sandwiches, while the *real* Elvis slept and exercised and rehearsed and finished a Master's Degree in Quantum Physics and appeared on stage wearing padded jump-suits to look more like what the fans, thanks to Alan Webster, expected.

It was a good plan and one that probably would have continued while Elvis worked on his doctorate thesis . . . if Alan Webster Curtis hadn't suddenly dropped dead that hot August night.

"Now, much as ah loved that man, and ah did . . . always thought'a him like he was Jessie, mah lit'l twin brother who died, cause he and ah looked so much alike. Ah blame mahself, really. Ah saw all the warnin' signs and ah do feel responsible. Ah mean, ah'm the one who got em hooked on peanut-butter n' bacon san'miches. Still do love them suckers, but in moderation. Yah know what ah mean?

"Ah shoulda got 'em some help, yah know, got'em off the pills'n booze, but ah was too busy tryin' t'tickle the dragon's tail

. . . that's a physics term dealin' with matter wave theory'n its applications.

"Thing is, Johnny, ah didn't know bout his heart or else *'Elvis'* woulda gone on a diet. Lord hep me but ah'll nevah forget that night. I heard this loud scream, then a thump and . . . and there was Alan, stretched out on the bathroom floor with four of these lit'l men standin' over him with autograph books in their hands and cryin' like their hearts were about to break.

"One o'em passed out when they noticed me standin' there, but after some explanation ah was able to convince'em about me bein' who ah said ah was . . . and about Alan. After hearin' all that and, being that they can read more'n a person's thoughts, they offered me a way out. And ah took it, Johnny. As far as the world would know, Elvis Presley was dead. That way ah could continue on with mah studies.

"Course, bein' human, ah just had t'come back and see if ah could pick up where ah left off. Ah though ah could have mah cake and be the King, too. So, yah feelin' better, Johnny?"

Mica took another sip and nodded. His Dad would forgive him for that.

"Yeah. Thanks, Al–El."

Elvis leaned back in his chair – just an ordinary club chair, identical to the one Mica was sitting in – and reached up to snatch a banana from the ring of fruit that revolved in the air above them. Gravity, he said as he was setting up the fresh fruit satellites, had been the easiest laws to bend.

"Ah'm still the same man, Johnny," he said as he munched away. "Although ah know it's probably a bit hard t'accept'n all."

"A bit," Mica agreed. "Um, Elvis?"

"Yeah?"

"Can I ask . . . I mean, shouldn't you be – I mean, you

look so . . . . Shouldn't you be olden than you are?"

"Sixty-six," Elvis said. "Ah'm sixty-six now, in Earth years."

"But . . . you don't look that old."

Elvis finished off his banana and tossed the skin into an ordinary plastic garbage container.

"Thank yah, thank yah verrah much. But what can ah say? Einstein was right, space'n time work differently out there."

Mica nodded again. He vaguely remembered some old *Twilight Zone* or *Outer Limits* episode about that. "Oh. Cool."

"Okay, Johnny," the big man said, scooting his chair forward beneath a floating bunch of seedless grapes, "can ah ask yah a couple'll questions now?"

"Yeah."

"Upstairs yah were ready t'kill me t'save mah soul, right?" Mica nodded. "Cause yah thought that sweet lit'l lady yah live with turned me inta a vampire?" Mica nodded again. "*Real* vampires, Johnny?"

Mica finished off the last of the iced-tea and gagged on the thick glob of sugar that poured down his throat.

"Yeah, but my name's not Johnny. It's Mica . . . like the –"

"Like the prophet Micah."

"Yeah . . . or the stone." Mica sighed and watched a pair of Siamese cherries disappear around a floating pineapple. "I am Mica and I met Allison, the vampire, in Hollywood and . . . it's really a long story, Elvis."

Elvis nodded and plucked a ripe peach out of the air. "Then you'd better get started."

Mica took a deep breath and did just that, "In the beginning, the Lord my Father had a plan for me –" and Elvis Aron Presley leaned forward and listened, while the orbiting fruit salad rotated around his head like a low-calorie halo.

❖

Allison rolled over and bumped her nose against the lining of her casket. *Ow – huh?* She didn't remember getting into her coffin. The last thing she did remember was getting squirted by Mica's little playmate . . .

No, wait, she wasn't *Mica's* playmate she was –

"Oh shit."

We've just got to do something about that mouth of yours, darlin'.

Allison blinked as the coffin lid opened and Seth smiled down at her.

"Hey, sweet-lips, welcome home."

Allison felt her nail rip through the satin lining as she stared up at him. There was something wrong with the ceiling above his head. The cracked plaster and overhead light was gone. Whatever this place was, it *wasn't* home.

"Where am I?"

Seth leaned back just enough to offer her his hand. "Where you belong, darlin'."

The Stud Farm. Fuck.

She swatted his hand away and sat up, managing to only rip out two seams of the real spandex-lace gown she was wearing. The small sandstone cavern was packed with her things, radiating outward from the coffin. The jade burial suit had been draped over King Tut which, in turn, lay upon an altar of books and Objects d'Art. Antonio, Tom, Christopher and Gary stared at her from over the edge of one of the boxes that had been dumped on top of her beautiful antique desk. Everything from her basement-sanctorum was there with the exception of her phone, computer and big-screen entertainment unit.

"Reception's really lousy down here anyway," Seth said, countering her complaints before she could say them. "And runnin' cable down here's more trouble than its worth. Besides,

I don't think you'll have much time for TV watchin' – you're gonna be busy, little girl."

"The fuck I am!" She tried to swat him away when he reached for her again and found herself hauled up and out of the coffin as though she was a rag doll.

"The fuck you aren't." Seth shoved his tongue half-way down her throat before releasing her. Allison stumbled back into a box of Objects d'Art and heard the sound of expensive crystal shatter. "I thought I made that clear the first time, baby. You're mine and you're here to stay until I say different."

"You can't do this."

Seth shook his head and walked over to the jade burial suit. Wrinkled up his nose when he touched it.

"You can't!" Allison repeated, louder, just in case he'd missed it the first time. "You can't just walk into my house and kidnap me!"

"Why?"

Um. "Because it's not right?"

Okay, she deserved the howling laughter for that one. It did sound pretty stupid.

"Shit, honey, you are so screwed up you should be sleeping in a tool box instead of a coffin. Besides, I didn't kidnap you, that was my Watcher. See . . . that's the sort of things they're supposed to do. Watch and keep us safe. By the way, what happened to your Watcher?"

Yeah, Allison wondered. *What?*

Al – *Elv*is had listened quietly to everything Mica told him – almost everything. Mica left out the reason why he'd been using an assumed name . . . but he told him everything else about vampires and Allison, about Luci and the Fur Pit. About Gypsy and Mrs. B. About being the Son of God.

The last fact made the big man start a little, but Mica

forgave him. After all, as the living Son of God that sort of thing was expected of him now.

"Vam'pars, here in Vegas . . . the undead right here under our noses. Blood-suckin' demons from hell who'll hunt us down like food. And that purdy lit'l lady o'yores is one o'em. Lord help us."

"Oh, He will, Elvis, my Dad wouldn't let us do this alone."

Elvis nodded. "Yeah, glad t'hear it. So what we gotta do is find your lit'l lady and her . . . group and destroy em. Yah gonna have a problem with that, John . . . Micah?"

"Of course not!"

Jumping to his feet, Mica's forehead slammed into a small star fruit and knocked it out of orbit. The force of the blow bounced it off a stack of *National Enquirers* and into a tiny inter-dimensional portal that Elvis had constructed in order to send things to his "friends" back home in space. Mica wasn't really familiar with the fruit, but hoped it was ripe enough for the aliens. He could already feel a lump raising under his scar and it took him a minute to remember what sermon he was supposed to give.

Aliens? No. Oh, right . . . *vampires.*

"They must all be destroyed in His name. And in His name shall we cast the demons back into the fiery pits of hell. For it is by the grace of my Father, the Lord God, that we have come together to save all of mankind . . . um, in Las Vegas from this evil. I did it before and we can do it again. For I am Mica – hard and pure as flint. We *shall* not fail, Elvis, for the Lord, my Father, is with us. However many there are, they shall fall."

The rest of the circling fruit managed to get out of the way as Elvis stood up. "Ah-men. So, how many do yah think we'll have t'destroy besides your Allison?"

Mica stopped to think – and that was a mistake.

He sat back down a little harder than he'd intended. He

knew Allison had to die, she was a vampire, after all – one of the monsters he'd just condemned in his Father's name – but hearing someone else say that same thing gave him a funny feeling in his belly.

"I don't – ah . . . "

❖

"You didn't answer me, baby," Seth said as he dropped the burial suit's sleeve and picked up the carved jade butt-plug. Figures. "Where'd your Watcher go? I mean, you're telling me all these things I can't do – I can't come into your house, I can't kidnap you – but you still haven't told me why your Watcher wasn't there to protect you.

"Or why he helped burn down your house."

Allison felt her body collapse on whatever happened to be under it at the time. More crystal shattered.

"He what?"

"Yeah, that's what I asked when my Watcher told me. Seems she was watching the *U-Haul* pull away -- with you and your stuff, when he comes running up, screaming like a Comanche and waving around a hammer and piece of sharpened wood." Seth tossed the butt plug into the air and caught it. "Guess we both know what he had in mind to do. So when my gal tells him you're gone your boy kinda went nuts. Desert-dry stucco burns fast."

"Mica was going to . . ." Allison shook her head. *Not Mica, he was too much of a wuss.*

"Well, that's what she said." Seth folded his arms over his chest and looked down at the suit. "Do you mind tellin' me why the hell you'd buy something like this for?"

"To be buried in."

"Well," Seth said, "if you run into that renegade Watcher of yours, you might just get your wish."

"Yeah," Allison thought.

". . . fuck."

"What's the matter, son?" Elvis asked, kneeling down next to the chair so Mica wouldn't have to move. "Yah don't look so good."

"I – It's Allison, Elvis. I – We've been together for so long. I – I don't want her to suffer."

Elvis took a deep breath, then sighed in what sounded like the beginnings of a song. "Yah love her?"

"No, of course not. I can't. She's dead. She's damned. She's cold. She's. . . ." Mica couldn't think of what else she was besides Allison. His Allison.

"Oh-oh. Ah know the Lord's acceptin' o'most kind o'love . . . but ah think that generally means the love between two consenting, *livin'* people. Ah'm not so sure about how He feel concernin' someone . . . lovin' summin that's dead. Ah know there ain't no Commandment or anythin' that says it's bad, but –"

Mica already didn't like the sound of that *but*.

"– but ah think that smacks o'idol worship and that *is* one o' the Commandments. One o'the big 'Thou Shall Nots'. Lord, boy."

Mica shook his head. "Just His Son for right now."

Elvis grunted something as Mica closed his eyes and clasped his hands together. A moment later he felt Elvis's hands close around his. They didn't feel as nice as Elena's hands, but they were warm and that's all Mica needed right now. Warm, *living* flesh against his.

"Dad?" Elvis grunted and Mica forgave him. "Dad, it's me, Mica. I know I shouldn't ask this of You, but sons are supposed to ask things of their fathers, right? I know she's dead and damned and that she forfeited her soul by her own free will, but . . . I don't want to hurt her. Ah hell, Dad, I'm going to need help on this."

Mica opened his eyes when Elvis's hands tightened around his. "Yah got it, son. The Lord'll have yore front and ah'll have yore back. And don't yah worry none, ah'll take care'a Allison for yah. A man shouldn't oughta kill the thing he once loved, no matter what."

"Thanks, Elvis," Mica said, "but that would be the easy way out . . . and the Lord, my Father doesn't like that. No, when the time comes I'll do what's right for Allison. But, I do need your help right now."

"Name it."

"I have to be baptized again before we start. I need all the power I can get. Will you be my John the Baptist, Elvis?"

The big man nodded and as he stood up, walked quickly over to a small side-by-side refrigerator, the hem and drooping sleeves of his kimono fluttering out behind him. "Uh-oh. Looks like all ah got is *Perrier*, unless yah'd rather use tap water."

Mica stood up and squared his shoulders. "*Perrier* will be fine. The water's not the important thing, Al–El. My brother, Jesus, was baptized by water that fell from his kinsman's hands . . . and that's what's important. I feel toward you as a kinsman, Elvis. And I am sorry I tried to kill you earlier."

"Think nothin' o'it. Ah'd probably'a done the same thing, if the roles were reversed. Yah ready?"

Mica slid onto his knees as Elvis twisted off the bottle's cap and walked back toward him

"I'm ready, Lord . . .*yikes!*" The bubbles caught him off guard, but only for a second.

"Sorry. *Ahem* . . . . 'We who were baptized into Christ Jesus were baptized into His death that like as Christ was raised from the dead through the glory of the Father so we also might walk in newness of life.' Amen."

"Ah-men," Elvis said as he steadily emptied the entire

bottle down on Mica. "'Mah bap'ism is external, phys'cal; it is justa type o'what He shall do in the spirit o'man. Ah bap'eyes the phys'cal body with water, but He shall immerse the spirit with the Holy Spirit, n'outta that immersion shall come the New Birth, and man shall begin a new life.'"

Mica squinted into the stream of bubbles and smiled as Elvis began to sing.

"We're caught inna trap . . . and can't back out. Because I loved yah too much, lady."

The words might not have been right (again), but Mica thought it was the perfect hymn for the situation.

Praise me . . . he . . . be.

Or something like that.

Allison picked up a shard of amethyst glass and crushed it into a powder between her fingers. No, Mica wouldn't kill me . . . we have a bond. *Had. He left, remember?* Yeah, okay, but he's only human. *Oh, there's an endorsement.* Look, dammit, he saved my ass back in Hollywood. *Because he wanted to hump it, but that didn't last too long now did it?* Well, we're just going through a rough patch right now, that happened to every couple. *He's a Watcher, you're what he's supposed to be watching. Slave and Master.* People change. *Vampires don't.* So? It's not like that's any sudden surprise. Why would he want to kill me now? *'Yo quiero Taco Bell'?*

"Oh? Yeah."

Seth was sitting on top of King Tut with the jade suit over his lap and a look of utter confusion on his face. It was the look more than anything else that pissed Allison off.

"What? Weren't you monitoring my thoughts?"

"I gave up. See, that's another reason why I didn't want females around. You're all too confusin'."

"Then why am I here?"

He smiled, fangs gleaming. "Because you disrespected m
in front of my boys."

"That's it?"

"That's enough, baby. I'm king here and you ain't nothir
but what I made you." His smile faltered a little around th
edges as he reached over and snapped off King Tut's symboli
beard.

"Hey! Don't do that! That's mine."

Seth looked at her as he tossed the piece of wood over hi
shoulder. "Yours?" Darlin' there ain't nothin' here that's yours
I made you, so that means what's yours is mine. No . . . I tak
that back, you do have something that's only yours."

Allison waited.

"That good ol' boy Watcher. He's *all* yours, honey. T
have n'hold . . . till death do *you* part."

Yeah, Allison decided. Till death.

CHAPTER 15

Refreshed, rebaptized and resplendent in the Caddie's solid embrace, Mica and Elvis had prayed all the way back to the bungalow:

"'That He would grant you according to the riches of His glory that ye may be strengthened with power through His spirit in the inward man: That Christ may dwell in your hearts through faith, to the end that ye, being rooted and grounded in love, may be strong to apprehend with all the saints what is breadth and length and height and depth, and to know the love of Christ which passeth' –uh

"'Wise men say you ain't nothin' but a hound dog hunkah, hunkah burning suspicious minds in the ghetto. But be down at a lonely county jail and all them cats began to sail away on blue suede shoes. Uh-huh honey stay away from the little chapel in the moment of sweet surrendah. Ah will love my good luck charm. A hunkah, hunkah river' – uh

HOLY SHIT!"

Mica grabbed onto the dash as Elvis pulled the Caddie in as close as he could to the smoldering remains of the bungalow and cut the engine. There was more noise in the neighborhood than

Mica had ever heard for a weeknight – the background murmur of voices from his neighbors and their assorted relatives, the gurgling of water rushing down the street and overflowing the sewers, the rhythmic click from the rotating lights of police cars, the soft, wet sounds coming from the remains of his house as masked firemen racked through the sopping remains, looking for embers, the call of one high-pitched voice.

"JOHN!"

Mica lifted himself out of the car as she ran up to him. Soot marred her golden complexion and the off-the-shoulder t-shirt dress she wore. There were ashes in her hair and fear in her eyes and the scent of smoke clung to her like a lonely ghost. But her arms were warm and solid as they wrapped themselves around him, and that's all that mattered.

"Oh, God, John, I didn't know . . . I came back to see if you were okay, you know and –" Her voice dropped to a muffled sob against his shoulder. "I was just so worried that she would do something awful to you. God, the way she looked . . . John, I – When I got here the place was on fire and I thought . . . I thought you were, that both of you were still inside. Oh, God, John."

Mica felt his arms tighten around her until they both stopped shivering in the hot desert night.

"She's dead?" he asked as Elvis got out of the car. "Allison?"

Elena shook her head against him. "No, but the police are looking for her. They're pretty sure she did it. Some of your neighbors saw her loading up a *U-Haul* and driving away right before the fire started."

Mica looked at the crowd, recognized a few faces and waved. "The bitch."

"Yeah," Elena said, smiling. "God-damn her."

"Hush now," Elvis muttered. "As good as terms as you are

with the Lord now, Micah, ah don't think He'd like t'hear too much blaspheme'n comin' from us."

Elena looked up, confused. "Mica? Who's Mica?"

"I am," Mica said. "And he's Elvis. The *real* Elvis. See, it was his fat body double who died when the aliens showed up and not him. Understand?"

The soot on her face made her look paler, her eyes wider as she pulled out of his grasp. "Uh-huh."

"Well, ah'll be more'n glad t'make your acquaintance proper some other time. Right now . . . I think we're about t'have company."

Mica turned and felt the sweat that had been gathering under his arms turn to ice. Which matched perfectly to the lump forming in his belly. One of the uniformed cops who'd been talking to a gaggle of neighbors was headed his way. Mica grabbed Elena's arm and pulled her back toward the Caddie.

"Elvis, we have to go. *Now.* I don't want to talk to the police. I know my Dad will protect me, but I – I wasn't completely honest with you about everything that happened in Hollywood."

"You've got a record?" It was either the exhaustion or relief at finding him alive, but Elena seemed very excited about that. "Wow. Did you kill someone?"

"No one alive," Mica said as he opened the door and motioned for her to move her pert little ass just a bit faster. "El?"

"Not to worry," the big man said as he slipped on a pair of near-clear shades and tugged at the oversized belt of his silver, bell-bottomed jumpsuit. Mica was just glad Elvis left the matching space helmet back in the lab. He didn't think Elena, or the quickly approaching cop would understand. "My lady here's all tricked out and rarin' t'go."

Elvis waved to the cop as he backed the massive car

between two rumbling fire trucks then gunned it into drive. The cop was on a dead run, a small notebook flapping in one hand while the other was reaching for the service revolver on his hip.

"Hey! HEY!" The cop was gaining on them when the Caddie roared away in a spray of wet gravel and exhaust. "Wait a minute, I want to talk to – *cough!*"

"Hated t'do that," Elvis said as he squealed the white-walls around a corner and headed west a couple dozen times faster than the posted *30-mph*. "Ah ain't personally never been in trouble with the law. Can't say the same for Alan, though, he did try t'ruin mah reputation some."

Mica could understand that. His own reputation had been spotless until he hooked up with Allison.

"So," Elvis said, braking the car to 90, "any idea where we're headin'?"

Mica hadn't thought about it until that moment – which was unfortunate, because he really had no idea where Allison, or her troop of vampires, might be. Las Vegas wasn't as large a city as Hollywood (and it's outlying areas), but it was plenty big enough for monsters to hide in.

"I – don't know."

A soft tap on the shoulder made him turn around. Perched on the edge of the massive back seat, her hair whipping around her face like ebony snakes, Elena handed him a soot-smudged business card.

"Will this help?" she asked, biting her lower lip. "I found it in the street with this. It's her's, your friend's, isn't it?"

Mica looked at the fake gold-plated necklace that dangled from her fingers, the small, lopsided heart swinging slowly back and forth. It was a cheap thing, a drug store special that cost him all of $12.95. He'd bought it at the end of their first week in town and Allison had worn it everyday for almost a full month.

He was surprised she still had it.

"Yeah, that's hers," he said and took the card. "You can have it if you want."

"Really?" Elena squealed and slipped it over her head. "Cool."

Children were so easily pleased.

Mica leaned forward until he could read the raised lettering by the dashboard light.

"The Stud Farm . . . Bust a bronc, break a stallion all in air-conditioned comfort. S&M? B&D?" He turned it over and squinted at the line map on the back. "I know what a B&B is, but what's a B&D? Bed and Dinner? Or is it a health club – Sauna and message? I never heard of Henderson."

"It's a small town just south of here," Elena shouted above the wind. "A straight shot down 515 and then west on 146."

Mica saw Elvis looking at her in the rear-view mirror as he turned around. "You've been there?"

"No," Elena said quickly, fingering the lop-sided heart in the hollow of her throat, "but I've heard about it. From friends. It's a bondage and domination freak house. I'm not into that scene for fun. Although I did . . . date this lawyer once who was a real sadist. He used to get hard just talking about whips. You think that's where your friend is, John? I mean Mike?"

"Mica," he corrected. "You think that's where she is, El?"

The big man shrugged under his silver shoulder pads, but turned the Caddie south, toward the freeway, at the next light.

"Good a place as any t'look, ah guess."

And then The King did something Mica wished he hadn't – he looked up. Which made Mica do the same. The sky was so black the Milky Way looked like an accessory to Elvis's outfit. Dawn was a *long* time coming.

"Maybe we should wait until morning," he said, trying to

keep his voice and bladder steady. "If she is there, with the others, they're going to be at their strongest now."

"Ah know," Elvis said, but kept the car headed steadily south.

"It's going to be bad," Mica said as they curved up the on-ramp to 515 South. "Believe me, El, I've seen what these things can do. We should wait until it gets light."

"The Lord don't need light t'see evil, Micah, but don't yah worry, ah brought us enough. Don't yah fret none, the Lord'll watch out for us. Yah believe that, don'tcha?"

"Of course, my Father wouldn't abandon us."

Mica watched the man's eyes shift toward him for a second before returning to the road. "Uh-huh."

"God-achoo-damned son of a bitch!"

Allison picked up one of the limited edition Hummels, that last listed in the catalogue for $18,000.00, and threw it against the wall of the cave. Poor little shepherd. His remains joined the growing pile of shards that littered the floor.

"Fucking asshole!" She picked up Tom Cruise's framed photo and flung it, Frisbee-style, at a different wall. It bounced off without damage. "DAMMIT! He thinks he can get away with this? I fucking made him my Watcher and he leaves . . . And burns down my house? MY house? God-*choo*-damn, mother-fucking shit!"

A Bohemian crystal goblet detonated upon impact with a stalagmite. It was a lovely effect, but it still didn't make her feel any better. Neither did destroying the lavender-jade dragon with emerald eyes, the 16-karat Thai-gold statuette of Ganesh or her original Jimi Hendrix LPs.

"He fucking up and leaves without telling me anything and then thinks he can just waltz back into my life after he's already taken it, telling me I don't know anything about being a vampire. Well, how the hell was I supposed to find out?" Her hand closed around a carved opal swan. "Fucking doesn't hang around to watch over me and then complains about it . . . burns down *my* house and tells me he owns me because he made me and —"

Allison cocked her arm and stopped. *Who the hell was she talking about? Mica or Seth?*

Shit, did it matter? They were both scum and deserved to die. One for the first time and the other forever.

The swan exploded against the jade burial suit.

"Threaten me, will you? You God-*CHOO*-damned bastard!"

She was looking for something else to destroy when she heard applause. Seth was leaning up against a melted-looking stalagmite near the cave's entrance, naked as the day he was born. Or died. Allison really didn't care about that point of history either.

"I really like what you've done with the place," he said. "But I'm afraid your interior re-decoratin' will have to wait. The boys are waitin'."

"For what?"

"Well, for the show." He snapped his fingers and frowned when she didn't respond. A moment later, Allison felt sharp claws tear at her guts. "You don't expect me to let you come back without makin' you pay for how you acted."

Allison wanted to shout and curse and pick up the heaviest object she could find and squash Seth like the already dead bug that he was. All she could do, however, was glare at him.

I don't want to come back. Your fucking little whore kidnaped me.

"Nope, just transported a corpse." He smiled and the pain in her gut went away. "But don't worry, she has a mortician's license for that – for when we go on trips and the like. See, darlin', that's what a *real* Watcher's supposed to do. Sure am sorry 'bout the one you picked."

As much as she wanted to keep her anger where it belonged – on Seth – she felt it slipping back toward Mica. The *living* bastard.

As opposed to the *dead* one.

Shit, shit, shit!

"You say something else, darlin'?"

"No," Allison said as she smoothed down the front of her lace gown and felt his eyes following her hands. "Just thinking to myself."

"Well, then, that's all right," he said, stepping away from the stalagmite and offering her his arm. "Just make sure you ask permission to do it next time, okay?"

"*Permission*? I–" A single claw nudged her belly from the inside. "Of course." She took his arm and smiled. "Sorry."

Seth patted her arm. "Sorry, what?"

And this time the pain in her belly had nothing to do with external, psychic forces.

"Sorry. Master."

That's my girl.

Allison kicked over her casket on the way out. Just because.

❖

You thinkin' again, baby?

Allison jerked back into a free-standing St. Andrew's Cross as a smirk appeared – Cheshire cat-like – in the air directly in front of her. The rest of Seth's face materialized a moment later, followed by his leather-clad body. Strips of her gown clung to the front of his studded jock-strap.

His outfit, and the fragments of hers, had been essential parts of the "Fuck, Buck, Suck and Whomp Allison Back into the Club" show. She didn't know exactly how much time had passed, but the "boys" each had more than one turn at her.

Allison couldn't remember ever feeling *that* much pain before, but at least now she was a quick healer. Which was good . . . considering this was going to be how she'd spend the rest of her eternity.

"I think I asked you a question, sweet thing," Seth said and subtly showed his displeasure by reaching between her legs and giving her clitoris a vicious twist. "You going uppity on me again?"

"No," she said, and it amazed her that her voice sounded relatively calm. Maybe an octave or two higher, but nothing that would cause a spontaneous sympathetic vibration in the "stable's" main cavern that would send it crashing in on itself. Dammit. "Just. Standing. Here. Waiting. For. You."

Seth smiled and released her quasi-penis, then began dry rubbing it. Allison saw no need to redirect any bodily fluids to the affected area. A little pussy juice might make it feel better and that wasn't what she wanted. Pain just helped her hate him all the more.

As if she needed any help.

Allison groaned in her throat and he, still a man, dearly departed or not, naturally assumed it was because of him.

"See, I told you, pun'kin. It's only good with your own kind."

"Mmm."

"And it'll only get better."

"Mmm?"

"When you stop actin' all high n' mighty and accept you ain't no different dead than you was alive. Men ride women for a reason, sweet cheeks. You beginnin' to understand that now?"

"Hmm mmm."

"Good, cause I feel the need of another lesson comin' on."

Oh joy.

Seth used the traditional "bowling ball" grip to walk her backwards to one of the padded hitching rails.

"Okay, darlin'," he said as he released her and spun her around, "lean over."

Allison had been able to figure out the fascination straight men had with anal sex. When she'd been alive, she'd let a number of men in through her back door — usually just before they'd decided that they "needed their space" or that "it wasn't her, it was them." And even though she still couldn't figure it out, at least now that she was dead it cut down on the shit — both real and verbal.

Allison leaned over the rail and relaxed. Unfortunately, her ass didn't. And reacted without prior consent. Her muscles constricted around the head of his cock with enough strength to crush walnuts.

And for a brief moment, the air around them flickered.

Hmm?

What the hell do you think you're doin', woman? Seth bellowed silently. *Open up!*

He cuffed her hard between the shoulder blades, and her body clenched.

This time Allison caught a quick flash of a woman, in a spandex cat-suit and cowboy boots, beating holy *(ah-choo. SHIT!)* hell out of Lance, Slave Boy #2.

Hmm!

Allison smiled and pulled her ass cheeks manually apart.

Now, Seth mentally purred, *that's my good girl. See how good it is when you play nice.*

"Funny you should say that," she said, looking up at him, "but I've changed my mind. I really don't want to play any more."

Hands clamped to either side of her hips and an angry red

light glowing from the center of his green eyes, Seth glared down at her.

"What the hell are you talking–"

She let go and her ass cheeks slammed closed with a solid, meaty twang.

"–aboOOOOOWWWWWWW!"

More screams followed as seven dozen women, of various age and dress and who suddenly seemed to materialize out of thin air, stared at each other and at the four "slaves" they'd been sharing throughout the night. Allison even thought she heard a few mumbled words about lawsuits and police before the herd of panic-stricken, hysterically screaming women headed for the EXIT.

It was an Exodus that would have made Moses proud.

"AH-CHOO!"

FUCK!

Seth made a grab at her hair, but Allison pushed back from the rail and ducked low, sucking her hair into a tight bob as she cranked down her anal sphincter to "vise-grip." This time his scream seemed to wake "the boys" out of their stupor. They still just stood there with their dicks hanging out and glancing from the women to their leader and back again.

Men, Allison thought. And giggled.

"What the fuck are you all standing around for?" Seth said through clenched teeth. Allison wondered why he didn't just think it, then decided it must be a *guy* thing. "Get this fucking bitch off me!"

The boys had something else to look at now – each other. Which they did, still with their dicks hanging out, until Shaft took a tentative step toward her. Allison tightened down to pea-shooter caliber.

"Ssssssshhhhhheeeeeee-IT!"

"Better tell him to stop," she said as sweetly as she could

from that angle, "or I'll tear it off. And let me tell you from experience that replacing body parts is hard work. But maybe it's different . . . you said we can only feel with our own kind, so maybe if we lose something to our own kind it stays lost. Might be worth thinking about, dick-head. No pun intended."

Allison felt Seth tremble. It was an interesting sensation, all things considered.

Without supervision, Shaft took another step and Allison turned and whipped her cargo into the railing. Ow.

Up to you, Sethie. Call him off or you'll become the first vampiric castrato. Sure hope you can sing better than you can fuck.

"Shaft – STOP!"

Shaft stopped.

And? Allison silently prompted.

"And the rest stay back."

The rest stayed back like the bunch of sheep they were. Damn, he was right after all. Regardless of the bullshit he'd been trying to feed her over the last 24 hours, Seth had been right all those months ago. It was better to go solo.

Well, she thought, *die and learn.*

"Seth! What the hell's going on down here?" Lance, who'd pulled registration duties again, came barreling into the cavern looking more pallid than he normally did. "We've got women running out of here still in their costumes and – Oh? Are we having another party?"

Allison clenched, Seth howled and Lance looked puzzled.

"No party, Lance," Allison said as he stepped away from the railing and literally hauled ass toward the softly glowing EXIT sign. "Me and the Boss Man are just going to . . . mosey along now. So why don't you just back up with the rest of your brain-dead posse and play with yourself a little."

Lance's hand actually moved in that direction when Seth, shuffling along on tiptoes, started ranting like a crazy man.

"You think you can tell my boys what to do, bitch? When I get loose I'm gonna find a fuckin' redwood and drive it through your heart myself! SHIT! You're nothin' but a piece of TAIL!"

Allison irised her sphincter down to drinking straw diameter.

"Yeah," she agreed, "but you have to admit, it's a *damn* fine tail! Besides, why are you complaining? Don't you know that women always lead men around by the cock?"

Any comment Seth might have made was lost in the sounds of pandemonium coming from above.

CHAPTER 16

When the first car, a brand-new Lexus wagon, appeared and swerved into their lane, Elvis had leaned on the Caddie's horn and fish-tailed out of the way, while Mica held onto the vinyl-covered dashboard and prayed. Loudly. That had been five cars ago and Mica hadn't stopped praying and Elvis hadn't let up on the horn.

The first two bars of *Love Me Tender* played over and over and over again until it sounded like the theme song for Hell.

For an out of the way, isolated dive – which they only found because Elena's friends had told her exactly where it was – it seemed pretty popular. Mica had never seen that many cars on the road except on The Strip. But there the cars were moving slowly, bumper-to-bumper so the tourists could take in the sights. Out here there were no sights and the bumper-to-bumper – and occasionally side-by-side – traffic was going 70+ mph. Or at least that's how fast Mica thought they were going . . . considering Elvis had the Caddie cranked up to 95.

"Have yah noticed something?" Elvis shouted above the blaring horn-song and rushing wind. "There're only women in those cars. What do you think that's all about?"

Mica stopped praying and felt his stomach cinch up tight against his ribs. It was Hollywood all over again. Allison had fallen in with another band of killer lesbian vampires who were probably just waiting for him to walk in there and show his pretty new face so they could strip him naked, tie him down and try their best to fuck him into the dark pit of everlasting torment.

His cock trembled at the very thought of it.

"'That through death He might bring to nought him that had the authority of death, that is the devil; and might deliver all them who through fear of death were all their lifetime subject to bondage.'"

"Ah-MEN!" Elvis shouted, but Elena didn't say anything. Mica didn't blame her, she probably hadn't heard the full prayer since she was sitting up on the edge of the Caddie's trunk and waving at the passing cars like she was the Grand Marshal in the Hollywood Lane Parade.

He turned around and shouted it at her again.

She heard it and pointed in the direction the Caddie was traveling. "Yeah! They're really into bondage there."

Mica nodded and turned back toward the windshield. There were still a lot of cars on the narrow road, but their numbers seemed to be diminishing. He thought about taking down license numbers, knowing the police would probably be able to use it when bloodless corpses started turning up, then decided against it. He couldn't afford to get involved with the police, not now – he and Elena had a new life to start and he didn't want to begin it from a jail cell.

Mica slumped back against the upholstery and closed his eyes.

"Okay, Dad," he whispered, wanting to keep the conversation as private as possible, "Your one living Son is about to go into a lion's den of lifeless, lascivious, carnal lust . . . so I'm really going to have to have Your help on this. You know I'm weak, but Jesus was weak, too and all You did was nail

Him to a cross. I'm going to have to face vampire women who'll try and make me sacrifice my . . . body before they take my soul. So You'd *better* be there, Dad, and I mean it. And it probably wouldn't hurt if You sent a couple of Your biggest, bad-assed angels down with a flaming sword or two. I know You didn't do it for Jesus, but, hell . . .this is the 21st Century, You know, and people expect a little more special effects in their miracles."

Mica felt his body jerked forward as the Caddie slid into a stop and opened his eyes.

"Amen. This is it?"

"That's what the sign says," Elvis said above the caddie's panting rumble, "but damn me . . . Oh, please cuse me, Miss Elena."

"Oh, that's okay," she said, sliding down into the back seat, "I've heard worse. Fuck, look at those bitches run! What do you think happened?"

Mica stood up in the foot well and watched a dozen women in alternative-lifestyle outfits throwing hissy-fits in the nearby parking lot when they discovered that they didn't have their car keys inside their corsets. A few similarly dressed women had already taken to the road, running as fast as their stiletto-heeled boots would let them.

It was a pathetic, terrifying sight . . . in a highly erotic way.

A white-haired old woman ran past wearing nothing but pasties and a thong. It was enough to snap Mica back to reality.

"Um, Elena," he said, "please try not to get upset but . . . Elvis and I are here to – to . . . um. Elena, the woman you saw today . . . who came into the bedroom when we were . . . My friend is a . . . a. . . ."

"A . . . a . . ." Elvis said, attempting to cover Mica's back like he said he would. ". . . a . . . a . . ."

"Yeah, a vampire, I know," Elena said as she stood up

behind Mica, her hand resting on his shoulders, fingers twitching with excitement. "Can I watch you stick her?"

Mica felt a chill move through the sultry night air as he turned around. "What did you say?"

Elena didn't seem to notice and pounded on a riff against the back of the passenger seat. She was smiling and the lights from the building glinted in her dark eyes. Mica had seen that look before.

Oh God, Dad.

"Hey, that's what you're gonna do, right? Stick her, right? Oh, oh can you cut off her head, too? That'd be way cool." Her smile dimpled. "What's the matter?"

Mica leaned back against the dashboard and saw Elvis out of his periphery reach for something long and pointed beneath his seat.

"Johnny?"

Elena fluttered her dark lashes at him. She looked so innocent, so pure. Mica saw the edge of the crucifix that Elvis held in his hand and swallowed.

"I never said Allison was a vampire."

Elena's lashes stopped fluttering. "Ah, sure you did. Or maybe he did . . . Elvis, I mean."

Elvis shook his head and lifted the glow-in-the-dark cross. A miniature Elvis hung from it instead of Christ, but Mica didn't think the minor blasphemy was worth mentioning at the moment. Especially since he thought the likeness was better than any he'd seen of his Brother.

"No, ah didn't," Elvis said, lifting the crucifix toward her. "Micah and me both were real careful not t'say anything 'bout it. We didn't wanta scare yah . . . but ah get the feelin' yah a'ready know more'n either of us bout this whole mess. She one'a em, son?"

Elena looked at the cross and wrinkled her nose. "Get this

out of my face. I had enough of these fucking things back in school."

"No," Mica said, answering Elvis, "she's human. And she's been blessed by my Father, the All Mighty."

Both Elena and Elvis gaped at him.

"Huh?" They said in unison.

Mica grabbed the plastic crucifix out of Elvis's hand and pressed it against Elena's wonderfully buoyant chest.

"The Lord, my Dad, moves in mysterious ways, El . . . and He moved through this beautiful woman to show us the way. Don't you see? 'Arise, shine; for thy light is come, and the glory of Jehovah is risen upon thee.'"

Elena blinked and whacked the cross out of his hands. It sailed through the air and landed on the blacktop a yard from the Caddie – where it was run over by a VW bug being driven by a blue-haired Biker Bitch.

Mica's hands were still stinging from the attack when she grabbed them and slammed his face into the front seat. The impact left Mica with a ringing in his ears and tears in his eyes, but he managed to clear both just enough to see the twin globes of her black-lace covered ass as she somersaulted out of the Caddie.

He didn't know she was so athletic. No wonder she was so good in bed.

"Wait," he said, wiping drool off his lips, "it's okay, don't be scared. My Dad likes you."

Elena backed away from the car as if she was looking at a crazy man. "Just kill that bitch and maybe my Master will let you live."

"Of course He'll let me live," Mica shouted back, blowing her a kiss. "He's my Dad."

"Uh-huh. 'Suse me for interruptin'," Elvis said and nodded toward the windshield as he gunned the motor. "But it looks like the party guests have arrived."

Mica heard Elena curse as he turned to see Allison coming out of the building with a tall, pale man on her tail. No, not *on* her tail, more like . . . .

"Holy fucking shit!"

Jealousy, though unwarranted, reared its ugly little head.

Along with something else.

Even at the beginning, when they were hot *(Forgive me, Dad)* and heavy *(I was led astray . . . like Jesus, in the desert . . . yeah, like that)*, Allison had *never* let him fuck her in the ass *(Not that I really wanted to, Dad) (Right, Bro.)*. But here she was, bent in half and waddling as fast as her long, luscious legs could carry her – heading across the near-empty parking lot with one guy up inside her and five other naked men following.

The God-damned lifeless slut!

"Bitch!" Mica screamed at her from over the windshield as he pulled himself to his feet. "You owe the Lord, my Father for your sins and I'm here to collect in His name! AMEN!"

He thought he heard a chorus of sneezes when Elvis reached over and hauled him back into the seat.

"Yah sure, Micah?" the big man asked as he tightened his grip on the wheel. "Bout wantin' her t'die with the rest o'em?"

"Yes! She deserves it! Peace, I mean . . . after her sins are burned away in the torments of Hell, that is." His words filled him with Heavenly, Everlasting, Radiant Power. For about a minute. "Uh, did you remember to bring stakes?"

"Got a better way, son," Elvis said, winking. "Ah did a lit'l checkin' on the computer terminal in mah room while ah was dressin' and transferred the data t' the Caddie's on-board replication unit. If yore sure, ah can destroy'em all without us havin' t'leave the car."

"I'm sure!" Mica shouted. "Of course I'm sure. They all have to die – *all* of them!"

"NO!" Elena shouted even louder. "You leave my Master alone!"

But before Mica could forgive her or tell her not to worry, Elvis popped the clutch and spun the car in a 180-degree arch that covered her in sand and sagebrush. Mica watched her cough, curse and dust herself off as the Caddie roared up the driveway going 50mph – in reverse.

When he turned around, he saw Allison, with bum-boy in tow, look up and mouth something, then instantly change directions, heading out of the parking lot and into the open desert. Mica's balls cringed when she, and the man, leapt the split-rail fence.

Damn, why must she always do things the hard way instead of standing still and accepting her just punishment?

"Go get them!" Mica yelled into the buffeting winds. "Don't let them get away!"

"Ah won't," Elvis yelled back. "Can't use mah heat-imagin' system, cause they don't give off any heat . . . but ah seen em and they ain't gonna get away. No sir. Woo-oh, DUCK!"

Mica looked up briefly until he realized that Elvis was making a suggestion and not observing a flying water fowl.

He ducked as split rails shattered around the Caddie's trunk and the car leapt onto the hard-packed desert floor. Sand spewed out behind the hood in two massive plumes. It wasn't exactly a Chariot of Fire, but it would do. If it had just one more little thing.

Brushing a sliver of creosote wood from his hair, Mica kneeled on the seat and raised his arms straight out to the sides.

"STOP!" He shouted and heard his Heavenly Father's Voice. "FOR I AM MICA! THE LORD'S AVENGING ANGEL!"

The Caddie was closing in – he could see Allison's face, drained of color and full of fear. The man directly behind her

"THAT'S RIGHT, ALLISON, YOUR TIME HAS COME. COWER BEFORE THE LORD MY GOD AND HIS LIVING SON!"

Elvis cleared his throat and goosed another few horses under the hood.

"AND A FRIEND!"

Elvis didn't say anything but "Better hold on."

"YES, I WILL HOLD ON TO MY FATHER'S HAND AS WE SLAY THE WICKED. 'DEATH NO MORE DOMINION OVER HIM, FOR THE DEATH THAT HE DIED, HE DIED UNTO SIN ONCE' – *umph!*"

Mica was propelled into the back seat, like a turnip, when Elvis stood on the brakes and slammed the Caddie into a stop. The last thing he saw, before the upholstery came up and French-Kissed him, was a bright, blood-red flash.

"Woo-wee, that was summin'." Elvis said as he grabbed the back of Mica's jeans and leveled him back into a position more suitable for an avenging angel. "Yah okay, son? Oh, yore bleedin' a mite."

Mica wiped his nose off on his arm and then wiped the seat. Other than that, a minor neck compression and possible internal hemorrhages, he felt fine. Better than fine when he looked past the Caddie's trunk and saw the five piles of blackened ash in the glow of the taillights.

"Is that?" Mica asked as Elvis helped him out of the car. "Are they?"

"Yep," the King said, swiveling his hips to work out the kinks. "That's all that's left of the vam'pars."

Using the Caddie as a crutch until he was sure his legs would support him, Mica walked up to the nearest pile and kicked at it with his sandal. It felt cold and greasy. Mica swallowed and tasted copper. Snorting up a mouthful of bloodied phlegm, he spit the glob into the closest pile and stumbled back when a hand . . . or something that looked like a hand, formed out of the ash and reached for the blood.

He made himself believe that the moaning sound was from the wind as it blew the piles of ash away.

"OhmyGodDad . . .El?"

"Yup," Elvis said, first slapping him lightly on the shoulder before patting the Caddie's trunk. "This is mah lady, right here. Ah a'ways give her the best o'everything. Ten coats of lacquer, hand washed and waxed. Dual carbs, radiant-convection coolin' system, top-quality halogen lights. It wasn't any trouble at all for the replication system t'reconfigure the normal light spectrum of the brake lights t'ultra-violet. Heck, ah once even programmed a red giant t'go blue for mah openin' night on Uuurhomphjjwqua. An' let me tell yah, Micah, if yah haven't heard *Blue Suede Shoes* sung under natural blue light, yah ain't really heard it at all."

Mica had heard it all now. "Um, Elvis?"

"Yeah?"

"I hate to say this."

"Go on."

"But there were only five piles of ash. There were seven vampires, six men and . . . Allison."

"Oh," the King said. "Shit."

CHAPTER 17

Allison grabbed the first wooden thing she could find – an oversized promotional pencil with the words *"Give Blood, Save Lives. STUD FARM/Henderson, Nevada"* stamped in red across one side – and pointed it at Seth's chest.

This wasn't exactly what she had planned, not that she had anything planned beyond getting as far away from the place as she could get. But thanks to Mica, her piss-poor Breather, this was about as good as she expected it to get.

"Back off," she warned, then added quickly, "no offense."

Seth, steaming like the smoke-cured ham he was, sneered as he continued to lurch toward her. He looked about as bad as she had only a few hours earlier. The scorching brake-lights had vaporized his backside from skull to heels, and eaten away the left side of his face. Allison had faired a lot better. The minute the pink Caddie broke through the fence, she turned and high-tailed it back to the Stud Farm, dragging Seth – still in tow – along with her. He was the only thing that saved her when the brake lights ignited the darkness, along with Rod, Lance, Shaft, Willie, and Cane.

He wasn't, however, very happy about that fact.

"You fucking cunt!" Seth sizzled at her. "Look what you did to me!"

Allison shrugged. "Sorry, but it'll grow back. Just think of it this way . . . I saved most of your miserable hide."

"And you're gonna pay for it with yours."

"You gotta be fucking kidding me," she said. "You're half the man you think you were and you're still making threats? Jesus."

They sneezed in unison and the left side of Seth's jaw unhinged. He didn't even bother trying to hold it in place.

"Sorry," she sniffed.

Right. Like you're sorry your Watcher didn't finish the job. You bitch, you led him here.

She only wished she had. Unless the guilt over burning down the bungalow had somehow kick-started his Watcher instinct, Allison had no idea how he found her.

But she was mighty glad he did. Though she wasn't about to tell that to her charbroiled Maker.

What's that about cooking?

Oops. "What do you mean, I led him here?" Allison shouted as she backed up, trying to remember if there was a back door to the place or not. "How could I? He wasn't there when your little Breather kidnaped. . . .

"Oh, wait a minute. If I didn't bring Mica out here and you didn't, there's only one person who could have." She smiled and tapped the point of the pencil against her chin. "Seth, I think you have a problem."

"Nuh-uh," a voice said from behind the reception desk, "he doesn't have a problem, *you* do."

Allison was already facing the reception desk when Seth turned around, lower jaw swinging like a black, pink and white pendulum against his chest, so she got the little enchilada's reaction. Which, in Allison's opinion, was priceless. The poor kid's jaw mimicked her Master's.

"What the hell did you do to him, you bitch?"

"Me?" Allison said as the girl jumped the glass barrier. She was holding a police baton that showed evidence of recently being sharpened at one end. The end currently pointing at Allison's heart. "I didn't do anything. You brought my psychotic Watcher out here, didn't you?"

"Wa?" Seth almost said.

"Only to kill you," the little Breather said, jabbing the air with each word.

"Ey navar . . ." Grunting, Seth walked over to the reception desk and, using an oversized metal paper clip, reattached his lower jaw. It wasn't a perfect fit and his back teeth clicked together a little when he talked, but it was better than having him in her head. "I never told you to do that. You were supposed to kill him and leave his body in the house when you torched it."

"Oh, so it was you, after all," Allison said. Turning, acting disgusted, she walked over to the door leading out to the hall . . . and tried to remember if there was an outside EXIT she could use. "You lied to me, Seth. And here I thought we really did have something special."

"We do have something special, baby," he lied. "C'mer and let me show you."

Fortunately, only he and Allison knew it was a lie, his little Breather, on the other hand – the one holding the baton – thought it was the truth.

"NO! You're mine!" She stamped her foot, the point of her improvised stake trembling in her hand as she aimed it toward Seth. "I – I brought him here for us. So he – he could kill her and we could be together."

Allison inched toward the door.

"What the fuck are you talking about?"

Boy, Seth . . . you really don't know anything about women, do you? The poor little thing's jealous.

"Fuck me," he said and looked at the girl. While the girl looked at him.

And Allison continued to inch closer to the door.

"I think that's what she wants, Seth," she said, hand reaching slowly for the knob. "So why don't I just leave you two lovebirds alone and —"

NO!

He might have lost half of his skin, but that hadn't lessened his control any. Allison moved away from the door and tossed the pencil onto one of the waiting room chairs. She had a better idea and slowly began stroking her body as she walked toward him.

Seth's green eyes followed her every movement.

"Okay," she said, "I just thought you might want a little private time with your Breather. You know, to Make her."

It was the look in the girl's eyes, more than the estrogen stink that rose from her, that made Allison want to puke. Little Ms. Chili Pepper loved him, really loved him — that would make things easier.

"Why the hell would I want to make her?" Seth mumbled, his unburned penis swelling as she stepped into his arms. "When I have you? She's just a Breather."

"And they're a dime a dozen," Allison added, making a face at the girl through the wisps of smoke rising from his shoulder blade.

"Less if you know where to look."

Allison backed away and patted Seth's cheek as the point of the baton erupted just above his belly button.

"YOU FUCKING BASTARD! YOU SAID YOU'D TURN ME!"

The girl's aim was way off, but it still hurt. Allison was rubbing her belly when Seth turned around.

"What the fuck do you think you're doing?" he asked.

"You – you said you were going to – that we'd be together forever."

Seth cupped the girl's chin in one hand. "I lied."

Allison saw the fear in the girl's eyes turn to pain as he tightened his grip. He'd done it again, he'd lied to a woman. *Fuck.*

With a battle cry of "Victim for Victims!" Allison jerked the baton out of his lower back and was just about to bring it down at the *right* angle when the front door suddenly burst open and –

"Ah–"

"'Behold, I stand at the door and knock; if any man hear my voice and open the door I will come in and sup with him and he with Me.'" Mica shouted, lifting the cross he'd made from two manzanita branches and a rusty length of bailing wire as he marched into the brightly lit waiting room. "I am Mica and I have come . . . and OH MY GOD, WHAT ARE YOU? GET YOUR HANDS OFF THAT GIRL, YOU MONSTER!"

The sneeze knocked the baton out of her hands.
"–shit!"

Mica stopped himself from blessing her, knowing how much she always hated that, and swung the cross at the horribly burned man. He knew it had to be a male vampire, no living man could have survived that . . . just as he knew the female wasn't Allison. The Allison he knew and had (Dad forgive me) once loved was gone. The dead woman who looked like her wasn't real – she was a vampire. A monster. A lifeless and cold thing that had to be destroyed.

He just hoped he could remember all that when the time came.

"I told you to get away from her," Mica repeated, cross upright and in the dead man's face. "Elena, are you all right?"

Elena had livid bruises on her chin and cheeks, and she'd been crying, her eyes were puffy and her nose red and dripping.

"Elena?"

"Go fuck yourself, asshole," she said, but Mica knew she was just distraught.

"It's okay, Elena. I've come to save you."

"Her?" Allison shrieked. "What about me? She only brought you out here so you could kill *me*."

Mica felt his heart almost burst with pride as he looked at Elena, his Elena. "I know. My Dad showed her the way." He felt something else when he looked at the creature formally known as Allison. Trading Elvis the crucifix for a manzanita stake, Mica squared his shoulders.

"I'm not going to say I'm sorry I have to do this," he told her. "You and . . . *him*–" The male vampire crossed his arms over his naked chest. "– are abominations onto the –"

"Yeah, yeah. Save me the rest of that speech, Milo. I've heard it before. So, what are you going to do, kill me?"

He took a deep breath and gagged as the scent of burnt vampire grew stronger. "Yes."

"Oh. Well, not to ruin your plans, but you may want to do him first," Allison said, jerking a thumb to the right. "Unless you want to deal with three vampires."

Mica knew that Allison had taken off, in a dead *(hah, good one, Dad)* run the second he looked away, but all thoughts of duty were forgotten when he saw what the burned man was doing to Elena. And what Elena was doing to the burned man.

"Elena, stop that! You don't know where that's been!"

But Mica had a pretty good idea.

Back arched, snatch exposed and panties down around her knees, Elena was fucking herself with one of his scorched ingers, while he, fangs buried up to the gum line, was busily sucking her neck.

"No!"

Draining her.

"NO!"

Taking away her right to everlasting Glory and turning her into another Allison.

But worst of all, stealing her from him. "ELENA, NO!"

Hips pumping as the monster fed, she looked at him and grimaced, her face a mask of pain and mortal terror. Mica had seen enough porno flicks to know that agony could sometimes be mistaken for ecstasy to the untrained eye.

Fortunately, for his Elena, his eye was trained.

Grabbing the cross back from Elvis, he raised it and the stake over his head and charged the vampire. Male vampires were a lot stronger than female vampires, he found out, when the monster moved Elena out of the way and lifted Mica off the ground by the balls.

A drop of blood glistened on one fang as he smiled.

"Mmm— that's some good eatin'," the creature said, smacking his lips. "Oh, and speakin' of that, where are my manners? Here we are, havin' a nice friendly chat and I haven't even offered you a drink yet."

He set Mica's feet back on the carpet and smiled. "Let me remedy that, shall I?"

Mica felt his fingers tighten on the bone-white wood as the vampire leaned in and kissed him, squishing his cold, slimy lips against his with the intimacy of a lover. *Rancid meat left out in the sun.* That had been Allison. And Mica would have given anything to have that taste in his mouth at the moment. Bile and mold mixed with shit slid down his throat before the warm, almost hot gush of Elena's sweet blood.

The cross and stake fell from his hands.

It couldn't have taken longer than a minute, but Mica' belly felt close to bursting when the vampire finished and tossed him aside like a used napkin. He began gagging before he hi the far wall.

"Oh, no you don't," the vampire warned. "I just had thes carpets cleaned and blood's the worst stain you can have. S just you swallow and –"

The vampire stopped moving.

Mica swallowed and pushed himself slowly to his feet. The vampire still didn't move. Elena's panties slid all the way of when she wriggled out of the creature's embrace.

"Master?" She said, too overwrought to remember to cove her breasts or tug her skirt back into place. "Master, what's th matter? Hey!"

She slapped the frozen face hard enough to make Mica jump, and squealed when Seth's bottom jaw flew off.

"Oh God – Sorry, Master. I'll get it. I'll fix it. Don' worry, Master." She started to go after it, but Elvis stopped her "Let me go, you fucking lunatic! And let my Master go!"

"He's not your master," Mica said, trying to calm her whil keeping a close eye on the still inanimate vampire. "And didn't do anything to . . . it."

"No," Elvis said, gently handing Elena to him, "ah did Now, if yah both'll just stand back a minute."

Mica had tried to hold onto her, but he was afraid to gral anything, given the disheveled state of her clothing, and sh slipped out of his groping hands.

"Don't you hurt him!" Elena screamed at Elvis. "I'l fucking kill you if you do!"

Elvis shot Mica a hound-dog look over the top of Elena' head and sighed. "Could you hold on a bit tighter this time Ah got some calculations t'do."

Coming in at ass level, Mica managed to catch th

hysterically strong girl around the . . . ass and lift her bodily off the floor. Unfortunately, the angle, or something, was a little off and they both toppled onto a small divan. Elena kicked and wiggled and beat her breasts against his face, but Mica held onto her. And thanked his heavenly Father for the opportunity to do so.

"Yah know," Elvis said, drawing Mica's attention away from his . . . duty, "ah gotta admit ah didn't believe yore story at first. But mah oh mah, these critters are real."

Mica watched Elvis tap one of the inert vampire's fangs and giggle.

"Elvis, for God's sake. Be careful!"

"Oh, it's a'right, yah don't haffa worry." the big man said as he punched some numbers into what looked like a palm-sized purple calculator. "It's just a matter'a . . . well, matter conversion, t'be more accurate. What ah did was t'momentarily phase this critter's essence outta sync with his body just enough t'hold him steady while ah crunch some numbahs."

"For what?" Mica asked around one of Elena's nipples that somehow got into his mouth.

"For this," Elvis Aron Presley said and pressed a button on the calculator.

Mica felt the ground move and heard a sudden high-pitched whirr . . . and the vampire disappeared. He didn't even realize Elena had stopped struggling until he stood up and noticed she was still sprawled on the couch, staring blankly at the spot where the demon had stood.

"You destroyed him?"

Elvis pocketed the calculator and sighed. "Matter can't be created or destroyed, Micah, but it can be transmuted inta another form. That's all ah did. Ah am sorry, though. Ah know how much yah wanted t'stake 'em."

"No problem," he said, feeling that there was still a very

big problem. "Are you telling me, he's still here?"

"Well, inna way."

"Where?"

The King winked and pointed to the ceiling. The sparkling acoustic tiles were covered with millions of fire-ants.

"That's him?"

"Yup."

"Vampire fire ants?"

"Uh-huh. Course with his consciousness pretty well divided among all those lit'l bodies ah don't think he can do much harm."

Mica wasn't so sure – especially since the army of ants was slowly beginning to crawl down the walls toward them.

"Uh, El? I think we'd better go."

"Mah thoughts exactly."

Moving quickly, but calmly so he wouldn't upset her any more than she already was, Mica turned around and held out his hand.

"It's okay, Elena. We're safe now."

She didn't move, didn't even shift her eyes toward him.

"Come on, baby. Let's get out of here."

Nothing.

"El, she's in shock."

Elvis slapped him lightly on the shoulder. "Ah think it's more'n that, son. Ah don't think that was the first bite that critter put on er. She might just be a zombah, son."

Mica looked down at the vacant, staring eyes and felt something tear inside him. He loved her, he knew that, and wanted to spend the rest of his life with her. *Oh Father* – but what kind of life could he have with a woman who was little more than a mindless doll without a will of her own . . . or any sort of opinions or judgments? A woman who'd always be available and would never have a headache or want her own life or argue with him.

What kind of life was that?

A freaking WONDERFUL life!

Thank you, Dad. Thy will be done.

Covering her breasts and straightening her skirt, Mica scooped her into his arms and carried her out of the building and into the hot desert night. Some day he'd tell their children about how he'd rescued their mother from the very jaws of hell.

Mica was halfway to the Caddie with Elvis running at his side, when he suddenly stopped and spun around. Elena's head and breasts flopped gracefully from side to side.

"Oh shit."

"What the matter?"

"Allison," Mica panted looking back at the building. He could see the ants, like a creeping shadow, moving along the front of the building. "Where'd she go?"

"Ah don't know. Anything dead come ottah there?" Elvis shouted and Mica was about to ask him how the hell would he know when a soft, lilting drawl answered the question.

"No. Perimeters in tack."

Mica turned around and stared at the Caddie. "It talks?"

"Like ah said, this is mah lady. Now, sweetheart, run a location sweep for Fem-Vamp I."

"Fem-Vamp I still within confines of buildin', but ah'm pickin' up numerous Male-Vamp traces."

Mica stared at the Caddie.

"Just a lit'l A.I. experiment ah been runnin'," Elvis said as he steered Mica toward the car. "It was something ah picked up from mah buddies up there."

Mica looked up at the sky, but instead of looking for little gray men, he saw a thin pale band just above the eastern horizon and felt a sense of relief wash over him. Dawn was coming and he figured he could forgive his friend anything by the light of a new day.

Don't worry, Dad, he thought as he carefully lay Elena down on the back seat. *I'll set him straight about what is and isn't in Heaven.*

"'Suce me, sir," the Caddie cooed to Elvis while Mica slid as carefully as he could into the front passenger seat, "but those trace Male-Vamps are about t'breach the first perimeter point."

"A'right, honey, go t'stand by." Elvis patted the steering wheel affectionately then turned to face Mica. "Last time, pard – yah sure bout yore Allison? We can try t'get er out fore we take care o'the ants, but yah gotta tell mah now."

Mica leaned back against the seat and took a deep breath. *His Allison,* it didn't even sound real anymore.

"No, I made myself and my . . . and the Lord a promise that I'd free her soul. She deserves that much. The dead aren't supposed to rise from their coffins until the Day of Judgement."

"Ah-men. Okay, honey," Elvis said to the car, "yah heard the man. Start up and prepare a fifty-second burst of formula LF-196-s at target area when we reach optimum safety range."

"Yes, sah."

Mica gasped and latched onto the dash board when the Caddie started by itself and backed away from the building in a cloud of alkali dust.

"Optimum safety range achieved," the caddie purred. "Commencin' firin' at four, three, two, one – firin'."

The Caddie shimmied and a stream of liquid blue-green fire shot out from under the hood ornament, completely engulfing the building in a ball of flames.

"Mah own recipe," Elvis said as he took back control and steered the Caddie out onto the blacktop road. "Hotter'n cheaper than most napalm products on the market. Should burn down to ash in bout a half-hour. Yah wanna say a few words?"

Mica closed his eyes and saw an orange-yellow reverse image of the fireball on his lids.

"Lord, my father, this is Mica. Your Son. Although I never knew her as a living woman, I feel that Allison was a kind soul and good person . . . before she condemned herself to hell . . . so I'm asking for that person she was, Father, for You to forgive her trespasses and allow her to enter Thy kingdom. After her sins are burned away, of course. I also ask that You bless and give Your protection to this poor, lost lamb, Elena. She's an innocent . . . as much as was the Mother of Your other Son, Jesus. And I think We both know that, don't We? Thank You, Father, for these, thy gifts. Amen."

"Ah-men. That was nice, Micah. So," he said, as the road curved gently to the east, "where to now? Yah wanna come back t'mah place till yah find a new place?"

Mica glanced over the seat at his sleepy baby doll curled up in the back seat. Her eyes were finally closed and she looked peaceful in the soft pre-morning light. His beautiful living doll. Vegas just wasn't the right place for a beautiful girl zombie. There were already too many of them wandering the Strip.

Besides, the police were probably still looking to question him about Allison and the fire.

And he somehow didn't think they'd like this explanation about what had happened to her. But he smiled as he squinted into the rising sun.

"No, I think Elena and I'll be moving on."

"Might be best," Elvis agreed as he fished a second pair of oversized sunglasses out of the glove compartment and tossed them to Mica. "Any place in mind?"

Mica slipped the *Officially Licensed ELVIS-WEAR (tm)* glasses and thought a minute.

"Might as well continue East, I guess," he said. "I think New York is just the place for Elena and me."

"Yeah. Me, too. Ah've a'ways wanted t'sing on Broadway. Hey, maybe even do a revival-type show of mah classics. Ah hear New Yorkers go silly for that sorta thing."

"But I thought you sang on Broadway, didn't you?"

Elvis thought a minute and shrugged. "Mighta been one o'mah clones. Pesky critters . . . a'most as bad as them vam'pars. They was the reason b'hind the whole Elvis Impersonator craze, y'know."

"No," Mica said, "I didn't. Really?"

"Micah, mah son, if ah'm lyin', ah'm dyin'. So, slap in some appropriate travelin' music, cause we're off."

Mica shuffled through the CDs with a song already playing in his heart. A whole new world was waiting for them – a world bright with promise and song and without vampires. Life was going to be good from now on.

"Got one," he said, slipping the disk into the player.

Elvis listened to the first opening bars and grinned. "Okay, but yah gotta sing along."

And together they sang, a la Alvis Ambrose:

'She looked like an angel.
And she walked like an angel.
And she talked like an angel, but we got wise . . .
She was a vam'par in disguise'

Uh-oh.

Mica felt a cold chill against the back of his neck as he turned to look at the beautiful traumatized woman-child in the backseat. Elena, *his* Elena. *Naw*, he thought.

Thank yah, thank yah, verrah much.

LAST ROUND-UP

The air was blasted out of the building in a single loud *whoosh* that took out the windows and blew the roof almost into the next county.

Allison watched the liquid flames pour down the stairs to the cavern, destroying everything – from costumes to equipment – in its path. Nothing was going to survive with the exception of a few metal hand-cuffs and wall restraints and her charred skeleton . . . which would probably give the local bars and county offices more than enough to gossip about for years to come.

She just wished she'd be around to hear it.

"Fire," she said out loud, even though she could barely hear herself over the train-engine roar of the hungry flames. "What the hell is it with these people? Are they all fucking pryromaniacs? I WOULD HAVE SETTLED FOR A STAKE THROUGH THE HEART, MILO!"

He wasn't there, of course. No one was there. It was just her, a few sex toys, and the fire.

Party.

"It's not fair," she said, thought she said – she wasn't sure anymore. "I don't deserve this. It wasn't like I killed without a reason. I DID SOME GOOD, DAMMIT!"

Something exploded at the front of the cavern and propelled her backwards into her "little room." Allison closed her eyes and offered up the last prayer she would ever utter,

"Fuck him good, God."

ah-choo!

By noon the next day, Mica, Elvis and the still dazed and confused, but beautiful Elena were pulling into a *Denny's* in Flagstaff, AZ, for lunch. They were in no hurry, had plenty of money (thanks to Elvis's ATM card) and had decided to play tourist as much as they could before hitting the bright lights of New York. They deserved it for ridding the world of a moral menace.

At the same time, one state over, a group of real tourists from Albuquerque laughed and snapped pictures of what they thought had to be the greatest advertising gimmick they'd ever seen this side of Disney World – a Jaded Mandarin wearing sunglasses and hitching for a ride. They knew it was a Jaded Mandarin because the wife of one of the couples had seen the touring "Emperor of China" exhibit when it came to Albuquerque, and had gone on and on and on about the burial suit and how it was supposed to ensure the Emperor's ascent into Heaven in such agonizingly dull detail that her husband and the other couple had seriously given thought to exchanging her for the sparkling hitch-hiker.

They didn't, of course.

First, they'd been warned by other friends and late-night news casts never to pick up hitch-hikers (no matter how well dressed), and second, they knew the whole thing had to be a set-up for the grand opening of a new "themed" Vegas casino. Although the expert-wife had voiced a concern about the "Jade-Man" as they roared past in a cloud of alkaline dust, regaling all (once again) with the knowledge she'd cribbed from her tour book. The jade pieces were so well interconnected, she shouted at them above the howl of the air-conditioning, that there was probably very little, if any ventilation in the suit.

Her husband quelled her fears by reminding her that it was only a publicity stunt to get them to stop so the man *inside* the pale green suit could try to strong-arm them into going to the new casino when they already had reservations at <u>New York, New York</u>, thank you very much. Besides, she'd had the same worry about the juggling Hotdog-on-a-Stick they'd seen on the Santa Monica pier only to discover the suit had a little AC unit built right in.

The wife suddenly remembered the incident and laughed. Her husband was right again, as usual, only a lunatic would be standing out in 120-degree weather.

Allison watched the dust on the highway settle as she lifted one hand and flipped off the occupants of the car. Of course, they wouldn't know she was flipping them off – jade mittens might be great at keeping out the sun, but it was hell on non-verbal communication.

The people in the car probably thought she was just waving them bye-bye.

"Damned tourist," Allison said and tried to brush at least the first layer of dust off her sunglasses. She'd found the glasses melting on the porch as she stumbled out of the inferno and put them on purely out of habit. The hot plastic had bonded with the hotter jade instantly which drastically reduced the resale price of the suit – not that she was complaining.

The suit was the only thing that saved her from the fire and was still doing a bang-up against the bright desert sun . . . and she still had miles to go before night . . . and probably a few more than that to go before she caught up with her ex-Watcher and his scanky friends and –

The blast of an air-horn and squealing brakes startled her off the center of the road and into a gully. The semi's red-faced driver was already in mid-rant when she turned around.

"You got a death wish? Hey, didn't no-body tell you Halloween ain't for another couple'll months."

Allison smiled at the sound her fangs made against the jade face mask. She always did have a weakness for junk food.

❖

And as the sun slowly continued west, the semi, with its jade-covered driver, continued to head east.

THE END

The best in all-new neo-noir, hard-boiled and retro-pulp mystery and crime fiction.

FLESH AND BLOOD SO CHEAP

A Joe Hannibal Mystery

Wayne D. Dundee

1-891946-16-1

The popular St. Martins hardcover and Dell paperback series is revived! Hard-boiled Rockford, Illinois P.I. Joe Hannibal is at it again, this time swept up in a murderous mystery in a Wisconsin summer resort town. Deception and death lurk behind the town's idyllic façade, when a grisly murder is discovered and Hannibal knows for a fact that the confessed killer couldn't have done the deed!

"Mike Hammer is alive and well and operating out of Rockford, Illinois."
Andrew Vachs

It'll take two fists and a lot of guts to navigate through the tacky tourist traps, gambling dens and gin mills to get to the truth, while dangerous dames seem determined to steer Hannibal clear of the town's darkest secrets. In the end, Hannibal himself, and everyone he cares for, may be in jeopardy as he learns that murder may be the smallest crime of all in this lakeside getaway!

WAITING FOR THE 400

A Northwoods Noir

Kyle Marffin

1-891946-14-5

They found the first girl in the Chicago train station, a dime-a dance and a quarter-for-more chippy. Suicide. A train ticket still clutched in her hand: Watersmeet Michigan, the end of line...

400 miles north, Watersmeet station master Jess Burton wastes away in his tiny northwoods depot with big dreams big city life, watching the high-rollers and their glamour gals hop off the train for their lakeside mansions and highbrow resorts. Till the night Nina appeared on the depot platform.

Nina...Big city beautiful and clearly marked 'property of'. The kind of dame that can turn a man's head, turn him inside out and upside down till danger doesn't matter anymore, till desire can only lead to death. Because folks *are* dying now, and Jess is in over his head, waiting for the 400 and the red-headed beauty to step off the train with his ticket out of town.

THE BIG SWITCH

A Brian Kane Mystery

Jack Bludis

1-891946-10-2

Hollywood, 1951. Millionaires, moguls and movie stars dazzle in the land of dreams. Money talks, when desperate glamour girls are a dime a dozen. There's a seamy underbelly beneath the glossy veneer. Scandals lurk in every closet, sins too dark for the silver screen. It's all a sham, everything's a scam, everyone's on the make, no one's who they seem.

This is Kane's turf. Brian Kane, Hollywood P.I.

It's a standard case, as un-glamorous as they come: Hired by a mega-star's wife to catch her cheating husband with another casting-couch hopeful. Till one starlet winds up dead. Then another. When Kane's client turns out to be an imposter, and thugs are trying to scare him off, he's suddenly suspect #1 in his own case. And the body count keeps growing...

But it's personal now, and not even a vicious murderer can keep Kane from getting to the bottom of the big switch.

Now try the finest in traditional supernatural horror!

...DOOMED TO REPEAT IT

D.G.K. Goldberg

1-891946-12-9

It's a miracle that sassy, self-proclaimed punk-cowgirl Layla MacDonald hasn't gone off the deep end: Her mother gruesomely murdered in one of Charlotte, North Carolina's most scandalous love triangles, 'Daddy-Useless' drinking himself into despair, another temp job leading nowhere fast, and the painful memories of her boyfriend's abuse still as fresh as open wounds. Till she meets Ian. And suddenly, dormant desires are awakened. Madness is unleashed. Surreal violence explodes.

Because Ian is a ghost...

...The wandering ghost of an 18th century Scottish rebel, compelled by dark forces neither he nor Layla understand, seeking vengeance for 300 year-old horrors from the bloody highland battlefields. Their fates are bound together, and Ian is driven to protect Layla, with violent consequences, as madness and lust simmer amidst the ethereal world of lost spirits. Now under suspicion for Ian's rampages, the law's on Layla's tail, and her only escape may be to join her spirit lover, both of them doomed to repeat an endless cycle of ghostly horrors.

MARTYRS

Edo van Belkom

1-891946-13-7

250 years ago, French Jesuits erected a mission deep in the uncharted Canadian wilderness, till they were brutally murdered by a band of Mohawks. Or so the legends say.

Today St. Clair College stands near the legendary massacre site, the mission's memory now more folklore than fact. Then St. Clair professor Father Karl Desbiens and his band of eager grad students set off to locate the mission ruins. The site's discovered, artifacts are found, the mystery of the Mohawk massacre may be solved...

...Till the archeological dig accidentally unearths an old world evil. There was no 'Mohawk massacre'. A malevolent demonic power was imprisoned in the remote Canadian wilderness by the original missionaries. But now it's been unleashed. Now the nightmare will commence. Father Desbiens has his own inner demons to struggle with, his own crisis of faith to overcome. He's an unlikely martyr to the faith he already questions, but the demonic presence has invaded St. Clair college, leaving a bloody trail of horror among his students.

The Horror Writers Association

BELL, BOOK & BEYOND

An Anthology Of Witchy Tales

Edited by P.D. Cacek

1-891946-19-9

Stoker Award winner P.D. Cacek brings you 21 bewitching stories about wiccans, warlocks and witches, all written by the newest voices in terror: the Affiliate Members of the Horror Writers Association. From fearsome and frightening to starkly sensual and darkly humorous, each tale will cast its own sorcerous spell, leaving you anxiously looking for more from these new talents!

A FACE WITHOUT A HEART

A Modern-Day Version Of Oscar Wilde's
The Picture Of Dorian Gray

Rick R. Reed

1-891946-08-0

Nominated for the 2001 Spectrum Award for "Best Novel": A stunning retake on the timeless themes of guilt, forgiveness and despair in Oscar Wilde's fin de siecle classic, *The Picture Of Dorian Gray*. Amidst a gritty background of nihilistic urban decadence, a young man's soul is bargained away to embrace the nightmarish depths of depravity – and cold blooded murder – as his painfully beautiful holographic portrait reflects the ugly horror of each and every sin.

"A rarity: a really well-done update that's as good as its source material."
Thomas Deja, Fangoria Magazine

"A startling study of human nature and of its most potent desires and fears...
Rick Reed is truly one of the best around today."
Sandra DeLuca, Graveline

GOTHIQUE

A Vampire Novel

Kyle Marffin

1-891946-06-4

International Horror Guild Award nominee Kyle Marffin takes you on a tour of the dark side of the darkwave, when a city embraces the grand opening of a new 'nightclub extraordinaire', Gothique, mecca for the disaffected Goth kids and decadent scene-makers. But a darker secret lurks behind its blacked-out doors and the true horror of the undead reaches out to ensnare the soul of a city in a nightmare of bloodshed, and something much worse than death.

"An awfully good writer...this is a novel with wit and edge, engaging characters and sleazy ones for balance, a keen sense of melodramatic movement and a few nasty chills."
Ed Bryant, Locus Magazine

"Bloody brilliant! A white-knuckle adventure filled with plenty of chills and thrills...this book just never lets up."
M. McCarty, The IF Bookworm

WHISPERED FROM THE GRAVE

An Anthology Of Ghostly Tales

1-891946-07-2

Quietly echoing in a cold graveyard's breeze, the moaning wails of the dead, whispered from the grave to mortal ears with tales of desires unfulfilled, of dark vengeance, of sorrow and forgiveness and love beyond the grave. Includes tales by Edo van Belkom, Tippi Blevins, Sue Burke, P.D. Cacek, Dominick Cancilla, Margaret L. Carter, Don D'Ammassa, D.G.K. Goldberg, Barry Hoffman, Tina Jens, Nancy Kilpatrick, Kyle Marffin, Julie Anne Parks, Rick R. Reed and David Silva.

"A chilling collection of ghost stories...each with a unique approach to ghosts, spirits, spectres and other worldly apparitions...Pleasant nightmares."
Michael McCarty, Indigenous Fiction

STORYTELLERS

Julie Anne Parks

1-891946-04-8

A writer who once ruled the bestseller list with novels of calculating horror flees to the backwoods of North Carolina. A woman desperately fights to salvage a loveless marriage. A storyteller emerges — the keeper of the legends — to ignite passions in a dormant heart. But an ancient evil lurks in the dark woods, a malevolent spirit from a storyteller's darkest tale, possessing one weaver of tales and threatening another in a sinister and bloody battle for a desperate woman's life and for everyone's soul.

"A macabre novel of supernatural terror, a book to be read with the lights on and the radio playing!"
Bookwatch

"A page-turner, for sure, and a remarkable debut."
Triad Style

"Genuine horror and the beauty of the Carolina wilds. It's an intoxicating blend."
Lisa DuMond, SF Site

THE DARKEST THIRST

A Vampire Anthology

1-891946-00-5

Sixteen disturbing tales of the undead's darkest thirsts for power, redemption, lust...and blood. Includes stories by Michael Arruda, Sue Burke, Edo van Belkom, Margaret L. Carter, Stirling Davenport, Robert Devereaux, D.G.K. Goldberg, Scott Goudsward, Barb Hendee, Kyle Marffin, Deborah Markus, Paul McMahon, Julie Anne Parks, Rick R. Reed, Thomas J. Strauch, and William Trotter.

"Fans of vampire stories will relish this collection."
Bookwatch

"If solid, straight ahead vampire fiction is what you like to read, then The Darkest Thirst is your prescription."
Ed Bryant, Locus Magazine

"Definitely seek out this book."
Mehitobel Wilson, Carpe Noctem Magazine

SHADOW OF THE BEAST

Margaret L. Carter

1-891946-03-X

Carter has thrilled fans of classic horror for nearly thirty years with anthologies, scholarly non-fiction and her own long running small press magazine. Here's her exciting novel debut, in which a nightmare legacy arises from a young woman's past. A vicious werewolf rampages through the dark streets of Annapolis, and the only way she can combat the monster is to surrender to the dark, violent power surging within herself. Everyone she loves is in mortal danger, her own humanity is at stake, and much more than death may await her under the shadow of the beast.

"Suspenseful, well crafted adventures in the supernatural."
Don D'Ammassa, Science Fiction Chronicle

"Tightly written...a lot of fun to read. Recommended."
Merrimack Books

"A short, tightly-woven novel...a lot of fun to read...recommended."
Wayne Edwards, Cemetary Dance Magazine

NIGHT PRAYERS
P.D. Cacek
1-891946-01-3

Nominated for the prestigious Horror Writers Association Stoker Award for First Novel. A wryly witty romp introduces perpetually unlucky thirtysomething Allison, who wakes up in a seedy motel room — as vampire without a clue about how to survive! Now reluctantly teamed up with a Bible-thumping streetcorner preacher, Allison must combat a catty coven of strip club vampire vixens, in a rollicking tour of the seamy underbelly of Los Angeles.

> *"Further proof that Cacek is certainly one of horror's most important up-and-comers."*
> **Matt Schwartz**

> *"A gorgeous confection, a blood pudding whipped to a tasty froth."*
> **Ed Bryant, Locus Magazine**

> *"A wild ride into the seamy world of the undead... a perfect mix of helter-skelter horror and humor."*
> **Michael McCarty, Dark Regions/Horror Magazine**

THE KISS OF DEATH
An Anthology Of Vampire Stories
1-891946-05-6

Sixteen writers invite you to welcome their own dark embrace with these tales of the undead, both frightening and funny, provocative and disturbing, each it's own delightfully dangerous kiss of death. Includes stories by Sandra Black, Tippi Blevins, Dominick Cancilla, Margaret L. Carter, Sukie de la Croix, Don D'Ammassa, Mia Fields, D.G.K. Goldberg, Barb Hendee, C.W. Johnson, Lynda Licina, Kyle Marffin, Deborah Markus, Christine DeLong Miller, Rick R. Reed and Kiel Stuart.

> *"Whether you're looking for horror, romance or just something that will stretch your notion of 'vampire' a little bit, you can probably find it here."*
> **Cathy Krusberg, The Vampire's Crypt**

> *"Readable and entertaining."*
> **Hank Wagner, Hellnotes**

> *"The best stories add something to the literature, whether actually pushing the envelope or at least doing what all good fiction does, touching the reader's soul."*
> **Ed Bryant, Locus**

CARMILLA: THE RETURN

Kyle Marffin

Marffin's provocative debut — nominated for a 1998 International Horror Guild Award for First Novel — is a modern day retelling of J. R. LeFanu's classic novella, Carmilla. Gothic literature's most notorious female vampire, the seductive Countess Carmilla Karnstein, stalks an unsuspecting victim through the glittery streets of Chicago to the desolate northwoods and ultimately back to her haunted Styrian homeland, glimpsing her unwritten history while replaying the events of the original with a contemporary, frightening and erotic flair.

"A superbly written novel that honors a timeless classic and will engage the reader's imagination long after it has been finished."
The Midwest Book Review

"If you think you've read enough vampire books to last a lifetime, think again. This one's got restrained and skillful writing, a complex and believable story, gorgeous scenery, sudden jolts of violence and a thought provoking final sequence that will keep you reading until the sun comes up."
Fiona Webster, Amazon

"Marffin's clearly a talented new writer with a solid grip on the romance of blood and doomed love."
Ed Bryant, Locus Magazine

Look for these other titles from The Design Image Group at your favorite bookstore. Or visit us at **www.designimagegroup.com** for links to your favorite on-line and specialty booksellers, or to order direct.

To order direct by mail, send check or money order for $15.95 per book, payable in U.S. funds to:

The Design Image Group, Inc.
P.O. Box 2325
Darien, Illinois 60561 USA

Please add $2.00 postage & handling for the first book,
$1.00 for each additional book ordered. Please allow 2-3 weeks for delivery.